Black Sky, Black Sea

15th Nov 2012

Izzet Celasin

Black Sky, Black Sea

Translated from the Norwegian by
Charlotte Barslund

MACLEHOSE PRESS
QUERCUS · LONDON

First published in the Norwegian language as *Svart Himmel, Svart Hav*
by Gyldendal Norsk Forlag AS 2007

First published in Great Britain in 2012 by

MacLehose Press
an imprint of Quercus
55 Baker Street
7th Floor, South Block
London W1U 8EW

This translation has been published with
the financial support of NORLA

A CIP catalogue record for this book is available
from the British Library.

ISBN (HB) 978 1 84724 643 1
ISBN (TPB) 978 1 84724 644 8
ISBN (Ebook) 978 1 84916 614 0

2 4 6 8 10 9 7 5 3 1

Designed and typeset in 10¾/16½ Caslon by Patty Rennie
Printed and bound in Great Britain by Clays Ltd, St Ives plc

To Ingeborg, Melis and Henrik

Sunday

Today is Sunday.
Today they led me out into the sun for the first time
And for the first time in my life
I stood immovable
Amazed at how distant the sky was
How vast,
How blue
Respectfully I sat down on the ground
Leaned my back against the wall
At this moment
No falling into revolting waves at all
At this moment no thoughts
Of struggle
Of freedom
Of my wife.
The soil, the sun and me . . .
I am happy.

Nâzım Hikmet, 1948

Part One

I

May 1977

The Byzantine aqueduct stretched from the outskirts of the residential neighbourhood near the central fire station, across the main boulevard, and arched down towards the back of the municipal theatre. Traffic flowed in four lanes through its still-sturdy arcades. Saraçhane Square lay surrounded by the park of the same name, the historical ruins of the aqueduct, the Şehzade Mosque and the City Hall. This was a busy and bustling area with thundering traffic, public offices, theatres and cinemas. However, the most striking thing about that day was not the absence of cars on the road, but the endless stream of people pouring into the square from all sides. Here, as in many other places, İstanbul was preparing to celebrate May Day.

I had sneaked out of school at ten in the morning with a group of friends from sixth form, all eighteen years old, all with butterflies in our stomachs. None of us had ever taken part in a May Day parade before. Rumour had it that the police would seal off streets in the city and arrest anyone they happened to find there. The prospect of being arrested sparked excitement as well as tension, so we laughed and hollered as we ran all the way down to Saraçhane Square. This place was the meeting point for marchers from our neighbourhood, and from there the crowds would descend on Taksim Square, where five or six parades from other parts of the city were also headed. Trade unions and various other organizations had declared today's to be the biggest May Day parade in living memory, while editorials in the bourgeois press had branded it a "trial revolution" and clamoured for the police to prevent İstanbul from being overrun by the Reds. When we reached Saraçhane Square the mood was already festive, with music, dancing, a sea of banners and red flags, speeches that only a few could hear over the constant hubbub, like a swarm of bees taking off from amongst the crowds.

Everything was new to us. We wandered from one group to another speaking to complete strangers. It was a unique sensation, sharing something so important with so many of my fellow citizens. Apart from at school, I had never seen so many women gathered in one place, and several of them were debating loudly, handing out fliers, selling newspapers, collecting money for something or other, or wearing armbands that suggested they were responsible for security. After a while we headed for the park, where the student union had gathered beneath their own banners. A fierce discussion about when the parade should start was in progress. It was coming up for midday and parades from other neighbourhoods had already set off according to plan. People were growing restless, rumours ran like wildfire, and the crowd was receiving chaotic and contradictory messages every other minute, but no-one really knew what exactly was keeping us. Every time a well-known student leader appeared, the buzz among the masses would soar only to fizzle out in disappointment. We were just as impatient as everyone else, but entertained ourselves by making snide remarks about the leaders who, in fact, looked just as lost as we did, including one man in particular who had clearly not been near an educational establishment since the early '70s. Despite the fine spring weather, he had slung a long black coat over his shoulders and was proudly strutting about, flanked by two bodyguards.

4

The bush telegraph eventually announced that it was a dispute between the Soviet-friendly organizations and the Maoists that was holding us up. We ran towards the aqueduct. There, in the middle of the street, representatives of all the political factions were engaged in a fierce debate, surrounded by their various supporters, who were enjoying the spectacle enormously. The mood was tense, obscenities rained down wrapped in political jargon. I failed to understand why they were so outraged at words such as "revisionist", "opportunist" and even "adventurer". My interest in political literature meant that I was not entirely unfamiliar with these terms, but they did not sound insulting to my ears. The representatives, however, were clearly of an entirely different mind and seemed offended by the political name-calling. I grew irritated at the parties' ill will and contempt towards each other, and I was not the only one. Here and there people started shouting "Stop it!" and "March United!" But the agitators and their supporters were in the majority. The Soviet sympathizers did not want the Maoists to be there and the Maoists in turn threatened to use all available means to monopolize words that belonged to the "proletariat". Impartial demonstrators – those who supported neither China nor the Soviet Union – tried in vain to broker an understanding, but the factions showed no signs of tempering their demands; to do so would be to desert the battlefield and betray the working class. The workers, for their part, were not sure who represented them best. One of them, a man in overalls, called out, "Toss a coin!" We laughed. Time passed and we were alternately entertained, bored and irritated. And while all this was going on, no-one saw any reason to point out how few police officers were stationed around the square.

When the procession finally set off, it was at a snail's pace. The student union found themselves acting as a buffer between the opposing parties, second last from the back. Behind us, the Maoists marched with their banners, megaphones and slogans. It was a war of words.

From the front, the evils of the Maoist Nationalists were impressed on us, while the marchers to the rear condemned the "Soviet Socialist Fascists". The independent demonstrators tried to enter into the spirit of the day, but were drowned out, sandwiched as they were between two extremes. I did not take part in the verbal sparring; I preferred singing to shouting slogans.

I gasped as we passed through the arches of the aqueduct, where the street began to slope steeply downwards: before me was a sea of people. The dull waiting was instantly forgotten, as were the tedious arguments, the thirst, hunger and heat. The masses that stretched out before my eyes filled me with pride. A giant had been roused and had stirred: you could almost hear his thundering footsteps. To be a single cell of this giant's body was enough to feel invincible. It would be a pleasure to confirm the worst fears of the bourgeoisie and claim Istanbul for our own, not from helpless Byzantines this time, but from a cruel, rotten and corrupt power. Sultan Mehmet would have had no objections. His proud army, which might well have camped right here in May 1453, would resemble a village outing compared to our band. It was tempting to fantasize and briefly forget that behind the city walls a much stronger enemy now lay in wait, one who would not surrender without a fight – and that our giant lacked Sultan Mehmet's cannons. However, the giant did not come with a declaration of war, but with a promise: "Look, we are here, and nothing will ever be the same again."

When we had crossed Unkapanı Bridge over the Golden Horn, the sea of people poured into the narrower arteries of the Old City and filled them. It was another long and demanding ascent towards Taksim Square. Time passed, and I despaired at the thought that everything might be over before we reached the square, before we experienced the highlight of the day. I leaned despondently against the railing and looked out at the dinghies moored at the quay, bobbing lazily in the brown water. At Galata Bridge a little further down and, beyond, a stretch of the Bosporus glinting in the afternoon sun.

Only a couple of my friends were still with me. They smoked and chatted, and looked just as pensive as I did. I wondered what had happened to the others; we had lost them in the crowds. Someone suggested that we might as well go back to school: this waiting was pointless and the teacher on duty might get suspicious if we failed to be back on time. We might easily have done so had the message not arrived that the delay was caused by a huge influx of people into the square and the effort required to organize and position them. Moments later the parade started to move once more. My optimism returned and I decided to stay on and experience as much as I could. My joy rose with every step, I felt happy to be on this earth. The good mood was infectious, every face around me wore a smile from ear to ear.

The bottleneck had eased and we jogged up Şişhane. Our progress was undeniably comic, everyone laughed and joked, and slowcoaches were mocked and encouraged to keep going. The sense of anticipation was not limited to the demonstrators: men, women and children along the pavements cheered and clapped, and a few threw flowers.

Once we had passed through Tepebaşi, the pace dropped again. The parade seemed to move with reluctance. Something up ahead was resisting the pressure exerted by the massed ranks of the crowd. The tension between the two forces caused our human river to divide at Galatasaray and pour into the side streets that led to the square. I stayed with the student union, but my friends were nowhere to be seen. And then, in a narrow alley just a few hundred metres from the square, we realized that we could go no further. Trying to push ahead was point-less; we were told that security guards were blocking the entrances to the square due to the huge number of people trying to push through. I was so close and yet so far away. My dream of being received by jubi-lant crowds, of climbing the Republic Monument and surveying the people who were the true owners of the city, was shattered. I sat down on the pavement, though there was hardly room even to stand. People were crowding around and constantly stumbling over me. But I was completely exhausted and I did not care.

Soon those standing closest to me sat down too, and I was provided with some breathing space. I listened to the conversations of my asphalt comrades. They were older than me, mostly university students. If the rumours were to be believed, the streets leading to the square were blocked because the Soviet-friendly trade unions wanted to keep the Maoists out. The students were angry with both sides. One of them said that he was glad that this was no Winter Palace moment: the minute the revolution started these idiots would be at each other's throats, and we would find ourselves in the midst of a fratricidal feud. The students could not imagine how anyone could think of celebrating May Day without their organizations being represented. They had their own concerns; I was mainly preoccupied by how deep and severe the rift actually was. Only this morning I had been optimistic, convinced of the unity of the working class. Perhaps I was just naïve, sitting in my ivory tower surrounded and protected by the school walls. Democracy could not be achieved without differences of opinion. There should be room for a range of ideas, I was just not sure how.

A cry of joy roused me from my musings. I instinctively looked at my watch. It was past 6.oo p.m. A young woman came running towards where we were sitting and told us, panting heavily, that the student union would be allowed into the square after all, but we had to hurry up because the streets would be sealed off again as soon as we had passed through. While we got to out feet and brushed the dust from our trousers, she ran on to spread the word. I was afraid that something might happen at the last moment to halt our progress, so I elbowed my way forwards and felt relief when the parade started stirring again. I stretched as tall as I could in the hope of seeing what was going on at the head of the column, my view obscured by a forest of flags and banners. The young people next to me knew no more than I did, but we marched all the same, and that was what counted. Soon I could hear the buzz that always rises from vast crowds of people gathered in one place; deafening waves of slogans rang out, louder and louder. At last I reached the end of the street and entered the square.

On either side were gathered dozens of full-grown, serious-looking men, supervising our parade. They were wearing tabards with the insignia of the Revolutionary Workers' Union. If they were looking for Maoists, they would not find any among us. Several students waved to them, but got no response. Not everyone was having fun today, some were still working. We quickly walked past them and took our first steps out onto Taksim Square, to great applause from the students. This was precisely as I had imagined. The demonstrators were on the pavements, on the roofs of the bus station shelters, they covered the grass of Taksim Park like a rug, clinging to trees and anything else you could hang from. I could forget all about the Republic Monument, it was no longer possible even to make out its original shape. The monument at the centre of the square was now decorated with countless people. A gigantic banner that read "Long Live May Day" had been hung above the entrance to the Culture House. It was clearly visible from all sides and displayed an image of a worker breaking his chains. Once in the square we flowed to the right, guided to the spot we had been allocated, which, according to my calculations, would be either by the Culture House or in the park. The columns moved very slowly. We walked past the Waterworks, past the commercial building where I had worked as a runner for a photographer in the summer of '73, and approached the Intercontinental hotel. It was a high-rise building that blighted its surroundings, but not even its hideous facade could diminish this moment. I felt happy as never before.

*

The first shots sounded like a hydraulic drill operating close by, but a lightning reflex alerted my brain that my senses were being deceived. Something similar must have occurred in the same instant to thousands of people across the square. At first everything went quiet, but when the shooting resumed, there was desperate shouting and panicked flight in every direction: the herd was now stampeding.

"They're shooting!" someone called out.

Several automatic weapons were fired simultaneously. I was thrown forwards by a powerful push to my back. It was then that I began to feel genuine fear. I thought I had been hit. It turned out not to have been a bullet, but the people behind me trying to get past. I was caught up in the momentum and carried away. It was impossible to stand on my feet. I was a helpless victim of the pressure from behind, and I pushed those ahead of me in turn, unable to think of what else I could do. Suddenly a tall young man stopped in front of me, waving his arms in the air and shouting, "Don't panic, don't run!" but he was instantly swallowed up by the stampede. I spotted through a tiny gap that we were close to Kazancılar, which slopes down towards Kabataş Quay. The hill was covered with fallen bodies piled on top of each other. I stumbled over a lifeless figure on the cobblestones, fell on all fours and hurt my knees. The pain shot through me, and together with the threat of the human wave behind me, triggered my survival instinct. I knew I had to do something or I would shortly be trampled to death. I crawled forwards as quickly as possible. When I finally stood up, the other demonstrators had lain down in an attempt to shelter from the bullets. They made up an enormous blanket across the square and were a clear target for anyone shooting from above. With my last strength I reached a safe place by the Republic Monument and threw myself to the ground as the next barrage of shots rang out.

"Be a man! Get up!" a calm but rather impatient voice commanded me.

I scrambled to my feet and the first thing I noticed were her eyes. They were dark and angry.

"Can you use one of these?" she said, showing me an automatic pistol and a revolver. I shook my head.

"Oh shit," she sighed. "Just hold on to this and try not to lose it." She lifted up a canvas shoulder bag, tossed it in my direction and looked around. A man came running towards us. He was tall, young and handsome.

"I'm so glad I found you," he said to her.

She said nothing, just handed him the revolver. He automatically checked the weapon.

"Where are they?" he asked, a little out of breath.

"I'm not quite sure. On the roof of the Waterworks, I think," she replied.

The firing of automatic weapons had stopped. All we could hear was the sporadic reports of smaller pistols.

"Look!" the man shouted and pointed at the Waterworks.

I followed his direction. There was movement on the roof, or at least I thought I saw something move, and a moment later the man began to shoot. So did the woman. I was standing next to her and I watched how she supported her right hand with her left before squeezing the trigger. Bullet cases spattered everywhere. One hit me on the cheek, burning hot. The pain enraged me. This was idiotic and pointless. The distance was too great – that much I did know about handguns.

"Give me the bag," she said when she had stopped shooting.

"No, I can manage," I sulked. Clearly she was not in the mood for a discussion.

"Alright, but give me a magazine and some rounds."

It did not take me long to find them; there was nothing but two spare magazines and some loose rounds in the bag.

"Who's the boy?" said the young man as he loaded his revolver. She shrugged because she did not know who I was, but she turned towards me, perhaps asking herself the same question as if she had just then remembered something.

"Stick to me like glue until I tell you otherwise," she told me. I did not like her tone, but did not want to say so. I was terrified and out of my depth.

Fresh cries of fear grabbed my attention. A police armoured vehicle with giant wheels had arrived on the square from Dolmabahçe by the Culture House. It drove mercilessly into the crowd, unleashing even more panic. Most managed to react in time and throw themselves out of the way to safety, but one woman stumbled and fell to the cobbles. The huge wheels rolled over her, one side of the vehicle lifting as it passed. The vehicle went on its way without stopping, now heading straight towards us. The young woman with the pistol and I jumped to the left. The young man ran to the right towards the Intercontinental Hotel entrance. The vehicle roared past. I saw him run after it. The crowd closed behind them and he vanished.

After these moments of distraction my terror was renewed. All I wanted to do was give the bag to the woman and get away from this place, but I just did not know how to, or where to go. In another time and another place I would have gone to help the woman who had been run over, but right now the only person I cared about was myself. My companion looked puzzled.

"Where are your shoes?" she asked. I looked down at my feet.

"Wait here and don't move," she said and disappeared back where we had come from. I was calm again. Time had lost all meaning, so I had no idea how long I waited, or what was happening around me. But I knew deep down she would come back.

If it had not been for the pistol in one hand and the shoes in the other, I would not have recognized her when at last she came running towards me. An odd pair. I just about managed not to point that out.

12

She had done her best, given the circumstances. When I tried them on, they were obviously too big, so I tightened the laces as hard as I could. She was almost smiling, and as I got up she took my hand and said, "Let's get out of here."

We walked towards the Culture House, but the road to Dolmabahçe was blocked by militia who were holding their ground for the time being, no doubt waiting for orders. I found my voice and reminded her about the side street we had taken to reach the square and how I had not seen any police officers there. She turned without saying a word. Going this way was a risk, for all we knew it might be crawling with police and soldiers by now. For the first time since she took me under her wing, I became properly aware of my surroundings. People were still taking cover behind the Republic Monument, cowering behind bus stops or in the park. Banners, flags, abandoned shoes and clothing lay strewn around the hill. A fine mist of smoke and sporadic gunfire made it seem like a battlefield. The people we were passing now seemed not to be injured, but there was fear and confusion etched on every face. I was hoping that everyone would be alright, including those I had left lying on Kazancılar and the woman who had been crushed by the armoured car.

"Is it safe now?" someone said. The woman hurried on without replying, hunched down and with me in tow. I copied her though I could not see how crouching would save us from being hit. But no-one shot at us – in fact, it had now been a while since we had last heard machine-gun fire. When we reached the corner of the street we saw a small group of security guards wearing the tabards of the Revolutionary Workers' Union. They were patrolling the junction with pistols in their hands and waved us down to the ground. We did not stop walking until we had reached them.

"Who's doing the shooting? The police?" the woman demanded in an authoritative tone. One of the men looked her up and down from head to foot.

"No, it's the bloody Maoists." he said, spitting on the tarmac. "They started shooting at us and we returned fire."

Or the other way round, I thought. There were plenty of bullet cases on the ground.

"What did they have? Machine-guns? Pistols?" she asked.

The man gave her an impatient look. "Pistols, obviously, like the one you're holding. Anyway, they've gone, we've driven them out." He was childishly pleased with his little exchange of fire, the imbecile, and clearly had no idea what had happened elsewhere. I was starting to get irritated with their banter and was about to say something when the woman tightened her grip on my hand and said: "Come."

We were an odd couple, running along the now-deserted streets, she with her pistol and me with my lady's shoulder bag. I did not look up once, but I could feel that people behind their curtains were staring down at us with terror in their eyes. Just before we reached the main road we slowed to walking pace. I did not protest when she took the bag and put the pistol in it. We waited while two police cars drove past, crossed the road and went into Tepebaşı Park, which slopes down towards Kasımpaşa.

"We'll take the bus from Kasımpaşa," she said.

For a while we walked in silence and for the first time I was able to observe her with eyes that could actually take something in. She was an adult, different from the immature girls I knew. Her face was framed by long, dark, tangled hair, she wore no make-up and was pleasant to look at. I could detect the white lace on her bra through a casually buttoned checked shirt. She had long, athletic legs, and was wearing pale jeans and suede shoes.

"What are you staring at?" she snapped when she realized that I was studying her. She must have decided it was her shirt, because she immediately buttoned it up to her neck.

"By the way, you look a sight," she said.

My hair was cut short, so there could not be much wrong with that. My face, however, I was less sure of. My polo-neck jumper was filthy, there was a big tear in one knee of my jeans, and as for my shoes, well, they were not mine.

"Likewise." Sparring.

She smiled, ran her fingers through her dishevelled hair, found a band and with nimble fingers gathered it up into a severe ponytail.

"Better now?" She looked older and more serious. I wanted to know how old.

"How old are you?"

"Twenty-one. And you?"

Being eighteen was nothing to be ashamed of. "Twenty," I said.

She raised an eyebrow in surprise. "You look much younger."

It was embarrassing, ridiculous. She had seen right through me. I shifted tack. "Are you a Maoist?"

She pretended to be hurt. "Do I look as if I have a thing for peasants?"

"So do you think it was the Maoists?" I really wanted to know.

"No," she said firmly. "They weren't even in the square. The others kept an eye on them the whole time, and yes, they do have pistols, but it's highly unlikely that they would have automatic weapons. What do you think? Do you think it was them?"

"No," I replied just as firmly. She had convinced me. Listening to her, everything seemed so obvious. She seemed so resolute and rewarded me with encouraging smiles. I, on the other hand, could barely hold it together and my hands were trembling a little. I carried my fear with me like an unwanted burden.

She was angry, she said, because no-one had managed to protect the crowd. Even though an attack had been predicted, more or less announced in the newspapers, it had ended in chaos. The group she belonged to never really had a chance. In this way she gave me an answer to the question I was too frightened to ask: why was she carrying a weapon? She looked an ordinary young woman. If I had passed her in the street, I would not for a minute have suspected her of keeping a pistol and spare magazines in her bag. We had left the park and arrived at the bus stop. Here people were strolling around the streets apparently ignorant of what had happened a few kilometres away. We waited in silence for the bus. For once it was on time. This surprised me because I had imagined that the whole city would have come to a standstill. On the bus she stayed standing, though there were seats, keeping a firm grip on her bag. There was something vulnerable about her as she stood there. Perhaps she was as tired and scared as I was. I wondered what she would do if the bus was stopped and searched at a roadblock. Would she let herself be taken alive, or resist and risk both her own life and the lives of innocent passengers?

Someone had gone on a hunting expedition today, someone who was ready to kill without hesitation, without even needing an excuse. Perhaps she was contemplating the same possibility. And when the bus stopped just short of the aqueduct, she got off without warning. I did not have a chance to say anything to her.

Through the rear window I saw her scan the traffic before crossing swiftly to the other side. The bus drove off, and my last glimpse was of her disappearing between the shops on the far side of the road. By ignoring me she might have been trying to protect me. That I could understand, even though it made me feel like a helpless child who needed to be looked after. What upset me most was that I had forgotten to ask her name and where she lived. But perhaps it was better this way: at least I had avoided the humiliation of being turned down.

Back at school a full range of emotions was on display, but by far the most visible were grief and anger. Most of my friends had turned back without having reached the square. A few of them had ended up in the park and had managed to escape unharmed. But when I failed to show up they feared the worst: according to the radio and television many had been killed or wounded. Precisely how many, no-one knew as yet. I told them an edited version of my story: I had been at Kazancılar when the shooting began, then I had run down the hill, away from the chaos, and finally ended up at Kabataş Quay. There I had sat for a long time composing my thoughts before taking the bus to school. Later, when I thought about it, this version seemed like the real one and anything else a figment of my imagination. Everyone agreed that I had been lucky, as many people on Kazancılar had been wounded or killed. They soon lost interest in my story and the conversation moved on to their own experiences.

I managed to sneak out and up to the dormitory, as dinner had already been served and devoured. Not that I was hungry anyway: all I wanted was to lie down in my bed. My body could take no more and I fell quickly into a deep, dark sleep.

Nothing would ever be the same again. The age of innocence was over for my generation. Perhaps it was the fault of the school; it had protected us too well from the outside world. I was eleven the first time I walked through its dark-green archway, which had admitted countless hopeful students for more than a hundred years. Once you passed through, you belonged to the community within its tall walls. It was no good crying for your mother or father, all the care and knowledge you needed would have to be found inside.

A century of integrity, authority and tradition. When you are eleven all this seems terrifying: the colossal buildings, the reading rooms, dining halls, dormitories and, not least, the teachers and your fellow students. But in time both the buildings and the people resume their actual proportions. You learn to fit in. Those who do not have no place here. You only get this one chance. In time, you understand that you are no longer lonely or poor but a part of a great community, one which proudly declares on a huge banner on the facade of the P.E. building: "Equal Education Opportunities for All". But you never forget that you were one of the few who passed through the eye of the needle.

Thirty-four killed and hundreds of wounded. Photographs from the square dominated the front pages of the newspapers. Bloody May Day. In one of the papers there was a picture of the massive banner that had covered the facade of the Culture House. It had come loose from one of its moorings and hung in disarray. In another newspaper, the lifeless bodies lying on the top of Kazancılar. In a third, a young woman holding a pistol. But it was not her. I was fairly certain of that. Between the lines in the right-wing newspapers you could detect poorly concealed glee behind a fake mask of grief, their delight that the "trial revolution" had been crushed. The radical left-wing papers were in no doubt that the shootings were an act of provocation, carefully planned and executed by the Contra-Guerrillas, a notorious paramilitary organization that had been responsible for kidnappings, torture and assassinations since the start of the '70s. Few of the victims had sustained bullet wounds: most had been trampled to death in the ensuing stampede. In one of the radical papers there was a blurred picture of armed figures on the roof of the Waterworks. However, the police were not interested in such information, they were too busy questioning the demonstrators that had been arrested in Taksim Square.

The tragedy had shocked me, in part because I had had no idea of its scope when I left the square. I felt I had failed, but could not say precisely whom or what. This enraged me. The murderers must be punished, ideally in a like manner, in an ambush, with death lying in wait for them. I was not alone. Revenge was mentioned more than once in heated debates, but (as is always the way) with time the temperature cooled. We were school children, deep down we were peace-loving boys who enjoyed playing with words, and words were hardly as lethal as bullets. Restless, I paced for days pondering how *she* would have assessed the situation. However, with mock exams perilously close, absorbed by my daily routines, I gradually calmed down. I looked forward to the summer holidays, to a life outside school, to everything that is exciting and unpredictable.

I told the truth only to Semra, because she would understand and because she was my best friend at school. Our friendship was characterized by rivalry. Competing for popularity with a girl who had both looks and intelligence on her side was no easy task, but we never hurt each other on purpose, and most importantly, perhaps, we did not envy each other. We could talk and argue about everything, forever sharing knowledge. The light tone I used to begin my story grew more and more sombre as the tale unfolded. As I relived for the second time all that had happened that day, my fear and grief returned. My intention was not to impress her, and I did not play up my own part. In my narrative there was only one saviour. She stood calmly holding her pistol, firing at the invisible murderers, before saving me and disappearing like a true heroine. I embellished the story slightly, letting her light a cigarette with steady hands and attributing to her as she stepped down from the bus a pithy parting remark: "See you later, comrade."

"All those dead people, those innocent people," Semra sighed, when I had finished. "The young woman you told me about, I could never be like her." She pinched my cheek in a good-natured fashion. "And nor could you."

2

June 1977

The Vegetable Market, located between the two bridges across the Golden Horn at Eminönü, was one of many venerable Byzantine buildings to be converted to commercial use. It was sturdy, divided into a series of bays where the vegetable traders bought and sold, with a high roof that leaked like a sieve. It was blissfully cool within its walls in the summer, and as I only worked here during the long holidays, I was lucky enough never to find out about conditions in the winter.

The city's total consumption of vegetables was transported here every day from the farming districts while everyone was asleep. The vegetables were bought by wholesalers who made vast profits by selling the goods on to the shopkeepers. From two in the morning until two in the afternoon it teemed with life; joy, drama and tragedy were all played out here. If you knew where to look, the market was a microcosm of the whole city and its attendant human destinies. I was one of those in the know, working for a friendly man named Ahmet. Ahmet was in his mid thirties, blond, tall and slim; a former porter who wanted to try his luck and risk his savings by becoming a wholesaler. For some unknown reason, he wanted to hire a good bookkeeper and had contacted me following a reference from a school friend who also worked in the market. My first impression of Ahmet was that he was a likeable villain whose enthusiasm compensated for his inability to make people trust him. It was easy to talk money with him – he promised me the earth, something that did not exactly increase my faith in him. I informed him that the tip-off about me he had received was misleading; I was not a skilled bookkeeper; on the contrary, I had no experience whatsoever in the field. He laughed it off at first and trivialized the whole thing, before admitting that he was chiefly concerned with honesty rather than skill. As long as I did not run off with all his takings, he would be a happy man. It was impossible to dislike him. I had nothing to lose, and trying something as hopeless as this might even be fun. Eventually we agreed on a trial period – a decision, he assured me, I would never regret.

Ahmet was a simple soul, from Nide, a sleepy town in the middle of Anatolia, and had received little by way of education. He smoked, swore, drank, fought, gambled and lived more or less exactly as his ancestors had. When I suggested a ban on gratuitous swearing, especially at customers and porters, he was initially flustered, then laughed contemptuously before finally accepting it. He agreed to my demand for a daily newspaper without objection, but judging from his crooked smile, it was regarded as just another eccentricity of the educated. Before long, I would find him absorbed in the newspaper every morning – in the sports section, that is. Neither the customers nor the money poured in quite as readily he had expected, but at the end of every day he had more money in his pocket than he had ever earned in a single shift as a porter. From this I took as much as I thought I deserved, we had no other salary agreement. I was completely responsible for the money and he had a strange faith in me. We laughed a lot and had a good time together. In a place where ancient rituals reigned, it was liberating not to take things too seriously. We had tomato fights in front of the old-timers in the market – who would shake their heads in disapproval – and ran after picky customers and pleaded with them on our knees while bystanders roared with laughter.

After much thought we also came up with an unconventional way of getting rid of the goods we had failed to sell that day. No-one would want to buy them the next day, so to keep prices high they normally ended up at the bottom of the Bosporus by the Golden Horn, or else floating on the surface. Ahmet could not afford to throw out surplus stock, and as far as I was concerned it was a terrible waste that proved beyond all doubt the greed of the middle classes. We found another way. Ahmet owned a battered wreck of a van and we started driving to the industrial areas around the Horn, selling tomatoes and grapes to the workers at wholesale prices. I was proud to have come up with this idea.

The summer holidays for me and many other young people were not holidays as such. It was a time for work, earning some money, supporting your family's faltering finances, spending a little of it yourself at the weekends and, at best, having a few weeks off before school started again. So it was great to have a summer holiday that lasted ten weeks.

One morning in June I woke to the insistent beeping of my alarm clock, and all I wanted to do was turn over and go back to sleep. Ahmet and his bloody tomatoes and grapes could take a hike. My mother had already risen for morning prayers. Her increasingly loud recitals of the sacred verses signalled that she was close to losing her patience. I had to switch off my alarm clock, get out of bed and leave the flat as quickly as possible.

Outside the market, normally bustling with customers, vans, porters with towering loads and street vendors shouting, there were few signs of life. The police had taken over the area instead. The sight of police officers in the market surprised no-one: it had its own police station. However, while the market's own police officers were essentially thuggish money collectors, the officers guarding the gates were of a different breed, with nervous fingers on the triggers of their automatic weapons. One of them stopped me and barked questions as though there were a personal disagreement between us. I was polite and helpful, but he did not appear to be satisfied by my answers. And when he eventually decided to let me in, his face still bore a strong hint of hostile suspicion.

Ahmet was beside himself. His normally sallow skin had taken on a faint pinkish tint, his hands gestured wildly, he jabbered in an attempt to regain his composure. I had never seen him so agitated before. It turned out he had every reason to be. Someone had been killed before his very eyes. He had just finished buying that day's stock when armed men arrived and started shooting at each other without warning. Fortunately he was not caught in the crossfire and had the sense to throw himself behind some empty crates and keep his head down until it was all over. When he had managed to scuttle out from his hiding place, there were three dead and four wounded on the ground. Not that he had examined their condition too closely – at that point he was mostly concerned about getting away from the scene of the crime. He had no desire to be hauled in as a witness. Thanks to Ahmet and people like him there were never any witnesses to such shootings.

The shooting was the result of a dispute between rival factions vying for supremacy. For a long time a clandestine war had been waged over control of the porters; providing them with protection and job security was a lucrative market that brought in hefty commissions. Since the motto was "winner takes all", such disputes were rarely settled at the negotiating table. Some called these protectors the mafia, others called them gangs. Mafia sounded about right to me.

Ahmet was upset by the incident, and in the days that followed his usual enthusiasm evaporated. He was forever sloping off and leaving me to do all the work. It was both frustrating and irritating. My complaints fell on deaf ears and, of course, our takings dropped. One day, when I had finally had enough, he returned with a parcel and waved me furtively up to his office, where he opened the package to reveal a pistol. I was too stunned to say anything. He was almost his former self again, in his "don't-you-underestimate-Ahmet" mood.

"Now we can protect ourselves," he said.

"Protect ourselves from what?"

His answer was vague. "All the dangers that lurk in a swamp like this."

But when I insisted on a proper answer, he changed his tune. Recently there had been tension between Turkish and Kurdish porters resulting in almost daily conflicts and fights. What did I know, he said, I who just swanned in and out as I wished? It was ridiculous. The Kurdish porters worked for us, too, though they were not very aware of their Kurdish roots. I could swear to that because whenever I chatted to them during breaks and was tempted to raise the political consciousness of a few of them, they shocked me by defending Turkey and the Turkish flag with almost Fascist ardour. They had assimilated far too much to remember their heritage. But then what about Ahmet? He had never before distinguished between Turks and Kurds: was he turning into a loathsome racist in his old age? No, the people he was talking about were not the same Kurds as those I was used to, but another tribe entirely, from a Kurdish mountain village far away to the southeast. They were stubborn, primitive and knew no respect. And no, he had not turned into a racist, but what was wrong with showing a bit of national pride? There was a reason why people voted for the National Party in Nide.

"Because Nide is a godforsaken place where you would expect nothing else from a horde of illiterates who long for the nomad days when they were free to steal, rape and drink horse's milk," I snapped.

I hated being arrogant towards uneducated and naïve people like

24

Ahmet and tarring everyone with the same brush, but I was sick of all this talk of national pride. Yes, I had recited my share of quasi-nationalistic poems about the flag and the motherland in front of my fellow pupils and assembled parents in primary school. For a while I had been fascinated by the history of the Ottoman Empire, and in my first few years of secondary school an older student with the nickname "Hitler Haluk" lectured us on the forgotten qualities of the Nazis and complained at how unfairly the world had treated them. Though Hitler Haluk was obviously a tragic figure and most of the time we simply laughed at him, we retained a certain sympathy for the Germans, whom we regarded as brothers-in-arms from the First World War – I had no idea whether the Germans had ever shared this sentiment. But these were all childhood illnesses, we grew out of them, and Hitler Haluk had long since turned into a radical left-winger.

As a child I was neither scared of nor excited by weapons. I was neither an idealist nor naïve. But history was full of armed conflicts and I believed it was necessary first and foremost to disarm history, so I wrote poems, rehearsed fine words and believed that words could change the world. Unfortunately I had forgotten that I belonged to a race that could be unbelievably brutal and yet, at the same time, produce the most beautiful love poems on earth.

I asked Ahmet to get rid of the weapon.

"Please come back with it if it can be used against the enemies of the people one day, but I won't allow anyone to use weapons in a dispute between workers," I said. It was pretentious and it sounded false to my own ears, not my usual style. Normally I tended to ridicule this kind of claptrap. Ahmet liked me, I knew that, and despite the disparity in our ages he rarely dismissed my views. I could say things to Ahmet that would have driven him into a furious rage coming from the mouth of anyone else. In my case he respected both the man and the acumen. His common sense told him to value in others the qualities he himself lacked. Now he was disappointed and indignant, perhaps he regarded this as an insult to his manhood; I do not know, but he made it clear that this business with the pistol was something that did not concern me. The gun lay in the drawer for two days. On the third day it was gone. It cost him a great deal of inner turmoil, but it least it had ended in a compromise we could both live with. As business returned to normal in the market, we slipped back into our old routines, with a cheerful Ahmet in his familiar role as top dog.

*

"Go on, give us a fag," Emel shouted.

I leaned over the balcony. There she was, one floor below, shielding her eyes against the afternoon sun with her hand, her smile revealing the whitest of teeth.

"Not until you give me a kiss."

"Forget it, stupid, or I'll tell my grandmother." This was an empty threat, even though her grandmother was a notorious gipsy. She was no longer a nomad, but her tongue was still as poisonous and her fists hit just as hard. But I was her favourite boy in the neighbourhood and Emel knew it.

"How can you kiss a girl when you're on the balcony above her?"

I threw one leg over the railing and pretended to climb down. Emel laughed. I lowered the basket we used when buying from street vendors and sent her a cigarette. We leaned over our respective balconies and smoked in silent companionship.

"Your girlfriend is coming," Emel called from below.

My girlfriend, I never called her "mine" but everyone else did. Every time I saw her cross the grass with tired feet, I was overcome with tenderness. She was small, innocent and defenceless, and on evenings such as this, when she stepped off the bus at the petrol station after a long day at work and started walking through the allotments towards

26

the development, it seemed as though she carried the weight of the world on her narrow shoulders. She smiled at my urge to protect her. She would not permit me to pick her up at her workplace and did not think the world was as bad as I made it out to be. She could look after herself. She worked in Bakırköy, approximately ten kilometres away by the Sea of Marmara, as a sales assistant in a clothes shop. Every now and then I would go to Bakırköy, sit in a café by the water and then wait for her at the bus stop after closing time. She would be both pleased and annoyed, pleased because I was there and annoyed because I did not respect her independence. I was punished with silence, but she rested her head on my shoulder all the way home.

*

I had met Ayfer the year before, one hot and dusty day in July as I meandered around the neighbourhood with only boredom for company. She was walking towards me with two other girls. They chirped loudly and laughed without a care in the world. Even at a distance her lovely appearance made her stand out, and I knew instantly that I had to stop and say something to her – anything would do. She did not look surprised when I let the other girls pass and blocked her path. Instead, she bravely met my eyes. She was pretty, the most beautiful girl I had ever seen, with shoulder-length curly brown hair, green eyes, high cheekbones and full lips. A floral summer dress of cheap material covered the slightly unripe curves of a very young woman.

"Who are you?" I asked, panting slightly. I was in that phase of life when you can still be captivated by unadorned beauty.

"Aren't you coming?" her friends called out. She giggled and waved them on.

"Don't you know me?" she said. "I know you. I've seen you on your balcony sometimes, but you're away a lot. People say you go to private school."

She spoke in a soft voice, shy, but at the same time not quite. She was a local girl who had grown up miraculously overnight as girls of her age are wont to do. I could not take my eyes of her.

"Why are you looking at me like that?" she said.

"Because I like you," I said.

"You're making fun of me."

"Will you be my girlfriend?" I asked her.

She giggled a little and then grew serious. "Don't know," she said and ran off.

I watched as she rejoined her friends. She turned and waved to me.

Perhaps this was the first sign. Later I spent much of my time on the balcony. Her block was just across the street, four storeys high, just as tall as ours. All the flats in this area were of the same design. She and her family lived on the fourth floor, too, and their kitchen balcony faced our front one. From time to time she would come out on the balcony, look in my direction, talk to the people on the other balconies, but never to me. Then she would go back inside to help her mother in the kitchen. I would stay on the balcony waiting for her to appear once more. I took every opportunity to read, eat and play cards with my younger brother out there. I did everything I could to catch a glimpse of her. So it could hardly be attributed to my mother's sharp wits when she commented on the time I spent on the balcony.

"Ayfer is a very young girl. Only fifteen. I know that because she is in the same year as your brother," she said.

My mother was not in the habit of giving me detailed information about the girls in the neighbourhood. I knew this was the prelude to some maternal advice.

"You mustn't do anything that might upset her," she added.

"How can you upset a girl by sitting on a balcony?"

She sighed and stroked my hair. "You never know with boys," she said.

In the evenings, after dinner, when the worst of the heat had died down, people would come outside. The adults would chat together on the grass with their teapots and rugs, children would play games, while teenagers eyed each other carefully. I would sit with my friends on a crumbling wall in front of the block and eat sunflower seeds. The girls gathered on the other side of the street. They would eat sunflower seeds too. While we boys were serious and spoke only a little, the girls would chat noisily, laughing and giggling. It was not until the adults and the children packed up their things and retired that the two groups of teenagers crossed the street to mingle. Then it was time for skipping ropes, stickball and singing, all the things we could not do while the young children were around. I enjoyed these hours, which were very different from my evenings at school, where we could not risk being seen playing. That privilege was reserved for children in the lower school.

Ayfer appeared on the scene some time after our first meeting. She had not been out at this hour before: perhaps she had not yet been accepted by the other teenagers. It was frustrating to see how she avoided me. She joked and talked to the other boys, but did not pay any attention to me, not even a single glance. To begin with I was wary of being intrusive, mindful of the gossip that was inevitable when boys and girls showed an obvious interest in each other. But one day I chased after her in a game, grabbed hold of her and flung her down on the grass. She panted hard beneath me like a trapped doe, but without a doe's fear in her eyes. On the contrary, she was smiling sweetly. Perhaps this was the sign she had been waiting for because in the days that followed, she made it clear to everyone that she was mine and I alone deserved her attention. She did not wait until the afternoon rituals had been completed and the adults were safely back in front of their televisions. She came over to me, sat down on the wall and ate sunflower seeds with me in silence. And as soon as the adults had gone, she held my hand and smiled affectionately.

Eventually we withdrew from the others and began living in a world of our own. We spent most of our time away from the development, lying in the grass among the daisies, cautiously side by side to begin with. I did most of the talking, telling her about my school and my dreams. She was modest, hesitant and a little sad because she was not good with words, but that did not matter. I liked the sparkle in her green eyes and I liked her smile. One evening when darkness covered the sky and the ground, muted the colours and blurred the contours, I took her in my arms and kissed her. Her mouth was soft, warm, sweet and salt at the same time. Her breath flowed over my skin, I could feel her heart beat. She snuggled up to me and held me tight, and we lay there in a long embrace until her younger sister disturbed us.

"Mum is going to kill you," she said.

"Go away," Ayfer said.

"I'm not going anywhere without you, and he there had better watch himself," she replied.

"You deserve a good thrashing," Ayfer said, stood up and brushed off the dust and straw. Then she chased after her younger sister. I heard them shouting and laughing, until their voices faded. I stayed where I lay on the grass with a blanket of stars above me.

My last carefree summer died of natural causes. September was meant to be a month of mourning for students, but it had never been like that with me. I missed school once the long holiday had exhausted the initial rush of freedom, and I was one of the first through the school gates when the new school year started. I liked to experience the emptiness and silence in the playground, in the dormitories and in the classrooms before it was irretrievably disturbed by the arrival of five hundred other students. But September '76 was a sad affair for me. While many others got over their homesickness in a few days, mine lasted much longer. It was Ayfer I was missing now. The boarding school had morphed from a sanctuary to a prison. Once I had thought up all sorts of excuses to spend my weekends at school, but now I could barely wait for the last lesson on Fridays to be over. Ayfer was impatient, too, so our reunions were just as joyful as our partings were sad. My reward was being able to hold her. Not with tired devotion, but with fresh enthusiasm filled with longing and love. I had much to tell her, everything that had happened at school, interesting and not so interesting news. She listened without saying anything because very little happened in her life. She was obviously not happy, and I suspected that she might think we were too different. Talking about books frightened her because she seldom read.

"Alright," I said, "we can talk about other things: about us, our future."

"Do we have a future?" she asked. "You'll be going to university soon. You'll become someone important and forget me."

This was slightly comical because doomed love between a poor girl and a rich boy, or the other way round, was a recurrent theme in '60s Turkish films.

"Real life is not the same as in films; besides, I'm not like that," I said.

"Like what?" she asked.

"I'm not rich yet."

We laughed. This was more or less how we spoke to each other. I did not toy with her as she might have feared and held nothing back. I said, "I love you." What worried me was that I was the only one to say those three words. She merely smiled, a little wistful, perhaps a touch suspicious.

Time flew for us, time spent mainly in each other's company. The winter stole our most valuable commodity: Ayfer could no longer come and go as she pleased, the grass was no longer green, the daisies and the stars were gone, the evenings were dark, wet and cold. I shivered out on the balcony in defiance of the elements. Her mother knew about us and acted with tacit acceptance for her daughter's sake. Her father was another story: we had no idea how much he knew. He worked long hours as a ticket inspector for a council-run bus company, came home exhausted and stayed in the background. Ayfer was afraid that her older brother would tell her father about us. If that happened, we would no longer be able to count on acceptance, tacit or otherwise. But as I defied the cold, Ayfer defied her fears, and every time I came home, she invented some excuse or other and ran down the four flights of stairs. I would see her familiar figure lit up in the stairwell. I would have flown if I could, so instead I took the steps three to four at a time. We met, hidden by the entrance to her flat, in the only place we could, and every time we heard footsteps, we jumped.

"Let's go down to the basement," Ayfer said one day.

It was dark there and it smelled of damp, wood and coal. Under the stairs there was a narrow broom closet and I shuddered at the dank surroundings. But no-one would find us there. The basement became our sanctuary and I grew to like it just as much as the grass above. Here we admitted for the first time that kisses were no longer enough. The urge to explore each other was irresistible. I had not touched a woman's naked breasts since I lay in my mother's arms. My hands were clumsy and rested hesitantly on her soft stomach. She had to show me, and, encouraged, I copied her and guided her hand. We changed, grew dreamy.

So our days passed and spring approached. At night I would lie sleepless in my bunk bed in the dormitory and think about her and the day she would be mine completely. One night I knew suddenly that I wanted to marry her.

She showed no sign of surprise, nor did she mention how young we were.

"Then you'll have to send your mother to ask for my hand," was all she would say.

We were secretly engaged, and I bought her a necklace, a heart-shaped medallion with two compartments, as an engagement present. She put photographs of us inside, and wore it proudly and bravely around her neck.

"You're much too young, my boy," my mother said without hesitation. "You still have your whole life ahead of you, and in that life you'll meet fifty other pretty girls, and trust me, you'll fall in love with every one of them."

I denied this, pleaded and made threats. I was going to abduct Ayfer if the adults would not see sense.

"Alright," she said at last. "And do you think your bride would like to sleep in the school dormitory?"

My mother had won – a hollow victory in a battle that wounded both sides.

I went to school and did not return for a long time. My shame was too great for me to meet Ayfer face to face. I had accepted my defeat too easily and betrayed her, and now, by staying away, I was making matters worse. But how could I pretend that nothing had happened and continue playing with her body? Worst of all was the likelihood that she would take the whole business calmly, as the submissive creature she was, and say "I can wait." In other words: "If you're not man enough to fight for me, I can wait until you've grown up." These were my thoughts in my wild rage, but I was being unfair. Ayfer was not someone who would knowingly and deliberately offend; she would use her common sense to assess the impossibility of the situation and the futility of saying, "I can wait." This line of thought did not calm my confused mind. The more I brooded, the harder the road back became. I was no longer her champion and I smiled bitterly at the thought.

I do not know what happened to me: I completely lost my grip. I stopped doing my homework and started reading newspapers and books during lessons. My grades, which were normally impeccable, plummeted. I devoted myself to physical activities and played football with unaccustomed brutality until all my energy was spent. This earned me many enemies on the pitch and the dubious honour of a nickname, "Oak", presumably because it was no use trying to reason with a tree. I flirted with all the available girls, became forward, shameless. The irony was that most of the girls liked me well enough and laughed the whole thing off.

One of these girls reminded me of Ayfer. One day I found her alone in the library and wondered how she would react if I kissed her, but she was reading so innocently, suspecting nothing, that all I felt was tenderness. She looked up and smiled cautiously when she noticed me. I asked if I could borrow a sheet of paper and a pencil.

"Here you are," she said, and I started to draw her.

I regarded myself as a decent draughtsman and would often draw portraits of my friends. A cartoon publisher had once expressed an interest in my work after my mother had sent it to the editor without my knowledge. He wanted me to become an apprentice, but I had no wish to become a cartoonist, a lowly profession in those days.

"I don't remember giving you permission," she said.

"Don't say something you might regret. Be patient," I said. I was careful and took my time.

"I'm going to go now," she said.

I asked her nicely if she would kindly stay. When I had finished, she admired the result.

"I thought you might be joking," she said.

"One should never joke with a pretty girl," I said. So why was I messing Ayfer about? That weekend I went back.

My mother was used to my moods.

"It's the Tartar blood in you," she said.

My sullen absence had lasted longer than usual, but this time the situation was a little different, she conceded, and she showed her joy at seeing me by cooking my favourite dishes. After we had eaten, the doorbell rang. Ayfer stood on the threshold with a bowl of pickled cucumbers. She was just as startled as I was, and we both stuttered.

"I didn't know you were home," she said as she handed me the bowl.

I felt awkward holding it and passed it to my mother, who had emerged from the living room.

"My mother sends her love," Ayfer said to my mother.

"We've become good friends, Ayfer and I. She visits me from time to time," my mother explained.

In order to get some peace and avoid my brother's snide remarks, we sat down in the kitchen. I opened the cheap red wine I had brought with me, little better than the wine vinegar the cucumbers were pickled in. Ayfer had not tasted wine before and wanted to make a cautious debut of only a few drops.

My mother entered, in a good mood. "You're nothing but bad news for this girl," she declared in mock reproach. "But as you're having a celebration here already, I can sin a little, too. Pour me a glass."

When my mother had left, I told Ayfer what had happened.

"I understand," she said.

I could see that she was upset, but she did not really want to talk about it.

"Your mother has been very kind to me," she continued. That was all she said on the matter.

I fetched my diary, eager to show it to her. Thoughts, dreams, mostly about Ayfer – I did not write in it every day. There was a photograph of her on the first page, followed by poems, my own and others. I had not given her many presents during the time we had known each other, so she was keen to have the diary.

"No," I had to say. "I want to write down everything I can't manage or don't get to tell you."

She leaned forward across the table and gave me a long kiss. This happened precisely one week before May Day 1977. One week before the bloodshed in the distant square.

After that the world we shared expanded beyond us. I gave her books, all about the world's oppressed. I wanted her to see the truth and join forces with me against the web of bourgeois deceit. This was a game she had no time for because she was too busy with more pressing matters, something she tried, but failed to communicate to me.

"Of the two of us you're meant to be the enlightened one, and I'm the worker you're meant to save," she said.

I was jealous. I had seen Ayfer with another boy. He was not from our neighbourhood, so he must have followed her home from Bakırköy. I waited for her at the petrol station. She got off the bus with the boy. I went right up to them. She knew all about my temper.

"It's not what you think," she said.

I wanted to call her a whore, and it was not decency that prevented me. It was the boy.

"She didn't want me to, but I insisted on taking her home," he said. "She said she had a boyfriend. I didn't believe her."

I was angry. I had been angry since the day I fled from Taksim Square. I was determined not to run away from anything ever again.

"Do you want to fight me for her?" I asked.

"No, I don't want to fight, not for anything," he said. He turned and walked away when I failed to shake his outstretched hand.

We argued. For the first time Ayfer challenged me.

"You can't go around threatening people. That has nothing to do with love," she said.

"Shut up," I shouted.

"No, I'm not going to shut up, not today. And next time don't act like a thug," she said.

I lost control and I slapped her. She was surprised more than anything else and stared at me, wide-eyed. I was the one who cried and it was she who comforted me.

"I know that you love me, you've just got to find other ways of showing it," she said.

The allotments we walked through smelled of newly turned soil. Soon another couple passed us. They nodded and smiled; everyone knew the local Romeo and Juliet.

Ayfer did not punish me, but she had been sad before and now she seemed sadder still. I felt as though something was slipping through my fingers, something I was losing forever. At the time I wanted to change the world. I should have started by changing myself.

3

July 1977

I was exhausted when I came home. A heatwave was suffocating the city – you could fry eggs on the pavement. I went out onto the balcony for a short while. It was unbearably hot, the whole street was deserted, there was not even a stray dog to be seen. It was cooler inside than out. My mother had gone to stay the night with her sister; true to form she had made dinner in advance and put it in the fridge. However, my energy and my appetite had both deserted me. My brother was working overtime at the leather workshop where he was an apprentice, so I had nothing to do but take my clothes off, lie down on the divan and drift off into a sweaty, troubled sleep.

Our doorbell did not work, so it must have been the knocking that woke me up. A cautious tapping that was nevertheless loud enough to rouse me. I must have been fast asleep for some time, because it had grown dark outside. Still drowsy, I pulled on my underpants. It had to be my brother, who did not have his own keys. That privilege was reserved for my mother and for me as man of the house. I went to open the door. Ayfer was standing outside and for the second time we surprised each other, she with her unannounced arrival and me with my Tarzan outfit.

"Why aren't you wearing a tie?" she said. She could be very funny when she wanted to.

I muttered something unintelligible.

"Alright, you're drunk, do you have some wine left?" She walked past me into the living room.

I was no longer groggy, but I was embarrassed and nervous and much more besides, which made it even harder to wriggle into my tight jeans and equally tight T-shirt. She smiled as she watched me.

"That'll do."

"What will?"

"Take off your T-shirt," she ordered me.

"But I've just put it on."

"Today I'm in charge, so come on, take off your T-shirt."

She loved playing games, and this had to be a new one, I decided, as I struggled with the T-shirt. She was not clumsy. With eager hands she unbuttoned her shirt, hung it neatly over the back of a chair and turned to face me, revealing small, firm breasts.

"And the trousers," she said calmly.

I nearly fell over, but managed to wriggle out of my jeans. It was a piece of cake for her to let her skirt slip to the floor with a single shake of her hips. When she said "underpants" in her commando voice, she failed to keep a straight face and started to giggle.

This was easier said than done, something was getting in the way. Oh, no, I groaned inwardly when I should have been overjoyed. If not now, then when? Never before had I tried to undress in such a hurry and cover up at the same time.

"What do you think?" she asked.

A question born of vanity. The moonbeams that fell on to her body carved out an ivory statue. She was a Venus, but I was no Apollo: no-one had ever seen Apollo cover himself with trembling hands. This was different from our fully dressed moments in the basement, which we jokingly referred to as "full armour minus the chastity belt". You were braver in the dark. The light brought out every inhibition and made you reticent, but I still preferred it. She was from another world as she stood there, naked. I wanted to drink her, become one with her, I would die for her, and yet I continued to stand there, rooted to the spot, paralysed.

"I came here to become yours," she said and broke the silence before gliding weightlessly past me and settling velvet-soft as a butterfly on the divan. What followed was diffuse. I was all over her like a bull in a china shop. I did not know what to do with the various parts of my body and had no idea whether I was in or out, but could feel that she was warm, soft and wet beneath me. My head was pounding.

"The door," she whispered.

What door? Was she referring to a certain opening? It was too late, something burning erupted from me.

"Someone's outside," she said, more clearly this time.

I raised my head like a wild animal that senses danger. Someone was hammering on the front door.

My brother was fuming, but he relished every single second of this opportunity to yell at me as I struggled into the rest of my clothes. Ayfer had finished dressing long ago and sat on a chair, smiling.

"You can't be a revolutionary if you shut out the real workers," he shouted. He was no longer angry, but baiting me. Since he had found a job and started earning, he had lost his respect for me. The time when I would have punched him to shut him up had passed. But this did not apply to Ayfer. They were not siblings, merely classmates.

"Shut up! And stop whining like an old woman." she shouted with unexpected force.

Slightly embarrassed, my brother pretended that he had only now become aware of her presence.

"By the way, what are you doing here?" he asked with the justified gravity of a host.

"I can come and go as I please, just like you. I'm his."

"His? Yeah right," my brother snorted. "Go wipe your nose first."

I watched this exchange of fire, helpless. My brother looked at his big hands, the embarrassing situation finally dawning on him and he decided that he had had enough of us. He came over to sit on the divan.

"No, not there!" Ayfer and I called out in unison.

"Bloody hell, what a mess," he groaned in disgust, and reprised the whole symphony about how horrified he was at such a shameless pair.

The whole thing culminated in helpless laughter. We were all hungry, so we went to the kitchen. Ayfer fetched the dinner from the fridge and heated it up while we set the table and opened some beers. We ate and chatted. The two classmates agreed that when they had finished school they would work to support me, the intellectual who would one day free them from their chains. They were having fun at my expense, and after a few beers, my brother gave Ayfer a hug and called her "my lovely sister-in-law".

"Get your hands off her," I said. Ayfer told me off for being a primitive and jealous Stone Age man.

She was serious when she left. She stood in the doorway, caressed my cheek and said, "Don't worry about what happened. It'll be alright next time."

*

"Take this ring, please," Hadji said, handing it to me across the vegetable crates. It was an eighteen-carat gold signet ring. I saw the hallmark as I examined it. The ring had always decorated the little finger on his left hand.

Hadji was a sturdy man, a Kurd from the distant mountains. I knew that he was young, but his weather-beaten face concealed his true age.

He was a good-natured and peaceful man, and he probably owed these characteristics to his Bektashi faith. He was a greengrocer, a loyal customer in the vegetable market and a friend.

"I can't do that, Hadji. I know how precious it is to you," I said.

He must be short of cash for some reason and wanted to pay for his purchases with his ring. Hadji was a man of honour and an unpaid debt was the greatest shame that could befall him. I tried to make him change his mind.

"There's no rush, Hadji. Pay me whenever you can."

"Keep the ring for now," he insisted.

"There's no need, Hadji. Unless you've bought a one-way ticket out of here," I joked.

He fell silent and rolled his worry beads between his fingers. "Well, brother, that's precisely what might just happen," he said.

As he was not a man to drop a hint that would arouse curiosity only to say goodbye before it was satisfied, he confided all his troubles to me. I wondered why. We knew one another from the market, but we were not close personal friends. Even though there was an unspoken bond of trust between us, he took a chance in choosing me. He was faced by a dilemma and felt terribly lonely. His family were going to abduct an underage girl the next day. This had occurred since the dawn of time in this part of the world; almost the entire Ottoman dynasty, who had reigned over the fates of generations, were fathered on abducted girls. I had myself threatened to abduct Ayfer, empty words of course and completely unrealistic. Even if I had done so, no-one would have been killed or injured; the feelings of those involved might have been hurt, but nothing else. Still, my adolescent flight of fancy stood testament to the legacy that centuries of tradition had left in our minds.

However, in the legend of Hadji – this was how his family would later refer to it – everything was far more complicated. Ballads had been sung and legends had been written about abducted girls. Every little clan and family had its own story, enshrined in family tradition, if the love was reciprocated. Hadji claimed it was mutual: the girl was fifteen and in love with his brother, but her family refused to discuss marriage plans. It was a large and powerful family that could trace its roots centuries back and was therefore held in high regard. They were notorious for finding it hard to give their women up and a long history of blood feuds bore witness to this. I could understand his dilemma; he was of a peaceful nature and feared the worst. On the other hand, his family held a loss of face to be an outcome far worse than death. Dying to preserve one's honour was always preferable. I wondered if anyone had thought about the two young lovers in all of this. What kind of life awaited them? Were they ever to be together?

"Don't do it, Hadji," I pleaded. "You must do everything you can to stop it."

I said other things as well, about how it had to end one day, that this was a great opportunity for him to break the vicious circle. It might be a drop in the ocean, but one drop was better than nothing at all.

Hadji was a very polite man. He listened without interruption, and when he was sure that I had finished, he said that he had not come here for advice. He had plenty of grey-bearded sages for that. There was a hint of sarcasm in his voice when he mentioned the sages. He just wanted to confide in a friend who had no connection to his culture. He spat the word "culture" as though it were a curse, so that at least one person would know that Hadji was a decent and peaceful man. He then tried to offer me his beads as a present.

"No, Hadji, you know I'm not a believer, it would be wrong for both of us," I said.

"Then give them to your dear mother," he said.

I had never told him anything about my mother: he must have taken it for granted that she was a believer. However, people who live exclusively for and in accordance with their traditions never mention a woman they have not yet met without good reason.

He smiled. "They are not just for believers, they also represent serenity and patience, and with a son like you, your dear mother needs plenty of both."

It was a kind thing to say. I accepted the worry beads and thanked him. He bowed his head and took his leave in the traditional manner by placing his hand on his heart. Then turned and left without a word of goodbye. I knew the beads signified something more. This gesture was his way of saying that he had no hope of ever coming back. It might sound strange, but he and his people had a kind of second sight: they knew when they were going to win and when they were going to lose.

When I picked Ayfer up from work, my heart was still heavy from my conversation with Hadji. It was a fine summer's day but with no suffocating heat, cooled by a refreshing breeze from the sea. The two other shop assistants waved, winked knowingly and said, "Have fun." As usual, the manager of the shop peered suspiciously at us, as though I were a potential shoplifter. It was common knowledge that he did not tolerate boyfriends loitering in the vicinity. Ayfer chatted nineteen to the dozen, and I let her. It was not difficult – all I had to do was relax my shoulders, make the right noises in the right places and admire her birdsong voice. I was not her only admirer: all eyes followed her Sophia Loren walk, which only girls from our part of the world are blessed with. Since most of those pairs of eyes belonged to would-be alpha males, I preferred to show them who was boss by putting my arm around her waist rather than by challenging them all to a fight.

"You're not listening to me," she laughed, pounding my chest with her small fists.

"Of course I am," I said, "but I can hear you better when you're close to me."

At the seafront the cafés were packed with couples and we no longer stood out. We ordered tea, which arrived in small glasses with feminine curves, fashioned no doubt by a glassblower with a healthy respect for nature's beauty. Nature herself stretched out before our eyes: the blue sea, the sky and the orange ball of an evening sun against the horizon. Ayfer grew silent like a bird that stops chirping when evening falls. She stared into her tea as though she expected to see something reflected in its surface at any moment. I could not ask her what she was looking for – it would have been a little too intrusive. I thought about the beads in my pocket, urging serenity and patience, qualities that Hadji, with true insight, had identified as lacking in me.

It was painful to lurch from joy to sadness, but each new state demanded a change of mood. I shuddered and looked at her face. Had I believed in curses, I would have said that eternal sorrow was hers. To my irritation it suited her, but then again there was very little that did not become Ayfer.

*

It was my mother who instilled in me the joy of reading. Every time I was ill she would surprise me with a new book. She believed strongly that a good book and a slice of chocolate cake would work just as well as the doctor's medicine. In addition, she would regularly borrow books from the mobile library that visited our neighbourhood, books that opened doors to a world where the most amazing things were possible. Alice wandered in Wonderland, Pollyanna found of set of crutches in a chest and was grateful that she did not need them; we trembled at the tense atmosphere on Treasure Island, and Jules Verne always had incredible journeys to offer. In time, debate arose about the characters we encountered in the land of imagination. We had differing views on the fates of Madame Bovary and Anna Karenina, and completely disagreed in our interpretations of the holy texts.

My mother was a believer on a very personal level. She was happy living in a secular society, as were most people of her generation, and regarded faith as a personal matter. We were offered religious education, but no-one ever pressured us. The only time my brother and I received any scolding on account of religion was when we chased after women wearing black tent-like chadors and made fun of them. My mother respected everyone who believed in a god, no matter which one, and deeply missed the Christian neighbours from her childhood and their colourful Easter eggs. She loved talking to us – to me mainly; my brother did not have the patience for anything that took time. We could discuss anything and everything. Well, almost anything. Love, for example, was one of her favourite subjects, but not sex. "I'm afraid you'll have to find that out for yourself, son," she said. Yet she had contributed to my knowledge of the secrets of the female body through our weekly visits to the local *hamam*, visits that ended abruptly when I was ten years old when the huge gipsy woman who guarded the entrance said: "Don't forget to bring your husband as well next time."

Up until I turned fifteen, my father went in and out of my life like a welcome guest, a tall, well-built man with narrow eyes and high cheekbones, strong, skilled working hands and a proud temperament. I had inherited my mother's appearance just as much as I had inherited my father's temper. Apart from these genetic legacies, he left no other mark on my life. He was rarely there at the times when a child needs his or her father. He worked long hours as an electrician in a large factory and as a film machinist in a cinema. In my childish mind he was the incarnation of something great and at the same time slightly terrifying, someone who demanded and received total obedience. But things changed. As I grew older we developed a more relaxed relationship, and it was a shame that fate conspired to cut it short. I wish we could have had more time for second-division football matches in small stadiums, where we could heckle politely "shame on you, Mr Referee, why do you blow your whistle at that?" For weekend trips to the fish restaurants along the Bosporus, and conversations where he would not get the last word. I was by his bedside when he died, hours after his third heart attack. I was fourteen years old and thought that he was free now, just as his ancestors had once been, riding their swift horses across the steppes of the Crimean peninsula.

My mother cut an anxious figure as she sat there on the divan with her knitting. I could not understand how she found the energy to knit in her spare time after all the sewing she was commissioned to do by the local textile factories. It supplemented her meagre widow's pension, as did my and my brother's wages, and, compared to the first few years that followed after my father's death, we were doing alright. What worried her these days was no longer money but my safety. The May Day events had left their mark on her – she scared easily these days. She was very protective and asked endless questions whenever she heard my friends whistle in the street. I tried to reassure her, but she had to understand that I could not spend the rest of my life tied to her apron strings.

"I didn't give birth to a son just to sacrifice him to the Fascists," she said.

Ever since the '50s, Turkish Fascists had been a weapon at the disposal of the authorities in their fight against progressive forces. Their ideology was simple and based on Turkish nationalism. It was they who had attacked the Christian minorities in the '50s, robbed them of all they had and forced them to flee the country. It was ironic that the Communists, and the country's cultural elite in particular, had been blamed at the public trials that followed in the wake of the violence.

By the start of the '70s, the Fascists had become the volunteer informants of the military junta. To begin with, political assassinations were rare: the Fascists were still learning their trade. In time, however, more and more intellectuals, journalists and trade union leaders were eliminated and their murderers invariably vanished without a trace. Eventually, when the Fascists had swelled in number and organized and armed themselves, they could no longer be bothered to select their victims. Anyone could be a target, from social democratic workers in factories to revolutionary students at colleges. They went about in armed hordes and shot down the first person they saw. Our school friend Ali lost his life like that: one day when he was out with his friends he was hit by a bullet.

In my mother's eyes the Fascists were responsible for everything that happened. She was convinced that they had been on the rooftops on May Day, firing at the crowds. In vain I tried to explain that it had to be the Contra-Guerrillas, agents provocateurs, who were behind this, and where would you start looking for them? To my mother it was utterly unthinkable that the state would start massacring its own citizens. She had grown up with the concept of a Fatherland that existed to be obeyed, feared and loved. When I pointed this out, she smiled and said: "It's a man's world, my boy."

She was terrified that I would get involved with an uprising against the government. It was just too dangerous. "I understand that you want to defend yourself against the Fascists, may God punish them, but don't go against the state. Nothing good has ever come out of that." She was referring to the two years at the start of the '70s when student rebels were jailed, tortured and finally hanged. As a child I would sit next to her while she read aloud from the Koran for their young souls, her eyes filled with tears.

I cared little for the Fascists. The fight against the Fascists was but one step on a long road. It was the narrow path that led on from that which troubled me. But as I sat reading my book beside mother with her knitting, I thought how cosy it was to seek shelter under her comforting wings. Her maternal instincts allowed her to sense the dark clouds that hid the sun from my gaze and asked me to confide in her: "Your worries are my worries."

I dismissed her with a comment I employed when something was my business alone: "It's nothing but the usual worries."

"You have to read this book, Mother."

"I'm looking forward to it already, son. What's it called?"

"*The Mother*, by Maxim Gorky, Mother."

*

The blood oozing from the gash to Ahmet's forehead had coagulated and it now looked as if a red patch had been stuck to the right-hand side of his face. He was disoriented, and while I tried to clean the wound with a cloth, he mumbled something incomprehensible. "I'll get the bastard. Oh God, I bet it's bad."

It was hard to get any sense out of him. The presence of his relatives and friends, who had gathered around us and were talking over each other, did nothing to help matters.

Finally I spoke up. "Haven't you got jobs to do? Go away! I don't need your help."

They were ordinary people who were used to taking orders as they had all done national service, and besides, the rules were clear, this was my patch, where I was in charge and no-one could challenge me. Soon we were alone and I could get on with my work in peace. I cleaned and dried the cut. It was a flesh wound and looked much worse than it really was. It was hard to say if it needed stitches, but it probably did not, so I decided to dress it. For once the first-aid training I had done as a Boy Scout came in useful. Apart from complaining about the pain a couple of times, Ahmet stayed mostly still while I tended to him, firmly and brusquely. When I had finished, I said calmly, "So, Ahmet. Can you tell me what happened?"

He was no longer in shock, but his pale-blue eyes still betrayed fear and confusion. Dazed, he looked down at his jacket and his hands, which were stained with blood.

"It's not serious, you've lost a little blood, but it definitely won't kill you," I said. I was trying to provoke him and succeeded beyond expectation.

He raised his head and gave me a furious stare. "What do you know? Those bastards wanted to kill me." He let the rest of the story pour out.

He had been picking out the day's porters, as he did every day. Only the big wholesalers had regular ones – the rest of us had to choose from whoever was available, a recurring source of conflict, as there were more poor men with families to feed than jobs going in the market. Ahmet claimed it was pure coincidence that he had picked only Turkish porters. This was probably true, but the Kurdish porters – "disrespect-ful and primitive, don't you think?" – saw things in a rather different light.

Harsh words and abusive language had escalated into a fistfight. Someone had punched him from behind, he hit back and suddenly the most aggressive of them was brandishing a flick-knife. Ahmet had panicked, grabbed hold of a plank of wood and swung it at random. Something hit his head, a stone perhaps, the blood spurted out and ran into his eyes. He sunk hopelessly to his knees, convinced he was done for. Then he heard a shrill whistle. Two police officers came running and seized his assailant, while the rest scattered. He knew the police officers from earlier; they were here to collect their "wages" from the wholesalers. Just as well, because the police rarely patrolled this area.

"Was that him?" they had asked Ahmet. He had nodded in the affirmative and they had set about beating the Kurd there and then before dragging him off to the police station.

"If you hadn't been so bloody stubborn and made me take that pistol back, I would have had it today. Sometimes it's enough to just open your jacket to show it, then no-one in their right mind pulls a knife on you."

Ahmet interrupted me firmly when I opened my mouth to ask what about anyone who was not in their right mind? He had not yet finished: "And another thing. Because of you that poor guy is getting the beating of his life down at the police station as we speak."

"Why don't you pack up, go home to rest and ask your wife to give you a couple of painkillers and make a good soup fit for an invalid?" I suggested.

He knocked over his chair in rage as he stood up and, to the amusements of onlookers, shouted, "You're the one who's sick in the head!" He continued to repeat this as he disappeared out of sight.

At lunchtime Ahmet returned with his tail between his legs. His wife was even less sympathetic than I had been when it came to his injuries; she had told him to go to hell and not come back until he was properly hurt. I chuckled discreetly, but as he seemed to be genuinely miserable I disguised my laughter as a coughing fit. We ate in relative silence: grapes, feta cheese, tomatoes, cucumbers and freshly baked bread.

Afterwards I noticed some unusual activity on the other side of the market hall. A knot of unfamiliar young men, roughly ten strong, had gathered in an open space. They seemed nervous, on the lookout, and the glances they aimed in my direction were not exactly friendly. At first I thought I was seeing things. But as their eyes were increasingly drawn towards me, I decided on another explanation. They had to be Ahmet's Kurdish "friends" from earlier that day. Ahmet was in the hut that served as our office. When I told him, he looked out of the window, and he was in no doubt.

"We're in deep trouble now," he said, sending me an accusing look as he reached for the telephone with slightly trembling hands to call for backup. Most of his relatives worked on the same aisle in the market. He also wanted to call the police.

"No," I said. "No more police. Let's try to sort this out ourselves." I was grateful that he did not ask how.

Ahmet's kin were soon formed up around our stall and the two rival groups faced one other. The situation was menacing and unreal. I did not want to believe that these honest and hard-working men could display such animosity towards each other, but it had happened before. Now they stood poised in a ridiculous show of swaggering machismo, waiting for the kick-off, which, in this case, would be that one word of provocation too far. You could easily imagine the rest. So what was I going to do about it? Strictly speaking, it had nothing to do with me. They had fought each other for generations without any help from me. What I needed to do was clear off. No-one would miss me and no-one would call me a coward, because I was not one of them.

"Alright," I said. "I'll go to them and negotiate."

I hushed the crowd with a commanding index finger to my lips, turned and crossed the aisle. My heart was pounding as though it were trying to escape my body. I could not blame it: the rest of me was also desperate to be anywhere else. Cold sweat made my old Scout shirt stick to my back. My mouth was dry, the bile rose all the way to my throat, and I was not sure if I would be able to find my voice.

The opponents hesitated; it seemed as if they had no idea what to do with this young man. I hoped they knew not to shoot the messenger, but history was full of messengers who had lost their heads.

"What do you want?" asked the one nearest me. I was out of luck here – he had the darkest stare.

"To negotiate," I said, almost choking on the word. My voice did not extend to sentences.

"And who might you be?"

"The bookkeeper," I said. Some smiled, others laughed out loud. I had no idea that bookkeepers were such an amusing species.

"Our business is not with you. Get out of here." said the spokesman, gravely. "Typical Turks to send the bookkeeper!"

I felt a profound sense of powerlessness. I needed a breakthrough, something that would impress them.

"I'm a revolutionary." It was delivered with all the dignity I could muster, but it sounded pathetic all the same.

"Makes no difference," the man with the dark stare said. At least he seemed to be taking me seriously.

"Who says?" one of the Kurds asked. It was a good sign that they were a touch divided. I seized my moment.

"Listen. If you promise to keep calm, I'll try to get your mate out of the police station."

This had a far greater impact than my claim to be a pro-Kurdish revolutionary. The silence was broken by fierce discussion in a language I could not follow. What if one of them were to spin around and stab me in the stomach without warning? I looked around for an escape route. Appearing hesitant and edgy might set off their already suspicious minds. The problem was that I did not know what the people staring at me were seeing. When someone grabbed my arm firmly I was jolted from these thoughts as if from a nightmare.

"Listen to me," said the man with the dark stare. "The one they took is my brother. I can handle him getting a bit of a beating, but if you don't come back with him soon, I'll regard you as just as responsible as those oppressors over there."

Ahmet's relatives did not look much like oppressors when I returned. The tense waiting had visibly frayed their nerves. Back in relative safety, I told them about my negotiations.

"How were you thinking of getting him out?" Ahmet asked. It was a valid question.

"Not me. You'll get him out," I replied.

"You're insane!" he protested.

I fetched the day's takings from the till – a whole bunch of notes – and stuffed them into the breast pocket of Ahmet's jacket.

"Use that famous charm of yours on your contacts and splash some cash around."

"Are you trying to ruin me?" he whined.

"Shut your mouth," Ahmet's cousin said to him. He was a short, sturdy, swarthy man who in terms of appearance was more closely related to the Kurds. "You've already cost us enough time and worry. Next time you'll think twice before you get yourself into a mess like this. Now off you go."

Ahmet was reluctant. His feet almost walked backwards, but he was on his own on this one. Cigarettes were lit and we waited. I looked at the men around me. If you were to meet them on the highroad and ask them how far it was to the next village, they would reply with the number of cigarettes you could smoke in the time it took you to get there. We were held in suspense for precisely three cigarettes. When Ahmet appeared at the end of the market hall with a bruised and limping man for company, a sigh of relief went through the crowd. There was even an element of comedy to the scene because Ahmet had his enemy's arm around his shoulder and was half carrying, half supporting him to the best of his abilities. The humiliation for both of them must have been complete. They were eventually put out of their misery when they were mobbed by the jubilant gang of Kurds.

I felt sorry for Ahmet – ultimately it was his blood and his money that had been spent. There was no point in asking him how he had got the Kurd out of the police station. He would act all closed and defiant for a few days, and then he would be back to his old self again.

*

"Make way for the Communist," Ahmet roared in his porter's voice, so that our end of the market hall seemed almost to reverberate with the echo. It was a miracle that the police officers doing their collecting rounds did not come over to start beating me up. I was in no doubt that he wanted revenge.

"Revolutionary," I corrected him. "Not Communist."

"Isn't that the same thing?" he said innocently.

It was obviously a distinction without difference as far as the working classes were concerned, but then again I did not expect Ahmet to know the lines of demarcation. I knew a few who called themselves Communists, actual members of the Turkish Communist Party. There was no disputing their bravery – membership was in itself sufficient cause for imprisonment, according to the law – but I did not understand how you could call yourself a Communist if you did not live like one. None of those I knew was a worker; at best they were students, and some had a middle-class background. They liked to talk like intellectuals, drink rakı and had nothing against money. I found it hard to believe that they were going to change society. It seemed almost as if they were waiting for a revolution to come strolling along one fine day. And then there were the Maoist Communists, who were distinguished by their steadfast rejection of all earthly pleasures.

The promise of a future paradise had not tempted me before, so why would it do so now? You only had to look at the Soviet Union and China. They lost their revolutionary zeal once power had been seized. I wanted to live well on this earth, to love, eat, drink, sing, enjoy peace and share the spoils equally. But I had seen enough to know that nothing comes of nothing.

Suddenly I could smell burning. Something close to me had caught fire. My newspaper was ablaze! The flames shot upwards. I threw down the remains of the paper and stamped on them to crush the embers. Most of the things that surrounded us were made from wood and a few errant sparks would be enough to start a serious fire. It did not take me

55

long to find the arsonist. Ahmet, still holding his lighter, could barely breathe he was laughing so hard. I looked around, got hold of a ripe tomato and hurled it with all my strength. Ahmet was fast, he ducked and the tomato missed him by a millimetre.

"You don't burn newspapers, you ape," I shouted. While I was busy gathering more ammunition, he had kicked off his clogs to flee barefoot and was already halfway down the aisle.

I had so much on my mind. My revolution gave me a genuine headache. What could be done to prevent it from suffering the same fate as all the other failed attempts in history? And what about Ayfer, who competed for the first place among my priorities? Then there was my future: my last year at sixth-form college was about to start, what did I want to be? A doctor, a teacher, an engineer? How could I best serve a new society, a new republic? And Hadji. Where was he? What had happened to him, if indeed anything had happened? So many kilos of tomatoes and grapes, so many prices, the figures flickered before my eyes. I struggled with thoughts that confused me and invoices that did not add up, without realizing that someone with the answers to all my questions was very close at hand.

"2,549. I think you missed out the figures in the fifth column."

She was standing behind me, leaning over my shoulder. She did not smell of perfume and she was quiet – that was why I had not noticed her. She must have been standing there for a while, long enough to complete the calculation I had been struggling with. I was not surprised. I knew that she would turn up some day, that we had not finished with each other. It was as if no time had passed at all. Same tight ponytail, same checked shirt, same jeans and same canvas bag. Her shirt had been unbuttoned in the meantime, however. She smiled when she noticed where my eyes fell and made no attempt to pinch the collar.

"Hello, brother-in-arms. How have you been?" she whispered into my ear.

56

Ahmet was overjoyed. He offered her his chair and sat down on an empty crate. He called for the coffee-maker's runner, ordered tea and asked her if she was hungry and wanted some toast to go with it. He did everything I ought to have done, and winked to me, thinking that it was my girlfriend who had come to visit. She watched the bustling crowds with a contented smile, and when the sugar had dissolved in the tea and we had taken our first sip, she began to talk. She was here with some other students to start a literacy course for workers at the vegetable market. They had met with opposition – from both porters and wholesalers – but eventually they had managed to get together a fairly sizeable group. At the end of that day's course, the Kurds in the group had asked if the students could do them a favour. When they saw that it was a woman who volunteered, they were slightly taken aback. She was here to talk to Ahmet. The Kurds had a proposal. If, from now on, Ahmet would employ Turkish and Kurdish porters in equal numbers, he could count on their friendship. I could see that Ahmet was proud to be at the centre of the conversation. He wanted to milk the situation for all it was worth and tried hard to create the impression that he was giving the matter his full and serious attention. Though he was a joker, he was a hopeless actor, so the whole thing merely looked as if he had digestive trouble.

"It's a deal," he said at last, and ordered a refill of the tea glasses to celebrate.

So, to fill her in, he started telling her all about the incident with the Kurdish porters. He awarded himself the starring role at every turn and made out that he had practically stormed the police station to free the poor Kurd, neglecting to mention the money that had changed hands. It was a textbook example of how a woman, by her mere presence, could bring out the hidden vanity in every man. Only a fearless knight would win the hand of the fair maiden, and now that Ahmet had realised that she was not my girlfriend, it was worth a try.

"How interesting," she said when Ahmet had finished and was waiting for her response. "Would you like to join our literacy course?"

I suppressed my laughter. Ahmet murmured something about already being able to read and write. I wanted to say "barely", but thought better of it.

She had some sad news for us as well. The Kurds had asked her to tell us that Hadji had been badly wounded in a shoot-out when his family had tried to abduct the young girl. He was now in police custody and risked a lengthy jail sentence. Ahmet forgot his wounded pride and went to fetch Hadji's ring, which he gave to her to send on to Hadji's family. I was keen to be alone with her, but Ahmet stuck to us like glue. It irritated me that she laughed at his monkey tricks and seemed as though she was enjoying the attention.

When he played his final card and invited us to dinner, I said: "Your wife called, you're having people over for dinner tonight." It was a half truth. She had called, but only to say that Ahmet could forget about a cooked dinner as she was visiting some friends.

"The more the merrier," Ahmet insisted, sending me a killer look, but she had got the message.

"Perhaps another time," she said politely. You did not get involved with workers who had a wife at home.

"We're not closed yet," Ahmet called out after me as we left.

"I'll work overtime tomorrow," I called back. A tomato – from the Marmara district judging by its size and colour – flew past my head.

"Is this how you do things here?" she laughed.

I had not seen her laugh at our previous meeting. She was attractive in a way teenage girls can so rarely match.

Silently I walked next to her. We seemed like friends with a long history, and perhaps we were. The road we walked now was merely an extension of our journey back from Taksim Square.

"Are you going home?" she asked.

58

"No, not straight away. We can sit down for a while if you like," I said.

She hesitated. "I don't know. We'll be meeting soon at the market for my next lesson."

"I see." I was disappointed.

She could hear it. "On the other hand I have plenty of time. It won't hurt to talk to you for a little while."

There was no reason to feel as happy as I did, it was just the way it was. We sat down in a café, a traditionally male preserve, under the bridge. Men smoking hookahs and playing cards or backgammon sent us curious and critical looks before returning to their pastimes. She clearly enjoyed provoking men, but it seemed as if these men had grown accustomed to the new times. The smell of fried fish from the dinghies along the quay, the cry of the gulls, and a mixture of exhaust fumes and salt water filled the air. I did not know what to say to her.

"Do you have a girlfriend?" she asked.

"Yes."

"What's her name?"

"Ayfer. What's yours?"

"Zuhal."

I told her my name. She did not seem to like it.

"I'll call you . . . wait a moment . . . I'll call you 'my little friend'. Is that alright with you?"

It was not. I wanted her to use my name to show that we were peers, equals.

"Don't get upset. I don't call everyone my friend, besides, we're brothers-in-arms, and that's what matters."

"What's in your bag today?"

"Only my books, but let's not talk about that now. Tell me about your girlfriend."

I told her about Ayfer. Almost everything. I only left out the day she

59

came to become mine. I did not understand why I opened my heart to Zuhal. Perhaps because she was a stranger. Or, conversely, because I knew her very well.

"Like Ferhad and Shirin?" she wondered.

"I prefer Romeo and Juliet."

"Same fate. None of them gets their beloved in the end. Drop her. Before it's too late."

Drop her? I was annoyed now. "Why do you say that? I love her."

She reclined with a smile that was neither teasing nor comforting.

"Love. It's an illusion. Love doesn't exist."

"Yes, it does," I said defiantly.

"Love between a man and a woman is only about sex, my friend."

She might know what she was talking about. I was tempted to ask if hers was the wisdom of dearly bought experience, but I was scared of offending her.

"We should only love mankind, and that has very little to do with sex."

She took out her purse from her bag and placed a bank note on the table. I protested. "It'll be your treat next time," she said, leaning over the table. "I'm serious. Drop her. You know she's not the right woman for you."

I wondered which woman she thought *was* the right one.

4

Autumn 1977

The end of August.

Little friend,

It was not me! Did you think it was me? The last place I was based carrier pigeons were the only means of communication. I have a feeling that I spoiled you a little when I called from civilization. Please don't get your hopes up every time the phone rings and you don't get there in time. I got two letters from you when we returned from the mountains. They were waiting for me in the hotel reception. Imagine how happy I was, and how you write! The poems were lovely. I presume they are your own. You will become our Mayakovsky, a pure revolutionary poet. But be careful, all your petit bourgeois dreams shine through the verses. And who is that woman you mention so often?

You should have come with us. I mean it, you should. Next time, perhaps, if there is a next time. What we have seen with our own eyes, you would not be able to imagine. I am not just talking about the landscape; it is amazing, the mountains, free, beautiful, wild, mountains not yet ruined by human hands. But the contrasts too! You come across them like an unexpected slap in the face. When you start the climb from the town – relatively civilized – it feels like you are entering another world. Up there you find only scattered villages with no roads, no electricity, no running water – unbelievable poverty (it's that which surprises me the least). Their wealth, however, is in their hearts. You should have seen the hospitality with which we were received. It's a shame I can't speak their language. Fortunately we have an interpreter, a student from this region. The other day we set off on a long walk across the mountains with a local girl as our guide. Without her we would surely have got lost in an instant. She was like a mountain goat, silent, stubborn and light-footed; I have a suspicion that she was secretly laughing at us city folk. And when one of the boys asked if it was almost time for a cigarette break, she looked up at him with ominously dark eyes and said, "We've only just started," in broken Turkish. Still, we were glad she was there: at one point the path disappeared completely, and a step further on there was a sheer drop of several hundred metres. The carcass of a cow lying at the bottom by the riverbank served as warning of what awaits anyone who loses their footing. Eventually we came across a family living in the mountains. The man of the house wanted to slaughter a kid in our honour. You can imagine how the girls screamed and squealed. He was a bit offended, but he had to give up. The kid was marked with a red ribbon, which means it will escape being slaughtered for all eternity. We are off on another walk tomorrow. If we can manage it!

I was not able to finish my letter and had to take it with me all the way to the Black Sea. Fatsa is a small coastal town. The people here are very politically aware. We are staying with friends now. We will be here for a while. You will find the address at the end of this letter, which you can write to. News: sweet music has started between Kemal and me (the young man from Taksim Square, do you remember?). Not that lightning has struck from a clear blue sky. It had been in the air for a while. The fresh breeze from the sea might have had something to do with it. Even though I have mellowed a little, I still don't believe in love yet. Jealous? You shouldn't be. He can have my body; my heart, never! There are mountains here, too. The two of us went for a walk yesterday. Green woods, blue sky, a glimpse of the sea far away. It rained a little at noon. "This is what I call a mountain. We can definitely start a guerrilla unit here," Kemal said. *The mountains of Dersim were too tough for the poor boy.*

How are things with Ayfer, by the way? Be nice to her and drop her. I know this irritates you, but you have to decide. Do you want to be a revolutionary, or a family man with five children?

Kemal was curious. "*What are you writing?*" he asked. "*I'm making notes,*" I said. *Not entirely untrue, I make notes as well. This might be a little childish, but I want to keep you to myself, as my secret. I don't trust men. They don't understand anything. Alright, alright. You understand a little. Got to go now. Write me a long letter.*

I miss you.

Hugs and kisses,

Zuhal

P.S. I miss Istanbul too, the exhaust fumes and the rubbish everywhere.

I missed her. I had missed her since the day she left Istanbul. She was part of a group of students who had gone to explore the country, or parts of it, and write dissertations about its social and economic conditions. I was not interested in going, only by the fact that she had left. She had entered my life like a whirlwind. She was funny and knowledgeable, she was direct, she loved to talk and had the courage to act. There was much more to her than just the pistol-wielding woman I had met in Taksim Square. My enthusiasm for her as a political role model knew no bounds. I was attracted to her, though she never appeared in my dreams. It was easy to fall in love with her and at the same time not so straightforward. She was good at making herself androgynous and deflecting unwanted desire. She treated me correctly, sometimes with a hint of flirtation, and made it clear that she valued me highly, once saying, a little solemnly: "Something happened between us on the Square, something that bound us together. If I had not met you again, I would have lived the rest of my life a sad woman."

She called me a couple of times from towns with exotic names. As the study trip had been extended, apparently with the vice-chancellor's permission, we started writing to each other. She sent brief, precise letters about the highlights of her trip. Mine were much longer, the last one sixteen pages, about all sorts of things. Her letters arrived haphazardly because she was constantly on the move, so I never waited for a reply before seizing my pen again. My letters reached her via a private postal system – someone was always going her way. This was how I discovered that I enjoyed writing. Being my mother's son I was fascinated by poetry and believed that it was the most complex and at the same time the most beautiful form in which mankind could express itself. Compressing a whole world into a few words was uniquely fascinating every time you succeeded. I was proud of and in time became dependent on her recognition of what I, in all seriousness, called my poetry. I do not know if it were true, the bit about them being petit bourgeois, but I hoped that my poems reflected unrequited love, longing, plenty of *tristesse* and a luminous optimism for a better world. The women were not her, not yet, they were diffuse, provisional and, unlike Zuhal, they were passive muses.

I grew jealous when I learned about her and Kemal, the way you feel jealous when you surprise your mother with your father or when your sister finds a boyfriend. Or at least, that was what I preferred to think. She had chosen Kemal and it could have been worse.

*

I went back to school in September. Saying goodbye to Ayfer was a sad affair. She embraced me as though I would never come back. I had seen very little of her in the last month. If I was not spending my spare time writing to Zuhal, I was out with my friends until late at night. I had a guilty conscience, but not because of Zuhal: there was no competition. They were two different women who met different needs in me. Ayfer and I went to the cinema or sat on the broken wall on the few occasions we were together. I made sure there were always other people around. Ayfer did not complain; she possessed the stoic calm of the believer, of someone who surrendered unconditionally to fate. I did not doubt that she was silently suffering, but I did not have the means to cure her. In stolen moments, when she could hold me and kiss me without being seen, she made her longing visible, not through words, but through her intense passion.

You were sheltered in your last year at sixth form, treated like an honoured guest. We deserved some respite after seven years' hard work. The teachers and the management overlooked most indiscretions, and exam stress and homework became things of the past. The younger students looked up to their heroes who had survived almost everything, and those among us whose ambitions were not high had the opportunity to drift without a care through autumn, winter and spring. Our first term in our "year of rest" was a cause for celebration. As final-year students we had earned our own dormitory. There were fifty of us, stacked in bunk beds; it was not a life of luxury compared to Eton, but we were quite content not to be sleeping in the same room as the rest of the school anymore. The important point was that this dormitory was not included in the duty teacher's nightly inspections. Money was collected, the wine guerrilla scaled the walls and sneaked off under the cover of darkness to empty the shelves of the local corner shop. The food guerrilla carried out a quick raid on the kitchen. When they had finished, a note signed "Arsène Lupin" hung from a meat hook that until then had held a thick leg of lamb. The bunk beds were moved and the festive table set at the far end of the room. The Arab entertained us with his guitar, which he had mastered like no other. He had been told in advance to play anything but Rodrigo. We were all fed up with being woken every morning by Rodrigo's guitar concerto. Bottles of cheap red wine were placed on the table, not a single one had been dropped when the walls were scaled. Chiko, the cook, and his assistants seared lamb chops in a frying pan on the paraffin stove. Our first toast was to this good old home of ours, accompanied by the strains of "Ciao bella". Anecdotes were retrieved from the darkest corners of our memories and contradictory versions retold. The days of quarantine during the cholera epidemic seven years before; the ghosts that haunted the ancient parts of the school; all the friends who for various reasons had left us over the years, fifty-five in all; the arrival of the first female students, which had made us the last all-male class in the history of the school; the month-long boycott in 1975 for the democratic and academic rights of the students; the police raids, arrests and expulsions we had witnessed together. A whole life – as then it seemed – from being a child to becoming an eighteen-year-old. When the Arab finally plucked the strings to play Rodrigo's guitar concerto, a new dawn was breaking outside. This was how we wanted to take leave of the school because we had no tradition of end-of-term celebrations. When the spring term finished in ten months' time, everyone would be on their way with a simple "see you later". We never said "goodbye".

The day after the party five of us were ordered down to the Headmaster's office. Lined up in rows were twenty-five to thirty empty wine bottles. The Headmaster was himself an alumnus of the school and known to have been a wag.

"The cleaner found these under your beds. What have you got to say for yourselves?" he thundered.

The others looked tired and bored, so I replied on their behalf. "I notice the bottles are covered by a thick layer of dust. They must have been lying there since the last school year. Poor hygiene, very poor."

"Get out," the Headmaster snarled.

I had put a smile on my friends' faces and earned myself a new enemy.

*

66

The last letter from Zuhal reached me in the middle of October. It was brief and informed me that she would not be writing anymore, but did not say why. It did not worry me. Worrying would change nothing; she lived her life on her own terms. I wanted to think that she knew what she was doing. I did not doubt that she would return, so I never wondered which direction my life would take without her.

*

I thought a great deal about Ayfer that autumn. My involvement in school life was fleeting and routine. I sat at the back of the class reading a newspaper. We collected money and bought all the newspapers every day. Few of us had the energy to keep up with the lessons until lunch had been served. The linguists had never been known for their style, we happily left that to the realists, those studying maths and the natural sciences. In the afternoon the Godfather entertained us with his Turkish-English via his Black Sea dialect. The Camel baited both him and our other teachers with poisonous remarks. The Locomotive was the only one of us who took learning seriously and brought some dignity to our lives as students. He was also the only one who had been given his nickname by a teacher. Our literature teacher, an energetic woman who was prepared to go that extra mile beyond the limits of the curriculum to keep her students interested, had called him the Locomotive for his tireless efforts in hauling us empty carriages along behind him. I woke up once, at the end of October, from my daydreams when the English teacher addressed the class.

"Your dear friend Oak earned himself an impressive score of seventy-five in the test, a mark which lies way above the rest of you. This alone confirms that *Sons and Lovers* was not an entirely dull book to study."

He had served up the novel for us on a plate with his own twenty-page analysis, although he had not expected that any of us would bother to read even these before a test. To his delight this was precisely what I had done.

"It's the little pleasures in life which help you preserve your self esteem as a teacher," he said.

5

Winter 1977

Zuhal returned at the beginning of December. When a younger student came looking for me to tell me I had a visitor, I thought first of my mother, who had not been to the school since my father's death. Every Wednesday during the early years we would sit outside on the low wall along the cobbled driveway and wait for our mothers. Mothers only, because the majority of the students were fatherless children. As one of us said later, not all of us had fathers, but there was no shortage of pretty mothers. My mother never missed a visiting day. She would bring a bag of apples, oranges and grapes, hug me, smell me and chat to me the whole afternoon. I fought to suppress my tears when it was time for her to go, but she cheered me up and told me that Friday was only two days away. Her visits ceased abruptly after my father's death, and I knew why. I was now the oldest man in the family.

As she stood there in her beret, boots, sheepskin jacket and long woollen skirt in the soft, heavy snow from the winter sky, Zuhal looked like a resistance woman in a French film. When I told her so, she laughed a little.

"Watch it, don't you try seducing me," she said and kissed me on the cheek with cold lips. I was delighted and grateful that she had turned up at a time when I needed her. She was my cousin, she said, that was what she had told the porter when she introduced herself, so how about giving her a kiss to make the family relationship more convincing? I gave her an exaggerated hug and lifted her up.

"Alright, alright, he can't be in doubt anymore," she laughed.

My closest friends, Levo and Gülnur, watched us with curiosity from a distance. I introduced Zuhal without going into detail. I was proud of having her here, showing her off to my friends and letting their imaginations run riot. Levo, a boy with striking green eyes, and Gülnur a sweet, gentle brunette, were sweethearts. Neither was particularly interested in politics.

"It can be a relief to be with people who don't have to talk politics all the time," Zuhal said when we left the school – another visiting-day perk for final-year students.

We had much to tell each other. The new snow squeaked under our feet as we walked along chatting. She was back for good now, back in good old Istanbul again, and visiting me was one of the first things she had done – I had to know that. It was lovely to be part of the student community again and she was lucky because, thanks to the dean of her faculty, so far she had avoided being expelled. I did not ask what she had been up to in the last four months. She would tell me when the time was right, or perhaps it never would be. The nearest café where you could sit with a woman without people staring at you was in the next neighbourhood. However, it turned out we did not have to go that far. She had a surprise for me, if I could be patient. We walked through the local market in Wednesday Street. It was an odd name for a street, but perhaps it was because markets had been held here every Wednesday since the dawn of time.

The street ended in the courtyard in front of the Sultan Mehmet Mosque, built in honour of the city's conqueror. The annexes surrounding the mosque had formerly been used to house and teach the clerics. I did not know why we were here – a mosque was not a place where people like us would go to talk. As she led me to one of the annexes, an old stone building from the fifteenth century, I told her how one day last year we had got drunk and played hide-and-seek around the mosque's courtyard. The whole thing had been innocent and harmless fun, as there were very few places to hide, but the Imam had not shared our sense of humour. Zuhal sympathized more with the Imam than with us, and declared that I ought to stay away from mosques, drunk or sober. As we climbed the stone steps, hushed by an atmosphere fostered by centuries of history, I was starting to wonder if we were here to visit a clerical relative of hers. Finally, on the second floor, she opened a heavy wooden door with her own key, just as ancient as the door, and said, "Welcome to my humble home."

The room was no bigger than a cell, the ceiling was high and it was very cold. It had probably been built for Allah's servants, who had few earthly needs, but the architects at the time had managed to let in a miraculous amount of light through several circular apertures in the outer wall. In the room were two beds, a table, two chairs and a rug laid over the stone floor. The rest of the space was occupied by books and clothes. The annexes had been turned into student accommodation – a rather unusual solution, but given the considerable housing shortage, no-one but the mosque-goers complained. They had a point – most of the students who lived here were left-wing radical atheists. Zuhal shared the room with another very serious but pleasant enough girl. I should not get my hopes up: she had a boyfriend.

A large room on the ground floor served as the refectory, but there was something oppressive about it, the weight of too much history, so we decided to stay in Zuhal's room and make our own tea. I could see no running water and wondered how they washed.

"We have our morning wash with the faithful who come to pray at the communal fountain of the mosque. It's a sight you must see. Or we go to the local *hamam*, but there is no way you'll get to see that," she said. She clearly possessed the ability to adapt quickly. She felt at home in these surroundings, but I couldn't relax in them.

"This is temporary," she said. 'I'll find somewhere else eventually. But right now I need to be in the community. There are serious rifts in the student movement, my friend. You'll see for yourself. But more of that later. Tell me what you have been doing with your life."

I began with the most recent news. "I dropped her."

The statement caused her to raise an eyebrow. "Who did you dump and why?"

I was disappointed. I had hoped she would recognize her own words, but perhaps she had more important things to think about than our previous conversations. When it came to Ayfer, only the ashes from the fire remained. I could talk about it without finding a lump in my throat or my voice breaking, without having to feign coughing fits to choke my tears.

That autumn I had come home every Friday, sat on the wall and stared at Ayfer's house. In the evenings I would stand on the balcony, waiting. One day her younger sister came and sat next to me.

"Don't wait for her, she's not coming. She knows what you want and she has nothing more to say to you," she said, and in doing so she brought me Ayfer's last message.

Ayfer's sister became my companion. She would sit quietly next to me, her small head resting against my shoulder while she ate sunflower seeds.

I had expected Ayfer to fly down the stairs and throw herself into my arms, talk to me on the balcony, knock on my door. From time to time I wondered if there was something she had expected me to do; if I had known what, I would have done it. I checked the basement a few times, but she was not there. My mother silently shared my grief and walked around as softly as she could – noise was associated with happiness. Emel, the girl from downstairs, came to visit and we played cards and smoked cigarettes.

"If it's that bad, I'll comfort you," she said.

"Your grandmother would kill me," I said.

"A kiss would be all you would get, you idiot," she laughed. She was being married off to a shoemaker soon and wanted to drown her sorrows in mine.

One day at the start of November it rained heavily. I stood on the balcony. My wet shirt irritated me, so I tore it off and shivered as the dense, icy drops washed over my bare body. The door to the balcony on the other side opened. I could not make out her silhouette in the dark.

"Go back inside, or you'll catch a cold," she said in her softest voice. I needed no more encouragement; I went inside and out of her life.

"Sad," Zuhal remarked. "But you'll meet many girls and you'll fall in love with most of them."

"You sound like my mother," I said.

Zuhal was a committee member of the student union. She had brought me along several times, as she had promised, to their dilapidated rooms in an old office block, stripped of all furniture apart from a table and some chairs, always packed with enthusiastic, constantly debating students, always thick with smoke. She had invited me there to show me how divided the student movement was. I had felt uncomfortable from the moment I walked in. Not because I was not one of them, no-one cared about that, but because of the bitter atmosphere: you felt as though you were caught between two spouses who were about to go their separate ways. It was unnerving even though the proceedings were democratic and different from any I was used to. At school I could say, "Well, it's not long since so-and-so was in short trousers," to silence an opponent. The speeches here were like duels, but with words instead of knives and bullets. Two themes recurred. Should you prioritize the struggle against the Fascists or against the oligarchy, and should that struggle be fought with peaceful means or with arms?

"Peaceful means?" someone snorted. "We're the ones doing the dying while the murderers enjoy the peace. How about changing that?"

Others were more cautious. They believed the struggle against Fascism was a tactical phase and that the main enemy, the oligarchy, was in no sense a paper tiger.

The contributors were good with words. They effortlessly quoted radical texts and I was speechless at their audacity, especially as there could be spies and police agents present. Zuhal looked unperturbed. Agents provocateurs were a fact of life. Some of them were bound to be present here among the most ardent speakers, but democracy and open debate were the main objectives now. And was there no-one here to represent the workers? I was confused. I had imagined that the May Day massacre would be a wake-up call, a turning point that would heal their rifts. Instead they had become much deeper.

Zuhal did not take sides when she spoke. She was calm and humorous, in contrast to the others, and quoted dubious tyrants rather than revolutionary heroes: ". . . and when the blood boils with hatred and the brain has been numbed, the leader will not need to take away rights from his citizens. On the contrary, drenched in fear and blinded by patriotism the citizens will hand over all their rights to the leader and do so happily. How do I know this? I am Julius Caesar."

She wanted to warn against armed struggle because of the way Caesar had used the threat of war to instil fear and obedience. She wanted to warn against underestimating an enemy who, armed with a little of Caesar's cunning, could trick the people into crushing their own hopes of freedom, leaving the dark night darker still, with all the brightest stars plucked from the sky.

Zuhal and Kemal, they were so different. While Zuhal urged calm, Kemal roused the gathering into frenzy. He cut an impressive figure with his long, lean, almost emaciated body, his unkempt hair, sparse beard and moustache, wearing a faded army parka and scuffed boots. He surveyed the young men and women gathered around him and opened his speech with his favourite opening line: "Not matter what weapons they have, we have our dreams." Then, in an ever-rising voice: "Will we let the Fascists, will we let the oligarchy win? Will we let history curse us?"

He was a poser, he was a fraud, and he irritated me constantly with his seductive, almost feminine, manners, but underneath his soft facade, he was fearless. One day I was in the office helping Zuhal paint banners and copy fliers for an anti-Fascist demonstration. Kemal arrived and announced as if it were an everyday occurrence that the police were on their way. Within minutes, they had the building surrounded. He helped us out through a back door and three to four plain-clothes police officers chased after us. They were right behind us and were liable to starting shooting at any moment. The previous day, police officers pursuing a mugger had opened fire on Galata Bridge in the thick of the crowds and killed an innocent young woman.

Suddenly Kemal disappeared from view. At first I thought that he had stumbled, but when I turned, I saw him run back the way we had come. He was arrested, but he gained valuable time for us so we could disappear into the Beyazıt Square throng. The police closed down the union. Two days later Kemal was released from custody with around a hundred others. We had heard much about torture and mistreatment by the police. He told us nothing. "What is there to tell? It's a natural part of the life of a revolutionary," he said.

The student union was resurrected under a different name, in new and equally dilapidated rooms in another part of town. Zuhal was elected as a member of the new leadership committee.

"If I'm arrested next time, it will be your turn to take over," she joked.

Kemal's selfless actions contributed to my slowly growing respect for him. Eventually I too acquired a faded army parka and a pair of military boots. He treated me with kindness, almost like a younger brother, without ever patronizing me. If Zuhal's obvious fondness for me played a part here, he never let on.

6

May 1978

The fruit trees blossomed in May. Quince, cherry, mulberry, fig. The acacia tree was veiled in white like a bride, as scented lilac encroached over the stone wall, leaving passers-by dizzy with happiness. There was almost too much life teeming in the backyard. Geese pecked at the windows, the two tortoises started their slow journey from the house to the wall, sparrows alighted in the trees, turtledoves declared their love for each other in the early morning, and even the house snake shook off its lethargy and slithered through the new grass. Spring cleaning began in our two-storey Ottoman-style house and all the other houses on the narrow alley where I had spent my infancy; nature and mankind were preparing for summer. May, in my childhood, was a wonderful month.

*

The dining hall at my school was like a big restaurant, built to seat and feed five hundred students. Eight people sat at each table; a teacher and a final-year student at the head and foot and six students from various lower years down the sides. In recent years this arrangement had been changed and the teachers now had their own high table, as was the way in English boarding schools. Each table was referred to by the name of its final-year student, and this year, in accordance with tradition, I was at last named king of my table. The others would start to eat, pass food around and fetch bread and water on my orders. I disliked this tradition just as much as I disliked the bullying of younger students. Fortunately, most of the bullying stopped when my year took over. However, in the dining hall the old traditions died hard. It was not easy to relinquish power, and abuse was considered acceptable as long as it did not extend to violence. At my table we lived by my rules. Jobs were allocated according to where you sat, not according to your age or year group. Everyone, including me, was responsible for ensuring there was enough water and bread on the table. My table was the meeting place for my friends when the regular placeholders had finished eating and excused themselves. Every day we would sit there chatting with the constant clattering of cutlery in the background. Boarding-school life was made up of routines and habits, and the huge dining hall played a large part in them.

That day in May, Levo and Gülnur joined my table after lunch. They had the most timid relationship in the world. They had never declared their love for each other, never held each other's hand, and had never kissed. But when they were each alone with me, Levo at night in the dormitory and Gülnur in spare minutes during the day, they would pump my head full of confessions of hopeless and inexplicable feelings. It seemed as if they liked the idea of love more than the reality. Personally I had little time for platonic love, or whatever it might be, and encouraged them to talk to each other instead of with me. My advice fell on deaf ears. I sat at one end of the table with the pair either side of me. The devil in me dared me to improvise a marriage ceremony to see how they would react. And perhaps I would have, had Semra not joined our little gathering.

"I see you're still head of the table even though lunch is over. How does it feel to be big brother?" she said before making herself comfortable on her chair. She was trying to wind me up and I did not want to look the fool.

"Would you like to swap places with me to experience this wonderful sensation?"

She was not the type to let others have the last word. "No thank you. There is more than one girl at this table who has a prior claim to that honour," she said.

It was well known that seven girls sat at my table every day. No other table could compete with this, either in terms of quantity or quality. The story behind it was very silly. As a member of the student council I, along with some other sixth-form boys, had the authority to inspect the kitchen, decide the weekly menu, and, at the start of the school year, devise the seating plan for the dining hall. At the student council meeting in question there had been no disagreement when it came to seating the boys, but when it came to seating the most popular girls, the meeting lost what little decorum it had enjoyed. People almost came to blows. I did not understand how seating girls you fancied at your own table would promote mutual attraction. Especially considering the mess the boys made, their twin bad habits of belching and talking with their mouths full. After several failed attempts to stop the row, I had left the meeting.

When I arrived for breakfast the next day, seven girls were seated at my table, three of them the blondest of blondes with the bluest eyes in the school, the other four younger, but no less beautiful. They looked just as surprised as I did. So this was the compromise the feuding parties in the student council had arrived at: dumping the coveted species at my table. This episode earned me another nickname, "Charlie", on which I came down hard and just about managed to prevent from becoming known to a wider circle.

Semra obviously knew that I had no more interest than she did in blondes of questionable intelligence, but she did not pass up the opportunity to find out if any interesting topics had been discussed at my table recently.

"Of course," I said. "I now know everything that goes on in the girls' dormitory."

"Rubbish!" she and Gülnur said in unison. "That can't be true."

I proceeded to give them concrete examples of who washed their hair each night and for how long, who wore the sexiest nightdresses and which girls fancied which boys, all to Levo's obvious delight.

"Oh, those nasty blondes," the girls said, again in unison. The two of them started debating the tales told by the blondes about the dormitory, and we laughed and gossiped until the Camel turned up, looking deadly serious, which was so unusual for him that the expression on his face looked like an ill-fitting mask. He had just heard on the radio that the Fascists had killed seven students and wounded many others in an attack at the entrance to Istanbul University. May, in my childhood, was a wonderful month. May, in my youth, was a bloody funeral procession.

I had to go there. I just had to be there with those who mourned their friends and I had to find Zuhal. I did not know the names of the seven victims; I kept seeing one face only. My Zuhal, my friend. I had to find her, touch her. My mind would have no peace until I did.

I stopped in front of the Deputy Headmaster's office. He was one of four deputy heads at the school, the kindest and most naïve of them, someone who never lost his faith that man is born honest and lives accordingly. While I was thinking, I heard footsteps behind me. Semra came running.

"I'm coming with you," she panted.

"Where?"

"Where you're going. The University."

I did not need anyone tagging along and I told her so. She was furious and it surprised me.

"You're not the only one who's worried, you arrogant ass."

"You don't understand. I'm looking for someone – they might be among those wounded or killed."

"Who?"

"A friend. A woman.'"

"A woman I know nothing about?"

"Yes, a very special woman."

My voice trembled, something rose from my stomach, up through my chest and got stuck in my throat. Semra gave me a baffled smile as though she was scared that I might start to cry.

"How are you going to get permission?" she asked.

"I'll lie."

"I'm an experienced liar," she said. She knocked on the door and walked purposefully into the office of the Deputy Headmaster. He was sitting behind his desk, busy with paperwork, and smiled when he saw us.

"Come in, come in," he said kindly. "What can I do for you?"

"My mother is seriously ill," Semra said in a flat voice. An experienced liar? I was an idiot for letting her take the initiative. This was the last time she would boss me around, she could clear off, go to hell.

"I'm sorry to hear that," the Deputy Headmaster said. "Do you think you can get back this evening?" He had already started filling in the permission form.

"I expect so. By the way, I'll take him with me."

"Oh, is Oak the next of kin?" the Deputy Headmaster asked with good-natured irony. If we had said yes, he would have accepted it as a fact.

"No," Semra said. "But he'll comfort me." It was an honest and rather romantic answer – at least the Deputy Headmaster seemed to think so.

Once clear of his office and the school gates with the permission form in my hand, my irritation resurfaced.

"You're mother is seriously ill? You haven't got a mother!"

"I took a calculated risk. The Deputy Headmaster can hardly know about everyone's parents, can he?"

"But he can find out, can't he?" I mimicked her.

"Then we'll claim it was all down to a big misunderstanding."

I gave up. Challenging her logic was like tilting at windmills. We caught the bus and once we had sat down, I forgot all about my exasperation. A bus on this route – I was on it at the time – had once knocked down a woman. It was a long time ago, but I remember clearly how the bus lifted – I thought it had mounted the pavement – and how people outside screamed and shouted. The human brain works method-ically and makes connections. I knew why I was remembering this incident now. It was linked to the woman who had been crushed by the armoured car in Taksim Square, who was linked in turn to my first meeting with Zuhal.

I did not know what I would find in Beyazıt Square where the entrance to Istanbul University was located. But life was proceeding as normal: the usual people, vehicles, street vendors, the same cacophony of urban sounds. Even the two police cars outside the gate were an everyday sight. The cynicism of life's indifference, that all traces of the shootings had been erased, baffled me. I stopped random passers-by, but saw only fear and compassion in their eyes, as though I were mentally ill. They shook their head and said, no, they had not heard anything about an attack. At last a street vendor called out "Come here, brother." The dead and the wounded had been taken away hours ago, he told us. Unfortunately he knew nothing about the identity of those killed.

"Come, let's try the Student Union. We might find her there, or someone who knows her," said Semra. She had to be there if she was still alive. Why had I not thought of that?

I wanted to send Semra back, to get rid of her, but it was too late. I would have to meet Zuhal with Semra at my side. I could imagine the disdain in her eyes. After what she had said about Ayfer I had no doubts that Zuhal would not tolerate any relations with other women.

In the narrow side streets the little boys working for the cobblers were looking tired. They still had many hours of work to do, would be given little or no food and were treated very badly. At the end of the day some of them – the homeless, the orphans – would sniff glue under the bridge and fall asleep huddled together for warmth. Further down, young women in blue boiler suits were smoking and chatting outside the textile workshops. They nudged each other and showed envious interest in Semra, the well-groomed, free and fortunate sister. They winked lewdly at me. All girls who worked for a living reminded me of Ayfer. I do not know if I reminded them of anything in particular. What would they have thought of me if I had said, "Come, let's go and pay our respects to those who were killed for your sake."

The student office was teeming with people. Due to lack of space large groups were gathered outside the building, like fans with no hope of getting tickets for a popular performance. They were an impenetrable wall blocking our path, and every time we tried to move a resigned voice would say: "Where do you think you are going, friend?" I ignored it and elbowed my way through. We managed to get as far as the landing.

I started calling Zuhal's name, quietly at first, then started chanting it as if I were at a football match. I do not know if I clapped along with my shouting, but someone near me, unable to suppress his herd instinct, joined in. The cry of "Zuhal" turned out to be just as effective as "Open Sesame". The immovable human wall parted miraculously and on the other side Zuhal appeared with an embarrassed smile and said, "You're unbelievable, my mad friend." People laughed, my little stunt proving a welcome distraction from the overwhelming melancholy of the day. The initial glow from our reunion soon faded as the gravity of the situation dawned once more on those present. Zuhal and Kemal were members of a committee that was thrashing out the details of the huge anti-Fascist demonstration planned for the following day. She chaired the meeting with the authority of an Amazon, displaying such assurance that the men around her could do little else but nod in mute agreement. I admired her. Semra, next to me, gave away nothing; she listened with her arms folded across her chest. Kemal was unusually quiet. He sat leaning back with his eyes closed, a sign of displeasure, perhaps. I hoped so, I hoped there were rifts between them.

Zuhal was concentrating purely on the problems in hand, the safety of the participants, the police and the lack of cooperation from the trade unions. She swore and called people "cowardly arseholes". I knew she was partly venting her frustration and partly putting on a show. Kemal knew it too, and he clucked like a hen. When it was nearly over and most people had left, the four of us sat down. No longer on her high horse as the general of the masses, she was once more the Zuhal I knew. Her eyes shifted between Semra and me, and finally the expected criticism surfaced in her eyes.

"You're capable of mobilizing the school for tomorrow's demonstration on your own, aren't you, my friend?" She stressed "on your own". We were on the same wavelength. She wanted to make it clear that I did not need a helping hand, not a pretty one like Semra's nor anyone else's – except perhaps her own.

"Moving hundreds of students through a hostile environment could be risky," Semra said. I could happily have kicked her, grabbed her by the scruff of her neck like a kitten and shouted, "Who do you think you are? Do you know who you're talking to?" But I really should have kicked myself for bringing her in the first place.

"I don't know you, friend, so I don't give a damn about your opinion." Zuhal said.

I could tell that Semra was confused. She looked to me for support:

she was not used to being treated like this. It came from unexpected quarter.

"It's Semra, isn't it? Yes, Semra is right," Kemal said. "Either we take responsibility for these students by providing them with armed guards, something we already know is a bad idea, or we keep them away from this demonstration."

I wondered privately what his intention was. Was it a delayed and perhaps overdue confrontation with Zuhal? And was that really so surprising? Why should they not have disagreements? Obviously my subconscious mind was willing a flaming row between them, political or otherwise.

"*Et tu, Brute?*" Zuhal said in a conciliatory tone.

I was disappointed and made sure that she could see it.

"What's done is done," she said, never taking her eyes off me. "We need everybody, anyone who wants to join us, students or otherwise. And they have to run the same risk as everybody else." Full stop. Not even Kemal could dispute that the subject was now closed.

"You're in love with her," Semra said on the bus.

"Not in the way you imagine," I snapped. I did not want to be dragged into a discussion about it.

"I see how you idolize her, with your eyes, with your hands, with your voice, with all of you. You're in love, admit it."

"Why do you have to torment me? You wouldn't understand it, anyway. What is love? A tangled ball of wool with no thread. Love like that does not exist. At most there is a sexual attraction between a woman and a man and that's all."

"So you're sleeping with her. Is she just as wild in bed as out of it?"

"I'm not sleeping with her." The admission came abruptly. I could have given a different reply, a more suggestive one. It made me angry

85

that she had forced me to tell her the less-than-glamorous truth. "What about you then? Isn't it terrible still being a virgin?"

She smiled. "Shall I tell you a secret? Being a virgin and teasing desperate boys is wonderful."

The smile turned into laughter so hearty it could disarm desperate boys, girls and everyone else.

"I'll admit to one thing," she said then. "I'm jealous . . . of Zuhal. She's the kind of woman men fall in love with. She exudes power, the power to attract anyone. You're no exception. You're in love. Love does exist. I know it. I just know it."

*

Countless times I sneaked around the corridors of the boarding school under the cover of darkness. Stealing exam papers from the staffroom, raiding the kitchen, scaling the walls to go on forbidden trips into town. The latter was not entirely without risk. I will never forget the time we returned from a soup feast at a local street kitchen that was open at night only to find our street blocked by police cars. We were taken by surprise and did not have time to seek shelter in the shadows, our customary allies. Someone shouted, "Stop", but you never stop for the police if you can outrun them, so we kept going. Reports from the machine-guns echoed like small explosions in the quiet night. No bullets whizzed past our ears, slammed into the tarmac or tore plaster from the walls. They were firing into the air, but the sound was enough to send the soup in our stomachs on a return trip. We had never before climbed over the wall so quickly and effectively. The irony of it all was that it was the Headmaster who had called the police because of Fascist threats against the students.

On excursions such as these I was always with the bravest and the funniest of my friends. On this occasion the Camel was there, as were the Godfather, the Tartar and the Twins. I was in safe hands – this was a group of people who would go to the ends of the earth for each other. This might have sounded like an empty promise had it not been tested by real-life trials, like the time the students from the Imam School had stood in front of our school shouting, "Communists go to Moscow." It was an irritating slogan as no-one had any intention of going to Moscow; besides, we were convinced that none of these ghoulish relics of the Middle Ages would even be able to find Moscow on a map. So we opened the gates and attacked them, twenty men against one hundred sheep, to show them where Moscow was. Those were the days when you could still fight with fists, sticks and planks and afterwards go your separate ways without anyone being badly hurt. This was before firearms took over the scene and the brave disappeared.

Levo was not with us. He was sleeping soundly in the dormitory, a dreamer whose elevated cloud floated high above the concerns of earthly politics. We liked him too much to involve him in anything that could be dangerous. He would happily sing to us when we were drinking, but we tucked him up under his duvet when we went out to save the world. We were heading back to the dormitory after a meeting with the other sixth-form leaders about how to mobilize for tomorrow's demonstration. I regarded the outcome as a defeat. At the meeting it had been agreed that only those who participated at their own risk could represent the school. I was far too loyal towards the will of the majority to want to impose my own views, and I was scared of splitting a group who, for once, would join the revolutionary ranks to honour the dead. I felt I could live with it and I was prepared to upset Zuhal, if necessary. This was bigger than us, much bigger.

At breakfast we sent word around the tables that all students should assemble in the conference hall. I was alone on the stage. Before me sat five hundred individuals ready to lose interest in one, two, maybe three, seconds, or instantly, depending on my performance. When I leant over the microphone I had a wonderful feeling that nothing could go wrong. The words took wings and flew in a steady stream from their nest. I spoke like the Mediterranean breeze, cool and embracing, I was unpretentious and avoided being melodramatic, but spoke movingly. I spoke to them about the deceased and those who had killed them. The audience was hushed – there was no whispering or coughing. They expressed their sympathy through dignified silence. I spoke softly, without recourse to jokes or irony; I was moved, but no tears flowed for me to hide. Nor did I stop when I saw the Headmaster march into the hall, his arms swinging in step with his long strides, his grey eyes bright with hatred. He grabbed hold of the microphone, but was unable to pull it from my hand. He leaned over it to block me and hit his forehead against the stand. "Oh hell," he said. Then, "This is your Headmaster speaking." His voice sounded strangled and he lost control of its pitch. "Leave the hall at once and go directly to your classrooms."

But the age of authority at school was over. No-one got up from their seats.

"Go back to your office," someone shouted.

The Headmaster was a man who had helped found the Academic Union in his day. But that was then. He had lost touch with the present, with progress, the students, and now the microphone. He was the only one who left the hall.

The students chose their representatives and together we went outside in the playground. I was a little nervous after the confrontation with the Headmaster and lit a cigarette with trembling hands. As I exhaled the first cloud of smoke I noticed the Headmaster, his hands on his hips, his long grey hair swaying in the wind, leaning against the wall of the old building, just a few metres away. He was with the Deputy Headmaster, the Falcon. He was trembling just as much as I was, and judging by his body language, he was out for revenge.

"You sack of shit. You'll pay for what you've done," he shouted in a loud and angry voice. For all his venerable appearance, he was known to be a rude thug.

Perhaps I should have dismissed the whole thing. He certainly should have gauged the situation before he provoked me. It was his misfortune that I was so full of adrenalin from my speech in the hall I was not thinking at all, let alone thinking straight. I attacked him with a war cry that even to this day sends shivers down my spine.

"Arsehoooole!"

I was close, so close that I swear I could see the surprise, the fear in his ashen eyes. Then my feet lost contact with the ground. At first I thought I had thrown myself forward to pounce on him like a tiger, but it was an American football tackle from two friends that had swept my feet from under me. The Camel and the Godfather, two sturdy lads, were lying on top of me, holding me down with all their strength. When they finally loosened their hold, the Headmaster and his Deputy were long gone. Thanks to the well-timed intervention of my friends, the proud history of the school would not be blemished by a fight between the Headmaster and one of his students.

*

Since the day Byzas had led his colonists from Megara and Athens on horseback to the crest of a hill, looked down at the Bosporus and pointed to the river that would come to be the site of the mother of all cities, history had several times witnessed the mother city's ability to take her children back to her breast and give them an eternal resting place in her fertile soil. Istanbul has always honoured her sons and daughters, celebrated her dead with bravura, music and song.

"Revolutionaries die, the revolution lives on." Prominent guests, dead but not forgotten, were in attendance: Ho Chi Minh, Zapata, Sitting Bull and Che Guevara, needless to say, still with lightning in his eyes. The workers were there in their overalls and despite the reluctance of their leaders, marched hand-in-hand with the students, all focused on a spot in the sky, on a better future. Tens of thousands were present, a hundred thousand perhaps – rumour had it that the crowd was a hundred and twenty thousand strong. Zuhal was lovely in her wild excitement.

"You're here. That's what counts," she said. I do not know if she could hear me over the roaring of the masses.

Neither Kemal nor Semra had joined us. I had not seen Semra since our visit to the student union and Kemal was busy elsewhere. There we were, Zuhal and I, and that was what counted. We marched hand-in-hand from Saraçhane Square down to Aksaray, up to Beyazıt and on to Istanbul University. The dead were with us and we showed them that our ranks had swelled since the bullets and grenades had torn them apart. I was smitten by Zuhal's elation and it did not seem wrong to be rejoicing on this day of sorrow. We were many, we were strong, and we would overcome.

My mood swung between pessimism and fierce optimism in those days, an emotional pendulum entirely dependent on her.

*

They threatened to expel me from school. There was only one month left – one paltry month until my escape from eight years of confinement. It had happened before to many of my predecessors and it could happen again. However, I was not about to let them destroy my mother's dream. I went on the offensive. "Anyone who wants to expel me had better think twice," I said.

The Falcon found me smoking in the boys' toilets. He had just come from the Headmaster's office. He was unpredictable, a chameleon, a strict disciplinarian towards the lower years, but friendly towards us in the sixth form. Falcon was not a nickname, but the name his parents had given him.

"Be sensible, my friend," the Falcon said to me. "You won't lose face by making a small apology to the Headmaster. He's an old man. A little sentimental. You apologize, make the right noises and we'll forget all about it."

There was something about his smooth amiability, artificial yet somehow genuine at the same time. I brushed him away as if he were a midge.

"Give my regards to the Headmaster. He apologizes and I'll forget all about it."

The Falcon smiled a cold smile as though torn between valuing the courage of youth and remaining loyal to his superior. I sensed that he liked me. This feeling grew stronger when, a few days later, he called the Camel and me out of a lesson, offered us tea in his office, chatted to us and gave us each a woollen jumper as a present. That same evening we were invited to his flat in the staff block. His wife served food and rakı. We talked about our plans for the future. He had plenty of good advice to give, mainly academic. Only once, raising his rakı glass and proposing a toast, his eyes narrowed by a slight excess of alcohol, did he touch upon the subject of our discussion in the boys' toilets

"Stay out of his way. You need to avoid him at all costs for the rest of the school year. That's the only condition."

Outside in the playground the Camel and I sat down beneath a hundred-year-old oak, smoked the last cigarette of the night and wondered what it would be like to sleep under the open sky, something we had not done for years. Eventually we decided that it was best left in the past.

"He likes us," I said as we got up.

"He's bribing us, trying to corrupt us," the Camel replied.

"Oh, you're an incurable pessimist. He likes us, I can feel it."

"I'm just a sceptic. But your condition is worse. You, my friend, are bloody naïve."

7

June–July 1978

I was exhausted. Completely exhausted. Five hours in a carefully supervised university hall, sealed off from the outside world. A letter, a letter with a sombre official logo would later decide my fate. Until then I had finished with the bastards. I threw a last glance at my fellow inmates, their heads bowed in obedience. No-one wanted to return my look, or perhaps they could not be bothered to.

"Bye," I mumbled. "Goodbye and good luck."

With my head held high I walked to the exit. No matter what I might have left behind, my honour was intact. The man at the door looked me up and down, just as sceptical as when he had let me in.

"I.D.," he snapped, with something I perceived as contempt in his voice. I.D. in, I.D. out. Under normal circumstances I would have crushed him like a cockroach with sarcasm, but there was no need to spoil a day that had been quite painless up until then. I handed him my I.D. card, which he took and held up to his eyes as though he were long-sighted, and studied it closely. He took his time. Either he was illiterate or he was testing my patience. When he finally finished, he gave me a broad smile.

"Best of luck with the rest of your life," he said.

I thanked him. Perhaps he was not a total bastard after all, just an ordinary clerk who took his job seriously.

I was blinded by bright sunlight the moment I stepped out into freedom. People went about their business without noticing me, some hurried, others at leisure, all ignorant of the world around them. What I needed now was a girlfriend, a girlfriend who could hold me in her arms, comfort me and help me glide into a long sleep.

"Hey, don't stand there like you've lost the plot. Come over here," Levo was leaning against a concrete wall. It seemed as if we were surrounded by nothing but concrete walls.

"How did it go, old pal?" Levo said as he pushed back his cap and wiped the sweat from his brow.

"No worse than expected."

"Same here. But that's good enough, I'm sure of it."

"If you say so."

We left. Out through the monumental archway of Istanbul University, down the steps, where insouciant pigeons searched eagerly for food without bothering to move for their superiors, and into Beyazıt Square, where the crowds pulsed and surged like blood through a pounding heart. With every step we put further behind us the university, the entrance exam and the papers we had sweated over for hours. They were now lying on the desk of the invigilator waiting to be read by . . . by whom? A machine perhaps? With this we had drawn a line under an important stage of our lives, the eight years at boarding school, puberty, early youth, and taken a fumbling step towards . . . what? This question did not disturb me unduly. I was more concerned with the fact that I had finished something. I was nineteen years old. I was on Beyazıt Square, I could do whatever I liked, go wherever I wanted. I would no longer fall asleep each night and wake up each morning in a school surrounded by walls. An eight-year sentence had been served. I breathed deeply the scents from the flower stall in the square. I could go wherever I wanted. I wanted to walk. Just walk.

"Hey, you're not listening."

"What?"

"Let's go and see Semra."

It would be good to be reconciled with Semra, but I was not in the mood for talking right now. I had faded out all the sounds around me. Levo's voice, cries from street vendors, car horns, the clinking and clanking from the copper bazaar, and God knows how many decibels of music from the loudspeakers in the record shop. Nâzım Hikmet was on my mind: how he must have walked, brimming with purpose, with his red scarf fluttering in the wind, with brisk steps and a poem in his head, deaf to everything else, perhaps down this very street. I had no poem in my head.

"She works nearby. Holiday job."

"I see." She had not taken the trouble to let me know.

"Let's pop in. Have a cup of tea. Have a rest before I take the bus home."

Levo was going home to his mother in a town hundreds of kilometres away. Gülnur had already gone home to her parents in another town. If he was pining for her, he did not show it. Instead he was trying to reunite me with Semra.

"Very well," I said. "Lead the way."

We crossed the road, exchanged unkind remarks with a taxi driver, laughed for laughter's sake the way you do when you are young. Then we fell silent and wandered on with our hands in our pockets. I do not recall the street or the building. It was one that houses shops for tourists, but for some incomprehensible reason the outlet where Semra worked was hidden away on the first floor, far beyond the scope of most tourists. At the top of the stairs the unmistakeable smell of leather from hundreds of jackets hit me. They hung on hangers in packed rows and from between two racks Semra suddenly emerged like a jack-in-the-box. Her joy and her smile were genuine and betrayed not a hint of surprise, as though she had been waiting for us. If she had told us off for being late, it would not have seemed in the least bit strange. She directed us to a leather sofa – everything was leather here – and ordered tea as we sat down to chat. Levo and Semra did most of the talking. I drank tea and watched her. There she was, a pretty girl, with a first-rate essay on Shakespeare to her credit, using her English to sell leather jackets to tourists. Pathetic, even though it was only a holiday job. It irritated me as if it were a personal insult. But why did she irritate me? She had a winning personality, intelligence, beauty. Every time I studied her, as I did that day, I was overcome with tenderness and love for her. I fixed my gaze on her with something I was sure resembled a Clark Gable expression. A teasing smile, raised eyebrows, cigarette dangling from my mouth – the lot. It was deliberate, I wanted to tease her. She clearly found it funny. Every time her eyes fell on me, she found it hard to suppress her laughter.

"Stop it!" she said at last.

"Stop what?" I said, feigning innocence.

"Pulling faces like that."

"Pulling faces? This was how Rhett Butler seduced Miss Scarlett in 'Gone with the Wind'."

"Scarlett? A mindless woman – selfish, jealous and a sworn racist. Seducing her wouldn't be something to boast about."

"You remind me of Scarlett nonetheless," I said.

"Oh, Oak, shut up for once and stop teasing her."

"It doesn't matter, Levo, it really doesn't matter," she said, and winked at me. She forgave me far too easily, even when I compared her to an impulsive and selfish woman.

"Very well. I just want you two to be friends again," Levo said. "But I've got to run now. My bus leaves in half an hour." His bus did not leave for another two hours. The traitor wanted me to be alone with her.

"I'll come with you, wave my handkerchief and throw water after you and weep and . . ."

"Shut up, you idiot. I don't need a farewell committee. Cry if you want to, but say goodbye to me here."

Semra said neither "go with him" nor "stay". She seemed slightly hesitant, slightly disinterested, as though it would make no difference to her if she got rid of both of us. I decided to stay.

"Alright, Oak. Take care. See you in September."

We kissed and hugged each other in turn. I seized the opportunity to kiss Semra.

"What? Are you going too?" She was genuinely surprised.

"No. I thought this was a part of the ritual, that we all had to kiss each other."

She laughed and accused me of taking advantage of the situation.

"Friends now?" Levo said by way of goodbye. And then he was gone.

We sat down under a walnut tree in Gülhane Park. I have loved Gülhane Park since my parents first took us there as children at the weekends. First a walk through the zoo and then up to a spot where you could enjoy the beauty of the Strait, kick a ball around and share a picnic. If anyone asked me where I wanted to go, I would reply "Gülhane Park", just as I did when Semra asked. It was a pleasant summer afternoon. We walked in silent companionship in the shade of the trees and climbed the hill to sit beneath the famous walnut tree. I was not sure whether I needed company. It was so peaceful here that I wished I had come alone. Until I heard her voice, that is. She was reciting a poem by Nâzım Hikmet, written in exile, filled with longing.

In Gülhane Park I am a walnut tree.
My leaves are like darting fish in the water.
Silk handkerchiefs are my leaves.
Pick one, my rose, dry your eyes!
I touch you, Istanbul, my beloved city,
With countless hands. I see you anew
With countless eyes. Day after day
I feel the heartbeat of the leaves.

I was moved. It must have been her melodic voice, the lines almost sung. It ran in the family: my tough father would cry when he heard his favourite songs. I had picked Gülhane Park, but she had picked the walnut tree and the poem. I had to ask why.

"Because I want us to be friends. Very good friends who share everything," she said.

So for once we talked without it turning into a war of words, without the competitive instinct of two tightrope walkers on the same line, each waiting for the other to fall. She assured me that as far as she was concerned there was nothing wrong with us disagreeing on issues of principle, such as politics, as long as ultimately we remained loyal to each other. I was relieved and understood how much I valued her friendship, so for once I was generous in expressing it. Smiling, she took my hand and together we walked along the path, two people at peace.

*

The final split in the revolutionary movement was now a fact. Those who had lost hope of continuing the struggle peacefully began a violent campaign. Armed groups all over the country attacked the Fascists. For the first time the number of Fascists killed exceeded that of revolutionaries. Panic spread throughout their ranks. There was an overwhelming surge in support for armed resistance among the young revolutionaries.

Zuhal worked tirelessly. I followed her from meeting to meeting and watched uncompromising activists with persuasive arguments winning the vote of the young every time. Driving the Fascists on the defensive in a short space of time had given them a huge boost of confidence. From the way they swaggered around the meeting rooms proudly displaying the pistols in their belts, you would have thought they had already won. Zuhal tried in vain to warn them – and those who had yet to make up their minds – against the state-sponsored terror that would inevitably follow. It was one thing to beat the Fascists; taking power from the oligarchy was an entirely different matter. Her speeches were drowned out by the usual slogans. "Down with the Oligarchy!" Zuhal had changed beyond recognition. She was unkempt, weary, aggressive and intolerant. Losing an ideological dispute hurt her much more than losing Kemal. She did not mention his name – she did not need to. Kemal was more than visible as one of the apostles of the armed revolution. He was forever surrounded by bodyguards, a living myth who would vanish after every debate as quickly as he had taken the floor, making it known to all that he was now an "outlaw". These carefully stage-managed speeches would be his last. Life as an underground activist awaited him.

I fantasized about such a life: being an urban guerrilla in the back seat of a car on a murky day, pistol by my side, waiting impatiently to strike at a target. Or in the mountains, resting around a campfire with a Kalashnikov in my lap. I could see how the romanticism of this would appeal to most of my peers because such fantasies always ended before any blood was spilt.

Optimism was high. Most people believed that the conditions for a revolution were present and that the oligarchy would tumble like a house of cards at our first breath. Only once did I have contact with

Kemal. He was on his way out of a meeting room and did not have time for pleasantries. His gaze drilled right through me. He was neither hostile nor friendly, merely indifferent.

"Take care of her," he said, and disappeared.

I was enormously disappointed at the split among the students, but this brief encounter proved to be decisive. I would follow Zuhal's path. That this choice was based on personalities rather than politics did not worry me. To be honest, I did not even consider the issues. My convictions were shaped by her strong character, and supporting Zuhal in an already lost cause was only natural.

I followed her everywhere. One day in July we visited a new shanty town on the outskirts of Istanbul. Migrants from the countryside hoping to find work in the big city had occupied government land and built houses for themselves. They lacked the most basic of infrastructure: no water, sewage or electricity. The students always supported the people here. They were kindly disposed to the left-wing radical ideas represented by the many different factions. The ideological split was beyond the comprehension of these simple people, but we knocked patiently on every door and told them about our road to revolution. They listened politely and served tea, as they always did when they had visitors. Some asked cautious questions. Why were there so many different roads? Zuhal answered with zeal. There were not many. There was one: the people's road. When the masses united around their own party, they would decide the outcome. And as long as the working class and the impoverished peasants were ready, the revolution had a chance. To my ears it sounded like a terribly long road. Neither did it sound very plausible. Quite simply, I did not share her faith in our fellow citizens. But it did not matter. I was there for her sake. I would have gone anywhere with her.

One afternoon we were told that there was an unusual amount of police activity around the shanty town. When we reached the last houses on the slope leading to the main road, we discovered that the road was blocked by several armoured police cars and two bulldozers. A demolition operation was in progress. I tensed up. I had read about such confrontations, but I had never been caught up in one myself. While I stood there with the silent men and women who would soon have to defend their homes against a superior enemy, I had the same feeling as with Ahmet and the Kurds. I was a stranger, I did not belong among them. It was their war, they chose the means, and no-one cared about what I thought. That was how it was. The poor workers were so close to me and yet so far removed. They had nothing to lose; but what about me?

As I looked down at the scene, calm before the storm, I realized how disillusioned I had become. And worst of all, how helpless I felt faced with such an imposing enemy. I could stroll quietly away and leave the battlefield without anyone lifting a finger to stop me. Why should they? Only the brave and those without hope were trapped here now. I was an uninvited guest who could leave if the wind changed.

This was what stopped me. No-one had invited me, I had come on my own initiative. I owed them a little loyalty. That was my first reason: the second was that I would never leave Zuhal. I would take my modest place in this last battle and then . . .

In the meantime a makeshift barricade of planks, old mattresses, tables, chairs and wrecked cars had been built by the silent men and women of the shanty town, and young armed men, just as silent, took their positions behind it. Not so long ago I would have regarded this scene as a romantic reprise of the barricades of the Paris Commune, but now it put me in mind only of the violence to come. A shiver went through my body. The two sides had taken up their positions with the almost leisurely movements of two medieval armies. The rest happened quickly. Suddenly one of the bulldozers was ablaze, someone fired a shot, sporadic echoes from several handguns followed, and soon the sounds of a gigantic firework display filled the air. I could not see much from where Zuhal and I had taken cover behind the barricade. Besides, my head was buried between my knees. But there were sounds, human voices, pitched high and low, terrified and commanding, a hail of bullets slamming against a tin roof, intermittent at first then like fingers on a fish-skin drum. When I lifted my head during a brief cessation of fire, Zuhal was gone.

I did not want to cry, I would not allow myself that humiliation. I could not tell if many minutes had passed or just a few short moments. Fear distorts your senses. Zuhal came crawling back. She had helped bring a wounded man to safety. Now she needed help. What did she expect from me? That I would operate on him? Save his life? Or perhaps she was just as scared as I was and did not want to be alone when faced with death.

The wounded man lay in a bed with surprisingly white, clean sheets in one of the shacks closest to the barricade. Two young women, shadows in the dim light, sat either side of him. They stood up and withdrew without a word when we entered. Zuhal had already cleaned and bandaged the wound.

"To his chest, not far from his heart," she whispered.

"He needs to go to a hospital," I whispered back, just to keep silence at bay – you do not give up your wounded to the enemy in a besieged city.

We sat down on opposite sides of his bed. I avoided looking at his face. He had a broad chest, which slowly heaved and sank. He was breathing with difficulty, but made no other sound. Perhaps he was unconscious. I clasped his wrist and checked his pulse. It was weak. Suddenly he took my hand and squeezed it. His grip was friendly and warm. My hand and arm grew numb, but I did not have the heart to pull back. I was very, very tired, with a dull ache behind my eyes.

I closed them and started dreaming, but not as you do in a deep sleep. I was still conscious of my surroundings, could still hear the shooting, but at the same time my senses were dulled and I no longer followed what was going on around me.

I was scared. Scared of taking a bullet to my chest or of turning to violence because of the anger I felt, the need to avenge the helpless man lying between us. I would not hesitate to shoot at random, kill the enemy and avenge every injustice on earth.

Revenge was an ancient inheritance dormant in the soul of every one of us and it was merely waiting to be roused. I could feel it stir, but I would not let the monster rear its head. I would stamp on it and bury it in the dark depths where it belonged. I was in no doubt now that it was a question of love. You could base nothing on hate, justice least of all. You had to build on love. "Everything starts by loving someone", a writer once said.

I would start afresh by loving someone. I did not know how far it would get me, but I knew one thing: I did not want to kill or be killed. I loved life too much, my life and the lives of others. For a long time I had believed that I was one of those destined to decide the fate of souls besides my own. The irony was that I had always despised the notion of elite rule. I was just one person on this planet who wanted to live in eternal peace, surrounded by poetry, music and love. I was ready now. Ready to love. Not in the way I had loved Ayfer, not just with my heart, but also with my mind, patient and enduring. I was no longer afraid of loving Zuhal.

He was dead. He must have been dead a while. His hand in mine had lost its warmth. The sounds of conflict had faded to ominous silence, and the encircled shanty town held its breath. Zuhal was standing next to me with her hand on my shoulder.

"Come on, we need to leave," she said.

The front door was opened hesitantly as though the visitor was unsure as to whether he was welcome. It was a young man wearing a bulletproof vest over a police uniform, holding a machine-gun in his nervous hands. He looked more like the hunted than the hunter.

"So, who's there?" someone behind him called out.

"Two suspects," he responded.

"Are they armed?"

"Not as far as I can see," he said. Then he spotted the dead man, examined him more closely and muttered, "May God forgive his sins," as though he were praying.

At first I thought he was going to kiss my hand when he bent over it, but then he sniffed it. He did the same with Zuhal's.

"These two haven't been firing weapons," he shouted towards the door.

"Take them away," someone shouted back.

"You," Zuhal said suddenly, "Aren't you ashamed to walk in on my rugs with your filthy boots? Is that how you enter your mother's house?"

The man apologized, "I'm only doing my duty, miss."

Zuhal winked at me and walked to the door with her head held high.

We walked along dusty tracks beneath an orange sky with police officers and soldiers on either side as though they thought one of us might throw a hand grenade at any moment. We grew in numbers as more prisoners were taken from the other houses. To begin with our guards kept a respectful distance and did not touch us – not until we were led to a police bus and had been handcuffed and blindfolded.

Someone brutally yanked my hair from behind. The guard closest to me barked out the order, and punches and kicks began to rain down indiscriminately upon me. Judging from the muffled sounds of violence, they were beating up all the prisoners on the bus. I did not know where Zuhal was sitting, I was not thinking of my own pain, only of her. I wanted to call out her name, to hear her voice, but I was afraid.

Then the beatings stopped. While the bus hurried through the city streets, the sirens howling in my ears, I thought of all that had happened that day.

I had come close to being arrested once before, at a folklore festival I had attended with Levo, Gülnur and Semra. Two policemen had picked me out from the crowd. I cannot think of any reason other than that they did not like the look of me. For a while I had sat in a police car with a policeman who knew no more than I did, only to be released without any explanation. On that occasion I could joke about what had happened.

Zuhal had asked me to take the incident seriously. All revolution-aries need to prepare themselves mentally for meeting the police. Staying silent under torture was the top priority. I was scared: anyone blindfolded experiences a natural fear of the unknown that awaits them. I had to conceal my fear at any price. She would never forgive me for humiliating myself before the enemy. The thought offered me no comfort, but I regarded it as fitting that I should have to go through this ordeal.

My thoughts were interrupted when the bus stopped. Unseen hands pulled me out of my seat. They led me away from the bus and up some stairs. Once inside the building, two policemen dragged me at running speed down an endless corridor. I could hear brisk footsteps both in front of me and to the rear. They haunted me as my escorts dragged me onwards, hauling me abruptly down a steep flight of stairs. The air on the floor below was oppressive and permeated with a mixture of sweat, urine and other less identifiable smells that made breathing difficult. It had to be some sort of basement. Brief remarks were exchanged between one of my escorts and a man who presumably worked as a guard below stairs. I heard a chair squeak. Then I was led on. I counted twenty paces. We stopped. After much jangling of keys, I heard the metallic click of a door handle being turned. My handcuffs were removed and my blindfold torn off, but before my eyes had had time to adjust to the light, I was pitched forward. The door slammed shut behind me. I felt as though I had been hurled from one manner of darkness into another. There was not much light here. It could only be a prison cell.

"Welcome, friend," a voice said.

I could not see him. I chose not to reply, waiting for my eyes to adjust to the darkness. They sat packed like sardines with their backs to the wall. Now I could make out the contours of their bodies.

"Do you have any cigarettes?" the same voice asked me. It belonged to the man nearest me, who was sitting to my right. Pragmatism determined the order of questions down here. I found my cigarettes and the lighter in my shirt pocket. It was strange that no-one had thought to take them from me. When I handed the packet to the man, a sigh went through the crowd.

"You're the first good news we've had for days," the voice said.

Only one cigarette was lit to be passed around.

"Be careful, don't heat it up too much," someone said. The basement in the police station clearly had its own rules.

I sat down on the concrete floor and started massaging my wrists. Light from the corridor stole through the tiny crack beneath the door. There was complete silence. I needed a pee, but how would I call the guard to tell him? I was startled by the sound of a male voice outside. The voice was not coming from the corridor. A prisoner, I thought. The voice shouted the same word at regular intervals. A female voice joined in. Rapid, heavy footsteps echoed in the corridor. Someone hit the doors, including our door, with an object as they passed. A violent struggle followed. Angry voices from the corridor and from behind the closed doors hurled insults at each other. When everything calmed down, I had long lost the desire to call the guard.

"It happens all the time," the man next to me said – he was the only one talking. "It's one of their psychological tricks. Ignore it. The art is to dream yourself away. So I suggest you try to get some sleep."

The air was dense and warm. I felt incredibly drowsy. Time passed without anything happening. I wanted to ask him questions, but he had already slumped forward and turned his back to me. I lay down on the floor. The draught from under the door cooled my burning face and I was soon asleep.

8

Police Station, July 1978

I opened my eyes and blinked, blinded by the light from the bulb hanging from the ceiling, which had now been turned on. I had been woken by a loud, rhythmic pounding on the steel doors to the cells. It must be standard practice to wake the prisoners that way. I looked around and counted my cellmates. We were nineteen. Fifteen of us were new arrivals; we had probably been picked up from the same place. I could tell because fifteen of us were fully dressed and looked relatively clean and tidy. The remaining four were dressed only in their underpants, wore several days' stubble, and lice crawled freely over their bodies. The man next to me was busy squashing some of them.

"Not that it makes much difference, but it passes the time," he said.

He was a young man, like most of us, but older than me, in his late twenties perhaps. Tall and skinny, you could count his ribs. He looked filthy and battered, with bloody bandages on both feet. It was as if all his strength was gathered in his eyes, which were bright, gentle and a little insolent.

"My arms are a bit numb, so we'll skip the handshake ceremony. I'm Sevim," he said.

"Isn't that a girl's name?" I asked. Someone laughed in the background; Sevim smiled a crooked smile.

"That's the whole point. I refuse to tell them my real name, it's my way of teasing them, do you see?"

It made no sense to me, but I did not want to reveal my ignorance. Instead I introduced myself to my new friend.

"Oak."

"And you thought my name was weird," he laughed.

I heard doors being opened and more footsteps in the corridor. What time was it? I remembered my watch and lifted my left arm. In the chaos surrounding our arrival, they had not had time to take these small, personal belongings from us. It was seven in the morning. I could hear approaching footsteps. The door was opened, revealing a man holding a stick.

"Toilet," he said without looking at us.

We went out together. There were more cell doors on both sides of the corridor. The man gestured with his stick that we should hurry up. It was a straightforward matter of following the smell. We passed two men sitting by a table watching us with indifference. The hatches in the cell doors I passed were shut. I wondered which one Zuhal was behind. It occurred to me, as it had on the bus, to call out her name, but it would only invite the guards' anger.

The toilets were to the left of the stairs. I tried hard to suppress my nausea. This was not a time for sensitivity. Carefully, so as not to step in the faeces that covered both the toilet hole and floor, I pulled down my pants and squatted. I urinated for a long time. The relief was enormous. My own faeces were watery, like diarrhoea. It had to be stress. Several warning blows hammered on the door while I pulled up my trousers. I quickly washed my hands and face and hurried out. A kick from behind sent me flying, amidst a tirade of threatening oaths. I did not dare turn around. There was only one thing to do. Get back on my feet as quickly as possible and hurry on.

What now? I wondered when I was back in the cell. Losing control over your own actions, your own destiny and being humiliated was like being cast into a well of endless confusion and anxiety. Now what? I stood facing the hatch in the door, missing Zuhal desperately. Two solitary tears, forced out by helplessness and rage, ran down my cheeks. As if in response to my suffering, the hatch was scraped open. The face that I loved looked down on me with curiosity.

"Be brave now, my only one," she said. She must have opened several hatches to find me. Someone hurried over to her and shoved her aside before I had time to say anything.

"You'll get a massive beating if you do that again," an angry voice snarled.

"Shut up, you Fascist dog," she shouted in return.

A hand closed the hatch and the voices in the corridor faded away.

"That's one tough girl," Sevim commented. "You're lucky. All the girls I meet just want to get married and stay at home for the rest of their lives."

He handed me a small carton of milk. "Well, my friend, it's time for some breakfast."

The meal consisted of olives, cheese and bread.

At 8.30 a.m. the corridor sprung to life. Names were called out, doors were opened and slammed shut, inmates screamed and swore and heavy footsteps echoed up and down the corridor. Sevim explained to us newcomers that they were fetching that day's unlucky candidates for interrogation. He drank the rest of his milk.

"It's important to drink as much as possible. You tend to lose a lot of fluid when you're being electrocuted," he said with a glint in his eye.

After a while we heard the guards approach our door and stop in front of it. You could not mistake the nervous tension. Everyone wondered if it was their turn. Being taken away for interrogation meant only one thing. Torture.

I could tell they were standing outside from the shadows they cast over the light creeping under the door. All was quiet now. I listened intently. All my senses were alert. I did not hear the key in the door being turned – it must have been left unlocked after our toilet visit. The steel slab opened slowly and noiselessly. The guard with the stick studied us one by one, and then he waved me outside. It was my turn. My heart pounded wildly, like a bird trapped in its cage. With my last strength I went outside. A few metres away stood a man with his back to me, smoking. The smell of smoke tickled my nostrils. The guard led me to a small room. There was yet another man waiting for me: it was hard for me to tell him apart from all the other men I had seen down here. Bizarrely, they all resembled each other. Sturdy, with short, dark hair, a moustache and a sour expression. The man was busy setting up some equipment on an old wooden table, the only furniture in that bare room. I looked at the windowless grey walls where the original paint had long since faded. Clearly no-one cared about appearances in here. I wondered why on earth I did.

Suddenly I knew why I had been taken here. The inkpad and the forms strewn across the table told their own story. With routine movements the man took my right hand and pressed first my fingers, then my whole hand on to the inkpad. It was not all that long ago that this whole process would have seemed incredible. However, recent events had left their mark. I did not feel criminalized, I felt nothing at all. I was simply impatient to get it over with. Totally indifferent to it all, I wiped my hands on a piece of tissue handed to me and stared at them blankly. They were still black with ink.

The fourteen other new prisoners, who had all been taken along with me, filed in and out to be fingerprinted and processed.

"This is a good sign," Sevim said after taking a deep drag of the cigarette that was doing the rounds. "The fact that they have registered you means the chances of you disappearing without a trace are relatively small now."

Sevim appeared to enjoy talking to me, he had barely exchanged a word with the others. I did not know why he had picked me, perhaps it was because of the cigarettes. He coughed like a terminal tuberculosis patient.

"I've got to give up this filthy habit soon," he said. "But, on the other hand, you've got to enjoy life while it lasts."

"How long have you been here?" I said.

"Two weeks – me and the other three."

"But the law states that the police can only hold you on remand for forty-eight hours."

"Who cares about the law? There are no laws and no god in here. Besides, I'm an unregistered guest."

Who can vanish without a trace, I thought.

He must have read my mind. "It's not all bad," he said. "They leave me alone now. They even treat my injuries." He pointed to his feet. "That's a good sign."

"But what did they do to you before they decided to leave you in peace?"

"Do you really want to know?"

I was not sure. But sooner or later I would find out. I surveyed his wounds. No words could express the violence that had been inflicted on him. Especially when you are trapped, rendered helpless, vulnerable and with no chance of defending yourself.

"Yes," I replied.

"I did not know where I was. I was arrested in the open as I was waiting to meet a friend, and I was blindfolded immediately. I did not get to the basement and this cell until three days later. On arrival they took me directly to a room on the second or third floor. The men who brought me there pushed me inside and closed the door after them. There was total silence around me. It felt as though I was alone in the room. I did not dare move for fear of stumbling over something. That must be what it feels like to be blind, a constant fear of stumbling. It had occurred to me at once to lift my blindfold and have a quick peek around. But what if there was someone in the room? Someone who was watching me? Someone waiting for me to make a mistake, like trying to escape, perhaps? No, I did not want to give them any excuse to accuse me of anything else. In the car to the police station the officers who had taken me had mumbled something about an armed robbery. They wanted to know where the weapons and the money were. I was tired. The moment I decided to sit down the door was flung open.

"I did not have time to react in any way. Hands pulled off my leather jacket, my sweater, my trousers, my underpants. I knew there was no point in trying to make them see sense, to tell them they had got the wrong man. The time for talking had passed. They were out to humiliate and break me. My brain could not even be bothered to ask how. Boundless shame and rage released my most primitive defence mechanisms. I screamed, hit, kicked out in every direction, until a merciless blow floored me. Before I had time to recover, my legs were lifted up and they pushed my neck to make me bend my head towards my knees. A round object was forced over my legs and head until it reached my thighs and shoulders. It smelled of rubber. I was sitting in a U-shape, trapped by a car tyre, with no room for movement. I did not have to wait long. The first stroke to the soles of my feet struck like lightning. The pain was sharp and searing. I know that they used a thin stick, but the effect was like being slashed with a razor. In sheer panic I rotated my feet, I flexed and pointed my toes in a vain attempt to ward off the blows. The pain in my toes was the worst, it felt as though someone was ripping off my toenails. I had already decided not to scream and give them cause to enjoy the spectacle. I heard the tormentor's laboured breathing and the swiping sounds of the stick cutting through the air. The strokes fell in a steady rhythm until they suddenly stopped. My feet must have been torn to shreds by now. All I could think about was getting some sleep. Then the beating resumed. The stick was in new hands. The strokes were harder now and came at regular intervals. In a last desperate effort I rolled over on to my left side. My resistance must have provoked my tormentors. The stick now hit my thighs, buttocks and my back. After a kick to my groin I lost consciousness.

"A metal spiral worked its way with lightning speed through my groin, stomach and lungs as it devoured my organs one at a time. I opened my eyes, but could see only the darkness of the blindfold. The pain that woke me was indescribable. I was lying on my back with my arms spread out and my legs apart and tied down. I tried in vain to wriggle loose. Then I felt the wires. One pushed up my anus and one wrapped around my penis. I heard a faint sound as if . . . as if someone was cranking up the handset of a field telephone. I knew it was the power source. The shockwave lifted my entire body and something exploded inside my brain. I was thrown up and down several times. The smell of burned flesh reached my nostrils. And bad breath mixed with a sharp smell of tobacco and sweat. All the time they kept asking me questions. I had nothing to tell them except when they asked me who I was. They had no idea who they had picked up. A man who had talked during his interrogation had told them where someone was supposed to turn up, but that he did not know who it would be.

"That was when I thought of the name Sevim. While I was chuckling on the inside, they grew even angrier. The current drilled its way through my spine. My body felt as if it were being torn into a thousand pieces. The shockwaves repeatedly sent me in and out of consciousness. My mouth felt terribly dry. It seemed as if all fluid had been drained from my body. I threw up, violently, nauseous from the stench of my own faeces. My whole body shook with uncontrollable convulsions. Eventually I was released from the wires and dragged out of the room, across the corridor and into a new room. There I was flung, like a sack, on to the cold floor. Someone covered my naked body with my clothes.

"Now it was the turn of 'the good cop'. He gave me a cigarette, spoke to me in a fatherly voice, complained about how primitive the others were and promised to help me if I answered his questions. 'Sevim,' was all I said.

"He smiled and watched me for a while, then he threw his cigarette stub on the floor, crushed it with the sole of his shoe and left.

"The 'primitive ones' did not keep me waiting for long. They had a surprise for me. I was suspended from a metal pole like a crucified corpse. Gravity pulled my body down. Every tendon, sinew and muscle in my shoulders and lower arms tensed up like the strings of an instrument being tuned. I was convinced my arms would soon be pulled from their sockets. Then my body, spurting blood, would collapse like a grotesque maimed lump while my arms would be left dangling. As my body grew heavier and heavier, my arms could no longer take the weight. That was when the real pain began. I could now differentiate clearly between types of pain. Blows, electric shocks and hanging all produced their own specific agony.

"My circulation and, with it, all feeling, had almost ceased in my upper arms. Thousands of tiny needles pricked my hands and fingers. But the all-consuming pain in my lower arms was the worst. Any kind of movement made everything worse. 'Do you know what this is called?' a voice asked me as bare wires were tied around my big toes. 'A Palestinian clothes hanger.'

"I heard the terrifying sound of someone cranking up the handle of the generator again. The shockwaves made me pull up my knees to my stomach as a reflex. I hung there, dangling, my body in spasms, a confused heap of muscles. A bucket of water was thrown over me. The next shockwave hit me with such violent force that it disengaged my brain.

"I don't know how long I was unconscious for. I had lost my sense of time long before. My whole body ached. My arms were no longer mine. But the worst thing was my thirst. Then I realized I was no longer hanging in the air. My feet were safely planted on the floor, I was in the other room and my right hand was handcuffed to a radiator pipe. It was completely silent outside. It was the end of the working day.

"So ended the first interrogation. I now knew what lay in store for me in the days to come and I was prepared. I even dreamed during my first night in custody. I lay naked on a bed. My head on a soft pillow with a white pillowcase. I watched my surroundings. The bed was the only object in the room. Everything was white. The walls, the window-sill, the curtains, the sheets, the pillowcase. Everything was white and clean. Peace descended upon me."

He had finished. I could see that he had managed to remain calm throughout his ordeal. I wished that I had the same will of iron. I knew that he had told me all the details with the precise language of an articulate man in order to prepare us newcomers for our inevitable fate. But, as he said himself, the time for talking was over. Yet there was one thing I wanted to know.

"Did you ever feel scared?"

"Fear, my friend, is not a good companion no matter where we are. The art is never to show it to outsiders."

I would have liked to have said the same, had anyone asked me. The difference was that Sevim was an expert and I was hardly that.

"Good morning, Miss Sevim. Have you been inducting our new guests, eh?"

In his tailor-made suit and gold-rimmed glasses, the clean-shaven and fleshy-faced man in the doorway looked more like a businessman than an underpaid bureaucrat. He looked down at his shiny shoes as though he were talking to them. "Yes, yes, we all have a job to do. How are we today?" The voice was soft and pleasant, ready for a friendly chat. He seemed almost educated compared with the rest of guards, who were unable string a sentence together without swearing. Suddenly I knew he was "the good cop". It was difficult to tell if the mood was artificial or if the two of them had built up something best described as a friendly enmity.

"I'm fine," Sevim replied. "How are things with you upstairs? Busy torturing people?"

"Now, now, my friend. Let's not give our new guests the wrong impression. I've never seen anyone being tortured in this building."

He chose to direct his smile at me. The light from the ceiling reflected off the gold frames of his glasses and blinded me to the extent that that I missed the expression in his eyes. But his smile, which was almost a snarl, told me all I needed to know. He was not interested in me. He focused his attention on Sevim once more.

"Pity. A bit of cooperation would have made all the difference. It's a matter of give and take, as in most other situations in life."

"This conversation is starting to bore me," Sevim said. "Please shut the door behind you unless you've got something sensible to say."

"Funny you should say that. I've got good news for you, as it happens. You'll be leaving soon. For a well-guarded prison, obviously. But anything's better than . . . than, well, you tell . . ."

Sevim was unperturbed. "I'll miss you," he said.

"Likewise, my friend, likewise." The man adjusted his glasses, nodded by way of farewell and disappeared behind the heavy steel door. He had delivered those last words with feeling.

*

The cell was an oven, hermetically sealed, suffocating, claustrophobic, a coffin containing nineteen gasping human beings. The heat became unbearable during the day. But I did not want to take off my shirt or trousers. It felt as if I would be buried alive here if I did so. No-one spoke anymore, no-one mentioned lunch, even though a fresh batch of cheese, olives and bread had been bought and paid for. The heat made us lethargic, fear and boredom took care of the rest. I jumped on the inside at every noise in the corridor, whenever doors were opened or closed. I avoided looking at my cellmates' faces, scared of seeing my own thoughts mirrored in them. I avoided all eyes except for Sevim's. They betrayed no fear, only the same unbreakable calm. He sat with his head leaning against the wall and his eyes closed. I wished he would talk to me, but I could not blame him. Two weeks' hell was nearly over; he had much to think about and wanted to be left alone.

I copied him, leaned my head against the wall, closed my eyes and thought. I thought about an age of innocence, safe behind the high walls of the school, ignorant of the world beyond them. The fierce winds of the storm blowing outside had reached our ears, but not yet touched our skin. I wondered if I would have been more prepared if I had not grown up within the protective confines of the boarding school. Perhaps, perhaps not. The knowledge I had acquired through halting curiosity, supposedly to prepare me for life's challenges, had been shattered like a defective heat shield by the merciless impact of my first meeting with reality in Taksim Square. I could have lost my courage there and then, but Zuhal had given me fresh hope to stagger on. I had believed that my dependency on her was temporary, like a child's reliance on its mother. It was an illusion. I had dropped whatever she told me to drop, stayed away from anything I sensed she did not like. And I had never been able to admit that all this was for the sake of one woman. I was scared of making a mistake and losing her. But now, with my freedom already forfeit, there was nothing left to be scared of. I would convince Zuhal of my love and win hers.

The guard called out my name. I opened my eyes. The time had come. I hated the fear of the pain that awaited me, hated that threats should be allowed to dominate my consciousness. I wished I could rise above it. My only comfort was that I had nothing to tell them, no matter what they might ask me and how much pain it would cost me. For once I thanked my lucky stars for my ignorance. Sevim placed a hand on my shoulder and whispered: "Remember what your girlfriend said. Be brave."

I followed the guard's instructions and faced the corridor wall. I was blindfolded, then left to my own devices. I do not know how long I had been standing there like that before I heard voices and footsteps approaching. Anything was welcome now. Anything but waiting. A male voice told me to take hold of the stick with which he was poking me.

"The wife's terrified that I'll give them all lice at home," he chuckled.

It was not easy to imagine that these people had a life with a wife and children. I stumbled up the first set of stairs expecting blows and abuse, but my escorts were completely silent. I was moved on without any words being spoken. After our ascent we walked down another corridor. It seemed that there were offices behind the doors to either side. In a strange way it was comforting to hear the familiar sounds of a normal workplace. But then I heard something indescribable, a hollow, dark and icy cry ringing out from one of the floors above. Deep from the throat, a pained, animalistic lament. I wondered about the source of it. I would soon find out. We were heading for it. We continued our journey down the corridor. However, when they finally stopped me, it was only the refreshing summer breeze that hit me like an unexpected slap in the face.

When they loosened my blindfold I was blinded by the sun, riding high in all its life-giving glory. The world was rendered in incandescent white; I could not make out colours or shapes. I shielded my eyes and gradually let the sunlight filter through my fingers. When I was ready I unveiled them with a gesture, a salaam for a long-lost friend. I was standing at the entrance to the Anti-Terrorism Department. Police cars and police officers moved in and out of my field of vision. I had no eyes for them. Zuhal was standing in the car park, waiting for me. I ran towards her.

If the kiss which brushed her lips surprised her, she did not show it. Her only concern was her joy at having me at her side. It warmed me, it warmed me more than the sun. We walked briskly down towards Mecidiyeköy, hand-in-hand. The afternoon rush had begun, with the usual pulse of life coursing through the offices and shops. People passed without a second thought for us and the hell we had just left behind. We talked over each other, out of breath, stole words from each other halfway through sentences and wanted to be the first to tell our story. We discovered sources of amusement we had not known we had regis-tered at the time. The torturers who panicked and hid under the table, terrified of being recognized, when the blindfold of one of their victims came loose. The prisoner in one of the cells who entertained his cell-mates with his jokes. The belly dancer who had been brought in for reasons unknown and who fretted about the evening's performance. The guard who smuggled in cigarettes and whispered, "stand firm, don't give up."

We both steered clear of our terror and fear. Our joy at our unex-pected freedom was so great that neither of us wanted to let those shadows diminish it. We wondered why we had been allowed to leave. While she waited for me, Zuhal had seen others from the shanty town being released. It was either because they knew that we had not used weapons or because they had brought in far more people than they could cope with. We did not know then that honest police officers had put huge pressure on the torturers. The police were split in two, progressive against reactionary forces, the same as the rest of society.

I invited her home, something I had not done before. We deserved a decent meal and a proper bath. We both looked like vagrants. In addition, she had an ugly bruise at her left temple. She made light of it when I showed my concern.

Zuhal prefered to meet my family under different and happier circumstances and suggested that we went to her student digs to eat and wash, and then organize everything else later. She got her way, as on so many other occasions. Suddenly we found ourselves in Taksim Square, both time and distance had passed unnoticed while we talked. We had arrived at the place where we first met. I could tell from looking at her that she was thinking the same thing, but neither of us mentioned it.

I found a telephone booth and called my mother. She was both worried and angry. I had never spent the night away without letting her know in advance. I could not tell her the truth, so I blamed an imaginary girl who had seduced me – something that made Zuhal giggle. The feminine laughter helped to convince my mother. I was allowed to spend another night with my femme fatale if I promised not to pester her about getting married when I came home.

"Your mother's very funny," Zuhal said.

I totally missed the longing in her voice. Nor did it occur to me to ask about her family. Instead I told her everything about my mother while we waited for the bus to Fatih, during the journey, and later as we bought eggs, sausages and bread in the shop.

Some older people were washing before evening prayers in the communal fountain in the courtyard in front of the mosque. There were many other people around, workers taking a short cut on their way home, couples with or without children out for an evening stroll, street vendors, pigeons. This courtyard had played an important role in the history of the city: as the venue of conspiracies against mighty sultans and, in the last days of the Ottoman Empire, the scene of reactionary protests against any progressive step. However, since the birth of the republic it had lost its political significance and become a showcase for the street life of the old city, now free from the militant imams and their rabid denunciations of traitors and apostates. Many of the new generation associated this enormous inner square with summer evening promenades, picnics and ball games. I associated it with death. Not because severed heads used to be displayed here as a warning to others, but because of a natural death. My father's funeral had taken place in this mosque. I had stood outside in a smaller, hidden courtyard where the coffins of the dead were set down on plinths before the final prayer, and later attended the ceremony behind the rusty fences. There had not been many mourners that day, a few friends and relatives. My father had been a hard man, difficult to get on with. It must have cost him friends along the way. I often thought of him as an aristocratic prole-tarian: all worn overalls and skilled hands when tuning electric engines on the factory floor, but always dressed in a suit and tie in his free time, shoes polished to a brilliant shine, grooming his impeccable Ottoman gentlemanly manners. I think he fell between two stools his whole life. He did not identify with the working class and he did not belong to the middle class. This may explain why I did not tell Zuhal about my father. I preferred to believe I was more like my mother.

In contrast to the courtyard, the annexes looked abandoned. Most students had gone home for the holidays, including Zuhal's room-mate. With her friend's belongings gone, the room was even more austere than I remembered from my first visit. Zuhal, who left her mark on most things, had not taken the trouble to turn her room into a home. No personal belongings, no photographs, posters, scent of perfume, no nightdress casually slung over the bed, nothing to suggest that a young woman lived here. It did not surprise me. I knew that this was her way of suppressing petit-bourgeois temptations and resisting conventional ideas of femininity. A glance, a slight sigh, perhaps, must have given away my thoughts.

"There's no point in putting flowers in a vase now. I've been given notice to leave," she said.

She did not seem too concerned, and I suspected her of taking the situation as another challenge – perhaps she was looking forward to moving on. She strongly disapproved of anything too established. The fact that she had to move was news to me and I wanted to know what she was going to do.

She hushed me. "Not now. Let's eat first."

She was illiterate when it came to cooking. This was how she put it, but I found it hard to believe. Any boy or girl who had been brought up tied to their mother's apron strings could cook a little. However, if she was determined to show me that she had long since dispensed with her traditional role as a woman, it was quite alright with me. I could easily fry a couple of eggs and some sausages. I found the paraffin stove and the frying pan and easily passed the test. We ate in silence. I thought how good it would be to have her at home with us. It was wishful thinking, but the idea came to me while I chewed my food and was fully formed by the time we had finished washing up.

"Come and live with us for a while," I said.

She burst out laughing. "Do you recall what your mother said? Don't pester her about getting married. What will she think if you turn up with a girl?"

She was teasing me. But the daring glint in her eyes said more: "Could you really do it? Could you really bring a woman home to your mother?"

I was not entirely sure. My mother did not like being dictated to by her sons. Could she handle the competition, the inevitable neighbourhood gossip?

"We'll go there together. If there's no room for you in my mother's house, then there's no room for me either."

It was the answer she had been waiting for – this time the glint in her eyes reflected her satisfaction. But she kept on teasing me. Where would she sleep? There was no spare bedroom in our flat, was there? Did I dare sleep beside her?

"You'll take my brother's room. He'll sleep with me in the living room," I said indignantly.

We decided to go there at once and started to pack her belongings into two worn suitcases. When we had finished, I stared at the pathetic cases; her whole life was inside them. No, this was an absurd notion. It was just her worldly possessions.

"I want you to be clear about this, my one and only," Zuhal said. "This is a temporary arrangement."

This was the second time within a few days she had called me "my one and only". Was this a form of address you used with friends or an indication of something more? Since we had arrived at her room, I had struggled to summon the courage to create the right atmosphere for telling her everything I had been thinking about recently.

"Kemal was right after all," she said.

"I love you," I said. We had spoken simultaneously. The words collided in the air and drifted towards the floor. A shadow fell across her face; she abruptly turned away from me and started pulling the empty drawers out of the chest. I did not know how I looked – like an idiot, most likely. I had chosen the very moment when the name of the man in her life was on her lips. "Kemal was right after all." Now her words hit me with their full force. The shots fired at the shanty town and the terror at the police station had made up her mind. We had pulled away from each other. She was ready to kill and to die now.

"You don't love me. It's just an illusion," she said, still with her back to me.

"How can you say that?" It was not meant as a response to what she had said. I wanted to go on, but something blocked my throat. It was hard to find my voice; any attempt would sound like the high-pitched whining of a pre-pubescent boy. I had lost the advantage of having shared something important with her and with it the chance to talk her out of a dead end. Now I had to contend with Kemal and everything he stood for, a man who did not even have to be with us to make his presence felt.

"He is not right," I said. My voice did not betray me. "Kemal is a mindless adventurer. He's walking into a storm that will blow him out of this world. He knows it and he likes it. Alright, so he's a brave man, prepared to face the consequences of his actions, but what use is it? Besides, he doesn't care about you at all."

The latter I knew nothing about. It was nothing but a blow beneath the belt. But it made Zuhal turn around to face me.

"You're wrong, my friend. He values me highly. That's why he left me in peace when I discovered that I did not love him. He is in love with only one thing: the revolution."

"You discovered you didn't love him? Weren't you the one who made fun of love?"

"Did I? How silly. Sometimes I try to sound tougher than I am. That's my secret. Don't tell anyone."

I was not sure if she was teasing me. Her serious eyes did not suggest so. After a whole year she was still an enigma to me.

"So you thought Kemal was an invincible rival for my love?"

I had done. But that was not the point now, even though I was pleased that I had been mistaken. I was a little confused; it felt as if we were speaking at cross purposes. The man himself might be out of the way, but not his ideas. And they were standing between us.

"He's got under your skin. That's what I'm fighting against. It's words against force. We cannot win this war with weapons, Zuhal. If we do, there will only be losers. With hatred, revenge and blood on their hands and in their minds."

"I didn't know you had turned into a pacifist. Our very own Gandhi. Are you that naïve? To the authorities in this country words are just as dangerous as weapons. The only ones who can hope to escape are those who keep silent."

"Do you think I don't know that? What's wrong with keeping silent and letting history run its course? They can't rule with force forever, can they? One day things will have to change. If not now, then in ten years, twenty."

"So what are you suggesting, then? That we all sit down together, holding each other's hands, and pray that the day will come quickly?"

"Something like that, yes. Or, if you wish, we can protest with our voices as our weapons and take the consequences. I'm ready to go on a long journey with you, anywhere, you pick, as long as I don't have to hold a weapon instead of the one I love."

"No-one talks like you, no-one I know," Zuhal said and caressed my cheek. "You're a born poet. Not a Nâzım Hikmet, perhaps, but a poet all the same. Poets are peace-loving. They are doomed to be so. But how sure are you that you love me?"

She was not expecting an answer. Instead she went to her bed, bent down and pulled out a white plastic tub. Then, like a good housewife, she walked back and forth fetching a large pan which she filled with water from a plastic container, lit the paraffin stove and placed the pan on top of it. I was curious, but received no explanation. Instead she sent me to fetch more water from the communal fountain outside the mosque. Equipped with two large plastic jugs I ran down to the court-yard. It was like the old days when we had moved to our new flat. Unsurprisingly, the housing association had built the houses with no infrastructure to speak of. While we waited for water to be installed, we had had to fetch water from the nearest factory. For us children it had just been a big laugh. We would queue with our plastic jugs and flirt with the girls. I remember that Emel fell for a steelworker who would sit on a scrap heap in his break, tug on his moustache and wink to her. The affair ended when Emel's grandmother caught them and gave her a sound beating – for nothing more than an innocent kiss blown in the direction of the amorous worker. I smiled at the memory.

"It must be a lucrative business, given your broad smile," said the young man sitting next to me, washing his feet.

"What?" I asked, baffled.

"Selling water," he said.

For a moment I was tempted to have fun at his expense. But he had a naïve and honest look.

"Oh, no. I just happen to be in love," I said.

"Oh, that's different," he said and offered me a cigarette he had just rolled. The smuggled tobacco made me dizzy. He turned out to be a porter from the market.

"You're joking!" I exclaimed. He knew Ahmet by reputation. We sat in the twilight in the poorly lit courtyard, smoking and chatting about the vegetable market like two old friends.

"Where have you been? The water has nearly boiled away." Zuhal was frowning.

"I had the chance to make big money in the water business," I replied.

She gave me a look that suggested I had been drinking. But my mood was infectious.

"You're mad," she said and laughed.

"Please tell me what it is you're doing?" I said.

"You're a man of words, I'm a woman of action," she replied enigmatically.

But I no longer needed an explanation. I had worked out what was going on. She had divided the room in two by hanging a sheet over a clothesline. We would wash and smarten ourselves up before she met my family.

"Ladies first," she said, and disappeared behind the sheet. I boiled water for myself while she washed. When she emerged once more, her hair and her body were wrapped up in two towels. Suddenly I felt shy and looked away from her. She did not pass up the chance to tease me.

"Why are you staring at the floor? Have you seen something funny? Your turn, lad. Come on."

I undressed, sat down in the tub and started soaping my body. It was wonderful.

"Do you need me to scrub your back?" she said behind me.

My mother used to rub my back with a coarse cloth, but Zuhal was not my mother.

"No, thanks," I said.

She bent down and picked up my clothes.

"Where are you taking them?" I asked.

"They're so filthy. I'll find some of mine which fit you," she said.

It would not surprise me: we were almost the same size.

"Do you think you could leave me alone now?" I said.

The room was warm, the water was warm and I felt warm inside. Warm with desire. I was hard in my hand, my mind replaying glimpses of her naked shoulders and legs. I dreamed of guiding it in between her thighs, but stopped abruptly, filled with shame. She would hate me if she suddenly walked in and saw what I was doing. I could never tell her that I wanted to make love to her. I was far too scared of being rejected.

I dried myself and wrapped the towel around my waist. We had to get out of this place. At home I would regain the composure I needed to take the next step. At home I would not be satisfied with her accepting my love without giving anything back. I would think it through, down to the last detail, until the simplest words would sound like lines from an epic poem. I would make her admit that she loved me. It would be a dangerous game and I risked losing her forever, but I had to take that chance. I did not want to continue as her young admirer, well liked, but nothing more.

I pulled aside the sheet carefully to ask her hand me some clothes. She was lying on her stomach on the bed, with her long curly hair spread out across the pillow, so that her face was hidden from me. I sensed that she had deliberately buried her head in the pillow to avoid eye contact, to forestall any awkward words and to let me watch her naked body undisturbed. I was drawn to her like a moth to a flame.

I knew it the moment I opened my eyes. Daylight crept in through the tall windows and fell like stage lighting across the bed. The unmistakeable smell of last night's lovemaking lingered in the air. I lay there for a while, inhaling what was left of her. Her chequered shirt and jeans – were they the ones she had been wearing that day on Taksim Square? – – lay neatly folded on the floor. The sheet on the clothesline and the plastic tub were gone. Gone, too, were the two worn suitcases.

Part Two

9

Summer 1979

I was no longer nineteen. A year had passed. One year since I felt the warmth of her skin. One year since she left me. Not that I fully understood it right away. She had gone, yes, but there had to be an explanation. I was too scared to try to find it. I chose to deceive myself and clung to other possibilities, no matter how unrealistic. The only way to trace her was through the student union. There were many new faces there, marked by suspicion. No, they did not know anyone called Zuhal. What did I think they were, the National Missing Persons' Bureau? Who was I, anyway, a police informer, perhaps? I knew that pleading would make no difference, nor telling them she was the woman I loved. It would only make the situation more embarrassing. Outside the office a young man came running after me.

"I've seen you with her once," he said. "Don't look for her. You won't find her. Not here, not anywhere. Do you understand what I'm saying, friend?"

I did. I walked away from him, and I kept on walking. Eventually I ended up in Gülhane Park, under the walnut tree. I sat down, looked out across the Bosporus and wept. While I cried I thought about the thin line between cowardice and courage. Was I a coward for choosing peace and love over war? Was she brave because she chose a different path without hesitation? Or was it the other way round? I reached a conclusion. I would wait. Wait for her to come back to me. Then we would find the answers together.

Support came from loyal quarters.

"You should have brought her here immediately," my mother said. "She would have felt safe with us."

I did not have the strength to say that it would have made no difference. She had taken her suitcases and gone. She did not want to submit to stifling conformity. I had never asked her what kind of home she came from. She had never told me about her family. Had I had the tiniest hope that she might have sought refuge with her parents or siblings, I would have looked for them.

"If she loves you enough, she'll come back," my mother said.

I did not expect her to say anything else. All I wanted was for her to cradle my head in her lap and to stroke my hair, while I listened to her calming voice and simple words. I imagined by now that she had become accustomed to my various forms of lovesickness. I did not know what else went on in her head, but her hands and her voice gave me the strength to bear the heavy burden.

I could wander the desert like Kerem, but I could not understand why a half-crazed character from popular legend on a hopeless quest for an equally hopeless love would appeal to anyone. Besides, I was far too happy and optimistic to seek out such a bleak existence. Trauma counselling was an unknown concept in those days, but then again I have always been a firm believer in being my own counsellor. My therapy was simple: fill every second of my life with activity. This was the only way I could prevent her from morphing from a departed lover into a haunting ghost. To help the time fly by, I started working for Ahmet again, with the same enthusiasm as before. He was blissfully ignorant of the storms that had ravaged my life, so avoided the obligation to put on a clumsy show of sympathetic participation in my grieving process. He had not changed, he was still a charming villain, good-humoured and relaxed. Only once, when a female student sashayed down the aisle towards the literacy course with every man's eyes on her, did he remember Zuhal and ask after her.

"Who?" I said, and carried on with my work.

"Lucky devil. Can't even remember all the women in his life," he muttered with envy, and lost interest.

In the summer of 1978 the letter with the official logo arrived. On the strength of my entrance examination I had earned a place at the Faculty of Arts. Under different circumstances I would have been overjoyed, but with Zuhal gone it seemed an empty prospect. I did not dare hope that she would suddenly turn up, with books in her canvas bag, to greet me in the corridor. I registered with the Department of English Language and Literature and attended the first lecture of the autumn term. With my heart pounding, acting as discreetly as possible, I asked after her, approaching anyone who might know her. No-one had seen her since the spring. No matter how slim my hopes had been, my disappointment was profound. Levo was there, at his faculty. We met in the refectory during breaks. He talked incessantly about Gülnur and Semra, who were both in their final year at school. I listened, but tried to appear uninterested and was incredibly inventive when it came to avoiding meeting the girls at the weekends. Levo's second favourite subject was the miserable state of student halls compared with living at home. I was lucky, he said, living in this city and not having to suffer like the other students. He had a heart of gold, Levo, but he never wondered why I kept so quiet during all of his chattering. Not that I was complaining; on the contrary, I found his stories refreshing and liked him even more.

The evenings were the worst. I read, I read a great deal, anything and everything. Nothing else could fill the void.

"All that reading will ruin your eyes," my mother said.

My eyesight did deteriorate, but I was not sure that I could blame it on excess reading. The glasses I bought with my savings gave me, in Levo's words, the intellectual touch he felt my appearance had lacked. While I, quite unintentionally, became an erudite student, the smouldering embers of civil unrest were rising to flame once more. Street fights and shoot-outs between Fascists, revolutionary students and the police had become an everyday occurrence. Teaching was interrupted for several days at a time as the buildings were occupied by political groups and turned into battlegrounds. I sided with the revolutionaries, went to their refectory, to their debates, but refused to take part in the violent clashes. They were so divided in their views, so fragmented, that even the most hardened militants eventually accepted me as a swatch of eccentric, colourful fabric in their patchwork quilt. The odd digs about cowardice I endured at first ceased when I did not panic and throw myself under the table at the first sign of gunfire. After all, I was more used to hearing shots fired than most. They thought I was a figure of fun with my strange theories about a utopian socialism where everyone was happy, shared the benefits equally, and lived in brotherly peace and solidarity.

"Where was it you came from again? Mars?" they would say and laugh. Young people who dreamt about the dictatorship of the proletariat laughed at my expense. It did not matter. I enjoyed being with them. They were like one big family I had inherited from Zuhal. And like a powerless paterfamilias I watched over them and wished that they would behave differently. How, I did not know. How do you stop Fascism from triumphing? By stopping the bullets with defenceless bodies? I had questions, but no answers. I had the feeling of rowing against the tide and felt sorry for myself and my generation. We were lost, and yet we were the finest this country had seen for decades. A lost generation who cared.

"What we need now is a decent utopia," I said, half in jest. There was only one thing I had no doubts about: Zuhal must have found the answers to her questions.

IO

Autumn 1979, a safe house somewhere in Istanbul

A bare table, a glass of tea (cold and untouched), breadcrumbs on the windowsill for the birds, a wood burner (unused) by the wall (in desperate need of a coat of paint) and the silence of self-imposed solitude. Echoes of the past, however, were ever present in her memories, sometimes happy in their carefree state, sometimes teasing in their irrefutability and sometimes irritating in their futility.

Zuhal liked her solitude. She was not short of company, had she wanted it. Her solitude was a shield against the outsider's lack of insight.

For several days she had pondered the one question she had not been able to find a convincing answer to. What would she say in the bank? She very much wanted to make an impression. On one man in particular. She had thought a great deal about him recently. Was her father the root of her beliefs, with his tireless sermons about justice? How credible they had been, distilled from genuine blood, genuine tears? Was it her father who had shaped her? Though eventually she had surpassed him, even in his eyes. The whole thing seemed like a drawn-out creation myth, with people linked to each other in a chain of influence, where some did not have the strength to keep up, while others, like her, threw themselves body and soul into the work.

Even though the desire to make an impression lay hidden deep inside her, there were times during the hours of introspection where she came close to admitting it. Surely a touch of vanity never hurt anyone? Besides, who had deserved it more than her, after nearly a year of self-sacrifice? It was no coincidence that she enjoyed a level of respect that only increased with time. True, there were still those whose eyes followed her with suspicion, the legacy of decades of inbred blindness to a woman's abilities. She did not care about that.

She compared her slight vanity to an artist's eagerness and urge to impress at first a few chosen admirers and then a wider audience. In itself it was hardly sensational to enter a bank, but a well-placed remark could change everything. She continued to struggle with this one problem. Everything she came up with sounded phonetically impossible to her ears. "To seize" for example. Or "to confiscate". Surely there had to be something that could do the job without sounding so pompous, something that would make an instant and enduring impression. After all, it was meant to be her signature.

Before she closed the door behind her, she routinely scanned the anonymous flat she had no reason to call her home. On her way down the steps she thought about the day the previous year when she and Kemal had walked side by side chatting as friends do – only this time their promenade was a matter of business and the conversation resembled an entrance interview. Kemal had seemed pleased to have her back with him: he made no references to their former intimacy and was a little superior in his role as an instructor. A half smile played at the corner of his mouth, his head was bent towards the ground and he spoke monotonously about theory and practice and about duties that she had taken for granted. When business was out of the way, he stopped and for the first time he looked her straight in the eye.

"You do know you can't see him any longer, don't you?"

She decided to feign ignorance because she had been taken by surprise, or perhaps she was embarrassed.

"Who?"

"That little lover of yours?"

If the statement was meant to be sarcastic, it had the wrong effect. He instantly looked remorseful, as if he had made a dreadful error, his eyes focused on the ground again. He was probably terrified of being taken for just another man driven by jealousy. She disliked his inappropriate rudeness, but she did not want to rise to his bait by confirming or denying anything.

"Wouldn't it be better for you to concentrate on the tasks ahead?" That was all she had to say to him, even though she was tempted to add she would be taking no lovers in the near future.

Later she breathed a sigh of relief when she was moved from Kemal's command – she was unsure whether it had been his decisions or another's – and sent to lead her own group. But she knew that their paths would cross when circumstance required it. It did not worry her. I will deal with it when it happens, she thought, and hoped that private disagreements would not compromise her work with Kemal.

She shook all this off as she strode briskly through the empty streets, like a woman hurrying to work before the worst of that morning's rush set in. Her stomach was rumbling with hunger. She had not dared to eat breakfast in case she threw up, and even though she walked past a couple of shops displaying freshly baked goods, she managed to resist temptation.

The car appeared moments after she had arrived at the rendezvous point. She appreciated this precision, pleased that her earlier rants at failed timekeeping had not been in vain. When the car pulled up next to her and the driver opened the door from the inside, she got into the passenger seat without registering its features or wondering how it had ended up in the group's possession. She had already discussed everything that was relevant with the four men who were now sitting in the car with her, so she merely nodded in approval like a teacher pleased that everyone in the class was present. She was immediately handed a parcel wrapped up in a cloth, which she opened. As always the steel that was revealed aroused conflicting feelings in her: disgust mixed with fear and a feeling of power. Having been unsure for a long time if she wanted to cross this line, she had at last reached the conclusion that fire must be fought with fire.

The four men packed into the car were waiting for her signal. They made no attempt to chat or tell jokes, but waited in silence with straight backs, tensed muscles, and beads of sweat at their temples. They were all young, but disparate in appearance – some with moustaches, others clean-shaven, some tall, others short – and together they smelled strongly of bad body odour. They looked so vulnerable and lost in their ill-fitting cheap clothes, and Zuhal felt compassion and a great urge to protect them. It was almost touching how they looked up to her, these fundamentally tough men who had most likely taken their belt to a woman or two in their time. To these men she was the nearest you could get to a field commander. She would do anything within her power not to let them down. She was ready. The only thing that threatened her hard-won composure was a dry mouth, a few heart palpitations, and the clammy, sweaty, slightly trembling but determined hands that held the Kalashnikov.

When the car turned into the street for the second time, the reconnaissance pass completed, Zuhal told the driver to park in front of the bank. They filed out of the car, Zuhal first, carrying the gun concealed in the cloth – a rice sack, judging from the name and logo of the producer. She and two others entered the bank, one man waited on the pavement as a lookout and the driver stayed in the car with the engine running.

The rest of the incident was a tangle of muddled images that she could not pull together in the right order after the event. She had no special recollection of the bank itself apart from the sharp, fluorescent lighting, the heavy curtains and the face of the woman behind the dark-brown counter. She walked towards that face in a trance, without any idea of what her two friends were doing. The woman was the only object in her field of vision. When she removed the sack and revealed the gun, the woman's smile stretched into a grimace and Zuhal's voice screeched in her own ears like chalk on a blackboard: "We're here to seize the assets of the bank in the name of the people!"

Silence. The woman's face turned into a question mark. It lasted until an object crashed down to the floor. Zuhal spun around towards the sound. One of her group, the man with the moustache, had managed to drop the magazine of his pistol and was busy picking it up, aghast. Almost embarrassed by his ineptitude and in a fresh attempt to take control, she cleared her throat and shouted, "Give me the money, woman. Fast!"

Fast was the key word now. Fast and efficient, but with no fumbling, without any fatal blunders. She did not know if anyone had called the police, and if so, how rapid and effective their response would be. Zuhal listened to her inner clock as she watched the woman behind the counter, whose trembling hands flinched whenever she touched the bank notes, as though she personally were robbing the bank. When the woman had finished, Zuhal took the sack from her with a smile, the only friendly sign she was capable of giving her, and hoped that she would not interpret it as contempt.

Their escape from the bank was lost to a gaping hole in her memory. The next thing she remembered was standing in the street with a raised gun. There was no hysterical screaming, no visible signs of panic. Perhaps it was because a woman was holding the weapon or because people were becoming used to living under such conditions. She reacted with something bordering on disappointment. No armed figures rushed out of armoured cars to take their positions, no sirens sounded to indicate an imminent battle. She heard her friends shout "get in, get in!" as they dragged her into the car. The car started with a jolt that sent her flying backwards, and when the driver unexpectedly slammed the brakes at the first bend, she was flung forwards and whacked her forehead into the back of the head of the man in the passenger seat. She bruised her forehead, the only casualty of the day, something that prompted ill-concealed laughter at her expense and lightened the mood among the nervous young men.

*

I gasped involuntarily. There she was, staring right back at me with black, innocent eyes, as though she were watching me. She was a younger version of herself: her hair was scraped back in a ponytail, strong eyebrows never touched by a pair of tweezers, a hesitant smile around her mouth. Zuhal at sixth-form college, pictured on the front page of a national newspaper. The reporter must have taken the photo from the police archives or talked it out of her stunned parents. We had no photos of each other. "No reason to update the police files, is there?" she had said. The huge headline on the front page referred only to her: "FEMALE TERRORIST ROBS BANK". It would not have surprised me if she had done it single-handedly. But the headline screamed out for attention and sensation. A female terrorist was much more interesting than four male terrorists. Below the photo were several columns about the robbery, written in the language of action films by a journalist who clearly could not decide whether he wanted to scold or admire her. The story was based on statements from so-called witnesses that explained how a woman and three men armed with machine-guns and pistols had stormed the bank just after it had opened, overpowered the staff and emptied the tills of money, by all accounts a considerable sum. Afterwards they had vanished in a waiting car with a fifth terrorist behind the wheel. It was later found abandoned in a side street some kilometres from the scene of the crime. It had been reported stolen the previous day. Police had been able to identify the woman due to an earlier arrest, the paper said. The four men were unknown. The journalist also quoted a spokesman for the police. He was convinced that the robbery was politically motivated and the robbers were members of a radical left-wing group. Police were looking for the terrorists and would do everything in their power to catch them as soon as possible. There was a photograph of the spokesman on the front page: more than anything he looked like a businessman. I wondered whether Sevim, wherever he might be, had read the paper and recognized his "good cop".

Zuhal was back. That was what mattered. I could relax. Waiting would be different now, less stressful. I could not hope for contact soon, for obvious reasons. Perhaps she was sitting with the same newspaper in front of her, thinking that I should regard this as a kind of greeting from her.

II

December 1979

"I think Shakespeare is overrated."

It was a deliberate provocation. I longed to see shock and irritation on her features. But I had misjudged her. She possessed restraint, a rare quality.

"You're too obvious, young man," she said. "Besides, everyone knows I have a weakness for my best students."

She was hidden in a cloud of cigarette smoke, buried in an antique armchair with a heavy, worn velvet cover: a small, slender woman with a tireless brain who navigated an ocean of knowledge every day.

Generations of students agreed that she was one of the few inspirations among our country's intellectuals. Emine Torgan, Professor of English Literature, referred to the late William Shakespeare as "my love". I did not doubt for one minute that she would have done anything to seduce the playwright had they been contemporaries. His rumoured homosexuality would have been a trivial obstacle. She had consumated this one-sided love of hers by publishing a book about the playwright's life and work. She regarded any criticism of her beloved as a personal insult.

"I mean it," I persevered. "The worst thing is that he's not even good. Think of all the banal stories he wasted his time writing. I can mention a hundred writers off the top of my head who are better than him."

She remained unperturbed; there was no hint of her famed professional rage. Her frail hand held the china cup, another antique, in a steady grip. She sipped her coffee, waved the cup in the air a couple of times before placing it upside down on the saucer.

"Life is full of banal stories. He turned them into superb poetry. Not even you can deny that *Romeo and Juliet* is a beautiful love story."

"An unrealistic melodrama," I said.

She raised an eyebrow, something she was apt to do when she wanted to be a little naughty. This woman, who was born as the Ottoman Empire foundered, still possessed the enthusiasm of a child.

"You think so? Well, then it's time for me to tell your fortune in the coffee grounds and reveal your secrets."

She could have knocked me down with a feather. She of all people, a self-declared enemy of everything metaphysical and beyond common sense, read fortunes from a coffee cup? I squirmed uneasily in my chair, where imperial greats had once been seated. She definitely possessed the ability to see through her fellow human beings.

"Right, it's as I thought," she said. "A sensitive soul with many burdens. A heavy heart." She showed me a dark-brown speck of ground coffee in the saucer.

"I see a long road here." A line had formed in the dregs as they ran down the inside of the cup. "You're going on a journey, you're looking for something, or somebody."

Her laughter was the loveliest thing about her. The years had left deep traces in her dark face.

"*Just kidding*," she said when she had stopped laughing. "Besides, it was my cup, wasn't it?"

She was being a little facetious; she hardly ever mixed Turkish with English unless for a specific effect.

"Tell me one thing. Are you fighting bravely for your beloved and preparing to sacrifice yourself like Romeo, if and when you are required to?" She had not asked if I had a beloved, but the question hit home all the same.

"She's gone," I said, rather than answering her question directly. She seemed content with this.

"Dead? Literally? Like Juliet? Or gone from your heart, home or country?"

"Just gone."

I enjoyed talking to her. The pleasure was mutual, I think. She had previously said that she was not in the habit of inviting students to her home. From the start of the autumn term she had been my tutor and when the Fascists had occupied the faculty buildings, she had given me work to do and assessed and discussed it during my frequent visits. The serving of coffee at such times was a signal that I could speak freely. Right from the first lecture I knew I had met the mentor I needed. I had never dreamed that I would be so privileged. I told her a great deal over coffee – she was a good listener too – but I had never mentioned Zuhal. The Professor was not a woman who needed to hear many words before she reached a conclusion.

"We have much in common, you know," she said. "For years I wondered if I had let down my friends. We were so few in the '40s and '50s. So few who believed in a better world. They did not have to kill us the way they're doing today. It was enough to impose a nightmare on us. Surveillance, torture and long prison sentences robbed me of most of my friends. I was a sensitive, peaceful soul like you. Someone who believed in but never participated in organized action. I was spared, perhaps in part because of my family's close links with the elite of the First Republic. Nevertheless I had to learn to live with my dilemma, a desire to change things without taking any risks. The feeling of having let down my friends – I would search their faces for accusing looks when I visited them in prison – was the worst I had to live with. Time passed. Some of those treated worst by the system did not hesitate to become a part of it later on, like the good citizens they were. I stayed the same, with my burning desire to change the world and remain incorruptible."

"Am I so important to you that you would tell me all this?"

I could see that she was prepared for the question, had almost been waiting for it.

"Every individual is important to me. In your case you should consider it a favour. For reasons I don't wish to go into."

No coaxing would make her more precise. Many before me had been sent home with their tails between their legs, having trampled thoughtlessly on her patience, but she did not want to send me home too disappointed.

"Sweethearts such as yours were lost to me along the way. Not necessarily because we betrayed each other; mostly because love dies. Some say that love will not die when the person you burn for is absent. I don't know. It sounds rather masochistic. Nor can I explain why I chose William for my last love."

She had a point. However, her raised eyebrow also suggested that I should not take everything she said literally. I, for my part, had no time for anything unrequited. I wanted to love Zuhal and be loved in return. It didn't matter how long it might last. That was the least of my worries. When the Professor escorted me politely to the door and out into a cool winter's evening, I was pleased to have spent the day with her.

An "idiot-soaker", fine and sneaky, fell from the dark sky. I liked walking in the rain. Running in the rain, like we used to do back at boarding school when we would put on our tracksuits after the last lesson of the day and throw ourselves into the puddles on the drenched football field, squealing with joy. As I walked along the wet pavement, my surroundings partly obscured behind a chiffon veil of mist, golden in the muted street light, all I wanted to do was sing. But not "Singin' in the rain" – I was not that light-hearted. And nor did I dance like Gene Kelly. With my hands in the pockets of my old reefer jacket, the collar turned up around my ears, I hummed an old Istanbul song about a plea for a kiss from a reluctant beloved.

It had stopped raining when I reached Beyoglu. Hotel Pera Palace was all lit up and there was a festive air along İstiklal Caddesi. Crowds flowed in both directions beneath constellations of neon lights, some merely taking in the atmosphere, others looking for the entertainment the night and the district offered. I followed the crowd to Taksim Square and wondered what it would like to buy a bottle of cheap red wine at a kiosk, sit on a wet bench in the park and spend the night like a down-and-out under the open sky. It was only a flight of fancy and held little actual appeal. If I wanted to sit down, drink and mope over Zuhal, I could do it without freezing my backside off. I turned around when I saw the glittering silhouette of Hotel Intercontinental, and retraced my own steps.

Çiçek Pasajı was packed almost to the rafters. An old whore was sitting alone at a small table in a corner. I had not guessed her profession looking at her, but she introduced herself as such when I asked if I could sit down. She was chatty and insisted on buying me a beer and a plate of battered mussels. No-one wanted to sleep with her anymore, no-one wanted listen to her. But I did. To listen, that is. She was a fake blonde, her hair was thin and dry as straw after years of bleaching and she had great stories to tell about what it was like to be a shameless young woman in the '40s. It was hard to understand why no-one wanted to hear them. Then it was my turn to buy the next round, but she had already had enough. Her head slumped onto the table with an audible thud. She was asleep. I ordered another beer and drank and smoked without thinking of Zuhal, distracted by the constant hubbub of this famous watering hole and by the straw-like hair of the woman sleeping next to me.

"I'm very sorry," said a voice in my ear later that evening. It belonged to a middle-aged man, well-dressed, polite. "She's my mother,' he said, pointing to the woman. "I'm here to take her home."

I helped him as much as I could. He found his wallet while we supported the woman between us, and left some notes on the table.

"I hope this covers it," he said.

Together we carried her to a waiting cab outside.

"She used to be a famous cabaret dancer, you know," he said by way of farewell from the back seat.

The money would have covered the bill for an opulent feast for several people. Perhaps it was payment for having shared the loneliness of a neglected woman and an offering to ease his conscience. The notes from a clarinet solo rose above the din, soft and playful, as though they were teasing my mind.

"Bravo maestro!" someone called out.

The clarinet was soon accompanied by an equally tender violin and the steady beat of a drum. People clapped, proposed toasts and bought drinks for the musicians. The music blended into the background after a while as I drank and watched a gypsy girl passed from table to table; she was either chased away instantly or groped. Then she stood in front of me. She was slender, dark, filthy, young and wearing an older woman's worn coat that was far too big for her.

"Shall I read your palm, brother?" she said.

I laughed out loud. Having lived my whole life without anyone looking either at my past or my future, I had received two offers on the same day. But unlike the Professor, the gypsy girl was deadly serious and my laughter offended her far more than the fingers that had pinched her.

"I'm a good fortune-teller, brother. I mean it. I can tell you what's going to happen to you and your girlfriend," she said enthusiastically. Members of her profession tend to assume that you have a girlfriend.

"Alright," I said, "take a seat."

She obeyed eagerly, delighted to have a customer at last, or perhaps she was just fed up with being laughed at or chased away.

"First we need to come to some arrangement," I said.

Suspicion flashed in her dark eyes as I took a note from the table.

"This will be yours if you—"

"I'm not sleeping with you," she said quickly. How old was she? Sixteen, seventeen? I did not want to find out if she would still resist if the number of notes increased.

"—if you let me tell you about my girlfriend."

I do not know if it was the most bizarre offer she had ever heard. Probably not; she looked visibly relieved.

"If you're paying for it, I can listen to you for a thousand and one nights."

This is what I told her: Zuhal was the daughter of a rich man, we belonged to separate worlds that could not be reconciled: her father would not accept a poor boy and she had been forced to go abroad, but she had chosen to be mine before she left.

The gypsy girl was a good listener. She only interrupted me twice, the first time to say, "How romantic, just like in a Yesilçam film," and then to ask, "So you actually went to bed together?"

My longing for Zuhal had in no way alleviated by the time the gypsy girl had left me. But the urge to tell an intimate story to a stranger I would never see again was satisfied. The clock would soon strike midnight. As someone counted down the seconds, I joined in the communal singing. "At Heybeli Island we row by moonlight each night." And with cheers and applause, 1979 gave way to 1980.

12

February 1980

I had no particular feelings about February. Perhaps because it is the month that passes the fastest. Grey, devoid of colour, the last gasp of winter, February's chances of making an impression were limited. But here was a glorious day that mocked my indifference. A day like this, when the sun shone without giving off heat, was something to be grateful for. The café outside the entrance to the university, off to the right before you reached the second-hand bookshops, where the Professor had annoyed many forbidding older men by smoking a hookah in her youth, was still closed for the winter. It was in this place that the city's poets used to meet and recite their work to each other. The poet who wrote "I am thirty-five, halfway through life," died shortly afterwards. Another, who wrote the unforgettable lines "I listen to Istanbul with my eyes closed while a young woman cools her naked feet in the Bosporus", fell into a ditch after a drunken night on the town. He, too, was barely halfway through his life. Did he listen to the sounds of his beloved city one last time as he died? Those poets still living had long since abandoned the café, like desperate citizens fleeing an invading army. Students had taken their place instead, delighted to sit in the refreshing shade of centuries-old trees rather than a smoky refectory that smelled of grease. In the winter, if you wanted to and the weather permitted it, you could fetch tables and chairs from the closed section of the café and sit outside.

We shivered a little in the cool breeze, but clung bravely to our freedom and the peace to be found at the worn wooden tables beneath the naked trees in the company of a few hungry pigeons. We shared our freshly baked sesame pretzels and warmed our hands on steaming glasses of tea. With red noses and cheeks, we giggled whenever one of us was stalled mid-sentence by chattering teeth. Levo was gently flirtatious, with an arm around Gülnur's shoulder. But only just. Aside from that his conduct was irritatingly brotherly. He was the self-appointed joker among us, telling stories and mimicking politicians and teachers with varying degrees of success. He was, if I had to be honest, the only man I liked unreservedly. Even his relationship with Gülnur distinguished him in my eyes. I myself was a woman's man. I loved them all and had done so since childhood.

Semra was very pretty in her red woollen hat and scarf. She sat close to me and warmed her hands in the pockets of my jacket while she laughed at Levo's jokes. This closeness was partly for show, to say to the world that we were good friends once more. The girls had left school a year after us and had now been accepted at different faculties of the University. Semra studied economics, but said she would love to swap with me as literature was where her heart was. She wrote poems, good poems, and would always give me a copy, on paper decorated with flowers and in neat handwriting. She insisted that I do the same. She was much more gifted than I, but somehow I was not jealous. It was strange, because I viewed other poets, especially those who had been published, as incompetent rivals. Hiding behind a facade of objectivity, I made sure I dismissed nearly everything I read. This did not apply to Semra's work. I could do nothing but admit that hers was genuine poetry – free from pretension, naïve, simple and pretty. Nothing came across as forced or chiselled, it read as though it flowed from a natural source. I was generous with my praise and encouragement. This was untypical of me.

Levo and Gülnur left, "to see if there was any news from the western front". That left the two of us. We had spent a lot of time together recently.

"Do you miss her?" Semra asked.

"Yes."

"Do you want to tell me about it?"

"No." I realized I may have sounded defensive, so I tried to correct the impression. "There's not much to tell. She's gone now and there is nothing I can do about it."

"No, there isn't." Her tone was even. "I've read about her in the papers," she continued. "Do you remember that I once said that I could never be like her?"

I remembered it; I also recalled her saying that I could never be like Zuhal either. She had been proved right. Not that it mattered much. She had gambled with safe odds and won.

"I don't want to change anything," Semra said. "I don't have the courage or the strength. The fact that she does, doesn't make her better or worse than us."

I knew where she was going with this. Not only did she want us to be reconciled, she wanted me to be reconciled to myself.

"You're brave for making the choice you did. And I'm grateful that you're with me all the same. I don't think I could bear reading about you in the papers." She put her arms around my neck in an unexpected embrace and kissed me lightly on my cheek.

"I'll take care of you. Forever," she said.

"Forever is a very long time," I said.

"I know," she said.

I was grateful that she was with me – it was like having an anchor. Perhaps her friendship was what I needed to get through the drawn-out post-Zuhal period. It would calm me to have a woman around I could rely on, whose warmth I could feel and be comforted by, a woman who would not burden my conscience with questions about infidelity. And when Zuhal came back to me she would have no cause to be jealous. She would discover her rightful place in my heart, and my friends would remain my friends. I smiled at Semra, but she did not see it. She sat with her head bowed, lost in her own thoughts.

I had never seen Levo this excited before. He was always excitable, but right now his enthusiasm was irrepressible.

"Come on, we're going, hurry up! We're finally taking the school back. The police are going to escort us in."

The university was still "school" to him. He was studying public administration, but spent most of his time in the folklore club, a habit he had brought with him from boarding school. We had already appointed him the future governor of Istanbul and teased him about the innumerable opportunities to enrich himself through bribes that would accompany his office. His excitement was infectious. As we walked, he told us that the university's management had agreed to end the illegal occupations and offer education to all, even though it meant allowing police to patrol the buildings. I was not as optimistic as Levo. It was a weak solution that did not address the deep-rooted conflicts between the student factions. Much blood had been spilt and peaceful coexistence with the Nationalists was no longer an option. I loathed the idea of being protected by the police, who had no business at a seat of knowledge. Besides, I did not trust them. But I was happy all the same and did not think to discuss my reservations with him. I, for my part, was looking forward to seeing the Professor back behind her lectern.

A large crowd of students had already gathered by the time we reached the entrance. People were arguing for and against the management's decision. Finally an agreement was reached to try it out but also make it obvious that the presence of the police was unwanted. Police officers were searching anyone who wanted to get inside. They were lined up like the trees in the avenue along the approach to the square. The officer in charge, holding a two-way radio, was running around like a sheepdog, herding the students into an obedient orderly flock. Levo was the first to break away.

"Come on then. Get a move on," he called out to me.

He was handsome, with his blond hair, carefree green eyes and the patchy beard he had left to grow. He was no political activist, never had been, just an impatient student who wanted his school back. I ran as fast as I could, but he ran faster than anyone. He was still a few metres ahead of me as we approached the entrance to the teaching block. I noticed shadows behind the huge columns, or I thought I did, like the shadows at Taksim Square. All I could hear as I ran was the wind, nothing else, so I was astonished when Levo suddenly froze, like a soldier dropped by a bullet. I did not have time to hold him in my arms. Something hard hit my chest and flung me backwards. When I landed there were so many sounds around me that I could not differentiate between them. I could see white cotton-wool clouds against a blue sky. The sunshine was so bright that I had to screw my eyes shut.

Then everything went dark. I could feel someone put their arms around me and rest my head in their lap. There was a scent of a woman. I was blind, I could not see her, but I knew that Zuhal had come to take care of me.

"Don't give up now," she said. "Remember, you're brave, you're immortal."

Something was dripping on to my forehead? Was it raindrops or was she crying? It did not matter. I was in safe hands now and I could rest.

*

Nothing made her stand out. She was no different from any other young woman. Same sad anxious eyes, same tired resigned body language. The only difference was that while everyone else had come outside for a well-deserved break from the oppressive atmosphere of the ward, she continued to sit on a bench in the garden, immune to the cold, staring vacantly into space. The others were free to end or prolong their stay outside in the fresh air, drain their cups, crush cigarette stubs underfoot or light up a new one with the embers from the last. Not her. She did not even smoke. While the winter lived out its last days, she sat on the cold bench, silent and paralysed, as though she were bound to it by invisible ties. There was nothing to stop her visiting and comforting the dying patient. Nothing but the spectre of Kemal. He pointed his finger at her as though to warn her. A sharp look that condemned any action that might undermine the cause. He stood between her and the entrance, wordless, but with his accusing finger and his gaze.

Zuhal did not know how long she had been sitting there, but at last she noticed the cold and pulled the fur coat she had inherited from her mother more tightly around her. She lived in an age where women inherited coats from their mothers and nothing was thrown away until it was hanging together by a thread. She thought about her mother, who, had she been here, would have said a silent prayer for the patient and – ignoring all obstacles, visible or invisible – would have gone inside to see him.

13

March 1980

I could see and hear once more. Everyone I saw and talked to confirmed it. My mother, my brother, Semra, the doctors, the nurses. This happened two weeks after I emerged from a state they described as a kind of coma, and one week after I had first opened my eyes. It was a complicated wound, the doctors explained as they showed me x-rays and described the trajectory of the bullet. It was complex. Two operations. They were clearly pleased with their handiwork – I was lucky to have ended up in their competent hands, but I was also a stubborn fighter. They feared no permanent damage, perhaps a slightly reduced lung capacity, which ought not to worry me given I was no sprinter – ha ha – and temporarily reduced mobility in both legs, which meant nothing more than a couple of weeks' rest at home with my mother. Who would say no to that? They were very positive and I had no reason to doubt them. A police officer visited me and asked if I would be able to identify the culprits. I would not. He was polite and wanted to do his job properly. I could look at some photographs if I wanted, he said.

"Only shadows," I said.

He shook his head pensively – he knew they were more than just shadows. At last he wished me a speedy recovery and left. I could see and hear again, but hardly spoke. No-one talked much. My mother contented herself with holding my hands, stroking my hair and kissing my face. Semra sat knitting, watching over me, trying to anticipate my every wish. I did not know that modern girls knitted. I suppose it was a distraction from unwelcome thoughts. Between them, my mother and Semra had developed something resembling a rota. One would leave when the other arrived. My mother had been working at a textile factory for the past year and was very proud to be supporting her family through a proper job. She took leave during the two weeks I was unconscious. Then she went back to the factory and returned to the hospital after work. It seemed as though they had reached another consensus – to talk as little as possible. It worked well: it was exactly what I wanted.

Gülnur visited. She was surprisingly calm and composed. She told me about the funeral. It had been far too solemn. Not in Levo's spirit at all. He was bound to have wanted singing and dancing and even some jokes, had he been able to choose. She did not want to shock the imam and the mourners by trying to sing one of his favourite songs, tone deaf she as was and in a strange, far-away town. So she had mainly stayed in the background. She kissed me goodbye, but turned in the doorway and came back.

"I loved him, you know," she said.

She was on the verge of losing her composure. Semra saw it, put her arm around her shoulders and escorted her outside. I cried when they left, but perhaps I should have sung instead. I promised Levo that I would one of these days, once I had recovered my singing voice. I wiped my tears away before Semra returned.

It started with Gülnur. Now I wanted to talk and listen.

"Zuhal was with me," I said. "She was holding me in her arms, she talked to me and gave me back the light when it had gone out."

Semra looked up abruptly from her knitting and stared at me as though I had fallen into a coma again.

"Do you think I'm mad?"

"I don't. But that wasn't how it happened."

I raised myself up on my elbows, trying to get closer to her, to stare through her pupils and straight into her brain.

"What are you looking at?" she said.

"No-one else has those yellow specks that flutter like butterflies in their pupils."

"It was me," she said, blushing. Perhaps because of the butterflies in her honey-coloured eyes, or possibly because she had held me in her arms. I leaned back my head on the pillow.

"You don't have to look so disappointed."

I was no longer listening to her.

Two days later the newspapers reported the deaths of seven national-ists in two separate attacks. "FEMALE TERRORIST STRIKES AGAIN", the headline said. There had been a woman among those who had mown down the seven men with machine-guns. It gave me no peace, it was no salve to my wounds; blood spilt for my blood did not quench my thirst for revenge because I felt no such thirst. I did not want to believe that Zuhal had killed in order to avenge me, but I had to acknowledge that this might be precisely what had happened. I had to find her. Get her away from this insanity and take her to a place where we could start a new life. I had to make plans for our escape.

When I asked to be discharged there were no protests from the doctors. They even offered to drive me home in an ambulance. I must have been popular, as transporting patients with temporarily reduced mobility was not the health service's responsibility. I declined politely and opted for a cab – any cab would be more reliable than the few ambulances still running. I was met by a huge welcoming committee in the neighbourhood and carried up the four flights by Dakan and my brother like an uncrowned king on his golden throne, enjoying the ride and lashing them with insults. Eventually they threatened to throw me down the stairs and cripple me for good.

I had missed my home. My mother had made up my bed by the wood-burner in the living room and decorated it like a bridal bed, with her own bridal pillows and sheets, not used for decades. After days of bland food from the hospital kitchens, where everything was boiled because it was the healthiest option, I could ask for any number of fried delicacies. I could hear my mother instructing Semra in the kitchen – alongside all the other reassuring domestic sounds. They got on well. My mother had said of her once at the hospital, "What a lovely friend you have." It was more than I could have expected of her. If she had an ulterior motive and was hoping this would help me forget Zuhal, she was skilled at hiding it. Semra, being the sociable girl that she was, quickly made friends with my mother. It did not take them long to discover mutual interests, not least a shared love of literature; they swapped books and discussed them with genuine pleasure. My brother treated Semra with respect and care, as the sister he had always longed to have. The rota was still in place. Semra arrived before my mother left, sat with me all day, ate dinner with us, and then went home to sleep. She took the opportunity to tell me about her life, her family and her home.

Semra lived in one of the new suburbs not far away, a quarter of an hour by bus, in the basement of an apartment building. Her mother had run off with another man when Semra was three; she did not remember her, she didn't even have a photograph. Her father had gone to sea shortly afterwards. He had sent money and the odd postcard from the ports he had visited, but he rarely came home himself. It was her grandmother, a tough and sprightly old lady, who had brought her up. She told me this as if it were a normal family history. I knew her well enough not to feel sorry for her. She was a girl who had overcome her misfortune through her natural talents.

What delighted me most after my homecoming was a visit from Ayfer. She appeared in the living room one evening after Semra had left, bearing the customary bowl of pickled cucumbers, a greeting from her mother, and sat down with a sad smile beside my bed. Not much had changed in her life. She spoke little, listened closely and was even more shy than the first day we met.

"You've grown into a beautiful young woman," I said, and it was the truth, though an ugly scar marked her left cheek, the result of surgery on an infected boil. She touched the scar with her hand.

"Don't worry about it, it will go away. And any man who doesn't want you because of a small scar is an idiot," I said in all sincerity.

"Your new friend is so attractive. I see her from time to time when she visits." There was genuine admiration in her voice and nothing else.

"She's just a friend, Ayfer. You'll always be my first love," I said.

I exercised hard, bending and stretching, greatly helped by my brother. The wounds to my chest still hurt. There had been a hole in my chest the size of a hazelnut kernel; it had healed and the larger scars from the operations were bandaged to prevent infection. When I lay awake at night I examined my mind for any after-effects. I wondered if death had succeeded in frightening me. Chronic pain and disability were prospects far more terrifying than the notion of eternal rest in some unknown afterlife. I had heard that you grew fonder of life as you aged, more determined to keep death at bay. Stories were told about the godless finding God on their deathbeds and non-believers bargaining in vain. This did not apply to the young, not the ones I knew anyway, and definitely not to Zuhal. I could not imagine that she consciously feared death. I had witnessed her defiance amid the violence in Taksim Square, and watched her scold the police on their home turf. Did she not feel fear? This did not necessarily make her insensitive, perhaps just a good actress with a will of iron. She dominated my thoughts even when they touched on fear and death, and she continued to inspire me. But there was one thing the thought of her could not displace. My anger – anger directed at myself, for having allowed Levo to die. I could not tear the final picture of him from my mind, and nor did I want to. What tormented me was that in time his memory would fade and disappear. I thought a great deal about betrayal and reached a point where I feared it was becoming an obsession. He was so defenceless that I ought to have foreseen it; I should have known how it would end. Challenging the faltering logic of my thinking made no difference. There was no peace to be found in common sense. I grew increasingly irritable and difficult to live with. Time passed. After two weeks at home I was able to stand up and go for short walks on unsteady legs between the living room and the kitchen.

A pleasant warmth spread across the room from the wood-burner, keeping the last gasp of winter at bay. March was an unpredictable month. In a few days spring would knock on the door like a longed-for guest. And with spring I would start looking for Zuhal again. Semra sat by my bedside, knitting. Her busy hands fluttered as the knitting needles clicked and whirred.

"I will find her. I know I will," I said.

It would make no difference, but I wanted her agreement nonetheless. A glance, a nod. She did not look up, just carried on knitting. Her silence irritated me, but I did not press her. The warmth from the wood-burner and her rhythmic hand movements made me drowsy. I had been in pain during the night and had slept fitfully. I had nodded off and woken with a start from my shivers a couple of times. Semra looked at me and smiled. I drifted off into the darkness again. In my dream Zuhal was sitting silently at my bedside holding my hands. I felt an inexplicable surge of rage when I opened my eyes.

"You lied," I shouted.

"About what?" Semra looked puzzled.

"About Zuhal. When you said she never came to the hospital."

"But it was the truth, my friend."

I did not want to hear any more of her lies.

"Go now," I said. "Please."

"Come on, be sensible," she said.

"Go," I said.

"I'll be back tomorrow morning. And by then we'll have forgotten all about this," she said cheerfully.

"You can go to hell and never come back," I yelled.

I heard my mother put down the shopping bags in the kitchen. She came into the living room.

"Feel how cold it is outside," she said and cradled my face in her hands. "Where's Semra?" she continued as she removed her headscarf.

"She's gone home. For good," I said.

14

April 1980

I looked around in an attempt to catch a glimpse of her amidst the sea of people. It was hopeless, impossible to pick out a face from the crowds. She was not late: it was I who was impatient to meet her. If I stayed here in front of the bus company's office as we had agreed, she was sure to turn up soon. But I loathed standing still for so long and I was starting to get edgy. If anyone aimed at me, I would be an easy target, as I had been when I saw Levo fall. It was best to keep moving, preferably with no pattern, in a zigzag, that would be ideal. But I did not zigzag. I had not gone mad. It was just my first day outside on my own.

I had felt this way for a while, during shorter trips around the neighbourhood and when I was on the balcony. Fear. Not of dying, but of an invisible enemy. Perhaps this was nothing new. Perhaps I had carried it inside me ever since Taksim Square. Was I actually haunted by fear? Was it the price you paid to have been shot and survived? Would I otherwise turn into a killer myself, sneaking in behind the enemy and shooting in revenge? I felt sick whenever I imagined myself with a deadly weapon in my hand and an unsuspecting person at my mercy, pulling the trigger and watching the blood and bone erupt. Could anyone with a conscience live with that? I had reached a conclusion. I would rather live with fear than inflict it on others. My advantage was to possess, not exactly a will of iron, but enough control to keep it at bay. So if I wanted to stand still, nothing was going to stop me.

I decided on a compromise. I would stop in front of a shop window, study the reflections of whoever was behind me, then turn around unexpectedly, stare into their faces and memorize them for all eternity. A little paranoia never hurt anyone.

I lit a cigarette. My hands were steady. The April sunshine was warm; it was spring at last. It was a fine day to be standing still and smoking a cigarette. The first few puffs were sheer bliss, but then my lungs said no. I dropped the stub and ground it under my shoe. I really ought to quit smoking for good one of these days. A hunch warned me that something was happening behind my back. I spun around quickly. She was coming towards me with brisk steps and a suitcase in each hand.

"Am I late? Did you have to wait long?" she panted.

I put my hands on her shoulders and kissed both cheeks.

"Do all women walk about with two old suitcases?" I said.

She was used to listening to silly comments. A boys' world, their language, their jokes. She smiled, a little tired, a little resigned.

"They're not old. I've just bought them, you fool," Gülnur said.

There was still one hour to go before her bus left. We handed in her suitcases at the cloakroom and sat down at an outdoor café next door. There was nothing here to remind me of the poets' café outside the university. The tables were cheap plastic, the trees entirely absent and the clientele open-mouthed peasants overwhelmed by the great metropolis. The tea they brought us could most charitably be compared to dishwater. Not that it mattered. Memories were the last thing you would want to take from a bus terminal.

"Are you sure going is a good idea?" I said.

"What is there to keep me here in this city? Look around. Oh God, so many brain-dead."

"City of zombies," I said.

"City of the living dead," she said.

I pulled a face and pointed to myself. We laughed.

"Oh, I'm sorry. I didn't mean it like that," she said. "I'm suffocating here. I need to go back home, take a break, I don't know. Anyway, that's not why I wanted to talk to you."

The moment of truth, which I had tried in vain to postpone, had arrived. I was unprepared, just as unprepared as when she called and asked to meet me. I did not know how much she knew, not that it mattered. Every word about to be exchanged between us would bring shame and pour salt in an open wound.

"I don't blame you," she said, and realized that she had started at the wrong end. "Oh hell, Semra doesn't blame you, was obviously what I meant. No-one blames you, you must know that." She paused to let me speak, but I had nothing to say. "Alright, she told me some of it, but not all. You must understand that everyone needs someone to confide in, so don't accuse her of being a gossip."

"I'm not in a position to blame anyone," I said. I had to say something so the conversation could flow, so we could finish it.

"Give me a cigarette," Gülnur said. She inhaled deeply with her eyes closed, as though no cigarette had ever tasted as good. "She's a shadow of her former self. She's suffering. You need to go to her, comfort her and show that you're the friend you claim to be." She blew a cloud of smoke into my face. A sign of impatience and irritation. "She feels rejected. Destroyed. Not hard to understand after everything she's done for you."

I was not prepared for this. I reacted as if I had been caught red-handed, and grinned sheepishly.

"It must be a dubious honour to make a woman so sad," Gülnur snapped.

I felt persecuted, misunderstood. "I thought you didn't blame me."

"Let's not change the subject. I came here to ask you to visit her."

"I don't know, Gülnur. You're full of bad ideas."

"For the sake of our friendship – for Levo's sake. I wish I had the same chance, the chance to tell him that he was my best friend."

"I don't know what I would say to her."

"Say what you like. Visiting her and comforting her is what matters now."

She waved from the window. I waved back. I had never said goodbye to anyone in a bus terminal. You stood there waving, wishing the bus would just drive off like it does in the movies, right on cue, without unnecessary delays. But instead it remained stationary with the engine running, as the driver bustled about checking a dozen invisible things. It was embarrassing to look her in the eye and keep on waving. I looked up at the sky, down at the ground, back at her, and waved again. She said something, her mouth moving silently behind the glass. Perhaps she was trying to tell me that I did not have to wait. I shook my head to say that it was alright, I would wait. When the doors had finally closed and the bus had left, I stood there relieved, with my hand raised in a final farewell. It was a strange feeling to watch someone leave your life after ten years of intense friendship. If she came back, I would forget this last goodbye and welcome her with open arms, because I was fond of her and because I owed it to Levo. But I had a feeling that she would not be coming back. Gülnur would build herself a new, predictable provincial life in her small town and from time to time she would wonder what it would be like to return. For her sake I hoped that she would have no regrets.

I was walking. It did me good. I ran in a zigzag for a while, conscious of the irony, then stopped and turned around unexpectedly to surprise those walking past me. Some raised an eyebrow, others smiled and showed some understanding of my game. And when a surprise shower put the weather forecasters to shame I started running in earnest. Many had sought refuge under the shelters at the bus station. The mood was good, as it normally is when you know the shower will pass and the sun will soon reappear. I exchanged a few comments with a middle-aged man about the latest high-profile city derby. A bus arrived. No-one boarded it – perhaps they were all there to escape from the rain. I looked for its destination. There were so many districts I had not yet visited. I made my excuses, pushed through the crowd and climbed on board at the last moment, just before the driver shut the doors. The rain ceased and the sun assumed the stage once more as the bus rattled along. When it stopped at the petrol station I could see our apartment block towering over the allotments and the lowlands. It was all too easy to alight here and not visit new places. The areas we passed through became less and less familiar as the bus continued its journey, and when I finally got down the surroundings were like something out of a vaguely remembered book. It is strange how life in the city leaves you with a constant feeling of déjà vu. I could have been here before, if she had asked me, if she had invited me. I crossed the bridge over the train track and noted that the local train would also take me here. Another shower began as I meandered down the street counting the house numbers.

The house was an ordinary concrete building, one of those that sprang up like mushrooms across the whole city in the 1960s at the expense of the old wooden houses – though I doubted that this area had been developed before the great exodus from the countryside had begun. I sought shelter under the awning of a grocery store, conveniently located right opposite the building. The courage I had felt when I got on the bus had deserted me. I lit a cigarette and looked across at the entrance.

"Are you waiting for anything in particular, son?" He was an old man with a grey beard. His characteristic skullcap told me that he was a Mecca pilgrim, his dialect that he came from the Black Sea and the apron that he owned the shop.

"No, father. I'm just waiting for the shower to pass."

"Rain is God's gift, son. It does you no harm."

He would know. It rained a great deal by the Black Sea. I lifted my head and stared pointedly at the awning. When our eyes met again, there was a mischievous glint in his. You could always rely on people from the Black Sea for a sense of humour.

"The sun, however, is a foretaste of hell."

I laughed and it did me good.

"I'm going to go now, father."

"I'm sorry, son. So many terrorists, bandits and robbers these days. God help us all."

"You take care of yourself," I said.

"May joy be with you," he said.

He stayed under the awning, watching me as I crossed the street. I wondered what he was thinking as I pushed open the door with the confident thrust of a resident and stepped inside. He had had last word, but I had won the round – thanks to the habit of leaving doors unlocked, which obviously died hard in this part of town.

The stairwell lay in semi-darkness lit only by the light that filtered through a small window in the front door. To the right were the stairs to the four floors above and to the left the steps leading down to the basement, where a solitary naked light bulb hung from the ceiling and defied the gloom with its dirty-yellow glare. There was a smell of coal, wood and damp, a challenge for my delicate lungs after the fresh spring air. There was only one door, with no bell and no nameplate. Had there been another I would have felt even more lost. I leaned in and listened out for the sound of slippers shuffling across the floor, music from a cassette player, a television, the clattering of cutlery and glass, muted voices or perhaps laughter. Silence. They were not in. I could turn around, go up the stairs, breathe in the fresh air once more, take the bus home and tell myself that I had tried. But it was no good. I would come back, listen again and . . . I knocked. It opened an inch, as though someone had been on guard on the other side. She might have done what I had done, listened with her ear to the door, wondering who was on the stairs. She looked like my grandmother; a white embroidered scarf covered her sparse grey hair. High cheekbones, pale eyes that had lost their sparkle, skin as dry as parched earth. Perhaps all grand-mothers look alike? Unlike my grandmother, however, she was alive.

"Yes?" she said, a question and an answer at the same time.

"Is Semra at home?"

"I know who you are. I saw your photo in the yearbook."

She despised me. An instinctive hatred, weary and resigned. At one time she might have had other ideas when a hopeful Semra showed her my picture. If she had invited me here before, I would have got to know her, charmed her in the way I charmed all older people. She would not have hated me any less after my harsh words to Semra, but I might have had something to say to her. As it was, all she could do was close the door, and I could go home, telling myself that at least I had tried.

But instead the door was flung wide open, taking with it the old woman and hiding her from my eyes. In her place Semra appeared against a background of naked walls and windows at street level, stand-ing in her white nightdress, fragile and reduced to a shadow of her former self. I had not managed to rob her of her smile.

"I've got a bit of a cold."

She swayed. I was scared that she would faint, so I quickly took her in my arms and lifted her up. She was as light and small as a child. She put her arms around my neck.

"How nice that you came, how nice that you came," she whispered.

The old woman showed me the way. I carried Semra and laid her down on her bed. The bedroom was cold and damp. The walls sweated in places. Rainwater leaked in where the hinges of the windows had come loose.

"Isn't it strange that we've ended up swapping roles, that now it's you sitting by my sickbed?"

I hushed her, tucked her in, and put my hand on her forehead.

"You've got a temperature," I said. "How could I do this to you?"

"Don't say that. Our friendship should be able to survive more than that."

How could I contradict her? It would have been easy to agree with her, but cowardly too. How quickly you could be transformed, your soul corrupted. A single bullet had changed me, even though I had only noticed the physical damage. The world revolved around me alone, it was only my loss, my love that mattered. How had I forgotten the compassion I had felt for Semra? I had not even thanked her for holding me in her arms, for spending days and nights with me in who knows what nightmarish agony. I had taken everyone and everything for granted. Even Zuhal. I was fortunate as far as Zuhal was concerned; she was blissfully ignorant of my selfish malaise. I owed Semra so much. I could not push her away yet again. Above all we were two human beings; we had to help each other get back on our feet.

"Please forgive me," I said.

"I can forgive you,' she said, "not for something you weren't to blame for, but for something you were unable to prevent."

How big was her heart? Had it no limits? How did Semra manage to contain her own ego? Was I, in my search for love, doing her irreparable hurt? I wanted to know the answers. As she lay there she had a new and optimistic glint in her feverish eyes and a contented smile played upon her sunken features. I could not disturb the moment and stir up something she may have laid to rest in the hands of fate.

"Have you written anything lately?"

"Plenty. Do you want to see?"

She rolled to one side and took the notebook from her bedside table. I read. It was touching how she had avoided her own problems and highlighted instead the suffering of the earth's dispossessed. Suddenly the tune of an old song was on my lips and I sang the first lines of her epic poem to it. It was wondrous how natural it sounded.

"I knew it was unfinished. Perhaps it was meant to be a song," she said.

"Levo would have liked it," I said. She nodded. There was still much to enjoy from days gone by.

Her grandmother had made herself scarce while we spoke. I had not heard her leave and I did not hear her return.

"Would you like to eat with us?" she asked. "It's nothing special, just some macaroni with minced beef and salad." She did not hate me.

"I love macaroni," I said, "but first you need to fetch me your tools. You need a man in this house. And that window needs a hammer."

15

May 1980

"You're the man of *this* house," my mother said.

"Nonsense, mother. You're the man of this house. And you always have been."

"Well, I can see that you've made up your mind. We've never been short of stubbornness in this family."

She was hurt. In her world children flew the nest when their wings could bear them; this usually meant when they got married. Not when they still needed their mother to tuck them up in bed, cook for them and wash their clothes, as I did.

"Semra will help me get started. I'll be fine. Please don't worry."

"So that's what she's been reduced to now. Your servant."

"You know that's not true, mother. She'll just teach me the basics a bachelor needs. Besides the Professor will help me catch up with the studying I've missed out on."

"Oh yes. The Professor."

Perhaps this was the rub. She had accepted Semra; the Professor, however, was a new, more formidable rival. She sat in her ivory tower among her dusty books, enticing young students out of their warm homes. This was so near the truth that I had to smile and laud her for her insight. My mother never ceased to surprise me with her uncut diamond of a mind. It was a shame that she had already singled out her enemy and taken up her position in the trenches. I had no doubt that under different circumstances the two women would have liked each other. But my mother's suspicion suited me fine. I did not want her around when I was thinking of diving in at the deep end without knowing what lay beneath the surface.

Sitting in her ivory tower like a lonely queen with no subjects: if she had heard it, the Professor would have hated this description – she was after all a genuine republican. But I always saw something of the sultans of past ages in her. She was a survivor, isolated and mighty, so mighty she could make heads roll, even in a man's world. She had not visited me at the hospital, but was waiting for me to come to her on my own two feet, because, she quipped, it was the custom in our culture that the young would visit the old and not the other way round. However, once we were reunited, she made no secret of the fact that she had not been able to bear the thought of seeing me lie helpless in a hospital bed. Nor had she believed that a cowardly Fascist bullet would be the end of me.

She was ready to listen to me. The eyes of an old woman might not be able to endure everything, but her ears were not as delicate as her eyes. It would have been pointless to leave out Zuhal. What was there to say if I did not dare admit who it was I lived for? I could tell from her eyes that this was a surprising twist to my tale, which, from the beginning, was meant to appeal to all her senses.

"Oh, this is something for my beloved. He would have loved it," she sighed.

Otherwise she listened without interrupting me. We sat among dusty bookcases, dusty furniture, and a dusty past as afternoon sunbeams cast a wall of stippled light between us through the voile curtains, until the darkness hid the details and left us alone with our

175

silhouettes. She did not get up to switch on the light until I had finished.

"What you need most of all is a base," the Professor said. "A base you can operate from. When you wish to explore the unknown, you cannot drag your domestic life with you, you understand. Whether you're ready to leave your mother's house, that's another question."

I had been contemplating it ever since I had made up my mind to find Zuhal. My mother was an anxious woman and as long as I lived at home, she would watch over me, protect me and make life difficult for everyone. I needed loose reins, a place where I could come and go as I pleased. She would worry no less, but when she grew used to the idea she would move on with her own life and I would not have to inflict on her the needless concerns our shared everyday life made unavoidable. However, I had no money, not even for such basics as rent and board.

"I have a solution, if that's what's troubling you," the Professor said.

She owned the entire house, six flats on three floors. On the ground and first floors were tenants who over the years had become part of the furniture, an extension of her family. Her mother had combined the two flats on the second floor into one, which the Professor had taken for her apartment, commanding a view of her beloved Bosporus.

On the ground floor, just as you entered and turned left, was a flat smaller than the others with a doll's-house-sized kitchen, a minute living room and a bedroom. The flat was waiting for its last resident to return. Yorgo the Greek was a gifted cameraman, sound designer, assistant director and editor and general jack-of-all-trades in Yesilçam before he had been deported from Turkey at the start of the 1960s. He had never officially applied for citizenship of the Republic of Turkey. It had seemed unnecessary to him because he could proudly trace back his ancestors to Byzantium and was thus a rightful and true citizen of

Constantinople-Istanbul, if not of the whole republic. His father, Theo, had been a patriot and just as angry as everyone else with the English and the French who had occupied the city after the First World War. He had transformed his tiny photographer's studio into an illegal printing press and distributed leaflets condemning the occupation. The father's politics did the son no good at all, and when the Cyprus crisis was at its height Yorgo was picked out alongside thousands of other victims and made a scapegoat. The Professor and Yorgo shed tears together before his departure, and her helplessness at such a great injustice remained one of the few black spots on her conscience. She and Yorgo, who by then was an old man, exchanged letters and she could read between the lines how unhappy he was in Athens and how his missed his home country.

After some years her letters to him started to be returned and at the same time Yorgo ceased to write. To begin with she forced herself to believe that there were other reasons, but slowly she had to accept that Yorgo was no longer among the living. For many others the story might have ended here, but symbolic gestures were important to the Professor. She had preserved Yorgo's flat as it had been the day he had left it, furnished with his things, but devoid of his soul and physical presence.

Obviously the Professor did not believe in fate, but nor did she want to dismiss the importance of life's coincidences, whether striking or incidental. In that sense she had not waited in vain. Yorgo and I had much in common – a longing for what had been lost and our hope to retrieve it. I could almost be regarded as his rightful successor. As such, I could take over Yorgo's flat indefinitely on the same terms: with nothing to be paid. The old furnishings were now out of fashion, but they could still be used. The Professor made sure a cleaner came to the flat once a month. She did not mind Semra's presence – on the contrary, a young woman usually brings light and joy. Nor had she asked questions about Semra's role in my story, partly because I had skipped over most of it, partly because she was in favour of friendships between men and women. The only thing she expected of us was that we would fill the empty rooms, give them a purpose and in doing so honour Yorgo's memory. I was overjoyed. This was more than I could have dreamt of.

However, she was not yet done. She was, as she put it, enjoying one of her moments of inspiration that could be triggered only by unique events. What remained was to find me a source of income that would not restrict my movements with conventional working hours yet still enable me to live on the right side of the poverty line. Would I like to assist her with a translation of Shakespeare or work for a dubious publisher hawking translations of cheap American magazines? I preferred the latter – out of respect for Shakespeare. That was the right answer. Shakespeare demanded everything a translator had to give, even her soul; besides the pay was derisory. But the hollow job that demanded nothing was well paid and I could do it in my sleep.

The day I moved out, my brother, proud to make use of his newly acquired driving licence, moved my belongings in a car he had borrowed. My mother did not come. This was in no way a protest, she said, and that was just as well because she had worked hard to get together everything I would need in the way of kitchen equipment, linen and clothes. She threw water after the car, a customary way of wishing travellers a speedy return. I turned in the passenger seat to catch a last glimpse of her. Obviously I would see her as often as possible, both here and at my place, but we both knew that the time when we had been branches of the same tree was over.

My brother talked incessantly about this, that and the other, seemingly unaffected by the strong emotions in the air. He did not mind in the least making a detour to pick up Semra. The longer we drove, the more fun we had. Semra was in a good mood too, and joked with my brother from the tiny space in the back she had managed to fit into.

She listened to my brother's comments about my opportunities to tempt lovely little lambs into my new den and retorted by pointing out the dangers of too much lamb meat for greedy old wolves. I smiled politely at their jokes, but deep down I was brooding and tense.

My mood improved the moment I turned the key in the lock and took my first step into Yorgo's flat. Everything – the sofa with the embroidered cushions, the old radio on the chest of drawers with the floral carvings – was straight out of a '60s film. The living-room window faced the main road and the Bosporus; the bedroom was simply furnished with a bed for an ascetic man, a moth-eaten Diyarbakır kilim rug and a wardrobe. A second window looked out on a small garden at the back of the house with fruit trees, a swing, grass growing wild, a small weathered table and two chairs, all surrounded by a fence whose missing planks formed a toothless grin. I did not know how I would divide myself between the Bosporus and the garden, something I had dreamed about having ever since I was a child. The kitchen was next to the bedroom, with a door that led out into the garden. It was slightly bigger than a play kitchen. I doubted that I would be spending much time there. I was surprised to find a bathroom with room enough to wash. I could boil water and . . . the image of Zuhal with her hair and body wrapped up in towels passed before my eyes.

I was desperate for Semra and my brother to leave so I could be alone in the flat. They had no such intention. Semra had brought home-cooked food and my brother surprised us by conjuring up a bottle of rakı. Their enthusiasm was infectious; after all, we needed a bite to eat and to celebrate and soon we were busy getting the garden ready for a small party. I ran upstairs to invite the Professor, but she was not at home. Perhaps she had decided to stay away so as not to give the impression that she was keeping an eye on my movements. We ate, drank and lit the paraffin lamp when the darkness spread over us like a blanket. They asked me to fetch the guitar my mother had bought for me – a childhood wish – when I was ill in bed. My playing was nothing to write home about, but my head was full of melodies. I had already composed tunes to three of Semra's poems, which I played for them. Then we sang well-known Istanbul songs together. In one of the songs a young woman walks to Üsküdar – this was a long time ago, at the beginning of the century – to meet her beloved Katip. This was a daring thing for a young woman to do in those days. She is surprised by a shower of rain, but as you might imagine carries an elegant umbrella, is wearing a long dress and a long coat, her fair face probably discreetly hidden by a veil. She does not care about rain or about gossip, she cares for nothing in this world but her Katip. When she finally finds him, he still has sleep in his eyes, dressed in a shirt with a stiff collar that suits him and a long coat, slightly soiled at the edges.

I forbade my brother to pour himself a third glass of rakı. The seductive aniseed liquor was harmless – as long as it remained in the bottle. My brother railed at me for introducing new rules in an old village. After all, passing your driving test in Turkey meant being able to drive home drunk and not kill yourself.

He had turned into a charming young man: tall, strong and hard-working. He had grown up with all the inequalities of our society and did not give a damn about his own safety on the road or that of others, but he had been raised to obey his big brother, even though there were times he felt moved to protest.

"Drive carefully," I said, as I walked them to the car. He revved the engine by way of response and spun the wheels until they stank of burnt rubber. I heard Semra's laughter from the passenger seat before the car had even driven off. I smiled and shook my head, but I was not genuinely worried. I knew he would slow down soon, that it would be alright, as it usually was. When I returned to the garden it was exactly as quiet and peaceful as I had hoped. A frog croaked and a grasshopper fiddled; the moon and the stars decorated the sky and the fireflies danced in the darkness. I sat there all alone in the world and relished it. But my stolen moment of peace in the small garden was artificial, staged. It was not real.

16

June 1980

It was like hearing the approaching footsteps of a giant. Bombs were detonated, young men on both sides were killed in attacks every day, and young women too. There were no women among the Fascist ranks – their place was at home, cooking, bearing children and so they escaped being targets. The women on the left, however, were a different matter: they were tough, among the bravest, and they led from the front. They planned and led operations, and had no great respect for men. They rejected feminism, a despicable middle-class ideology. For them women's liberation was a natural part of the class struggle. I agreed. I liked them, even though they wanted everyone to address them as "sister", which raised the risk of mental incest if you happened to find them attractive. Yes, I liked these new women – the Zuhal type, though I was grateful that she had laughed off all that "comrade sister" nonsense.

The summer of 1980 was dominated by unrest, prolonged martial law, heavy police patrols on the streets, random arrests and torture. Zuhal and Kemal made the front pages on several occasions and were among the most wanted people in Turkey. I was running out of time. Every day that passed without me getting closer to her added to my frustration. I was looking for a woman whom even the police, with their vast resources, could not manage to hunt down. I spent my days wandering the streets – especially in the areas the newspapers had last reported sightings of her – in the hope of running into her by chance, even though that would require nothing less than a miracle in a city like Istanbul. I was no dreamer, just a desperate man who had nothing else to cling to. People in the Student Union had grown used to my regular visits – it had become my habit to visit the places where she had left her mark. They regarded me as a hopeless romantic.

"Perhaps you'll find her if you go into hiding . . . No, we're only joking. It doesn't work like that," they said, and laughed.

I needed a passport photo of Zuhal, so I pestered the Professor. She had always been loyal to the institution she worked for: ethics and duties were something she took seriously. But she also took her adoption of me seriously. One day she broke her principles and went to the university's archives. There she found Zuhal's file and with it the contact details for her next of kin. The passport photos that I had wanted to get hold of and which should have been in the file were missing; presumably the police had already taken them.

The Professor went so far as to offer to accompany me on my visit to Zuhal's parents. A professor, concerned about the well-being of her students, would trigger fewer worries in already anxious parents than a young man who would find it hard to account for himself. Since she had opened her house to me, she had become less critical. She did not question my judgement, but never failed to offer advice and suggestions that once considered I could not dismiss. So I asked myself what I would get out of a visit to Zuhal's parents apart from satisfying my own curiosity? Was it not morally reprehensible to stumble into the lives of two people who were suffering already because they had a daughter who had been branded a terrorist? But I wanted to meet them. To be able to give her a history, a background, a family like most others, would make her less abstract in my mind.

A retired general was the last person I expected to find as Zuhal's father. As he sat there in his armchair, his back straight, his face grave and his eyes fearless, in a room furnished with heirlooms, the walls decorated by pictures of himself in uniform, you could not help but feel the aura of power he radiated. In his day he had led men and done so with a natural authority. But what surprised me the most was the way we were received: as long-awaited guests. It was a fine day when the Professor and I set off, warm with a cooling breeze from the Strait. We had decided to walk to where Zuhal's parents lived, an area for the city's wealthy families. I was nervous and had prepared myself to be met with resistance, to be told in no uncertain terms that we were not welcome, perhaps to have the door slammed in our faces.

My fears proved groundless. We were received with polite hospitality when we introduced ourselves and were led into a large drawing room. Zuhal's mother was round and jovial, and, like most housewives, proud to show us her home and demonstrate her talent for baking. The General was a skilled conversationalist with a wide range of interests. He spoke exclusively to the Professor, and discussed in a stern voice the latest developments at the university and his guest's most recent Shakespeare translation. I felt his sharp eyes on me while I leafed through the albums as Zuhal's mother commented lovingly on each page. "Zuhal is three years old here, isn't she lovely in that princess dress? She's five here, in the garden where we used to live. This is taken on her first day of school. This is our Zuhal . . ."

I thought the General might be avoiding me for some reason and that I would end up leaving without having exchanged a word with him, when he suddenly said: "Do you smoke, young man?" It sounded almost like a trick question and I was not sure whether the right answer was yes or no.

"Yes, I'm afraid I do, General, sir," I mumbled. I never would have believed I would address anyone as "General, sir." However, it seemed natural in his case. He smiled faintly at my response and looked pleased.

"That settles the matter," he said as he got up from the armchair. "We'll have a cigar on the balcony while the ladies carry on talking inside."

There was no doubting whom Zuhal took after. Her father had the same ordinary but pleasant features and the same olive skin tone.

The large terrace that ran the length of the apartment faced Emirgan Park. He lit my cigar and his own, then pointed out and described the surroundings as though delivering a briefing: an ancient sultan's villa in the middle of the park, the tulip garden, where it was lovely to go for a morning stroll on the beautiful, peaceful paths. It was like listening to someone you had known for a long time. The awe I had felt for him at first was still there, but I was starting to feel relaxed, and at home.

"We knew that you would come," he said. "She told us."

He did not look at me; his gaze remained fixed on the paths in the park.

"She came here to say goodbye before she went into hiding and she asked us to welcome you as a member of the family when you came. We've never denied her anything, you see."

He did not know who I was, yet he opened his house to me because his beloved daughter had anticipated it and asked him to.

"Do you think you deserve her trust?" It was an odd question.

"I love your daughter. The fact that she is apart from you, from me, is her choice, and there's nothing I can do about it."

He nodded in understanding. He knew his daughter well and perhaps he had come to regret bringing her up to be more wilful than was good for her. But he could not know that I had not told him the whole truth, that I could have chosen to stay with her.

"It's a dirty war out there. It's dreadful to think that she's alone in it."

He was not blaming me for having abandoned her; the reproach was aimed at himself. He knew more about dirty wars than most. As a young army captain he had been sent to Korea by a government keen to appease the United States in order to gain membership of N.A.T.O. He had been sent to a distant country to fight in someone else's war. From day one he had loathed everything about that conflict and felt like a mercenary serving arrogant rulers. His only aim had been to protect his men as well as he could, but his hopes were undermined when his company was ordered to cover the Allied retreat. It had turned into a nightmare that had lasted several days, and when it became clear that they were surrounded, he realized that they had long been written off by their own commanders. One night the company decided to shoot its way out. They were one hundred and fifty men. He had spoken to them, and no-one had voted for the alternative, which was captivity. They broke through, but only five men reached their own lines after marching for several kilometres through hostile terrain, each bearing the mental and physical scars of his ordeal. They went sent home as heroes. He kept the medals well hidden in a chest in the loft. Eventually he became a general who detested conflict, and many years later his own daughter found herself in a war without fronts or even uniforms, barely able to distinguish friend from foe. He respected the courage of the young in the face of a superior enemy, but he did not share their optimism. Yet he hoped that they would one day need an old general. This was the only way he could hope to see his daughter again.

For a while we sat in silence, each with a heavy conscience.

"She doesn't want you to look for her. This was the message she asked me to pass on to you." He was still avoiding my eyes.

"Someone has to stand up to her," I said.

His eyes, which he had raised to meet mine, were just as dark as Zuhal's and they lit up as though he had suddenly discovered an exceptional soldier within the ranks.

"Don't think it's going to be easy. No-one can help you. And you might lose her for good the day you find her, if you try to pull her out of it. Nor can you be certain that she loves you and by looking for her you risk her rejecting you. What do you say to that?"

"Do you have something, anything at all, that could help me get started?"

He thought; he thought hard. I could see that he was trying to penetrate every nook and cranny of his tired brain to retrieve something from his memory.

"There was a girl. The two of them were inseparable. She used to come here when times were different. Then suddenly she vanished. It's likely to be a shot in the dark, but there's no harm in trying. Her name is Tuba. I know where she lives. I drove Zuhal there once."

He got up to fetch a pen and paper. I seized the opportunity to ask if he had a passport photo of Zuhal. He did not ask why. When he came back, he had brought with him a piece of paper with Tuba's address and two passport photos of Zuhal taken a few years earlier.

"Do you know what Zuhal means?" he asked.

"No, I'm afraid I don't," I said.

"It means Saturn. Strange name for a girl, isn't it? But if you think about it, Saturn, with its mysterious rings, is the most beautiful planet in our solar system." He sat down and relit his cigar, which had extinguished itself in his absence. Then he said, as if speaking to himself, "Perhaps it's not so good to be that beautiful and that superior. The rest of us are doomed to live in her shadow."

17

July 1980

Last night I had a strange dream. We had gone out, we were strolling around and had ended up in a bar. I know that you normally drink in moderation. However, this time you looked as if you wanted to experiment, test your limits, or you wanted to make a fool of yourself. Or perhaps there was another reason. Despair. Despair at being in love with a shadow. I would not say that being drunk suited you. You grew strange. You spoke incoherently, about all sorts of things, but not about her, you never mentioned her, not even a word. Then you became unusually tender, but it was not convincing. You know I have mixed feelings about alcohol. I like a few drinks in the company of friends. But I am also scared of getting drunk, scared of losing control and letting myself go. In my dream I drank a little, I wanted to look after you. Then everything was chaos.

Everything happened in slow motion, as it often does in dreams. You need to do something urgently, but you never get to do it, and things suddenly vanish. I panicked when you vanished. I tried to call out for you, but I had no voice. I remember that I ran everywhere, but not back to the bar. I was running in an open, empty, indeterminate space. Then suddenly everything was back in place, but you were no longer there. I had lost you. I do not know if there is a similarity, but I decided to emulate that woman in one of

Graham Greene's books (I cannot recall which one). I promised that I would leave you alone if you came back.

I regretted it as soon as I woke up. I should not have promised anything. What else is left for me, except your friendship? I am not complaining. Being with you is difficult, but very rewarding all the same. I know what I wrote was unfair, "despair at being in love with a shadow". No doubt to you it is a light that calls out to you. That you respond to its calling means that there is hope. But now I need to leave you alone. For the time being, while you look for your light.

One day at the beginning of July, after Semra had left my apartment, I found the letter in an envelope placed on Yorgo's chest of drawers. My first thought was how empty life would be without her. It was then I realized that I did not want to be left in peace, I did not want to be alone. I depended on having people around me who cared. Dependency did not sound very attractive, but over time I had grown attached to Semra, and with her to lean on had found peace. Everything that had happened from the day I threw her out of the apartment to the day I found her letter was confusing. I fluctuated between liking, disliking and liking her again. The shame that haunted me was not enough to prevent me from wanting to recreate the tenderness she stirred in me.

I did not know if Tuba was a student or had a job, so I decided to visit her address on a Saturday. She might have moved elsewhere. It was a depressing thought that I tried to brush aside as I walked down a steep, cobbled hill along a narrow street with houses to either side that practically leaned into each other to meet in the middle. The street widened a little as it levelled out at the bottom and opened on to a small square. In the centre was a fountain under an awning, with walls decorated with old İznik tiles and inscriptions in Ottoman lettering, clearly built in bygone times to honour a prince or a princess.

The house where Tuba was supposed to live lay to the right of the square, one of a row of the low, squat houses that had once character-ized the city and which were miraculously still standing. It was coming up for noon and the sun shining right above my head was an intense ball of light, warning of a new heatwave. The heat, the deserted square, the scent of various flowers cascading from pots on the windowsills – the effect was altogether soporific. A bee bumbled past like a contented sleepwalker. I sat down on a marble bench by the fountain, quenched my thirst and washed the sweat from my face. I was no longer as deter-mined as when I had left home; I could not be sure who would open the door if I were to knock on it. Even if it turned out to be Tuba, I no longer knew what to say. "Hello, have you seen Zuhal lately? Please can you help me find her?" If this woman was still in contact with Zuhal, my curiosity would arouse suspicion. The more I thought about it, the more I grew convinced that any attempt to talk to her would wreck my chances rather than help them. I had to think of something else; I could not sit here by the fountain forever. I took in my surroundings a second time and saw my salvation on the left-hand side of the square. There was a teahouse that stood out from the other houses because of its large front window. It lay almost diagonally across from Tuba's house – the perfect lookout post.

It was just as muggy inside as out. A few old men were playing cards. I greeted them and the owner of the teahouse. He was standing behind the counter drying glasses with a tea towel. They returned my greeting in unison and followed me with their eyes until I took a seat at a table by the window. The house across the square was whitewashed, with a green door. I could see flowerpots nestling behind the metal bars that guarded the two ground-floor windows. I looked out at the white house.

"What can I get you, sir?" The owner had come over and was leaning forwards with his notepad and a pencil in his hand.

"Tea. A cup of tea with a slice of lemon, please."

He licked the pencil and noted down my order slowly, as though it presented him with something of a problem.

"Tea it is, sir. We always have fresh tea here."

"Nonsense," an old man wearing spectacles called out. "That tea has stewed for at least three hours."

"Your eyesight is failing you, Uncle Fuat," the owner snorted. "I've just made a fresh pot. It's brewing now. Of course, you can't smell it. At your age you've lost your sense of smell as well."

Uncle Fuat muttered something; it must have been funny because it made his fellow players roar with laughter. The owner was clearly used to being teased and he did not reply. Eventually he returned with a glass on a tray.

"I've not seen you here before. Do you live locally?"

"No. I'm only here for the day. I'm studying architecture and I wanted to see the houses in the streets here with my own eyes. You have many beautiful houses in this area."

"Very true. And we'll keep it that way. No fat-cat businessmen will be allowed to tear them down as long as I live."

"Just wait until you get a fat-cat offer from a fat-cat businessman," Uncle Fuat said. More howls of laughter followed.

The owner returned to his glasses and the players returned their attention to their card game once more and I lit a cigarette and kept watch over the white house. The tea was fresh, the right strength and its fragrance reminded me of the mountains by the Black Sea. Time had stopped in this hidden corner of the city. I could sit here for hours and do nothing; my brain was not processing anything but the ticking of the clock on the wall. I could live here for years, like Uncle Fuat perhaps, and do nothing but shuffle back and forth between the teahouse and my home. It was just as absurd a notion as knocking on the door to ask Tuba if she had a room to rent. This peaceful, sleepy neighbourhood would have bored me, suffocated me after a few days. But it was very easy to pass the time of day there.

She was tall, thin and otherwise ordinary-looking with shoulder-length dark hair and glasses, wearing a white blouse and a cream skirt – all in all no different from the description Zuhal's father had given of her. As soon as she had locked the door, looked to either side and started walking briskly up the street I had taken to reach the square, I knew that I would follow her. It did not matter where or how far. If this woman were going to help me, it had to happen without her knowing. I put some money on the table, hurried outside and heard Uncle Fuat call out after me: "Watch out, son. That lady is a tricky bird to snare."

I did not hear the laughter that undoubtedly ensued. I was already halfway up the hill, terrified of losing sight of her. It was not easy following a woman in these deserted, narrow streets without being spotted, so I had to allow sufficient distance between us. Every now and then I would stop on a corner, wait, then run as I saw her disappear around the next corner. To curious eyes watching me from behind the curtains, I must have cut quite a ridiculous figure. To me this pursuit seemed more dramatic than amusing. My adrenalin levels rose, my heart pounded and I struggled to breathe. If this had been a game, I would have asked her for a cigarette break. Every corner brought the risk of losing her. When we finally reached the high street, I exhaled deeply, but from relief. Her tall slim figure was approximately one hundred metres ahead of me. We both reduced the pace in order to adapt to the flow of people out doing their Saturday shopping and the traffic thundering by with rush-hour intensity. We took our respective places, not far from each other, among the crowds getting ready to race across the four lanes at the first gap in the traffic. I practically collided with her when she stopped because of an inconsiderate driver.

The bus stop was packed with passengers of all ages. The bus was late. If it arrived, if it still had vacant seats and stopped, and if she caught the bus, there should not be a problem. The problem would arise if she suddenly decided to flag down a cab. But on this hot summer's day I had no cause to complain about my luck. She walked on after the crossing and headed for the entrance to the University Hospital. She was either on her way to visit a patient or she was ill herself. In both cases it was a matter of maintaining contact between us, resuming my pursuit when she had finished and hoping she was not planning on going home right away. I could now tell anyone who cared to listen that what we see in films or read about in crime fiction about tailing someone was just nonsense. It was hard work to walk, run, hide and make yourself invisible while keeping the other person in sight.

She was heading for the maternity ward. Pregnant women, women with new-born babies, fathers-to-be, new fathers and other visitors flowed in both directions through the corridor, and laughter, crying and children's screams merged into a painful cacophony. The scene confirmed me in my belief that there should be no rush to bring children into the world. I made my way carefully past women of varying shapes, but when I found myself at the end of the corridor, Tuba had disappeared. She must have entered one of the rooms – it was impossible to say which. Flustered, I retraced my steps. She had to be here somewhere, it was a matter of keeping my nerve; sooner or later she was bound to turn up. I could choose between waiting on a bench in the corridor or waiting outside, lighting a cigarette and keeping an eye on the entrance to the ward. The tannoy that sprang to life saved me making that decision. "Doctor Tuba Karan, please go to delivery suite 1. Doctor Tuba Karan . . ." The crowd parted to let Doctor Karan pass, her white doctor's coat flapping like the cape of the heroine in a movie. I smiled at my good fortune as she raced past me with a worried expression on her face.

I could go home now. Her shift was unlikely to end until late in the evening. Hanging around the hospital for that long held no particular attraction for me. Besides, I expected that she would go straight home to sleep. All in all the progress made in one short day was not to be sniffed at. Tuba, Zuhal's old friend, did exist; I could imagine them in happier times, walking side by side, chatting, laughing, swapping silly stories about boys. Were they still in touch? Did they still share secrets, or had they lost one another in the gathering storm? I had a lead, no matter how tenuous it might be. If I could succeed in following it without making a fatal blunder, I would find my answer. I knew where Tuba lived and worked. If this got me nowhere, I would just have to knock on her door and say, "Hi, have you seen Zuhal lately?"

A bloodied head and a torso in a blood-stained shirt were lying at my feet. The rest of the body, his legs, were still in the cab. I had very nearly stepped on him, but at the last moment I had snapped out of my daydreaming. The cab driver was busy trying to force the man out onto the pavement. I shuddered in the heat at the incredible scene. The world seemed to have taken leave of its senses.

"What are you doing? Can't you see the man's bleeding?"

The unconscious man was a heavyweight, and the cabbie, who was slight in build, was struggling to drag him out of his vehicle. The sweat was dripping from his face. In his eyes he had the resigned look of a man who profoundly regretted poking his nose into someone else's business. With my intervention, I had poked my nose into his and was about to be on the receiving end of a rant.

"Let me tell you something. That fat pig has bled all over my cab. You should never lend anyone a helping hand nowadays. I find him bleeding like a sacrificial lamb in the street. Good heavens, I think, he needs to go to a hospital right away. So I drive him here with my foot on the gas pedal the whole time, and what does he say when we get here? Come on, guess! 'Sorry, brother. I don't have any money on me.'

So I'm asking you: Am I a taxi driver or a charity? Who's going to feed my kids if I ferry everyone who is bleeding to the hospital free of charge?"

Curious onlookers had already gathered around us and were already taking sides.

"He's right. Who'll feed his kids?" some said.

"My God, what's happened to us Muslims?" others said.

"Alright, alright. How much?" I said.

"How much what?" someone in the crowd asked.

"Mind your own business," I responded. "I'm asking the driver. How much did the trip cost?"

The cab driver had already forgotten his more serious concerns. I could not tell if it was down to his guilty conscience or his sense of justice, but he mentioned a reasonable sum.

"He's all yours now, brother. Hope you get some use out of him. But I doubt you'll get your money back even if you manage to sell him."

Those were his parting words, after which the cab sped off to find new adventures. It was easy enough to disperse the rest of the crowd. All I had to do was ask them for money towards the injured man's fare. When only the two of us remained, I knelt over him.

"Can you hear me?"

"Loud and clear, mate."

He had a round face, short hair, a thin moustache and gentle eyes, and his smile revealed bloodstained teeth.

"Life's a circus and we're all just clowns, don't you think?" he said as he got to his feet, still slightly groggy. I asked if he felt alright. Oh yes, he had never felt better. As long as you could count to ten, you were out of danger. No, he was not a boxer. Yes, he had heard everything. That vile maggot of a cab driver was lying: he had not bled all over the cab, he had pressed a towel against his wound the whole time. The only blood-soaked object in the car was the towel on the back seat which the driver had driven away with.

He was a sturdy chap and not fat either once he was standing upright to his full height, though you might say he was thickset. He agreed with me that we ought to pay a visit to casualty to see if he needed stitches, though he was sure his cuts were no more life-threatening than donating blood – he would be fine. He gave the impression of being someone who did not take life very seriously – except perhaps where his honour was concerned. That maggot would pay with his car, if not his life, because he had not believed that the cab fare would be repaid immediately. It was an unforgivable insult. I asked him to forget about the driver and concentrate instead on his injuries.

"As you wish, sir," he said, and saluted me sharply. From now on everything I asked for would be considered an order. I laughed at his big words. If I wanted him to, he would swear on his mother's grave. Or even better, if I let him hit me over the head we could become blood brothers. He might have been a few years older than me, but he treated me as his big brother. As I grew more confident about his health, I started worrying more about how we would pay for his treatment in the casualty ward. I only had thirty lira left in my wallet.

"Our problems are over, just you wait and see," he said.

We did not have to wait long. He was received like some kind of celebrity.

"Welcome, Soldier. What's happened to you this time?" the nursing assistant said.

The duty police officer brought us two glasses of tea and wished him a speedy recovery. While the doctor stitched his head, he drank his tea and smiled at me. They gave him a good wash and found him a clean shirt. When they had finished, he looked like a hale and hearty young man despite the bandage around his head. Afterwards we sat on a bench in the hospital park. It was time to say goodbye, but he had stirred my curiosity.

"Why did they call you Soldier?" I asked.

Oh, it was a legacy from his time in the Foreign Legion. Once a soldier always a soldier, you see, and now he was a soldier for one particular family, if I got his drift. And what had just happened was a family matter. He was an idiot who had only gone and let himself be robbed of the house's takings – a considerable sum, by the way. We introduced ourselves properly. He was not surprised that I was a poor student: he believed that students, young people with knowledge, were the future of this country. And he hoped that we would show mercy to people like him when we took our place among the great and the good. I did not think he was being wholly serious.

The house he referred to was a casino, bar and restaurant that belonged to a family that operated an entirely legal gaming business as well as offering protection and sexual services. Beyond that his lips were sealed: no-one could make him say that there was anything illegal about their set-up. He was a kind of day-to-day manager and had been on his way to bank the takings from the previous night when he was mugged. It was an occupational hazard in his line of work. But, enough talking, it was time to enjoy ourselves, and I must never forget that being alive was in itself worth celebrating. I was his guest and he wanted to show me the city's dark, but oh-so-attractive underbelly. I would gamble, drink, eat and choose freely among his girls. Wait a minute – there was this new girl in town, never been touched, she would be only too happy for her first time to be with a handsome young man such as me. Soldier might have been bragging, or perhaps not. His invitation was undeniably tempting, but one ought to decline certain things in life. Besides, a poor student such as I had to work for his daily bread and boring translations awaited me at home. Soldier seemed hurt, but my mind was made up, it was not even worth discussing it.

"Once a student, always a student, eh?" he said. Then he asked me to do him one final favour: give him some change for the telephone and wait for him. He would be no more than half an hour.

The car arrived after twenty minutes. It was a Mercedes – brand-new, it looked as if it had just rolled out of the factory. The driver, in uniform, opened the door for me, and I got in next to Soldier in the back. I did not doubt that he was capable of intimidating his enemies, but his proud and joyful smile and his bandaged head made him look more sympathetic than threatening in my eyes. We enjoyed the drive in silence. Eventually the car stopped on a back street in Beyoglu where I had not been before, outside a "house" decorated with coloured lights and a large neon sign announcing to visitors that they were about to enter "Casino Las Vegas". He hugged me and kissed both my cheeks.

"Come by one day, any time. If you need something, or even if you don't."

He opened the door of the car. "Take this gentleman anywhere he wants to go," he told the driver.

I took hold of his arm before he got out. "One thing. Be nice to the girls," I said.

He smiled, a little goofily this time. "Will do," he said, and closed the door behind him and waved from the pavement.

I leaned back in the leather seat and asked the driver to take me home. He was a middle-aged man with long sideburns and a huge moustache; he glanced at me at regular intervals in the rear mirror with dark, cold and intrusive eyes.

"Did you want something?" I said when the staring became uncomfortable.

"No, sir."

Then, without taking his eyes of the road, he handed me an envelope. Inside I found a wad of bank notes, the value of which exceeded the fee for countless pages of translation.

"I can't accept this," I said, handing the envelope back to him.

"That's what Soldier said, that you wouldn't accept it. But he also said that I would lose my job if I came back with the envelope."

I badly needed the money. I did not want an unemployed man on my conscience and I did not want him spending any more time wondering what kind of idiot he was driving around. I leaned back in my seat and discovered that it smelled of real leather.

18

(Still) July 1980

Beads of sweat trickled down her forehead and into her eyes, blurring her vision and forcing her to stop to wipe them away with her shirt-sleeve. Still, she had made the right decision in turning her back on the sun to avoid being blinded. A large black fly kept buzzing around her head, as if intent on further aggravating her, but she was lucky compared to the two men next to her, who were being attacked by a whole swarm of them. As she squatted on the hot earth she wished the heavens would fill with dark clouds and deliver a sudden shower to drive away the intrusive creatures and the intense smell that was attracting them. She turned her head to one side and saw that the man lying on his back was still bleeding from his leg. She looked away quickly. Not because she could not handle the sight, but because she had other things to focus on – pulling the trigger, resisting the recoil against her shoulder and watching as the empty cartridge case was ejected with a metallic click. A bleak, barren plain opened out before her: the trees had been chopped down to make way for the new shanty town. Only rust-tinted heaps of soil remained, forming desert-like waves, and the shimmering heat of the midday sun rose from the tarmac road as it faded into the horizon

The police car lay on its side in the ditch, roughly a hundred metres away. Zuhal took aim and the distant sound of lead penetrating metal assured her that the bullet had embedded itself in something inanimate. Not that there was any danger of hitting anything living; the policemen had flattened themselves against the ground, occasionally shooting into the air without raising their heads. Zuhal knew that they were awaiting reinforcements, no doubt delayed by the crowds of people blocking the road further down. Her group should have retreated long ago, but one of their number had been wounded in the opening exchange of fire when the police had first arrived. They had to help him, but with more police on their way it was time to withdraw. She turned to the man next to her.

"Are you done with him?"

"Yes. I've stopped the bleeding, but he has lost a lot of blood," Kemal replied as he wiped his hands on a strip of cloth.

She was glad that Kemal, who usually kept his cool in a crisis, was part of this operation and that they had temporarily merged their two groups in case it did not go as planned.

"Then you'll take him and you'll leave first. Are we sure that the gravel track is still passable?"

"The locals have just said that it is. But they also say the track is not suitable for motor vehicles."

"Just drive. We don't worry about the suspension of stolen cars, do we?"

She thought she saw something resembling a smile on Kemal's normally grave face, but he was already busy giving the group the signal to assemble. Then he did something unexpected – he took her hand. There was tenderness both in his eyes and in the gesture, but also concern.

"He's going to need a doctor."

"You know where you can find one, don't you?"

"Yes," he replied with slight reluctance.

"Then do it. And goodbye."

"Goodbye. Take care of yourself," Kemal said as he let go of her hand.

Zuhal watched them carry the wounded man to one of the two cars. Further down, a lorry was parked, abandoned and stripped of its goods. Kemal's car disappeared in a cloud of dust, and she was left wondering when or indeed if she would see him again. When the moment of sentimentality she had allowed herself was over she switched the setting of the gun to automatic, stood up and fired towards the police car. A few seconds passed and no shots rang out in reply; she sketched a circle with her right hand above her head. Her group instantly responded to the signal to gather together. All four of them appeared to be unharmed.

"We're done here, comrades. *Vamos!*" she said cheerfully. It became obvious that none of them had read Wild West comics as children. They stared at her in expectation.

"Oh, forget it. Let's go, guys. Let's go!"

*

The garden had become my sanctuary. This was where I ate, read and worked, but I felt that the serenity was fraudulent, that my garden was an oasis of calm in a city under siege. This feeling continued to grip me when I sat on the wooden chair and listened. No matter how hard I tried and how much I pricked up my ears, the noise from the street fighting remained inaudible. The battles were fought in secret, but they were no less intense or bloody for it.

Pride had made Zuhal foolhardy. I tried to put myself in her place, to think as she thought. I failed, but I could understand the attraction. It could not have been an accidental choice. She must have planned it. I also tried to imagine how they had gone about hijacking the lorry. Nine men and women hide by a road and wait. They know exactly where the lorry will be at any moment as it follows its daily route. Somehow they cause it to stop. The driver suspects nothing; after all, it is not as if he is carrying gold.

What do they do with him besides threatening and terrifying him with a pistol pressed to the back of his head? The woman sits in the passenger seat of the high cab and a man takes the wheel next to her. The powerful engine starts with a roar and they drive the lorry to its new destination. The rest of the unit follows them in two cars. The new shanty town on the outskirts of the city has not changed. It is just as dusty, bleak and impoverished. The woman asks the driver to stop the lorry in front of a house where two years ago a young man died with a bullet in his chest. Soon the women and children who live there are gathered round the vehicle. Young armed men jump out of the cars, open the back doors of the lorry and begin to distribute the food. The woman stands on the roof of the truck. She wants to explain to the people why they should accept goods from a hijacked lorry.

"Today revolutionary forces have seized these goods from the bourgeoisie, goods which were stolen from you and which ultimately belong to you." She stops abruptly. She did not come here to make a speech. She leaves the lorry, the boxes of food and the women and children and places her troops in strategic positions, securing the escape route. Then she waits. This time she will decide where the battle will be fought. Special Forces sent to the shanty town will walk into an ambush and find themselves caught in a heavy crossfire. She has equipped her men with all the firearms she has at her disposal for this operation, machine-guns and hand grenades. She leads the attack from the front.

Eyewitnesses say that she stood tall, spraying bullets from her Kalashnikov, then replaced the clip and opened fire again. I had no difficulties visualizing her. Not in the way the newspapers portrayed her, as a mystical Joan of Arc figure, but as the woman she was: fearless and loyal and above all real. No matter how arrogant her actions seemed, I was sure that she had come back to the shanty town to show her solidarity alongside the people with whom she had tasted defeat. She had done it her way, by humiliating the enemy in the very place where he had previously been victorious. "A DISPLAY OF POWER", "WHERE'S THE GOVERNMENT?" She made the headlines. It was a miracle that no lives were lost in the brief but intense exchange of fire. And it was an embarrassment for the government that the terrorists were able to leave the battlefield as easily as if they had been out for a stroll on a summer's day. I bought the newspapers and studied closely every line about Zuhal with a mixture of admiration and anxiety. Even reactionary journalists afforded her legendary status. But her pride and careless disregard for her own life worried me.

I had stagnated. It was like having legs of lead, though the lead was mainly confined to my brain. No matter how much I pondered. I made no progress. Tuba was a dead end. What connection could there be between a hospital doctor and self-declared professional revolution-aries? A professional revolutionary had only one mission and sacrificed to it both their private life and their family. Even if Tuba were a sympathizer, she would not be in contact with Zuhal. But what else did I have? I could not stand guard outside every bank in turn in case she decided to rob one of them, nor watch over cars she might steal or move to her favourite shanty town in the hope that she might be plan-ning another raid. I spent insane amounts of time dreaming up absurd ideas such as placing an advert in the paper: "Oak seeks Saturn. Meet me at this or that place, in a week from today at . . ." Then again, spies in novels apparently get results this way.

One Monday morning, in the middle of July, I called the hospital. They could not answer questions about the shifts of individual doctors, but normally a daytime shift would end around 5.00 in the afternoon. At 4.30 p.m. I took my place outside the maternity ward. At 5.10 p.m.

Tuba came out of the building with two other women. They were in a good mood, chatting and laughing, relieved perhaps that another hard day's work was over. They were absorbed in a world of their own and did not notice me or anyone else. I was relieved when they joined the queue at the bus stop in front of the hospital. Tuba had plans that evening, she wasn't going straight home from work. I decided to allow myself one last attempt before letting it lie. If it turned out to be just an innocent shopping trip where only her purse would suffer, I would say a quiet goodbye.

It was the middle of the rush hour and the passengers on the Bakırköy bus fought a merciless battle for standing room. Surviving the trip was almost entirely a question of creating air pockets around yourself. Everything was tight and clammy, the windows were of a type that could not be opened and bodily fluids evaporated in the heat. People's nerves were as taut as the strings on an instrument and everyone was on the verge of a collective breakdown. Arguments broke out here and there, mainly between men and women, the women complaining of unwanted physical contact, while the men defended themselves by asking what alternative there was. If some of these men were innocent, others, no doubt, were borderline sex offenders. They seemed to be of a particular type, and I wondered if they might not be solely respons- ible for the unbearable rush-hour chaos. The driver did not want to miss out on the fun and played his part by driving straight past a couple of stops. The confusion and mayhem that followed suited me just fine. With everything that was going on, Tuba was unlikely to notice me. The only disadvantage was that on the rare occasions when the driver actually bothered to stop I risked losing sight of her and might not see if she left the bus. By the time we had reached Bakırköy, the crowd of passengers had thinned out. Tuba's two friends were no longer with her; they must have got off along the way.

She was now standing alone by the middle door, holding on to one of the poles for balance, swaying lightly to the rhythm of the bus. She seemed to be studying her fellow passengers and for a brief moment our eyes met. She fixed her gaze on me, investigative and curious. I looked away, a little too quickly, panicking possibly, and stared out of the window. She did not get off until the final stop, which made it easier for me to tail her. She was in no hurry. She strolled at a leisurely pace down the street and stopped frequently to look through shop windows. She also stopped in front of the shop where Ayfer worked, but she did not go inside. She continued her walk and entered a small boutique a little further down.

I crossed the street. On this side, too, there was an unbroken row of shops. I had walked here countless times and never noticed any of them. I stopped in front of a lingerie shop, right across from the boutique Tuba had entered, using the reflection in the main window to keep an eye on the entrance opposite. Ladies' underwear proved interesting. I had never studied in detail the shapes of so many bras and pairs of knickers.

Tuba took her time, but eventually she came out. In the window I could see her standing on the pavement, slightly hesitant as to what to do next. After a few moments she crossed the street. I was unprepared for this move. She stood next to me, so that there were two of us attracted by the small, sensual garments. I felt it more than I saw it, how her gaze moved from the display to my profile. It was so intense that it almost burned into my skin. I could no longer pretend to be absorbed by the display, so I turned and met her smiling eyes. There was something in them that made me feel we had just been introduced to each other. I almost expected her to hold out her hand and start making polite conversation, but she did not. Still smiling, she entered the shop. I was in no doubt that she was on to me. It was difficult to tell how. Perhaps the men in the teahouse had warned her or perhaps she had known the whole time. I felt nervous. I lit a cigarette and waited. There was no point in hiding anymore. I leaned against the wall of the shop and soaked up the afternoon sun. I amused myself by trying to guess the jobs of the people who walked by, and whether they were single or married, happy or sad. After three cigarettes there was still no sign of Tuba.

The temperature inside the shop was pleasant and the atmosphere friendly. The few customers and the shop assistants spoke in hushed tones as though lingerie was uniquely deserving of reverence. The room was much larger than it appeared from the outside; it opened out to the right into an L-shape. This part of the shop was invisible to anyone looking through the front window. Tuba was not among the customers, nor was she in any of the changing rooms, all of which stood empty with their curtains pulled back.

"Can I help you?" a young shop assistant asked.

"Yes, please," I said. 'I'm looking for a friend who came in here a little while ago. A tall, slim woman with glasses."

"Oh, the one from the Fire Service. She was here to inspect our emergency exits. She went out through the back door and didn't come back."

"That's strange. We were supposed to meet outside the shop. Never mind, I'm sure I'll find her. By the way, where does the back door lead to?"

"To a courtyard which leads to another street. We comply with every regulation, you see."

"Very reassuring," I said kindly. I wanted to laugh out loud at the way Tuba had tricked me. "You've got some very nice garments here," I said.

She blushed.

"Many thanks for your help," I said and hurried outside before she started asking questions.

There was no point in racing around the neighbourhood. She would not be hanging around waiting for me. I had lost her. I wondered why she had gone to the trouble of losing me in that way. Causing a scene in the street would have been much easier. She might even have attracted a couple of young men who would have been only too happy to rough me up in order to defend a young woman's honour. The logical explanation was that she did not want to draw attention to herself, that she was clever and had experience of losing anyone who followed her. What was she afraid of? Did she have something to hide? It was just possible that I might be on to something after all.

Ayfer was standing outside her shop smoking a cigarette.

"Hello, stranger," she called out.

I waved to her, but did not have the energy to cross the street again and begin a tense conversation. When I reached the bus stop I knew one thing. I was no longer an anonymous shadow following in Tuba's footsteps.

*

"I want to borrow one of your girls," I said.

If he was surprised he hid it well behind the permanent smile on his round face. After all, Soldier must have seen and heard it all in his time. He had welcomed me like a close friend, a brother almost. Before my arrival, I had secretly feared that Soldier's fraternal enthusiasm had been of the moment and that he had forgotten all about me the second he had turned his back. The gruff manners of the sturdy bouncer I met at the entrance were not encouraging. He scrutinized me from head to toe when I mentioned Soldier and asked me to show him some I.D.

"I'm over eighteen," I said, but he just repeated "I.D." like a parrot with only one word in its vocabulary.

Frequent police searches meant that I always carried my I.D. card. He was more suspicious and more thorough than all the policemen put together. His expression suggested he was trying hard to find discrepancies between my physical presence and the person depicted on the card. At last, with a brusque gesture confirming my suspicions about his command of language, he signalled that I should remain where I was, then disappeared through the heavy velvet curtains. Shortly afterwards Soldier made a theatrical entrance, flinging the curtains aside, running towards me and embracing me while he called out: "Welcome, brother. What wind has blown you here?"

He had that right. Without an ill wind to guide me, many months might have passed before we saw each other again. He returned my I.D. card to me and apologized for that rude ass, the bouncer. The next time I came, he would salute me: he, Soldier, would see to that. The ass pouted like a cat that has spilt its milk. He said nothing, but the poor chap had surely only done as he had been told. However, as they say around here, "Every cockerel crows the loudest on his own dung heap."

We passed through a well-lit corridor and entered a shadowy room. Red lamps on the tables and a few recessed wall lights provided the only sources of illumination, just enough to stop you stumbling into the furniture. It was early in the evening and the restaurant was still largely empty. Soldier picked a table near the stage, where a scantily clad young woman half-mimed, half-danced to recorded music. I never saw Soldier make any signs, but two waiters, quiet and unobtrusive, laid the table with meze dishes: sliced honeydew melon, feta cheese, stuffed vine leaves, aubergine salad, grilled *köfte* and rakı, served neat of course, the proper way. A crystal carafe of water and a bowl of ice cubes arrived in case the guest preferred his rakı diluted. The conversation was relaxed. Soldier was trying to present me with a respectable facade, so he steered clear of subjects such as gambling and sexual services. As well as the woman on stage, there were a couple of girls sitting with the customers, but it was hard to tell whether they were guests themselves or employees.

Soldier's reticence wrongfooted me; I had hoped that he would spontaneously make me an offer.

"I want to borrow one of your girls," may not have been quite the right way to put it, but I was an amateur and the words, appropriate or otherwise, had already been said.

Behind his smile Soldier cleared his throat softly. He seemed uncertain as to what tone he should use with someone like me.

"Well, brother, as you've come straight to the point only one thing remains: what's your type? Blonde, brunette or very dark?"

"The smartest one you've got."

Thinking did not appear to be Soldier's strong point: the furrows in his brow indicated intense brain activity and considerable confusion. I owed him an explanation, but the whole truth would only confuse him further. A few white lies, on the other hand, surely would be no major crime in his world and, besides, they would make matters simpler for everyone concerned. So I told him about a friend of mine who had a problem. He had a wife, a little wild, unfortunately, who ran around with no sense of shame. My friend was tearing his hair out, worrying about her cheating. We had come up with a plan. Following his wife for a day would solve the problem once and for all. But she knew both of us too well, so we couldn't do it. That was where the smart girl came in. She could follow his wife without being noticed. All she would have to do was keep an eye on the wife until she reached her destination and report back. My friend and I were willing to pay for this service.

Soldier was happy with my explanation. He offered his own services if the brazen woman needed to be taught a lesson. That would be going too far, I assured him. Besides, my friend loathed violence – he would simply file for divorce if it turned out that his wife had a lover. I could tell that Soldier did not agree with this and that he did not think much of my friend.

"Well, that's settled," he said. 'Is there anything else I can do for you while you're here?"

I did not know how much I could expect of him in return for the small kindness I had done him, if there was a limit to the favours you could ask in his world.

"Listen to me," he said. "I'm not calling you my brother for nothing. You helped me that day with no thought of a favour in return. I'm not used to that, you see. I always expect crap from other people. You've gone some way to correct that. You're like a brother to me now. And brothers don't keep score of what they do for each other. So out with it."

I came out with it. I had a girlfriend, a minor, even though she looked quite mature. Her family was set firmly against any serious relationship for the time being, but we could not and would not wait. I was planning to go abroad, but not without her. So the thing was that we both needed passports without going down the bureaucratic road, if he got my drift. I did not know if this was his area of expertise, but hoped that at least he could give me some good advice. When I had finished, I had a guilty conscience for having lied so much to him in one day.

"Did you bring passport photos?" he asked, getting straight down to business.

I had. I handed him the photographs, mine and Zuhal's. He studied them for a while. He was no longer smiling: he already seemed pre-occupied by the magnitude of the task. When he had finished with the photographs, he looked up, was about to say something, but changed his mind. When he finally spoke, his smile was back in place.

"She's lovely. Now I understand why you're not interested in my girls."

He fished out a notebook from his jacket and carefully placed the photographs inside it.

"There is very little which is not within my area of expertise, brother. Consider it done. However, it might take a bit of time, good craftsmanship always does. But no-one's after you, are they?" His smile grew even broader. He was getting closer to the truth. Someone was definitely after Zuhal, but as long as I did not know where she was, there was no rush.

"Any particular names you want in the passports?"

"Do you know, I hadn't thought about that. No," I said.

"Alright. I'll pick new names for you."

"I insist on paying," I said.

He laughed and slapped my cheeks with affection. "You don't give up, do you? Fine. You can settle the bill when you leave. And don't think it will be cheap either. When you've done that, we're quits. O.K?"

I nodded.

"Consider it done. Finding a smart girl among my lot is another matter. I have tested most of their skills, but never their intelligence. Quite unnecessary in this business, you understand. Let me see what I can do. In the meantime enjoy yourself. I have work to do elsewhere in the house, so I'm unlikely to come back. Stay as long as you like. If you want anything, just snap your fingers. O.K?"

I nodded again and thanked him. He gave me another bear hug and disappeared through a door by the stage. I never had to snap my fingers: a waiter stayed at a respectful distance and exchanged plates, poured rakı and lit my cigarette before I had time to think about it myself. The unaccustomed attention mixed with the never-failing effect of the rakı went straight to my head. I leaned back and enjoyed the temptations promised by money and power. The working class would forgive me this one indulgence. The room was almost full now and on the stage a dancer had replaced the singer. She was blonde, perhaps genuine, perhaps not, a young woman with long legs and lovely curves – and unlike the singer, she knew how to use them. Her sensuous dance turned out to be the prelude to a striptease act. She took her act literally and teased her male customers with brazen glances, blowing kisses, winking, pouting and licking her lips shamelessly and flaunting her breasts and hips. She peeled off her clothes and threw them at the audience. I had never seen anything like it and I worried that aroused men would storm the stage. However, they seemed to know, from previous bad experiences perhaps, where to draw the line, because they stayed obediently in their chairs, groaning and sighing, and, judging from their expectant faces, hoping that one of her garments would land on their head. When she had stripped down to her knickers, which were more like a piece of string, and a minimalist bra, the room fell completely silent. It had to be the climax of the act. She prolonged deliberately the moment and the torments of anticipation suffered by her audience. The stage lights were dimmed when she finally turned her back to the audience and nimbly unhooked her bra. When she turned to face us again her breasts had been liberated and were swaying to the rhythm of the music and her movements. The next thing I knew, her bra was flying through the air, coming to rest in my half-eaten aubergine salad. A collective groan went around the room, the audience applauded and whistled with vigorous enthusiasm. She curtsied like an actress after a stand-out performance and blew more kisses to her admirers. Then she ran down from the stage and came over to my table.

"Bad throw, eh?" she said and sat down nonchalantly on my lap. All this was happening as though she had rehearsed it. It was clear that she did this every night with her chosen customers. I was without a doubt the most envied man in the room at this moment and most certainly not the only one wondering why she had chosen me.

"Hi, I'm the smart one," she whispered into my ear and licked my earlobe. "You're not gay by any chance, are you, sweetheart?"

"No, I'm not," I stammered and was instantly silenced by her tongue, which forced its way into my mouth as she rotated her hips on my lap.

"Oh, yes. There it is. The beast awakens," she said, taking a break from kissing me, and grabbing the "beast". I did not want to be rude, but I longed to put an end to this performance, which was causing much merriment and whistling among the audience.

"You've misunderstood your job. All you have to—"

"Hush, lad. I know exactly what to do. So you're turned on by the usual things?"

I had passed the test. She told me that you could not be too careful these days. She did not mind gay men, but could not stand perverts. You never knew with men, they might suddenly pull out a whip. Not a game she wanted to play. Still flirting with me, she asked for my permission to leave in order to change into something more decent, and in the meantime could I be a good boy and not let anyone else sit on my lap? She took her time in coming back, which was just as well because I needed a few moments to recover my lost dignity. When she arrived she was so presentable she could have been taken to any event, however conservative the clientele. She had removed her heavy make-up, her dark hair, scraped back in a pony tail, was no longer covered by the blonde wig, and the simple dress she wore did not reveal even a hint of cleavage.

"I feel like a nun, but this is the best I could come up with for the occasion," she said.

"It's fine. And you've never looked lovelier," I said.

She laughed and flattered me by saying she had liked me from the first moment. She was not exactly repulsive herself, transformed into a chatty and witty girl, her striptease manners left behind in the dressing room. She asked what it was like to be a student and listened with interest. I did not ask about her life and she appeared to be grateful for that.

"So you're the one who converted Soldier?"

"Converted?"

"He used to be a real bastard. There's hardly a girl here who hasn't felt his fists. Then suddenly, he changed. He only uses his mouth now. Between you and me, I'm not sure that's a change for the better. His swearing could bring on a heart attack. He said the change was down to you. So I had to be nice to you."

"I think Soldier is rather exaggerating. It must be the latent goodness in him which has finally broken through."

"Ha ha, very likely. But credit where credit's due. He protects us against most things. And there's a lot of bad people around, I want you to know that. Let's get down to business. He said I'm yours for as long as you need me. So, I am. Shall we go, darling?"

"May I ask where?"

"Well, you must have a place somewhere, haven't you?"

We were never given a bill, but I tipped the waiter generously. The bouncer politely said goodnight to us. We took a cab home. Leyla – she assured me it was not her stage name – had brought with her a large shoulder-bag. In it she had packed two wigs, sunglasses, a pair of trousers and a vest; she referred to them as her props. The rest, a pair of knickers, a nightdress and a toothbrush, was standard equipment for a brief stay with a stranger. So there we stood in front of the only bed in my flat, in nightdress and pyjamas respectively. She asked if I wanted to make love. No sadly, I had a bit of a headache. That suited her fine: she was exhausted after all that "housework". But it would be lovely just to sleep next to a man. We decided to give it a go. I lay on my left side and she snuggled up to me and put her arm around me. The last thing I noticed before I fell asleep was her calm, even breathing.

Leyla was a blonde once more. Her wig suited her pale skin surprisingly well and did not make for a grotesque contrast as is often the case. You would not mistake her for a real blonde, but she could pass everywhere for a good fake. She sat quietly next to me on the bench licking her ice cream, a little nervous perhaps, she no longer twittered like a bird. This time I had picked a discreet spot, approximately one hundred metres from the entrance to the maternity ward, covered by a large tree. We had checked it out in advance to be sure that Tuba would not be able to see me, but that I would still have a good view of the entrance if I leaned against Leyla's shoulder. A loving couple would not be first on Tuba's list of potential tails.

Tuba emerged from the building exactly the same time as before, at 5.10 p.m. She was alone and on her guard, taking her time, scanning her surroundings before walking off at a brisk pace. I was already hiding behind the tree, crouching behind Leyla. She needed no further instructions. I had drummed Tuba's appearance into her and warned of how she had tricked me in the lingerie shop. When she got up and brushed invisible specks of dust off her dress, I wished her good luck. She winked and waved, then wriggled her hips in a final farewell, adopting a rather less eye-catching walk as she ambled off and was soon swallowed up by the crowd.

*

Leyla was humming an unknown song. She did not have time for me, she was too busy in the kitchen. My job was to relax and look forward to a culinary experience I would never forget. She had faith in my openness towards new things. In a mountain village by the Aegean Sea her mother had taught her this dish, as well as the songs she was humming. The past was the past and it was nothing to cry about. You could honour it, as Leyla did, with your mother's old recipes and flavour it with charming mountain songs.

We talked about everything but her mission during the meal. The food was different, exotic almost, and it tasted delicious. I could praise her without having to lie and toasted her mother's memory. She entertained me with quaint and amusing stories from her village. When we sat back and lit our cigarettes, she was finally ready to satisfy my growing curiosity.

"That friend of yours, my darling: he needs to find himself a new woman, unless he's the type of guy who can live in the shadow of a rival."

*

It was an ordinary four-storey block of flats, anonymous and dull, one of many on the street. Life progressed at a slow pace here compared to the hectic tempo of other parts of the neighbourhood. Both the traffic and the people became laid-back once they had torn themselves away from the constant chaos on the main street. I was one of the few who were still restless. I had already paced up and down the street twice. Leyla had written down the address and described in detail how to find it, so there was no doubt that I was in the right place. Where I had failed, Leyla had proved truly resourceful. She had the advantage of being a woman and she was genuinely inventive, thanks in part to the speedy clothes-changing skills required by her profession. If her explanation were to be believed, it had all gone like clockwork, almost too easy, perhaps even a little dull. I suspected that she was trivializing her own skill, her remarkable ability to be the centre of attention one moment and completely anonymous the next. Soldier had not erred in picking her.

Tuba had returned home by a different route, taking the opposite direction, towards the city centre. After having got off the bus at Beyazıt, she had strolled down to the Grand Bazaar. Leyla did not for one minute believe that Tuba was at all interested in the tempting jewellery or pretty Persian and Turkish rugs in the display windows, even though she had spent plenty of time in front of and inside the shops. On a couple of occasions Leyla had dared stand next to Tuba and study the same jewels to check if the other woman was wary of her sisters. She was not. Even though Tuba had glanced frequently both left and right, her eyes usually followed the movements of nearby men. In a clothes shop Leyla had entered the changing room next to Tuba's and seized the opportunity to whip off her wig and exchange her skirt for a pair of trousers.

When they came out of the Grand Bazaar, Tuba had taken the local train from Sirkeci. Leyla sat in the same carriage and busied herself in crocheting, apparently absorbed in her handiwork all the way to Bakırköy. After a round trip through the city, they had finally ended up in the street where I was now pacing up and down. Tuba had appeared absent-minded and exhausted by then; she no longer bothered looking over her shoulder at regular intervals and she went straight into the anonymous, dull building without a backward glance. Leyla could have returned at that point, her mission accomplished, but she was not a girl to do things by halves, so she did not hesitate to push open the entrance door and follow the "brazen wife" to the very end. Her determination was rewarded when she came up the stairs just in time to see Tuba being let in through the door of a first-floor flat. Before the door was closed, she caught a glimpse of a man whom she could not describe in detail. This was sufficient proof of the debauched life of my friend's deceitful wife, wasn't it? No doubt about it, I said, and helped her clear up. I planted a friendly kiss on her cheek before she left and promised her that I would definitely catch her bra next time.

Despite what I had said to Leyla, I was haunted by a great number of doubts as I stood outside the building. I had an address that might just be the home of Tuba's boyfriend. Her guarded behaviour could easily be attributed to the conduct of many girls when they have a secret lover, or better still, maybe she really was deceiving a husband who was waiting for her at home in blissful ignorance. There was only one way to find out. Knock on the door. If a strange man opened the door, I would say: "Is there a Miss Zuhal living here?" And if he answered in the negative, I would apologize for the inconvenience and leave. End of story. The bottom line was that anything except the miraculous appearance of Zuhal herself in the doorway would mean the end of the road.

I raised my hand to knock, but the man on the other side of the door pre-empted the movement, as though he had been expecting me. It took me a few seconds to recognize him. I had time to lower my hand and so avoided being frozen in a ridiculous position. In the street he could have passed by me unnoticed, he could have been anyone. Here I might have expected to meet him, which made it possible for me to place him. He had changed a great deal in a relatively short time, but it could not be time alone: his own efforts must also have contributed to such a dramatic transformation. His long messy hair was now cut short and carefully combed; the Che Guevara beard which had flattered the sunken features of his face was nowhere to be seen – he was clean-shaven now. He no longer had the slim, gaunt figure that, to my annoyance, had lent him an athletic look. The army parka and the jeans had been replaced by a clean white shirt and suit trousers. For a moment we looked at each other: I surprised; he with superior calm.

"Come in. I've been expecting you," Kemal said, finally breaking the silence.

He had to make the first move, as I was lost for words. My brain was working overtime. If Kemal was here, Zuhal had to be here too. It was the logical conclusion. Perhaps it was not love, but they had found each other in the struggle, and it was hard to imagine one without the other. I felt like a child, a helpless child, and did not know what I would do if I found her waiting in the middle of the room. I would not be able to throw myself into her arms in Kemal's presence, nor could I just stand there like a paralysed idiot. The torment lasted only a few seconds. My fears were not realized: the living room was empty but for the two of us. It looked as if it had been furnished in great haste with items from a flea market. Nothing looked directly ugly, worn or second-hand, but everything was badly positioned, as if someone had picked out a few bits and pieces and thrown them in the air, not caring where they ended up or whether they matched. Kemal stood with his back to the window, which was shrouded by a net curtain. I realized why he had been expecting me. He must have seen me on the pavement.

"You've changed," he said. "But not so much that I couldn't recognize you."

He no longer had the dreamy look that had characterized his time as an idolized student leader. Tough experiences along the way had hardened his eyes.

"Sit down," he said with the voice of one forced to be polite to an unwanted guest. I would have preferred to have remained standing, and told him to cut out the small talk and get to the point, which, as far as I was concerned, was Zuhal and Zuhal alone. But I was scared of irritating him, scared of saying the wrong thing, of making him clam up. So I obeyed and sat down in an armchair that creaked under my weight, and watched as he sat down on the sofa opposite. He wore an expression of visible discomfort as though physical pain made his every move agony. Otherwise he looked well, better than ever; was I the source of his discomfort?

"Let's get this over with as quickly as possible," Kemal said. "How did you find this address?"

I told him about the journey that had begun with Zuhal's parents and ended here. When I had finished he looked angry, with me, with himself and with everyone else involved.

"It's unbelievable that it would be so simple," he said. "I'm almost pleased that it's you sitting here. If that old soldier had tipped off the police rather than you, I would have . . ." He stopped himself, there was no need to state the obvious.

"He would never do anything that might hurt his daughter," I said, defending the General.

"No, that's right. Not him. But what about you?"

"I don't have a daughter. Not yet," I said.

Something resembling a distorted smile lit up his face, and then he relaxed and smiled more freely.

"So, here you are," he continued. "And the damage has been done. We can't use this place as a safe house any longer and we need to evacuate as soon as possible. Secondly, we need to cut contact with Tuba. If you can find her, so can the police. You understand that your eagerness will prove costly for us, don't you?"

"Aren't you being a little paranoid now?" I said.

"Not when lives are at stake."

"Then it might be time to change the way you live your life. Do you still think that the actions of a small group of armed individuals can ignite the fire of revolution among the masses and rouse them from centuries of doing nothing?"

"What else would rouse them?"

"I don't know. But certainly not violence. That will make a bad situation worse. Those people who want to cling to power at any cost will use this as an excuse, and—"

"Listen, my friend. You can't teach me anything. You have chosen your way. That's fine. But don't think that peace will win the day if we lose. They will find plenty of excuses for crushing any resistance, be it guns or pens. No-one will escape."

I did not need to be persuaded to admit that he was right. My path was no more honourable than his – remaining a spectator was not a viable alternative to countering force with force. There had to be other ways, more peaceful ways, but as he said, no-one would escape. So it was understandable that he had chosen to defend himself with a gun, rather than a pen. I, for my part, had not even chosen the pen.

"It's too late, anyway," Kemal said. "All the signs are there. The generals are preparing a military coup. When it comes – not if, when – someone has to resist and show them that they can't walk all over this country."

I shuddered involuntarily, not at the words, but at the way he said them. I could imagine the tanks rolling through the streets. And I could also see that he had long since embraced the role of would-be martyr. Now it was even more urgent that I reached Zuhal.

"Please help me find her," I said.

He must have seen my despair. His expression softened and he replied in a mild comforting voice.

"I can't. Not because I don't want to, but simply because I can't. We were together for a long time. But then she joined another unit. In an organization such as ours you don't know everyone, you only know what you need to know."

"But what about Tuba, then? Perhaps she can help?"

"Tuba came here at my request. Trust me, she knows no more about Zuhal than I do. Come on, let me show you something."

He jumped up from the sofa and headed for a door, opened it and stepped aside to give me a full view of the room. It was furnished more austerely than the living room, with a bed, a bedside table and a wardrobe along one wall. The curtains had been carefully closed, the light in the room was dim, but I could make out the shape of a young man lying in the bed, either sleeping or unconscious.

"He was shot and injured," Kemal said. "Not fatally, luckily. But he lost a lot of blood. That was why Tuba was here. Her experience of Caesarean sections proved very useful. He is on the mend now. We should be able to move him soon."

He closed the door. The man on the bed had brought back suppressed images of another young man and of my time in hospital.

"You don't have to move him right away. You can trust me," I said.

222

Kemal appeared to be preoccupied. It was a while before he replied. Then he held out his hand. His grip was friendly.

"It'll be fine. Don't worry about it."

I said goodbye to him and turned to leave the flat.

"Wait a moment," he said. "I can't promise you anything, but I might run into her if the situation demands it."

I gave him the address of the Professor's flat. He repeated it a couple of times to be sure he had memorized it correctly. With this unexpected gesture he resurrected my hopes, a small candle in a sealed room. Not enough to light up the darkness – more like a distant lighthouse glimpsed from turbulent and hostile seas.

19

August 1980

Nothingness is an agonizing vacuum. When you are waiting for a specific event, you often fill your time with countless other activities. But they are all irrelevant, you live for one thing only, you wait for only one thing to happen. Nothingness is an implacable force that poisons, crushes, degrades and tramples everything else. Food becomes tasteless, sleep no longer refreshes you and words make no sense no matter how many times you read the same paragraph. Songs sound sad and spoken words inadequate; old friends are barely tolerated. Even a seductive woman, only half pretending to be holding down her skirt in a gust of wind, does not warrant attention. Nothingness goes hand-in-hand with boredom. When nothing happens, everything becomes an endurance test.

I was optimistic to begin with. She was bound to run into Kemal at some point, take my address and find me. The days passed, and each one found me waiting in anticipation, pricking up my ears at the slightest sound in the hallway. I jumped every time the front door slammed shut. Once, hearing footsteps die down just in front of my door, I ran to open it, only to find the Professor, who remarked that this was the fastest response she had ever had to a visit. She must have read the

224

disappointment in my face. She demanded, and received, an explanation.

That day we spoke about love again.

"Love can be a solitary business," she said. "But the waiting and the pounding heartbeat should be cherished, because it is also exciting – your feelings are set in motion, kept in a state of alert. This stage of love is the most creative and even though you feel lost, hope and faith will help you survive. It peaks when you get your heart's desire, and then, sadly, the intensity has an unfortunate tendency to fade as love becomes routine. Love needs nourishment, challenges and change. If you stumble from time to time and lose your jewel, how much greater is your delight when you find it again?" She envied me and would like to be in my shoes, waiting with strained nerves instead of killing time with dusty books. Secretly, I doubted if she would swap her books for anything.

I had become familiar with the sounds of the other residents. Quick, soft, heavy, light footsteps, coughing, laughter, rows, voices. Things I had not noticed before – had not needed to notice. I settled into a sort of calm once I got to know the sounds and they no longer startled me. Boredom took over. My apartment and the garden became once more my world.

The Professor took matters into her own hands and ordered me to visit my mother. This turned out to be a mistake. I felt even worse when I failed to respond to my mother and brother's well-meant attempts at entertaining me. While they were at work, I sat on the balcony in the summer heat and stared down at the deserted street. Something heavy pressed against my heart, where the bullet had penetrated. I was too young to worry about my heart, but I took other concerns seriously. What if Zuhal had picked this day to seek me out? My every thought magnified this remote possibility until at last I could no longer bear to stare at the street. I went home before my family returned from work and found my flat just as empty as before.

The Professor would not give up. This time she decided that I was in need of a proper change. When had I last had a holiday? I had never been on anything that could be described as one. Precisely, the Professor said. She had a cabin she had inherited, not far from Istanbul, by the Sea of Marmara. I argued neither for nor against it, perhaps I was just grateful that someone was willing to take control of my life. The Professor picked out the clothes I needed and packed them for me. The next day we took the bus to my first holiday destination. It was a dilapidated cabin in a row of equally dilapidated cabins, a few hundred metres from the beach. I half expected the door to fall off its hinges when we opened it and that we would be met with cobwebs and a thick layer of dust, but it was surprisingly clean and tidy inside. The Professor explained that her housekeeper visited once a month to make sure the place remained relatively habitable in case the Professor felt like taking a break from the noise of the city. Here there were no signs of elegant décor, in contrast to the Professor's flat in the city. The cabin's two rooms served as bedroom, living room and kitchen. In addition there was a narrow toilet; as for bathing, you would have to improvise an appropriate solution. The two beds were the only fittings that real money had been spent on. They seemed comfortable when I tried them. Apart from that the rooms were furnished with only the most basic of household effects. This suited me fine. I had never felt comfortable with extravagance.

I spent the first day exploring my surroundings. There was sand, sun, sea, and people everywhere. Not much peace to be had, perhaps, the Professor said, but if you took the trouble to go for a walk, it was always possible to find sunflower fields and the odd deserted beach. We ate lunch at the local restaurant, which consisted of a roof to provide shelter against an unlikely shower of rain, a wooden floor for keeping the sand out and a few worn tables and chairs. The owner caught, grilled and served the fish himself. The food was good and cheap. After lunch the Professor introduced me to my nearest neighbours as a nephew who was taking a well-deserved holiday after a tough year of study. It was an outright lie, but it satisfied the neighbours' curiosity. In the cabin to the right lived an older couple, both retired, who were worried that I might be a fan of loud raucous music. My answer went some way to reassuring them: a single guitar was not such a terrible thing, provided I did not take it into my head to play after midnight. The cabin to the left was let by regular holiday tenants – a charming family: mother, father and two teenage children. The girl of sixteen and the boy of eighteen took after their mother, a gentle beauty. The teenagers chatted freely, talking over each other, delighted to have a young man for their nearest neighbour. They asked what kind of music I liked and were thrilled when I told them about my guitar. People here were clearly interested in music. The Professor did not want to stay the night. She could not tolerate the heat, and mosquitoes were her worst enemy. She already longed for the breeze from the Strait. She tended to come here in the spring and autumn when the heat, mosquitoes and crowds were not so stifling. I escorted her to the bus and before she left she promised to keep her eyes and ears open for anyone knocking on my door.

The family to my left adopted me instantly and without them I would have been a lonely man. I had never met such a harmonious family. The mother was an industrious woman, the head of the family and a superb cook. The father, a modest, almost shy, man, was in love with his wife, his children, his books and his fishing. He also competed with his wife when it came to cooking. His role as a quiet, devoted father was some-thing both unknown and surprising to me. While many would have called him henpecked, his unusual status within the family made me warm to him immediately. The liking was mutual. Many men would not have tolerated the sight of another man near the family's women, but he made it clear that I was always welcome. The relationship between brother and sister was the very ideal of sibling love. While Nehir was the family pet, Deniz was praised to the skies as the family's big brother. Despite all this attention, they were surprisingly unspoilt; two lively teenagers with good manners and respect for other people. I would either be in their cabin or they in mine – at least the teenagers would. On the days I was not invited for dinner, food was brought to me. But usually we would light a fire in the evening and barbeque outside. We would sit around the fire, under the stars, and talk. Before we went to bed, one of them would always ask me to play and sing. They all agreed that my guitar-playing and my singing were unlikely to bring me fame, but the songs were some of the best they had heard. Eventually Nehir took over the singing and brought her own talents to Semra's lyrics and my music. She had a voice that matched her name, which meant "river" – at first soft, calm and shallow, and then exploding with strength; it was wild, deep and unbridled. I was the only one to be surprised at the almost-mature voice of this young girl, a voice with such range; the others merely remarked that she had always been the songbird of the family.

My apathy gave way to a rather melancholy state and I spent my time and energy writing new lyrics and tunes. It was agonizing. The melodies were there in my head, but I struggled with the words. No matter how I twisted and turned them, all the lyrics had the same theme: a hopeless search for love. I lacked Semra's talent for word-play, for making the personal relevant and universal, and for all my lethargy and brooding, my songs weren't really much good.

One day Nehir came to wake me up with freshly baked bread and a pot of tea. I had had a tune in my head and I had drafted some new lyrics. I was less dissatisfied with this one. Feeling an acute urge to be praised, I suddenly wanted to hear her opinion, or rather have her express her enthusiasm. I reached for the guitar, signalled impatiently that she was to sit down and played the tune, but did not sing the lyrics. When I had finished, I stared at her in anticipation.

"Isn't that too much like 'Bridge over Troubled Water'?" she said. There it was: the honesty of a child.

"It was 'Bridge over Troubled Water'," I said.

"No, it wasn't," she laughed.

Then she wanted to see the words. She made many suggestions, transforming the words from an unfinished poem into simple, accessible lyrics. She definitely knew a lot more about music than I did – she told me she had taken private singing lessons and was preparing for her entrance exam to the conservatory. We worked together and at the end of the day we had one complete song. It was not "Bridge over Troubled Water", nothing groundbreaking, but it had a pleasing melody – a little wistful and yet remarkably optimistic at the same time, with a catchy chorus. In the days that followed we went through my earlier tunes. Semra would have been spinning in her grave had she not still been among the living.

Deniz looked like his sister, but they had very else little in common. As far as he was concerned, music was just something you listened to. He lacked his sister's insight, confidence and ambition. On the other hand, he was a conscientious young man fully engaged with Turkey's complex political issues. In many ways he reminded me of my eighteen-year-old self. I enjoyed his company much more than I enjoyed Nehir's. With Nehir I always felt I was walking on thin ice. Even though she behaved impeccably at all times, she was an attractive young girl, very aware of her body and generous when it came to exhibiting it in scanty clothes in the summer heat. Once on the beach in a bikini she became a magnet for men's eyes. I never imagined that she hoped to seduce me, but the uncomfortable feeling remained that she would not have protested if I had taken her in my arms during the hours we spent alone together.

We went for long walks, Deniz and I, and, as the Professor had promised, we discovered sunflower fields and quiet, isolated beaches. We had plenty to talk about. Deniz was a romantic, both politically and emotionally. He did not want to carry on with his studies after his school exams. His dream was to become a trade unionist once he had served an apprenticeship in a factory. Becoming a worker like my brother and Ayfer was something that had never even crossed my mind. It struck me that I had never protested when they joked that it was up to me to gain power and influence and free them from their chains. I respected Deniz for his working-class romanticism and did not attempt to lecture him on the value of higher education. I think he appreciated my ability to listen, because that was what he needed – to talk and to be heard. His family knew very little of his future plans.

Deniz was in love with a girl who had gone away herself, so this holiday was just something to be endured. He was convinced he had found the love of his life. Nevertheless he asked me if that was possible at his age. My mother would not have hesitated to tell him that he would meet another fifty pretty girls at least. I was more diplomatic. He was a sensitive boy with a kind word for everyone and a warm smile that could melt even the iciest heart. At peace with himself and the world around him, he was still learning, and had not yet entered into any unfortunate relationships. But something was about to happen that would have a profound effect on the rest of his life.

It was a lovely evening, with millions of stars lighting up the sky. A cool breeze drifted in from the sea. The heat of the day, which had paralysed us, had faded as dusk fell. Deniz and I decided to seize the opportunity to stretch our legs. The free and unforced conversation, the darkness and the unfamiliar surroundings took us far away from the holiday resort. Suddenly we had reached the motorway and could make out lights from a residential area. We were not entirely sure where we were, but did not worry about getting completely lost as long as we could see signs of civilization. It was a pleasant surprise to find a teahouse on the outskirts of the town. A number of men were watching a football match on the television; others were sitting in the garden, a tangle of fruit trees and tall grass, the air thick with the sounds and scents of summer; it was a garden from the past. There were no lamps outside: you had to make do with the light that escaped through the windows and door of the teahouse. This made it possible to sit undisturbed and soak up an atmosphere that sharpened our languid holiday spirits. Tea was served by a quick but careful waiter, and everything around us was blissful. Deniz was as happy as a little boy to have made this discovery and spoke about bringing his family there the following day to share with them this idyll. The place would probably look like any other in the light of day, but for now it was a pleasant change from sun, sea, sand and run-down cabins.

Everything was so peaceful that we sensed no danger when a group of three young men suddenly appeared out of the shadows. I just about had time to throw a glance at them when they started shouting something that was incomprehensible at first, as any collective noise is, then became clear: "Death to the Communists!"

Fascists! My brain started working feverishly. It is good to feel fear, but not to be numbed by it. I took a quick look around. Two of them had entered the teahouse. I could see through the windows that they were moving from table to table, gesturing and shouting. The third, who had remained in the garden, was still screaming "get down, get down!" Several times in recent months, Fascists had attacked teahouses in the city and executed people at random. I knew that this was about to happen here. No-one would stop them, so we had to get out. I hated the thought of being a helpless victim waiting to be slaughtered, and, for the first time, I wished that I carried a weapon. At the same time I realized that I was not nervous, that I refused to die in this way.

Then I registered the terror-stricken expression on Deniz's face.

"Wait for my signal, then run in a zigzag as fast as you can. Don't lose sight of me, but don't get too close to me, either," I whispered to him.

The Fascist in the garden was coming towards us.

"Get down, get down," he screamed, waving his pistol.

He was no older than Deniz and judging from his reeling walk and vacant eyes, he was high on something. He was nervous, his hands were shaking and I felt a strong urge to punch his nose with my bare fist.

"Get down, get down," he screamed again.

I had warned Deniz not to lie down at any cost. If someone wanted to shoot us, they would have to look us in the eye while they did it. The Fascist appeared to hesitate. He jerked his head impatiently backwards and from side to side as though he were waiting for the others to come to his rescue. Suddenly he turned around and ran to another table.

"Why haven't you lot got down yet?" he shouted.

This was our chance, perhaps the only one we would get.

"Now!" I said to Deniz. We knocked over our chairs as we got up and ran off into the dark.

The shots he fired served only to frighten us. After a while I was struggling to keep up with Deniz, my lungs hurt and I found it hard to breathe. He stopped, shaken and confused, to allow me to catch up. I took his hand and together we started running again. I recalled the time when Zuhal had taken my hand during another escape. Now it was my turn to take charge. We made our way through the fields of tall sunflowers.

It took us forever to find our way back to the holiday resort. The peace here was a surreal contrast to what we had just witnessed. I thought about all the tragedies that occurred every day without us being aware of them. For a while we sat silently on the step to my cabin. Deniz had calmed down. He was no longer scared, but he was angry.

"Someone's got to stop them," he said eventually.

I had heard that one before. Perhaps from Levo.

"I'm going to do it," Deniz added. "By any means necessary."

Not with their means, I ought to have said, but I had neither the urge nor the conviction. Instead I asked him not to say anything to his parents.

I did not sleep that night. My thoughts were with those left behind at the teahouse. The attack had frightened me even more than being hit by a bullet at the university. I never even saw my assailant that day, nor heard the shot being fired. But a few hours ago I had sat defence-less in front of a man and looked into his eyes, a terrorist with a pistol in his hand and murder on his mind. Tolerance was largely an alien concept in our society, but the sheer brutality of killing an innocent person at point-blank range, perhaps in full view of the victim's family, was still shocking. Every time I thought about it, I saw images from Nazi newsreels of German officers amusing themselves by executing prisoners. I couldn't understand how someone would be able to do the same thing only forty years later.

What confused me the most was Zuhal's role in all this. She was a conscious player in an armed conflict. Could she justify killing unarmed men to avenge fallen comrades? Could she banish all perspective and reduce her struggle to a primitive and almost religious blood feud where the only thing that mattered was taking an eye for an eye? I would soon know the answers to my questions. I had eventually worked out when she would come to me. She was waiting for the final show-down. When the tanks rolled through the streets and the enemy started his grand offensive to crush all opposition, when the last entrenchments fell, when there were no longer any safe houses left, then she would come to me. She would not expose me to danger until then. All that was required of me was to be patient and loyal, and to be ready and alert when she came.

I rose at dawn and packed my things. After making sure that the cabin looked relatively tidy, I sat down to a breakfast of bread and cheese, then waited for my friends to stir. They were surprised at my decision to leave so suddenly, but they understood. My vacation was nearing its end, there was not much entertainment here for a young man and they themselves would be going back in a few days. Nehir gave me a warm hug and asked if she could write to me. I scribbled down my address on a scrap of paper. In time and under more normal circumstances we might be able to establish a friendship based on our music. Deniz made do with a simple handshake, perhaps because he was feeling abandoned. The cheerful glint in his eye had been replaced by something darker and more determined.

20

September 1980

On September 11 I went to a wedding. This was a rare occasion for me. Very few in my circle had married – we were still far too young. These weddings were exotic affairs, a fusion of East and West, with the extravagant white dress, a band and the happy couple's first dance on the one hand and, on the other, folk dancing, kissing of hands and cheeks, and decorating the wedding dress with banknotes.

For the first time the invitation bore my name and not my mother's, and it was solemnly delivered by Soldier's own driver. It was for Soldier's wedding. I had no idea why on earth he had invited me. Alright, he liked me, but we were hardly best friends. When I entered the ballroom of the Hilton Hotel, wearing my one suit and tie, I realized that he had invited half of Istanbul. A couple of B-list celebrities and a few actual celebrities could be found amongst the crowds, but the guests of honour were a colonel from the army in full ceremonial uniform and a notorious police superintendent. They were seated behind a long table in front of the stage, surrounded by men who exuded a V.I.P. aura and were attended by a pack of bodyguards. They could only be "the family". I felt like a fish out of water and went on a desperate search for a familiar face, though I rated my chances at close to zero. But he who seeks shall find. Somewhere in middle of the ballroom, in a jungle of dancing guests I collided with Leyla, who, it turned out, was looking for me.

"Oh God, at last," she said. "I was starting to think that you would never turn up. Let's sit down before someone takes our table."

She looked lovely. Her natural hair was on view and she wore an elegant ball gown with a deep slit down the side that revealed most of her long legs. I took her in my arms, swung her around to the music from the band and commented on the risqué dress. She laughed and said that I was not the only shark circling her. A great many fat men with fat wallets had already enquired, but she had been saving herself because she had heard from Soldier that I had been invited. The girls she had arrived with had long since divided up tonight's goldmines, but Leyla had no plans to work tonight, she just wanted to drink, dance and have a good time. When the dance was over she steered me to a small table for two, strategically placed with a view of the whole room. Leyla wanted to know the latest news of my friend and his wife.

Perhaps I should consider a career as a scriptwriter: the flat she had seen Tuba enter belonged to my friend's cousin. The inevitable confrontation between the two men ensued and ended in a fight. At the hospital the wife had repented, but my friend, who was there with a broken arm, had refused to forgive her. She had left the hospital with a broken heart. Seeing her leave in tears my friend had run after her and taken her into his arms, well, into one arm at least. So in the end the couple kissed and made up, and no-one ever knew what happened to the cousin.

It was touching to see Leyla go from being shocked to tearful and then smile broadly at this corny tale that was surely small beer compared to what she experienced on a daily basis. She was clearly entertained by my story, so I did not feel bad for having lied to her. Then she told me everything she knew about some of the guests, scandals that would have shocked even a seasoned hack.

It was time for the newly weds to make their entrance. Soldier looked almost handsome in an impeccable dress suit, and the bride, well, it goes without saying that she was as beautiful as any model.

"Not 'as'. She is a model," Leyla remarked enviously, and then shed tears of joy as the happy couple danced their first dance. Afterwards the couple did a round among the guests to be congratulated, hugged, kissed and showered with gifts of gold, silver and other precious metals.

Selecting a present had proved to be a real headache. I finally settled on *The Godfather* by Mario Puzo, which suited my wallet and Soldier's sense of humour. I was not mistaken. He roared with laughter, gave me a bear hug and said that the film was like an episode from his own life and that Al Pacino was his hero. Leyla, meanwhile, decorated the arm of the bride – already laden with countless chains of gold – with yet another bracelet. Soldier looked as if he would rather be sitting with us, and he chatted and joked until the bride started showing signs of impatience.

"I've got a present for you too," he said and slipped a packet into the pocket of my jacket. Then he gave me another hug and whispered into my ear: "Have a nice trip, brother. But take care of yourself. I see that your liaisons are just as dangerous as mine. Next time, trust me and bring her along with you. I like a woman with balls." Then he was gone. He was an odd man, Soldier, and he had just surprised me by revealing that he read beyond the sports pages.

"He looks happy," I said to Leyla.

"He certainly was very happy when he tried to screw me in the toilet earlier tonight," she sighed.

"The bastard!" I exclaimed. "So what did you do?"

"I told him I was having my period. Fortunately the pig only has a taste for the kind of blood he can beat out of people."

"Are you really having your period?" I asked, nosily.

"Do you want to find out? The toilets here are terribly smart," she said.

"Let's save it for my wedding."

The rest of the evening proceeded as a wedding should – with the guests having a better time than the happy couple. While Soldier and his model bride sat politely and respectfully with their families, Leyla and I danced the night away, floated in each other's arms, rocked and rolled, and, after several drinks, Leyla seduced the whole assembly with a belly dance that revealed more than a little of her stripteasing talents. She stole the show and ended up with at least as many banknotes sticking out of her dress as the bride. But drunken men digging deep in their pockets and even deeper into her cleavage irritated her. The mood grew ugly and created the right setting for a fight, the almost obligatory climax of any wedding. Some were ready to ravish her there and then, and others were ready to defend her virtue.

Everything calmed down when I came over and led her back to our table. These men who a moment earlier would have killed for her favours made way without protest for a man whom she obediently followed. One of the ancient codes of the male world, Thou shalt not offend a woman who has male company, had come to our rescue. We had eaten, drunk, danced and come close to starting a small war, so now it was time to say goodbye. The taxi we took dropped me off first. Leyla would not hear of me paying: I would have plenty of opportunities to pay her cab fares once I had a decent income.

I had not had such a good time for ages. When I sat down on the edge of my bed, I felt pleasantly intoxicated, enough for the room to sway slightly, but not so much that I couldn't pull off my clothes. Soldier's packet was still in my pocket. I opened it. The passports showed good craftsmanship, just as he had promised. To be on the safe side, they were "used", showing many entry and exit stamps as well as desirable visas for a couple of wealthy European countries. I put them under my pillow, slipped under the duvet and drifted off to sleep without worrying about cleaning my teeth.

*

The next morning I woke up with a headache. It was 10.35 a.m. and all was quiet, both inside and outside my apartment. The usual sounds of my surroundings – footsteps on the stairs, doors being opened and slammed, thundering traffic on the main road and horns hooting – had been replaced by an ominous silence. I felt nauseous, thirsty: something was wrong with me and with the world around me. I stumbled out of bed and over to the window. It was overcast outside, dark clouds moved across the Bosporus. They were the only things that did move. Devoid of its usual traffic of large and small vessels, the Strait could now be any stretch of water, and the motorway was deserted. It was as if all life had been spirited away. Mesmerized, I stared at the deserted scene. There was something very peaceful and very scary about what lay before my eyes, as if a deadly weapon had eliminated all life while I slept off my hangover, leaving me, for some reason spared, the only survivor. I waited. Nothing happened. Then, in the distance I heard sirens. I never would have thought I would welcome the sound. The sirens grew sharper and sharper, then a police car raced along the empty street, followed by another. It was not the sight of the first vehicle in the convoy – a quite ordinary jeep with a driver and an officer in the passenger seat – that snapped me out of my reverie, but of the second, third and fourth; in all twenty of them, heavy military vehicles full of uniformed soldiers. I took cover as though I had suddenly found myself under fire. It had begun, the big offensive. The generals had made their final preparations and inspected their troops while I had danced myself into a sweaty lather. Someone had pushed the button while I slept the sleep of the innocent.

Yorgo's colossal radio, which he must have sat in front of during the

239

long nights of the Second World War, craning to hear the latest news from the front, stood silent on the chest of drawers. I had used this powerful short-wave radio to listen to foreign voices and foreign languages from foreign places when boredom threatened to strangle me. It always took time to respond when the tuning dial, worn by Yorgo's touch, was turned, no doubt waiting for some element inside to warm up. I continued to nurture a faint hope. The music of old Istanbul songs would soon fill the air; I would hum along to them while I made tea and smoked a cigarette looking out over the Bosporus. Life would go on as normal.

As was often the case, I was startled when the noise from the radio finally hit my eardrums at full blast. A military march burst into the room. I listened to it without reacting, without turning down the sound, leaning against the chest of drawers, my head slumped between my shoulders. I waited, waited for the march to end, for a voice to take over.

"State of emergency announcement from the headquarters of the 1st Army in Istanbul.

Dear citizens,

Today, September 12, 1980, Turkey's Armed Forces took control of the government and thus fulfilled its duty to protect the Constitution. The National Assembly has been dissolved and all political parties and all forms of political activity have been declared unlawful. We ask all citizens to obey the curfew and remain in their homes. The aim of the military action is to crush illegal extremists, separatist organizations that . . ."

I switched off the radio. I thought about Salvador Allende lying lifeless in a chair, covered by the national flag. Of the Chileans who were stopped in the street and kicked and beaten. The young men and women who were arrested in their own homes and driven to a football stadium.

There were soldiers outside, armed to the teeth, going from house to house, checking their lists and picking up anyone who had joined a demonstration, thrown a stone, written slogans on a wall or sung protest songs. They would gather them like a flock of sheep at the Dolmabahçe Stadium between the Faculty of Technology and the Barbarossa Monument at the Bosporus. Perhaps a soldier's voice would read a pseudo-poem aloud over the tannoy: "What does the roar of cannons signify? Do not doubt, it is the fleet of Barbarossa returning from its last raid."

I imagined the stadium and remembered past football matches; Galatasaray was my favourite team. While at school we had gone to matches, a treat courtesy of our English teacher, who also coached our team. He was a true Englishman, an eccentric who brought his guitar to the classroom to teach us English through music. At matches he would shout "good ball, good ball" every time someone made an incisive pass; apart from that he was a quiet man. He was not much to look at, but he won the most beautiful woman at the school, a teacher from east London, a blue-eyed blonde with a short skirt and long legs. They married, two lonely Brits. An odd match, we used to think, but they did not have much choice in a boarding school far from home. After they were married, they moved to a country that was mostly desert. One day we heard that she had been found dead in the sand. Some said she had an unknown serious illness. Others that her husband had killed her out of jealousy. Such a shame, we all said. I was young: I did not want to die. Not in that stadium.

I was startled by the knock on the door, firm, almost military. I had not had time to scare myself thinking about it. They had come far too soon. The knocking continued as I hurriedly put on my trousers. I needed something to defend myself with. What was it Kemal had said? "Someone has to show them that they can't walk all over this country."

I fetched a knife from the kitchen. I inhaled deeply: I was ready. Just as determined as whoever was knocking, I opened the door.

"Congratulations," the Professor said, and smiled.

I was speechless. All I could do was marvel at her habit of turning up when I expected her least and others most.

"You're cooking, I see." She pointed to the knife. "Why don't we join forces?"

She held up her shopping bag. Moments later she was in the kitchen softly humming an old tune. She worked quickly without talking to me, without commenting on the knife. I made my bed, left the passports under my pillow and cleared up the worst of the mess while she set the table and poured tea.

She started talking again during the meal. She had been outside to break the curfew. Someone had to show resistance. There were street patrols everywhere. Young soldiers, hesitant and nervous, had called her "mother" and told her to go home, but she had gone to the local shop. The shopkeeper was furious. How would people buy their bread now? He did not give a damn who ruled the country as long as they did not dream up such nonsense as curfews. While they were chatting another patrol arrived, headed by a young lieutenant. He was polite but firm. The shop had to shut: no-one was allowed out today. He chose to overlook the old lady. Besides, no-one would starve to death because of a one-day curfew. They could make no promises, obviously, but the army would do everything to avoid unnecessarily inconveniencing "our dear citizens". She mimicked the lieutenant with glee, enjoying herself as if this was all a game.

"Have you seen anyone being taken?" I asked, to stress the gravity of the situation.

"No. They didn't want me and there is no-one else around, not even a cat."

"It's bound to happen. They're gathering people at the stadiums."

"This is no banana republic."

"That's what they said about Chile."

"We have a more civilized army." She smiled her crooked smile. No teasing this time, just sadness. Then she leaned forward and took my hand.

"Don't worry. Not yet. We'll have to wait and see. My guess is they'll go about things quietly."

"They're making a lot of noise on the radio."

"They always do. The last time they called it 'Operation Sledge-hammer'. But they carry out their sledge-hammering at night. Remember, this is my third coup."

After eating we played chess in the garden and talked. It was another world, one that military marches and the state of emergency could not breach. Gardens have always played an important role in my life, I thought. The Professor told funny stories from previous coups. About the time a group of completely innocent and harmless writers and academics were accused of having sabotaged a boat that had been in dry dock for ages and of having started a fire in the Culture House during a performance of "The Crucible". The Culture House reminded her of a joke. I had never heard the Professor tell jokes before; anec-dotes yes, but not jokes. There was this self-made millionaire who thought money could buy him anything. He was getting married and was looking for a suitable venue for his wedding. One day he drove past the Culture House and liked what he saw. He went inside and asked how much it would cost to hire rooms for a wedding. No, unfortunately, the rooms were only used for cultural events. He was disappointed. A few days later he drives past the building and sees a poster for "The Marriage of Figaro". He is furious, storms inside shouting: "So I wasn't good enough for you, but you'll hire out your rooms to this Mister Figaro, eh?"

"The day we all know our Figaro there will be no more coups," she said. It was a new take on the subject. The academic's perspective.

If we could have sat in this garden, never to be disturbed, we would have enjoyed everlasting peace. Or perhaps not. The jokes would dry up, we would get bored with playing chequers. We humans are social animals. We might as well go out, sit on the steps outside our house and chat to the soldiers on patrol.

It was not possible to talk to them. They looked with suspicion at anyone who ventured out in front of their house or on to their balcony. Apart from making a few half-hearted attempts at chasing people back inside, they were silent. But they were definitely worth watching. Farm boys, wide-eyed and shy, marching in close formation as if to seek shelter and protection from the dangers of the big city. They held hands on a few occasions, oblivious that it could mean they were gay. There were the ones who carried their guns dutifully but as though bearing a heavy burden. Others were more self-assured, from the smaller and larger towns around the country, and they were much less predictable in their behaviour. Some made no effort to hide that they longed for the end of their watch, for food and a bed. They looked bored, their helmets were shoved back, their guns slung nonchalantly over their shoulders. Others walked, fingers on triggers, with angry, prying eyes, ready to kill to earn themselves a medal. And then there were a few who smiled, winked to young women and hummed revolutionary songs to signal to those in the know that they did not support those behind the coup.

We went back inside in time for the evening news. This time we went to the Professor's flat, where she had a television. We sat down in front of the screen with cups of tea. I had not looked forward to a T.V. programme with so much dismay and anticipation since the heyday of "Dallas". After the obligatory introductory sequence – national anthem, flag-hoisting and sundry announcements – five generals sat down behind a table. The black-and-white images ("nothing will be thrown out until it has been used up" was the Professor's motto) made every-thing look old-fashioned, as though what was taking place on the screen did not belong to our time but to an unknown past. The Chief of Staff made a speech, while the other four men from the four branches of the armed forces sat like ornaments or trained animals. Their efforts to communicate with the viewers were limited to looks and gestures that at times gave the impression that they were attempt-ing mass-hypnotism, unless of course they were simply trying to entertain themselves with a little game of "who blinks first". The speaker did not disappoint us. His commander-on-campaign manners were highly amusing.

"A tree stump would have more charisma," the Professor remarked.

According to the Chief of Staff, elected representatives of the people, who had been sent home before they had time to open the National Assembly after the summer recess, were to blame for the state of the nation. And the terrorists, of course. No-one else had anything to fear. This point was relatively easy to understand. We had yet to hear his most astonishing remark: "What will you have us do? Shall we feed them in prison forever rather than hang them?" When we switched off the television and watched him fade from the screen, I wished that he could disappear from our lives in the same way – at the push of a button.

My brother arrived early the next morning. I had politely declined the Professor's invitation to spend the night in her flat. My initial bewilderment, caused by the feeling that I was alone in the world and faced by a huge enemy, had eased off and been replaced by anger. What authority did these stuffed military shirts have to rob us off our already restricted freedoms? None. They just had more guns and ammunition than anyone else. This was the only thing that turned them into patriots and the opposition into terrorists. And these incompetent individuals, who had undergone their brain-shrinking training by an army that had long planned on civil war, would decide our fate. I lay down to sleep. Against all the odds I slept surprisingly well.

My brother had come to collect me. My mother was worried about my safety. I did not try to argue with him; he was just the messenger. After a brief goodbye to the Professor, who agreed that the most comforting place right now was in a mother's arms, we set out in my brother's borrowed car.

Life in the streets appeared to go on as normal, but only on the surface. The curfew was suspended between six in the morning and midnight. I remembered what the Professor had said: it would all happen under the cover of darkness. Through the car windows I saw men and women, buildings, shops, banks and commandos wearing blue berets flashing past. What was really going on inside the heads of the people on the streets? Were they anxious or relieved? Or were they indifferent, like the Professor's shopkeeper, living their lives in accordance with the motto: "The snake that doesn't touch me can live forever"?

The complacency that had dulled this nation's senses for centuries was surely part of the answer. Zuhal would no doubt hate this thought and call it defeatist, but as we drove through the city I did not see columns of the people's army marching to face the enemy. The only thing that marched forwards, invisible and silent, was the fear of anything that signalled authority. Not all that long ago a theatre company, dressed in home-made uniforms, had stopped passers-by at Beyoglu, carried out body searches and humiliated people with strange orders. No-one had protested or asked them who they were. The actors had been wearing uniforms, it did not matter what kind. Uniforms were there to be feared, even fake ones. I sensed that the people now walking on the other side of the window were scared of everything and anything, and were ultimately relieved that someone in a uniform had taken control.

246

"Has there been any resistance in the factories?" I asked.

"Sporadic, as far as I know. Pickets at a few sites. Rumour has it that most of the trade union leaders have already been locked up inside the barracks of the 66th armoured division. I drove past the fence this morning and it was teeming with soldiers and vehicles. Something is definitely going on."

This was no banana republic. Who needed football stadiums when they had already invested so much in military garrisons?

"They've taken Dakan," my brother said, "and some other boys from around here. No-one knows where they are. They can keep them in custody for up to three months now. You know what that means, don't you?"

His expression was serious, and that was unusual for him. He had always been the joker of the family. Once he pretended to have died after I had hit him and did it so successfully that I fell for it and wept by his side. He loved to tease and wind me up, always with glint in his eye, always good-humoured, a quality I probably did not possess to the same extent.

Dakan was more his friend than mine – the two of them had linked arms and carried me up the stairs when I came home from the hospital. We both knew that three months' custody meant torture and abuse in a place where they might already have hung the notorious poster: "There is no God here."

*

The figure in the black coat looked much older than she remembered, but despite the distance she was fairly sure that it was the same man. Though the only detail she could make out was the thick moustache that hung from his upper lip and looked like it was dragging his whole body down with it, that was enough for her to read his pain and sadness. His trademark long black coat, which had once fluttered in the wind at the front of demonstrations, now hung like a ragged cloak on his emaciated body. Under different circumstances she would not have hesitated to put this impression from a distance down to illness or ageing. But his body language of humiliation and naked fear, like that of a cornered animal, helpless in the shocking knowledge that its freedom was forever lost, left little room for doubt about his fate. She had recently seen far too many images of broken members of the resistance on T.V. to be mistaken. He *was* a cornered animal, and his entire being screamed it out: anyone who comes near me is walking into a trap.

A bus stopped in front of her, blocking her view while bleary-eyed passengers stepped down and others, who had been waiting alongside her, pushed towards the entrance doors. When the bus drove off, she was the only one left standing there. Across the street, at the corresponding stop, the man in the black coat was swaying between |two alert young men who were surveying the surroundings with sharp eyes.

Zuhal knew she had been a whisker away from being captured. Only her vigilance had saved her. From the moment she had received Kemal's message via an intermediary she had had a bad feeling about the whole situation. Kemal's instructions had been clear: Tuba and the man from the trade union were to join her group. Both were reliable people who could no longer operate alone. Zuhal needed no persuading. She knew them both well: Tuba was her friend from university and the trade unionist was a trustworthy individual with working-class roots, which was a rarity in their circle. They had been committed to the cause during a difficult period, but they had never before participated in an armed struggle. That was something that would normally have labelled them a security risk – it was no secret that police kept an eye on revolutionary sympathizers in order to track down active militants, who were otherwise extremely hard to find – but Zuhal found it hard to believe that Kemal had not assessed the risks. He must have felt forced to make this decision and, with no opportunity to discuss the matter with him, all she could do was meet them.

She had taken the precautions she thought necessary; she had dressed for the occasion as a meek, working-class woman, with a head-scarf, glasses, discreet make-up and a worn handbag, but decided to leave her Browning at home. If she walked into a trap, her chances of shooting her way out of it were negligible anyway. She had arrived earlier than arranged and stayed at a distance to recce the area and evaluate the situation.

She felt calm, without fear or panic. The man in the black coat must have spoken under torture and taken his torturers with him to the meeting place. She did not blame him – on the contrary, in a strange way she wished she could comfort him. Her composure might be down to her belief that she had a high pain threshold and to a simple conviction she held fast to: no-one would ever be able to break her. But she was terrified of being captured. A life in a cage was unthinkable and might be harder to bear than physical torture.

She now faced a dilemma. She could leave the meeting point and let an unsuspecting Tuba walk right into a trap or stay here and try warn her. Zuhal strained to identify more enemies in the crowd. In vain. Apart from the two fine specimens who guarded the man in the black coat, they were all well camouflaged. They had clearly learned the art of blending in.

She spotted Tuba walking down the opposite side of the street, tall and thin, her slender figure clearly visible in the otherwise homogenous crowd. There was still time to cross the street, prevent her from reaching the bus stop by pretending to be an old friend meeting her by chance, and then turn around with her and walk her to safety. She almost smiled at the thought that it might work out after all and took a step forward. Two strong hands stopped her.

"What are you doing here?" an authoritarian voice, accustomed to interrogations, demanded.

Zuhal knew she had to play her part to perfection and, to begin with, avoid eye contact with the two men who might otherwise detect hesitation in her eyes or recognize her features from all the wanted posters. Shyly she looked down at the hands holding her.

"I'm waiting for the bus. Have I done something wrong?"

"Perhaps," one of the men said. "The bus has just left. Why didn't you take it?"

She searched for a sensible reply as she watched Tuba's progress towards the man in the black coat. The way she tossed back her hair and increased her speed revealed that she had already spotted him, the man who matched the description she must have been given in advance. But she did not have Zuhal's experienced eyes and was blind to the danger signs.

"That bus was packed," Zuhal said. "I'm not in a hurry. I decided to wait for the next bus so I could get a seat."

The time was right for a quick glance. She turned her head randomly to the right. The man's skin was like a rugged moonscape, scarred from "oriental acne" as it was known in the region he was probably from. Nevertheless his eyes were most revealing: hard, with a penetrating stare, always hunting for public enemies. She smiled bashfully at him.

When she turned, Tuba was leaning towards the man she had come to meet, as if they were having a private conversation. Then she froze in that position and disappeared from sight behind several men who had disengaged themselves from the crowd and made a beeline for her. A sky-blue Ford minibus appeared out of nowhere and hid them from view. Zuhal and the two men with her stopped to watch the scene that was unfolding in front of them, and when the moment had passed, the man with the horror-movie face turned to her in a renewed attempt to make eye contact.

"Do you know what's going on over there?" He had bad breath and an incurable Kurdish accent.

"Me? No."

She had already started her litany of denial. Deny everything: her name, her address, her contacts, weapons depots, everything. For a second she imagined herself in the torture chamber, tearing off her blindfold, spitting at the scarred Kurd in disgust. The other man's voice snapped her out of it.

"Let's go!"

"What about her?" the Kurd tightened his grip around her arm.

"Her? Forget her," the other man said. "We've got more than enough to do today."

The Kurd released her arm reluctantly, unwillingly, and ran after his friend. When he was halfway across the street, he glanced over his shoulder, disappointed, as though he had been deprived of something he had wanted.

Zuhal waited until the Ford minibus had driven off as quickly as it had arrived. Then she took a cab home.

Beams of sunlight poured through a gap in the layers of cloud and hit the window in violent haste, bouncing off at all angles. The strong reflection blinded her, so she moved to see if the curtains were open or closed. She was in the habit of leaving them open, but now she could not remember if she had left them closed, as they were now. For the first time she feared the presence of the enemy. Had they taken Kemal?

Her superior, the link between Kemal's group and hers, was the only person who knew this address. Had Kemal talked and given him up, and had he, in turn . . . ? She needed to concentrate and gather her thoughts. What next? The solitude she normally enjoyed suddenly became her worst enemy. She felt terribly alone, with nothing left to cling to.

"Is anything the matter, my dear?"

It was an old woman whose eyes held genuine concern. Zuhal must have looked ill, which was precisely how she felt. For a brief moment she was tempted to say "yes", lean against the old woman's body, walk a little with her and talk about everyday things, anything to take her mind off a world in turmoil.

"No, auntie," she replied. "But many thanks for your concern."

"Go home, my dear. Lie down, have a rest."

Home? As well as the details of the meeting with Tuba and the trade union man, Kemal's messenger had also given her Oak's address. Even though she had no idea how he had found Kemal, this was a clear sign that he had not given up hope and was still looking for her. A moment of weakness on her part had given false hope and foolhardy courage to a man who could never play a significant role in her life. Yet somehow the message filled her with a strange joy. She had a place to go if the pressure became too great, but not until then. Right now she had to pull herself together, forget about the blasted curtains and take responsibility for her own life and the lives of her team.

The car was in the street where she had parked it the day before. She unlocked it, got into the driver's seat and put the key in the ignition. To her relief it started immediately. While she sat there listening to the calm humming of the engine, she was reminded of the first driving lesson she had taken from a comrade, fumbling through it until she grew confident enough to drive on her own. And how, in a market square, he had taught her the art of stealing a car right from under the owner's nose. Cars might be easy to steal, but they were also unreliable, like weapons that jammed and people who betrayed you, so she had to be sure it would work if she needed to make a quick getaway. She just hoped that the engine would start as smoothly the next time. She left the key in the ignition and the doors unlocked and wondered if a twist of fate would see a second thief steal an already-stolen car.

Feeling optimistic, Zuhal flicked the switch, but the light failed as it always did and the stairwell remained in darkness. She inhaled deeply several times, trying to lower the adrenalin that had disturbed the rhythm of her breathing and heartbeat, and when she had regained an acceptable balance, she listened for any movement on the floors above. Everything was surprisingly quiet, but she chose not to take this as a sign of danger. She attacked the stairs at speed to deny herself time for any more distracting thoughts and reached the second floor within a few seconds. When she stopped outside her own front door, her breathing rapid but silent, she allowed herself one final thought: if they were waiting inside, she would never manage to get back to the car. Her head finally clear, she bent down and put her ear to the door. When she was finally convinced that nothing would break the silence in the immediate future, she put the key in the lock and turned it.

21

October–December 1980

The days passed quietly. My mother was pleased to have me home. She pottered around me as I sat on the divan with my books or at the table busy with dull translation jobs, like a kind of paterfamilias of whom no-one had any major expectations. She was finally convinced that I was not involved in any uprising against the state, but could not understand why I did not want to resume my studies at the university now that the occupation, according to her, was over. Her expression displayed a mother's patience and tolerance towards a stubborn child when I insisted that the occupation was ongoing, that soldiers had taken the place of Fascists.

I wish I could have brought her there, even though she would never have made it past the guards without a valid student card. The entrance had become a military guard post, a kind of Checkpoint Charlie, complete with the same eerie atmosphere, where anyone who approached was examined and treated as a potential terrorist. Inside the walls you could feel in your bones that you were being watched, a sensation that made you treat all strangers as possible police informers. It was like going to jail voluntarily without knowing if your stay would be temporary or permanent. The Professor was no longer teaching there. She had been forced to retire, while several other academics had been dismissed.

"I've tried to go back," I said to my mother, "but I always come to the conclusion that the ban on students' beards is completely insane."

While my brother laughed at this understatement, my mother looked puzzled. She was not particularly up to speed with the humour of the younger generation.

"But, son, why are you upset about that? You don't even have a beard,"

I said that I had just made up my mind to grow one.

I did indeed grow a beard, and with it gained a valid reason for not attending classes. After the best part of a month, I started wondering whether the generals might not know best after all. A beard did not suit me. It needed trimming and without constant attention it curled in every direction. It weighed heavily on my face, looked false in the mirror and itched infernally. If Semra, who refused to kiss me when she returned from her self-imposed exile, was to be believed it suited me just as much as a beard would suit her. I admitted that I preferred her without one and to satisfy them all I shaved there and then, to my mother's and Semra's delight. I kept my moustache as a memento.

Semra's laughter warmed my soul, and showed me how much I had missed her. She had first come to see me at the Professor's and then turned up at my mother's, having decided that the coup was a good enough reason to break off her fast – as she referred to staying away from me. This had nothing to do with religion, she assured me, even though meditation had proved very helpful. Oh, there was no need for me to get alarmed: it was no different from sitting still and staring at the wall. She brought with her all her warm and tireless optimism at a time when we needed it most. I ended up competing with my mother for her attention.

We went for a walk. There was a chill in the air, as you would expect in October. The noise from the wind drowned out the roar of the traffic from the motorway and lent an impression of serenity that you did not usually associate with a big city. We sat under a tree and the leaves fell and mingled with the foliage that lay beneath like a soft quilt.

"Are you scared that she might come while you're gone?" Semra said.

"If she comes and finds I'm not there, she will come back. Besides, I would know. The signs will tell me when she's coming."

Semra looked at me. How could I explain to her that I had not taken leave of my senses, that I was not talking gibberish?

"You speak as if you're waiting for the Messiah," she said.

"Waiting makes you wise."

She nodded in agreement. This was a notion she found easier to accept. Then she said, "I want to go away."

She studied my reaction with an insistent but slightly uncertain gaze. Perhaps she was gambling on the hope that I would say, "Don't go." The thought that she might leave for somewhere far away upset me. She was a part of me. Without her my life, such as I knew it, would start to unravel and nothing would be the same again. As long as she was within reach, I was safe. If she left, I would lose my last link to a time of my life that had now passed.

"Where?" I asked.

"Anywhere. Somewhere abroad."

I thought of the passports lying under my pillow in Yorgo's flat. She was like me. We both regarded leaving as the last resort.

"I've had enough of this country," she continued. "Enough of seeing pictures of corpses splashed across the front pages."

I could not blame her. I had stopped watching T.V. and reading the newspapers. They had become the mouthpiece of the generals.

"But most of all I'm scared of finding your bloodstained face in the papers one day. I know it could happen. I know that you would do anything for her."

She was right. We were co-conspirators. Anyone who helped, hid or loved a terrorist could be shot and tortured too. It could happen.

Semra was awarded a scholarship and a place at a university in England, not Cambridge or Oxford, somewhere less-well known. She would start the following autumn, but thought that was a long time to wait and grew impatient. Her enthusiasm and obvious excitement hurt me. England would blind her with its picturesque villages, its museums crammed full of stolen treasures and its literary heritage no other country could match. In the not-too-distant future an Englishman with a dry sense of humour might charm her with lines from a dead poet after a few beers in a pub. I struggled to hide my jealousy, but she had developed an uncanny ability to read my mind. She asked what was wrong, laughed at my discomfort and said she was unlikely to meet anyone wittier than me or with more poetry up their sleeve. She could have said plenty of other things which were not nearly as flattering, but who wants to be told the whole truth?

*

In the middle of December she surprised me with the news that she would be leaving at the end of the month. She had applied for and secured a job as an au pair. She was sorry she had felt the need to do this in secret; she had been afraid that I would try to discourage her. Desperate, with time so short, I tried to make amends for all the hurt I as a confused young man had caused her: a single rose from a flower stall, a book she had mentioned that she liked, tickets to a good film, a song dedicated to her, a friendly kiss . . . All this made her smile. I realized too late how easy it was to make her happy.

I stood in front of the mirror that night, two days before New Year's

Eve, combing my hair just as carefully as when I was sixteen, satisfied that keeping my moustache had been an extremely good decision – it gave my face a more distinguished appearance and helped to hide the last rumpled traces of adolescence. A little later I left the house, pleased with my appearance and ready to escort Semra to her evening flight to London. I wished we could celebrate New Year's Eve together, in Çiçek Pasajı for example, where I had found myself the year before with a drunken old woman, a gypsy and a band of musicians.

It was dark and cold outside, with the odd cotton-wool snowflake in the air. More snow had been forecast; I hoped it would not fall until Semra's plane had taken off. People had hunkered down in their homes and abandoned the street to the darkness, which was never properly challenged by the gloomy light from the street lamps. The bus stop was some distance away, but I liked walking in the frost, feeling it nip my skin. I saw two men standing in front of a Ford minibus stamping their feet. Smoke billowed from the exhaust pipe as the engine ticked over. More people who preferred the fresh air to the oppressive heat of a car, I thought. Perhaps I already knew that they were waiting for me when I saw them stamping impatiently on the ground.

No-one would react if I called out and I would be shot in the back if I ran. I walked towards them. They blocked my path and studied my face carefully to see if I met their expectations. Someone opened the car door from the inside and said, "Get in."

I did as I was told and sat down opposite him. The minibus started as soon as the two men outside had climbed into the back seat. The man sitting facing me no longer wore his gold-rimmed glasses – perhaps I had only imagined the frames when we had last met. This time he was wearing large, round plastic spectacles. It was hard to see if his shoes were Italian because they were covered in mud. His formerly round face was haggard now, the eyes behind the glasses tired, and he was wearing two days'-worth of stubble.

"We've met before, I think?" he said, and looked at me for confirmation. "Do you remember Sevim? He's back in my basement. Calls himself something else now, a man's name this time. Still stubborn. I like him."

I turned, looked out of the window and wondered why I had not been blindfolded. I did not want to talk, but I would have to say something soon.

"All we're missing now is Zuhal, eh?" he said, certain that he would get a response this time. They did not have Zuhal, so I could talk.

"Are you busy at the moment? Do you have enough time to torture all the people you're picking up these days?" I said. I sensed a restless movement behind me. He stopped the two men with a warning glance.

"We don't do things like that," he said amiably. "In fact, I vote for the Social Democrats. Well, I voted for the Social Democrats," he corrected himself.

"I never had much time for them myself," I said.

He laughed. I felt like laughing too, because I was not scared. I had nothing to say and nothing to fear.

"Tuba says you're not involved, it's just love. Should I trust her?"

So they had Tuba. And through her me. I still had nothing to be scared of.

"I imagine people say a lot of strange things under torture."

"She also says that Kemal broke off contact with her because of you. You've cost us a great deal, you understand. Do you want to see Tuba? You've got to see Tuba. She's become very chatty lately."

He would show me Tuba, battered, bloody, the soles of her feet torn to shreds, wires attached to her nipples and genitals.

"What good would it do?" I asked.

"Oh, who knows? You go in. You see. You start to think: 'Is it worth it?' You want to be left in peace. But there's a price to be paid for peace."

"What price?"

"Let's just say it's not cheap. At the moment it might be a shot in the dark. But you never can tell when it comes to love. She will never go to her parents. But she might come to you. You will contact us. Yes, that will be hard to live with. On the other hand, you'll be saving her life. What's a relatively short spell in prison compared to a bullet in the head?"

He spoke like an old sage, a little weary of life. Or perhaps he was just tired of turning the handle on the generator.

"A relatively short spell in prison?"

"A civilian government after military rule would have to introduce an amnesty."

"She will hate me for the rest of her life."

"Perhaps, perhaps not. That's the risk you have to take."

"What if I can't take that risk?"

"I have nothing against you. You can get on with your life. But her?"

He shrugged indifferently. The minibus had stopped in the car park where I had once planted a fleeting kiss on Zuhal's lips. We were standing outside the vehicle. The plumes of breath frost rose from our mouths.

"You can still see Tuba if you like," he said.

"What good would it do?"

"You might be right. What good would it do? Besides, I'm tired. Time to go home. See you soon."

The two other men had gone inside the building. He got back in the minibus.

"Take me home," he ordered the driver.

"Happy New Year," he said to me.

I stuffed my hands into the pockets of my winter coat, walked down the hill and hailed a cab at the main road.

*

"She left fifteen minutes ago," Semra's grandmother said.

I turned to leave.

"Don't," the old woman said. "She's grown used to the idea that you never come."

Outside the snow had started falling more heavily.

Part Three

22

February 1981

I don't know why you didn't come to say goodbye. You must have had a good reason. I prefer to think that you could not bear to say goodbye, that you were scared to show your feelings, afraid that you might cry. Do you ever cry? I do, frequently. I must admit that I cried a little when I fetched pen and paper and sat down to write. So if you notice stains on the paper, they are tears, not drops from a drink I have spilt. "The little angel" has just fallen asleep. She really is an angel, little Victoria. We liked each other from day one. Even though my experience with children is minimal, she is easy to get on with, very polite and obedient. And – to tell tales – desperate for attention. We talk a great deal. She laughs at my mistakes and loves to correct them in a charming, precocious manner. Those who claim that the best way to learn a foreign language is in bed with a stranger are wrong. Nothing beats a child as far as that is concerned. She is so trusting, my little friend. I get broody and want to have children of my own when she falls asleep in my arms listening to the Turkish fairy tales my grandmother told me when I was a little girl. Her mother is a rather reserved woman, always busy with one thing or another. She calls me "darling" and is terrified of coming across as patronizing. Hurrah! Someone is finally calling me "darling". Should I try my luck with girls, do you think? I see little of the father and so I have little to say about him. He pretends I'm not there and avoids talking to me directly. Any messages for him must be passed through the mother. "Nannies" might be off-limits to husbands in England, for all I know. So the chances of him harassing me sexually or indeed in any other way in my room at night are currently looking slim.

Besides, I have plenty to do. Taking and picking up the child from nursery, cleaning, shopping, cooking and so on. Life as an au pair is not exactly a "piece of cake", you know. (You'll have to get used to a bastard language. Besides it sounds quite "posh" – don't you think?) However, despite it all, I have managed to visit the British Museum. It is incredible how far they have gone in stealing what belongs to others (I'm still under your influence, do you see?). Tons of stone from antiquity on display, brought here from Egypt, Greece and Asia Minor! One room is dedicated to a Greek monument "brought to Britain with permission of the Sultan". The Sultan in question was known to have wondered what on earth the infidels were going to do with all those stones. The term "stone" is the Sultan's and not mine, just so you know. Talking of stones, a little anecdote: When the poet known as "the Fisherman from Halikarnasos" was exiled to the Aegean Sea, he was horrified to learn that the monument had been brought to England. So he writes a letter to the British Museum and requests politely that the treasure is repatriated as it best suits the deep blues of the Mediterranean. The reply is swift. "We have considered your request and we will be painting the room where the monument is displayed blue." And the room really has been painted blue! You cannot say the English have no sense of humour. In order to gain further experience in this area (to your express horror), I also visited a couple of pubs in London. However, I will be an old woman before I make any friends. The men mainly stick with other men and seem to manage very well without female company. The only man who plucked up the courage to approach my table turned out to be a Turkish Cypriot. He owns a restaurant and is as interesting as the labyrinthine London Underground. Ten minutes later he had offered me a job as a waitress in his restaurant. What do you think? Don't say anything. I know it sounds creepy.

But God and everyone else know that I need some money before I go on to Wales.

Otherwise it is lovely to wander around without bumping into a general here or an armed unit there. I recommend it.

Please write back. A long letter, if you please. Take care of yourself (I mean it!).

Hugs and kisses.

Semra.

The letter was addressed to Yorgo's flat, so she must have guessed that I would return there before the spring. I had already decided to move back when a change in my family circumstances occurred and made the decision for me. At the beginning of January my brother was called up for his first round of national service as part of that summer's draft. His worst nightmare was coming true. He was restless for days, the mere thought of it tormented him; he lost his spark and became a shadow of his former self. I could not imagine him as a recruit in the coup-maker's army, but I tried to keep quiet because I had the option of deferring my national service for as long as I was a student. He was just a working man and had no option but to serve. My mother tried to offer the consolation that generation after generation had offered before her – the idea that military service was a patriotic duty. She received little by way of response. In the end it was she who came up with the first and only practical solution. Her youngest son would go to Germany, to her brother, who had already been living there for years with very little contact with his family in the old country. Anyone who worked and lived abroad was entitled to postpone his national service.

She did not enjoy contributing to the break-up of her small family, but a mother could not expect to keep her sons at home forever. She proved to be true to her word, arranging everything, writing immediately to her brother, who was only too happy to be of use for once and promptly issued an invitation. With this in hand my mother could argue tooth and nail for a deferment at the local recruitment office. And when it was time to apply for a passport I asked casually if it might not be a good idea for my mother to travel with my brother. Going abroad just once in her life had always been her dream. My thoughtfulness made the tears well up in her eyes and she kissed me, unaware that I was also thinking of myself. I would have one thing less to worry about once she was far beyond the borders of Turkey.

The day of their departure I stood waving on the platform as the train for Germany rounded a bend and disappeared from view. I was thinking that I could now move back to Yorgo's flat without worrying about men in Ford minibuses tracing me through my family. Now I could begin the final period of waiting. However, I was no longer sure if I wanted Zuhal to return to me. I had grown used to living without her. I longed instead to be on the train with my mother and brother as it left Central Station.

Then I received Semra's letter. It arrived at a time when I needed a distraction. I wrote back and told her about my dreams – clichés such as world peace, equality, brotherhood and solidarity. And about a future where I could feel and hear music in a way that no-one had before. And my dream of loving without being disappointed or disappointing the other person. I did not mention Zuhal. When Semra was reading my letter no shadows should fall between us. It should bring me to mind like the scent of home. Our letters should build the foundations of a solid friendship, raised above convention, intimate and special, something that would belong to us alone.

The second letter was from my mother and my brother. They had each written a section. My mother was thriving in the little town just outside Frankfurt where her brother lived. They got on surprisingly well after all the years apart and as he was a life-long bachelor he had invited her to stay for as long as she wanted. My mother wondered if the manager at the factory where she worked might be prepared to extend her leave. She did not miss her home country because the town was almost a "Little Turkey". The sight of our fellow countrymen and women in their colourful, traditional clothes parading down the main street of the town on Sundays was a fine spectacle. The only thing she missed was her eldest son. My brother spoke of one thing only: German girls. His latest news was that he had got a job in the tyre factory where my uncle worked. There were still jobs available if I was interested.

I had always enjoyed receiving and writing letters, but I had not realized how important they could be in your life. My loved ones were so far away that this was the only way my need for communication could be met. I obviously could not afford a telephone. The Professor, who eventually discovered my letter-writing activities, sought to improve the quality of my writing by lending me a volume of Rosa Luxemburg's letters to her beloved. Up until then I had thought of Rosa Luxemburg as a hard woman of action. The raw passion in her letters surprised me.

It was the third letter that confused me. The envelope revealed no sender. I sat down at the table, afraid to open it. The handwriting on the envelope was quite ordinary, with no distinguishing features. I tried to recollect Zuhal's handwriting. If it turned out to be Zuhal or Kemal who had written the letter – no-one else apart from Semra and my family knew this address – it was unlikely to offer mildly amusing, everyday stories from the underground. It would be bad news, I could feel it, but no matter how much I stared at the envelope, it did not reveal its secrets. I picked it up, held it tight and carefully tore it open, as if the paper inside might spring to life and fly out of my hands.

The letter was stripped of any attempt at a greeting. The language was factual, a little formal and purely informative. I was right about the envelope containing bad news. Nehir was writing to me about her brother. I had forgotten her, forgotten that I had given her my address, which was why her name had not even crossed my mind when I wondered who the sender might be. And, as though she had anticipated that I would struggle to remember her, she began by introducing herself as "Nehir, from the holiday resort".

The rest of the letter was about Deniz. He had grown strange after the holiday, introverted and quiet. She could not recognize him as her brother and for the first time in their life she suspected him of hiding something from her. It was this suspicion that had made her search his room. The pistol she found under the folded clothes in his wardrobe gave her the relief of an explanation more than it frightened her. She could not betray him by warning their parents, so she confronted him instead. At first Deniz was angry, accusing her of being a horrible snitch, but then he calmed down and told her about that terrible night at the teahouse. That was when she understood why he had started speaking about me as though he owed me something. She understood his frustration. He had feared for his life and been humiliated, and he was scared and angry. However, she could not think of her gentle brother as someone who would conceal a lethal weapon. She tried to comfort him, tried to be there for him to prevent him from doing something he might later regret. It made little difference. He grew increasingly restless and distant; he spent his time with new friends who wore army jackets and looked too serious and sombre for their age. He returned home late from raids, his hands stained with paint from writing anti-Fascist slogans on walls. One evening he came back in a very agitated state. He had to tell someone what had hap- pened, so he told Nehir that there had been an exchange of fire with the Fascists and that he hoped some of the bastards had been hurt. For the first time, Nehir had been truly afraid. That was when she decided to contact me. And then everything happened at once. Their father had a heart attack and she spent all hours at his bedside. The family was preoccupied with her father's slow recovery, and she barely had a chance to speak with Deniz, who had become even more silent and secretive after the military coup. Nehir did not automatically interpret this as a bad sign, because her father's illness had affected Deniz just as much as her. He went out less at night and pretended that he had nothing to say about the coup, even though everyone seemed to have an opinion about the country's future. However, one evening he failed to come home and as the family began to worry there was a knock on the door. A heavily armed police and army unit stormed into their flat and ransacked it. They behaved like an invading army, sneering and shouting orders, showing no respect and refusing to answer any questions about Deniz's whereabouts and what they were looking for. Unmoved by her mother's pleas and tears, the officer who was leading the raid snarled: "Just be thankful your son's not dead, woman. He was arrested for being a member of an illegal armed organization."

Deniz spent a month in police custody before being transferred to a military prison at the beginning of February. The ban on visits had just been lifted. Her father would unable to cope with the stress and her mother refused to see her son behind bars. Nehir disagreed with her mother and felt it was important to show Deniz that the family was on his side. Besides, she blamed herself for having neglected her brother. But she was nervous and not confident that she could summon up the courage to visit him on her own. So she was asking me if I would be prepared to accompany her on this intimidating journey. Deniz respected me and would surely value my presence. She concluded her letter with a telephone number in case I wanted to contact her.

I did not. I did not want to get involved with something that was none of my business. I had no moral obligation to do so. The boy had chosen his own path. I felt a growing sense of irritation towards him. Why did he have to play at being a freedom fighter? Why did he think that weapons could bring about justice? I had no intention of being his mentor and decided not to reply. She would be disappointed, but she would forget me, just as I, in time, would forget them both.

I woke up in the night and after a failed attempt at getting back to sleep I got up and stood by the window. The central heating was switched off for the night and it was cold. A full moon, a little blurred, a little foggy and trembling, hung above the Bosporus. I wondered if Neil Armstrong really had walked on the moon or whether it was a gigantic propaganda stunt, one huge deceit. All we had to go by was the word of the Americans and some flickering black-and-white images. Ultimately it made no difference – even the Americans got bored with the moon eventually. But who had thought up Armstrong's famous line? "One small step for man, one giant leap for mankind." They were beautiful words that deserved their place in history regardless of whether they had been spoken on the moon or in a studio. When I heard that Armstrong had managed to break his leg while looking for Noah's Ark on Mount Ararat, I had lost what little faith I had once had that he had spontaneously uttered those unforgettable words.

One giant leap for mankind. Had Deniz hoped to make such a leap? Had I not, when I was his age, hoped that gravity would cease to exist for me? And believed that I could move mountains? Why was I tolerant of Zuhal but so dismissive of Deniz? Deniz had made the leap I had dared not risk, which I did not believe in. I would never know what I had lost. I envied him. This was the real reason I was refusing to help.

I called Nehir the next morning. She answered immediately and told me she had got up early to wait by the telephone; today was visiting day, a fact she had deliberately left out of her letter. I should be able to make up my mind without any pressure. The joy in her voice was my reward, a gratifying feeling of not having let her down. I had already disappointed too many people in my life.

We agreed to meet at the bus stop. She was on time, wrapped up in a sheepskin jacket, woollen cap, and scarf. She was noticeably slimmer and her face had lost the puppy fat of six months ago. Her discreet make-up complemented her appearance. We stood together, not really knowing what to say to each other, smiled politely and dutifully and then stared in the direction from which the bus would arrive. We were like two strangers accidentally placed next to each other at a dinner party. Her reticence irritated me. As always when I grew irritated, I neither tried nor succeeded in hiding it.

"I can see you're bored. I'm sorry. I'm a little nervous. And scared," Nehir said.

I nodded to show I understood, but did not try to be more sympathetic. I was a little nervous too, but we had to get through this without upsetting each other unnecessarily. We were silent during the journey, and when we got off the bus we found ourselves in the middle of no-man's-land. I asked a passer-by for directions to the prison. He knew nothing about the prison, but we were not far from the Hasdal garrison so it was just a question of walking until we found the entrance. A barbed-wire fence ran along the road, an avenue lined by tall trees. Even in winter, when the trees were bare, this was a serene and beautiful place. Nehir must have felt the same; she took my arm and smiled at me. I do not know why I paid attention to my surroundings – this was not a place I intended to return to.

There was hardly any traffic on the road. A military vehicle and two civilian cars drove past us, but apart from that there was no-one to disturb the silence as we walked along arm-in-arm. We soon reached the entrance, just as the man had promised, and when we stated our business at the main gate we were sent down a drive that ended at a wire fence. It was different from that which ran along beside the road; it was in several sections and armed soldiers patrolled the ground between them. The buildings behind this fence were grey and anonymous. We were referred to one of them and encountered a group of people, men, women and children at the door.

"You're late. We've already let in the last group of visitors," the sergeant said. He was sitting at an empty table by the entrance to a small bare room. It was three in the afternoon, and for some reason we had not considered the time.

The sergeant said this more as statement of fact than from any desire to send us packing. He looked tired and miserable.

"Which one?" he asked.

Nehir replied.

"Relationship?"

"Sister," Nehir said.

"Cousin," I said.

The sergeant looked up at me. "Only close family," he said.

This was something I had feared, but had deliberately not mentioned to Nehir. I shifted uneasily from one foot to the other. The sergeant looked up and scrutinized me more carefully this time.

"Are you really a cousin?" his eyes asked, not quite suspicious, just more a little curious. "Just this once, brother. Do you understand?" he said.

I nodded. He got up and went over to a bare wall painted a dirty grey, and opened a door of the same sombre colour. He stood in the doorway, his hand still on the handle, his head tilted as though he were wondering if we would take up the challenge. For a brief moment I thought he might close the door behind us and never let us out again.

The second room was like the first, bare and dirty grey. A new sergeant was sitting at a table covered by a large logbook; he checked our I.D. cards and registered our details. He carried out his job like a conscientious secretary, displaying no emotion. There were also two private soldiers in the room. While one frisked me, the other was content just to look through Nehir's shoulder bag. We were that told fruit and clean clothes were allowed, but sadly not the books we had brought.

The third room was different. It was divided by a mesh partition that stretched from floor to ceiling. Mesh set the tone for this place, without it the room would have been nondescript, grey and dull, rather than disturbing. There were two layers of it, and in the space between them vigilant soldiers were listening in to conversations between the relatives on one side and the prisoners on the other. It was buzzing like a beehive in here. It was a race against time, with everyone trying to say as much as they could before someone stopped the clock. We forced our way into a corner. The prisoners on the other side were all young men. Some were my age, others a little younger or a little older. Most were smiling and laughing as they gestured and talked, but their mothers, fathers and siblings looked anxious, and some were crying. Suddenly Deniz's face appeared in the crowd. His eyes moved from side to side, scanning the room eagerly before finally resting on us.

"Deniz, Deniz," Nehir shouted.

He raised his arm in a greeting and made his way towards us.

"Hi, how are you doing?" he said casually, as though we had accidentally bumped into each other in the street. He had not changed much – on the contrary, in a strange way the spark had somehow found its way back into his eyes. This was the Deniz from our carefree days at the holiday resort. He talked like the forever returning waves on a wild shore, asked about his parents' health, joked with his sister and called her the loveliest creature on earth. Nehir stood clutching the mesh with both hands, looking intensely at her brother as though she wanted to move him with her eyes, as though she wanted to drag him through the fence and take him home.

"You've grown a moustache. It suits you. I'm so happy that you could come," he said to me. So was I. Even though his cheerful tone might be a front, it was reassuring to see him in such a good mood.

"They're treating us well here. We even have a T.V. But there's a rumour going round that this is just temporary, that they're getting another prison ready for us," he said.

The nearest soldier raised his index finger to his lips to hush him and nodded in the direction of the non-commissioned officer who had entered the visiting room.

Deniz carried on regardless: "They intend to break us there. Do you know something? We're looking forward to it. We want to show them that they'll never succeed."

That was when I realized that his good mood was not a front. It was an expression of pride. The battle had not ended with his captivity; it had only just begun. I looked around with fresh eyes. The sergeant at the entrance, these soldiers who initially had come across as eavesdroppers and informers, were unwilling prison guards. They just happened to be in the wrong place at the wrong time because their once sleepy military base had suddenly been turned into a prison. The same might even apply to the non-commissioned officer who, in a gentle voice, was trying to console an old woman. But somewhere not far away expert hands were preparing a real prison for these young men. I shuddered involuntarily. What I was witnessing would fade into a comfortable memory compared to what awaited them. Oblivious to my thoughts, Deniz told us about the farce that had played out in the military court of interrogation, how they had formally been arrested without any evidence apart from statements from the police. He said nothing about his time in police custody, presumably to protect Nehir from the truth of it. She wanted to know when he would be let out. Deniz shrugged as though it did not matter in the slightest.

"Take care of her," were his final words to me as he was led out of the room.

We were not alone when we walked back down the avenue; there was a sense of solidarity based on shared sorrow. I was overcome by newfound concern for Deniz, and felt closer to him than ever. He was my brother and I naturally belonged among these people. I talked to a father who had come a long way to catch a glimpse of his son; Nehir talked to a young woman, strangers came up to each other and struck up conversations. Once we were back on the bus, Nehir and I fell silent. But this was a different kind of silence. We needed time and peace to reflect. Nehir looked as though she was thinking very hard about a decision she needed to make.

*

It started raining as we stepped off the bus. At first we discussed going to a café, but then I, or perhaps it was Nehir, suggested going home to my place instead to make proper tea. We took a cab. I helped her out of her jacket, cap and scarf. There was steam coming from her hair and she was shivering. I took her in my arms to stop her trembling. I had no other intentions, I would swear on it, but when I looked down at her flushed cheeks, lowered eyelids and half-parted lips, I knew that she would allow me to kiss her. I could have stopped there and left it at an innocent kiss, but I could not bear to let go off her. With fumbling fingers and thumbs we got rid of our clothes. Her small, firm breasts were a pair of rosebuds above a flat stomach, a narrow waist and smooth hips. Her skin was velvety. I kissed and caressed her whole body. She was cautious, shy and scared.

She sat on the edge of the bed, staring down in wonder as though she had discovered her Achilles' heel. A sudden urge to protect her came over me. The world was a dangerous place; here with me she would be safe.

"I have to go home," she said.

"There is something you need to know before you go," I said.

"There's a woman you forgot to mention?"

"Something like that, yes," I said.

"Where are your cigarettes?" she said, leaping around the room like a playful deer. She found them and fetched an ashtray, placed a pillow behind my back and straddled me.

"You're my horse, I'm going to ride you," she said. Then she lit a cigarette, inhaled deeply without coughing and placed it between my lips. The smoke stung my eyes. "Don't look so shocked. Today's is my day for trying new things. So tell me."

I would not have been surprised if she had made a scene, cried or at least rebuked me. But she seemed happy as a child listening to a new story. I was used to telling several versions of it. In this version I emphasized the loss and the longing. Love was an abstract, almost intellectual curiosity. Zuhal was well hidden in the shadows. I imagined her as a dream. And just as I had realized that my dream was over, that my waiting was in vain, and that Zuhal never would, never even wanted, to come, Nehir had floated into my world.

She placed a soft hand over my mouth.

"No more. I liked your story as it was. Without me. I liked your story, she repeated. "It taught me much more about you that I could hope to learn in a lifetime."

This was evidently not true. But she had her way of simplifying things. I did not know whether or not this was to my advantage.

"My turn," she continued. "And you need to listen carefully. You owe me nothing. If you had not come with me, I never would have dared to visit Deniz. It's more important to me than you can ever know."

She stopped as though a small pause were necessary to emphasize that what would come next was crucial.

"You're a good man," she said. "No, don't protest. You are, and I feel safe with you. Today, when I saw my brother in that room, I realized something. I could not carry on being an innocent virgin in a world that lost its innocence a long time ago. I thought about it when we were on the bus. There was no reason to delay it. You were sitting next to me. You were the first to come along. I decided there was no reason to imagine I would find anyone better. No-one writes better songs than you, by the way. So don't feel guilty, blame yourself or whatever. Don't declare premature love to me, I would be very insulted. And don't contact me unless you're serious. Will you promise me that?"

What could I say? If she meant what she was saying, she was more mature than I was.

"Yes," I said.

"Good. We'll say no more about it. Anyway, we're going to get married some day. But one thing at a time."

She leaned over with a spark in her eyes, as though she were joking with me and with the whole world.

"And now I'm going to ride you."

23

20 February, 1981, at the Black Sea

"Wake up."

Someone was shaking her. It was the lookout. He bent over her to make sure she was really awake before moving on to the next person. She had drifted in and out of sleep all night. It was impossible to get a good night's sleep in these conditions. That blasted rain, she thought. It poured down, persistent and freezing cold. It penetrated the makeshift roof of spruce branches, soaked through her blanket and camouflage uniform and settled on her skin in a vile and moist film. What irritated her most were individual drops that found their way past her collar and trickled icily down her body. The hood of her uniform had slipped off during the night and exposed her face and neck to the rain. She threw aside the blanket and shifted herself into a sitting position. All her joints were stiff. I'm growing old, she thought. She had just turned twenty-five.

The need to urinate announced itself almost instantly. She took up her Kalashnikov, a weapon known to work in any weather. She used the butt for support and carefully took one step at a time down the wet slippery slope. At the stream she loosened her belt and squatted down.

The urine stung as it coursed from her body. She must have picked up an infection: the last few days had been agony. She washed herself laboriously in the stream. The fresh cold water boosted her circulation. When she returned to the camp, everyone was up and ready for morning exercises. Kemal was extremely strict when it came to staying in good physical shape, so as his second in command all she could do was obey and act as a role model to the rest. A political commissar, she thought with a touch of irony. There had not been much time for ideological activities recently. Since their whereabouts had been discovered, their days had been spent marching indeterminately through varied terrain pursued by the army's crack troops. Apart from a couple of insignificant skirmishes, they had yet to come into contact with the enemy. She looked around and examined the faces of the men and women gathered together in a circle. Most of them were in their early twenties. Only three were over thirty, all local men, weather-beaten, quiet peasants who could endure severe hardship without complaint. They had grown up in these hills and guided and led the group through the tough terrain to the most suitable places to camp with an innate precision that did not rely on maps and compasses. Their relatives and contacts in the villages provided the group with food and information.

There were three women in the group. Zuhal did not know the two other girls well, as they were locals too. She admired these girls as she admired the local men, for their unaffected attitude, stamina and optimism. She knew two of the men in the group well because they had come with her from Istanbul. She trusted them implicitly as she did Kemal and his men, who had come to form a guerrilla unit. The three remaining men were perhaps the group's weakest link. They were from Ankara and had complained about everything from day one. The food, the weather, the terrain, the weapons, the ammunition. She could not blame them for their concerns over the equipment, because their stock of weapons was poor, to say the least. Two Kalashnikovs, two French-made automatic pistols, the peasants' hunting guns, three shotguns, some hand grenades and a limited supply of ammunition. The three men had each brought a pistol. They were particularly critical of the distribution of the Kalashnikovs and questioned their being in her and Kemal's possession. Kemal just told them to scavenge weapons from the enemy. She disagreed with his approach. He ought to be stricter, use his authority as the group's military leader and get them under control before they became a threat to discipline. Kemal had no faith in bourgeois hierarchies, as he called them. These men were simply having trouble adapting and everything would get better with time. She wished she could share his optimism.

Things had not gone well in Istanbul. She was still unable to grasp how the military coup could have taken their organization by surprise. She had always believed they were rock solid and prepared for anything. The reality had proved her badly wrong. At the end of December she had been summoned to an extended planning meeting. She had never cared much for meetings and had always led her group as a flexible and mobile unit. Her task was armed propaganda and they were well equipped for it, both in terms of ideology and munitions, an elite unit of a few highly competent men who never questioned her leadership. Harvesting the fruits of their efforts, organizing support and recruitment were the responsibilities of other elements within the resistance. She was proud of her group, which had carried out several raids with no losses, humiliated the enemy and occupied more column inches in the newspapers than any other. Her superior, the link between her cell and the central leadership in the city, sang her praises and spoke of the thousands of activists all over the country ready to rise up against the coup makers. She had no reason to doubt him and had arrived at the meeting with a carefully prepared plan: they had to demonstrate that someone was prepared to resist the new regime, and they had to do it immediately. Her proposal was to carry out a surprise attack on a military garrison in the city, preferably an armoured division, seize tanks and other armoured vehicles and occupy factories and public communication buildings. If they could successfully cut off the European part of the city from the rest of the country, they stood a good chance of organizing and regrouping in preparation for civil war. If they held Istanbul – it was after all the heart of the country – the remaining major cities might in time fall like dominoes. She had all the figures: a hundred well-armed men should be able to execute her plan. She could contribute seven of her own. They would need skilled drivers and mechanics with army experience. You could expect a certain number of deserters among the private soldiers in the garrison they were targeting. The rest was up to the political apparatus of the organization. They would have to work very hard among the working classes to gain support for armed resistance. Without that support she could not guarantee an immediate victory.

The committee, eight men, had listened to her in total silence. The only one she knew was her superior. He appeared to be deeply embarrassed, and many of the others were suppressing wistful smiles. The chair of the meeting, a bald forty-year-old man with a thick moustache that lent his face an air of exaggerated gravity, was the first to speak.

"I don't doubt that you mean well, comrade, but are you talking to us from another planet or have you merely lost your senses? Can you tell us where to find one hundred armed men? We have lost forty in the last few weeks. They've been arrested and we've no idea how. What we do know is that they are now under torture in enemy hands and that we must be prepared for further arrests. Your group is one of the few still active and your job is to make sure it remains intact. The last thing we need now is another failed Moncada attack – Fidel Castro already tried that. We need to take steps to limit the damage and help us survive this period. I won't hear any more of this nonsense when we can't even guarantee the safety of this meeting."

She had felt like an idiot, patronized by a man she did not even know. The smoke-filled room made her feel nauseous, and if they had told her to cook the dinner, she would have left without a second thought. But they had not. She found her superior in the kitchen, emptying tin cans into a large saucepan and mixing the contents into an unappetizing mess.

"I'm sorry," he said, evidently still embarrassed. "I was just trying to be supportive."

She despised this man, all the more for her former trust in him, but she had a question that need answering and he was the only one who owed her anything.

"Where's Kemal?" she said.

To her surprise, he smiled as he stirred the sludge in the pan.

"Kemal has already had his meeting. In fact, you're here to replace him."

He told her that Kemal had gone to the Black Sea to organize a guerrilla group, with or without the blessing of the organization. She thought tenderly of Kemal, of all the invisible ties that bound them. She wanted to be transferred to the Black Sea. The committee refused her request and decided that she would be sent to Europe to speak for the organization abroad.

Time passed. In the chaos that followed they either forgot their decision or simply failed to arrange safe passage for her. Had this happened before the coup, she would have been horrified and accused her superiors of incompetence. But nothing surprised her anymore. Had she wished she could have arranged to flee the country on her own, but she had never wanted to go abroad. Instead she spent her time planning and executing two successful attacks with her group. She attracted the organization's anger for having acted without the leadership's approval; besides, with censorship in force, the media could no longer report her activities. She was threatened with expulsion. She did not like being threatened and started rethinking her original garrison attack, albeit on a smaller scale. Without being aware of it, Kemal came to her rescue. He needed reinforcements. This time the central leadership in the city was more than willing to send her, a pair of volunteers and a feeble cache of weapons, as reinforcements to a guerrilla leader they had lost all faith in.

They had stolen a truck for the long journey towards the Black Sea. Zuhal sat well hidden behind some empty crates, her gun lying within easy reach. She read a book by the dirty yellow light of a torch. The excitement surrounding the first few days of the coup had long since faded and the soldiers at the roadblocks could barely be bothered to stop them. The few times they were held up, Zuhal's men talked their way out of trouble by offering the soldiers cigarettes and telling them their load consisted of empty crates to be filled with hazelnuts and leaf tea from the Black Sea. After several checkpoints and twice that number of comfort breaks, a few kilometres after the exit from the main road, the vehicle stopped at a spot high above sea level where the gravel road suddenly gave way to dense woodland.

Even though it was the middle of January and cold and wet outside, Zuhal and the two men left the warmth of the truck, stretched their legs and inhaled the fresh mountain air. A little while later Kemal appeared with a peasant and a mule. The peasant turned away, embarrassed, when Zuhal and Kemal embraced each other. They loaded the mule and left the truck for the peasant to drive to the nearest village, then set off on foot along the crest of the ridge towards a deep valley. She felt as if she had finally come home – this was the area she and Kemal had visited when they were two students in love. It felt as if a hundred years had passed.

The first day's march, which left Zuhal with aching and weary legs,

ended at a farm on the outskirts of a village. The rest of the group was
waiting for them inside the farmhouse.

Fifteen men and women were sitting on the ground in a rough circle.
Zuhal had forgotten the damp and the pain, and was entranced by
Kemal, who was updating them on recent events and new plans of
action. There were two other groups in the area, whose leadership and
rank-and-file were drawn from the local populace. They were to
contact each other if the need for joint actions arose. At best they could
mobilize some sixty men, all more or less armed. Kemal leant over a
map and briefed the group with calm authority. He was their leader, but
he did not rule with an iron fist: this was a group of volunteers who
participated in all decisions. He asked them to appreciate the gravity
of the situation. They were not here to play at being guerrilla soldiers
– the time for romance was over. He could promise them nothing but
blood and hardship and their only reward would be the satisfaction that
came from striking a well-aimed blow that would weaken the military
rule. The safety of the group was their first priority. There was only
one crime: treachery. And only one punishment: death. Anyone who
objected was free to leave there and then. Everyone deserved one last
chance to be honest with themselves. It was a relief to see that everyone stayed.

Zuhal listened with the same admiration she had felt for him in
their student days. Although many had regarded him as arrogant and
vain, a bit of a prima donna, Zuhal had always believed him to be loyal
and honest. She was glad that she had not been mistaken. She was glad
of this chance to be together. Kemal had not shown any particular
interest in her after their first meeting and had treated her as one of the
group. She was not offended, she knew that old acquaintances counted
for nothing; everyone should have the same starting point for building
a new community. After the meeting she stayed behind with the other

women. For the first time since leaving Istanbul, she took her diary out of her rucksack, leafed through it to the first blank page and wondered for a long time what her opening words would be.

*

Istanbul, the same day

I sat at the table looking at the books Nehir had forgotten to take. Two volumes of *Memed, My Hawk*, the story of the lonely and reluctant killer who became a popular legend through his ability to shoot his way out of the most incredible situations. I did not read newspapers, did not listen to the radio and did not watch T.V. The Professor, still worried about my intellectual nourishment, updated me regularly with all the enthusiasm she had once brought to her lectures. There had been skirmishes by the Black Sea. The army had moved major divisions, with helicopters and reconnaissance aircraft, to the area. Memed, who had never encountered more than a handful of soldiers, would not have survived that. Did the handful of guerrillas evading capture in the mountains – defying a harsh winter and a vastly superior enemy – stand a chance? What drove them? Desperation or courage? I stopped thinking at that point. The third book was called *The Factory*. I had read that, too. A story of love, betrayal and lost ideals.

I had been unfaithful. I had been unfaithful to Zuhal and my conscience was clear. I dwelt on this for several days, sitting at the table with a packet of cigarettes in front of me, thinking. Or perhaps not so clear. Several things troubled me. I wondered if I should write to Semra about it. But how could I explain Nehir? I could insist in my letter that she just had to understand me and weep for me for being so pathetic.

I owed Zuhal nothing. I did not even remember her face, her body, what it had been like to make love to her. But I remembered everything about Nehir and I was incapable of thinking about anything else.

*

By the Black Sea, the same day

The rain had stopped. Zuhal could finally feel her body warm up. She helped the two girls prepare the food. The women had been automatically allocated the cooking. They had accepted it as a natural part of a woman's role and everyone else seemed happy with the arrangement. She decided to discuss this with Kemal and suggest that they reorganize the cooking so that everyone took their turn, as they did with guard duties. Lighting a fire was strictly prohibited, the risk of giving away their position too great, so she had to suppress her craving for a decent cup of tea. She chatted to the girls as she sliced the black bread; it was tasteless, but it kept forever. The meal was simple and consisted of two slices of bread, some goat's cheese and a dried apple. They would have to find more provisions soon. The two girls asked if she was married or had a boyfriend. It was the first time she had talked to them about anything personal. She was not sure how to answer, so decided a "no" was the safest option. They thought that was a shame given how pretty she was. She smiled, amused by the white lie implicit in their remark. One month in the woods had already wrecked her appearance. Her hair was stiff and matted with dirt, her face was covered with scratches from branches and bushes, the skin on her hands was cracked and her feet suffered from blisters that grew larger every day, the result of the endless marching. A few more years here and I will turn into a witch, she thought, and felt ashamed. There was no place for vanity here. The strange thing was that when she was in the city and wore her hair loose like any other bourgeoise woman – though that had been in order to blend into the crowd – she was just a "comrade" to the men around her, admired and respected, but androgynous. Here, however, she was never short of attention. A week ago, when she had been washing her naked upper body in the narrow river that ran through the woods, one of the men from the Ankara group had suddenly appeared, the most thuggish of them all, a man who called himself Lucky Luke. She could not have been more repelled if a snake had slithered out from the bushes. He had simply stood there with an expression that told her he had no idea what his next move should be. She had picked up her gun, loaded it, rested the butt against her shoulder and aimed it squarely at him, then turned and walked away without caring what other facial expressions he had in store. She wondered if she ought to warn the other girls about him, but they were self-assured, tough girls who could take care of themselves.

There was nervous anticipation in the air. They knew they would confront the enemy today. Zuhal was more relieved than anxious. She was tired of being hunted; she wanted to be the hunter for once. The plan was simple. They would position themselves for an ambush not far from the camp and wait for the army's scouts, who were hard on their trail. Kemal would be the first to shoot, the signal for a lethal barrage of gunfire to begin, and with the enemy in disarray they would retreat in good order and march without stopping until nightfall.

The group arrived at the planned location after two hours of steady marching. The gravel road that ran along the edge of the woods was the only way in or out of the area. The wooded terrain sloped upwards, dense and impenetrable, west of the road, and there was a sheer drop of a several hundred metres to the east. Kemal positioned his unit along a gentle curve following the outline of the woods. Zuhal took her place on the flank nearest the road. Kemal stood on a mound, a hundred metres behind her, ready with his binoculars. The others were concealed behind trees and rocks. The plan was to hit the lead vehicle, which normally drove slightly in advance of the main convoy, when it was level with the centre of their position. This meant that when the signal came, Zuhal would have to aim for the rear of the vehicle. Her nearest neighbour was one of the peasants, who had, on this occasion, taken over Kemal's Kalashnikov. Kemal would use the peasant's hunting rifle, with its accurate sights, to take out the driver if necessary.

Zuhal was crouched behind a rock that kept her well hidden. From time to time she would look up to check the road that wound its way along the crest of the ridge. From here she had a commanding view of the terrain. Their orders were to retreat immediately if the convoy held a close formation. She wished they had two-way radios. It started to rain, falling fine and sharp, like icy needles. She pulled her hood over her head, curled up and blew on her hands to warm them up. The only thing that comforted her was the scent of spruce. She imagined being in Istanbul, in a café, with a view of the Bosporus and a warm cup of tea within reach . . .

After they had been waiting in the rain for several hours, the weather turned. First there was a refreshing wind, rising into a near gale that howled in her ears and whipped raindrops and dirt into her face. The light was smothered by a thick layer of cloud. Everything was dark, the clouds, the woods, the road down to the valley. In a flash everything was charged with brilliant white light. Forked lightning danced across the mountain tops. The rain petered out as though frightened away by the angry sky. The wind, however, held firm. For a long time she lay curled up, wondering if she would ever again feel the warmth of a fire on her skin.

Suddenly she jerked upright as though her heart had stopped for a fraction of a second before resuming its pulse. She panicked, afraid that she might have nodded off. The sky was lighter now. A thick band of milky fog hung over the mountaintops, undulating like a dirty-white bed sheet. As though it were trying to tear itself loose, Zuhal thought.

The fog detached itself silently from the peak and started to roll heavily, like an avalanche, down the side of the ridge. Instinctively shielding her head with her hands, she was swallowed up into a white dream world. It was hard to breathe; invisible particles of ice scourged her nostrils every time she tried. She found her handkerchief and tied it around her nose and mouth.

Zuhal imagined that she could hear scraping sounds. The fog gave voice to a mournful sob, as though it were clinging with its last strength to the cliff. Visibility was zero, and this was what made up her mind. She would either have to leave her position and move up into the woods on her own initiative, or somehow request new orders. Shouting would be no use: her voice would be lost to the wind. Rummaging around in her rucksack, she found a ball of string, tied it to the rock and, very carefully, one step at a time, walked towards the nearest guerrilla. It was as if the fog resisted her movements, as if it wanted to keep her for itself. When she heard Hamit call out "stop, or I'll shoot", she was less than a metre from the muzzle of his Kalashnikov. White fog wafted from the weapon, his clothes, his hair and his moustache. He nodded to show that he understood her message about seeking new orders from Kemal.

"String. Good idea," he said, smiling as he vanished into the fog. Zuhal made her way back to her rock and sat down. She looked into the fog. If she stared hard enough without blinking, perhaps it would give up its secrets.

An hour later, maybe two – Zuhal had lost all track of time – a gust of wind, much more powerful than any that had come before, swept in to lift and drag the fog from its hold on the mountain. Once more she convinced herself that she could hear its claws scrape and grapple as it lost its grip and sank into the valley with a final desperate cry.

Ten, fifteen metres down the track a jeep appeared before her like a ghost ship at sea, a machine-gun mounted like a mast above the rear axle. She stepped out from behind the rock, knowing full well the effect she would have on the driver and the two soldiers manning the machine-gun, a faceless, hooded wraith, sent straight from hell like death itself. She fired a long salvo and felt the recoil jar her stomach. Empty cartridges were spat from the mechanism as she aimed her sights at the tracer rounds tearing orange strips through the air. Her bullets punctured the right front tyre, riddled the grille and the wind-screen and ricocheted off the heavy body of the machine-gun. She knew she could have taken out all three, but the bullets spared them. Zuhal ran towards the jeep. Her next move would decide who would die and who would be allowed to live.

The fleeing soldiers had already covered good ground, but the convoy of trucks was still a couple of kilometres away. Zuhal emptied the rest of the clip and saw them dive for cover. They were not neces-sarily cowards, just young men who had not yet been hardened by war. Perhaps the next time they came under fire they would be able to control their fear and panic and remain behind their guns. Zuhal replaced the clip, loaded and climbed inside the jeep. On the floor lay a crate of cartridge belts for the machine-gun and a box of hand grenades. Time was short, but she had to take as much as she could. The machine-gun would not move and she did not know how to dismount it so she pulled and kicked at it with growing frustration.

"Let me do that. I used to man machine-guns in the army," Hamit said.

The man had a peculiar ability to smile in any situation; it was his trademark and it never failed to inspire warmth and confidence. He dismantled the machine-gun with skilled hands, and with the help of two other men he carried the weapons and the ammunition towards the woods, with Zuhal covering them all the way. The mortar barrage started as they reached the first trees. From the mound where they turned to watch, they saw the shells falling closer to the jeep with every attempt, sending the soil flying and leaving small craters on impact. When a well-aimed round finally hit the target, the jeep lurched into the air, seemed to hang suspended for a brief moment, then tumbled over the precipice into the valley and was lost in the fog.

24

25 February, 1981, Istanbul

I wrote two letters, both with the same contents. One I sent to Semra; I had no address for the other. I decided to be honest and tell them that I had become obsessed with a very young woman. And that I felt no guilt or shame. I was innocent; I had been struck by lightning, a bolt from the blue. Semra would understand and support me, or at least I expected that she would. What Zuhal would think, if she ever received her letter, I could not begin to imagine

I was obsessed. I lay awake at night dreaming about Nehir. I dreamed that she lay with her back to me, that I embraced her and did things with her I hardly dared fantasize about. At the same time I was gentle and careful, as though she were made of crystal and could break into a thousand pieces the moment I let go of her.

It remained a dream. Nehir seemed puzzled and distant the first time I called her. She said she was not feeling all that well and would not be able to meet me. The second and third time I called her mother answered the telephone. She was polite, but reserved and said that Nehir was in bed with flu. I felt abandoned, used and discarded. I was angry, sad, sick with longing and pent-up desire, and I was terrified. If I had had the courage I would have gone to see her, but I was scared that it would only confirm my worst fears. I finally succeeded in speaking to her at my fourth attempt. Confused and impatient, I accused her of staying away deliberately. I whined like a child and made a fool of myself.

"Call me tomorrow," she said before she hung up.

I could not live without her, I had to find a way of getting her here, abducting her if need be.

She refused to come to my flat when I called the following day.

"I know what's on your mind," she said. "But I'm very busy with my own thoughts. Why don't we go to a concert tonight? I can tell you what it's all about then."

I did not want to go to a bloody concert, but I could not afford to say no. In fact, my vocabulary was limited to the word "yes". The thought of being able to see but not touch her was agony. I carried my pain with me the whole way to the concert hall and when I found her at the entrance, I took her hand without saying a word and led her to the shelter of a doorway. My kisses were forceful, desperate.

"You've missed me that much?" she panted.

I grabbed hold of her hips and pulled her towards me, my fingers buried deep in the fabric. I whispered my forbidden fantasies into her ear.

"You really want to do that?" she asked in surprise.

We found our seats inside the concert hall. I sat down. Nehir remained standing, scanning the audience. I started to worry and when she waved to someone, my jealousy was instantly inflamed. I turned to look and was relieved to see a young woman waving back. The choir, which consisted of final-year students from the Conservatory, sang surprisingly well, performing a selection of classics, alternating old Byzantine-Greco lyrics with Turkish variations. The audience showed its appreciation and for the first time in ages I could relax my shoulders and enjoy something publicly, with Nehir's hand in mine. At the interval we went out into the lobby where I left Nehir to order drinks from the bar. When I returned she was with the young woman from the auditorium. She introduced us. I was surprised to learn that this rather pale woman was Deniz's girlfriend. Trying to hide my disappointment, I chatted to her a little. Her general air of misery was infectious, and I eventually fell silent as though I had done my duty, like a guest at a funeral once he has expressed his condolences.

I spent most of the second half of the concert wondering if this meeting really was pure coincidence. I did not see the young woman again when we left the hall and she was instantly forgotten when Nehir said she would spend the night with me – she had been given permission by her parents to stay over at a friend's house. I could not hide my excitement.

"You're like a child," Nehir said.

Yes, I was like a child who had been given a surprise present. Some passers-by smiled, others shook their heads in disapproval and a patrol of three soldiers looked at me as if I were an enemy of the state. I glared back at them. The eyes of one were glued to Nehir's hips, and that was all the excuse I needed.

"What are you staring at?" I snarled, ready to fly at him without thinking of the consequences.

"Bloody peasant, never seen a city before in his life," a young man said. He and his friends were on my side.

"Sorry, brother," one of the soldiers said, and dragged the other with him as he continued down the street.

"We should have given them a good seeing-to," the young man said.

I thanked them for their support and we walked on. A little later Nehir stopped me.

"You've got to learn to control your temper," she said.

"No-one stares at you like that and gets away with it," I said.

She held my hands and looked at me with bright eyes.

"Only you. I promise that I'll never make you jealous. But if you want me, not just now, but for as long as you want, you have to earn it."

"Tell me, fair princess, how can I serve you?" I joked.

It was not until we were inside the warm bus that she lowered her voice and started talking. The young woman I had met in the concert hall was wanted by the police in connection with Deniz's arrest. For the time being she was safe with friends, but she did not know how long that would last and she was desperate to leave the country. I did not need to hear the rest of the story. Nehir had found the passports under my pillow and had thought of nothing else since.

"That passport is meant for Zuhal. You know that, don't you?" I snapped, suddenly flaring up.

"She's not coming. You said so yourself," she replied.

"We'll need a passport photo," I said.

She opened her bag and showed me an envelope. Her self-assurance and faith in her own talents of persuasion were admirable. Or perhaps it was just an unshakable trust in her fellow human beings and their capacity for unselfish acts.

"It might go wrong," I said. "I haven't done this before. What if I end up damaging the passport when I try to swap the photos?"

She took my arm and leant her head against my shoulder.

"I'm not worried about that. You're an artist," she said.

I tried to concentrate. Beads of sweat trickled down my forehead and stung my eyes as I watched the steam billow out from the spout of the kettle boiling on the stove. I mopped my brow with a hand towel, took a deep puff of my cigarette, passed it to Nehir, and held the passport above the steam with trembling hands. I was nervous. I did not know how long to hold it there, so I quickly removed it. The plastic covering the photograph and the personal details on the first page stayed firmly in place. My impatient second and third attempts also failed. At my fourth attempt I tempted fate, held the passport in the steam for a good few seconds and did not remove it until I saw drops of condensation forming on the plastic. I breathed a sigh of relief when it allowed itself to be peeled off the paper. Worn out by the tension, like a surgeon after an operation, I held the precious sliver between my fingers. I asked Nehir to dry it carefully and examined the passport. No damage had been done. I repeated the same process with Zuhal's photograph. The glue offered more resistance, but it finally released its grip with the help of a razor blade. The paper was becoming damp now, so I told Nehir to dry that too.

I sat down at the table with a piece of cardboard, a pencil and the razor blade. My next task was to make a stencil for the quarter of the official stamp that had been imprinted on Zuhal's photograph and was missing from its replacement. I studied Zuhal's gentle eyes. She looked at me with a smile: a little wistful, a little pleased, a little accusing. I placed the photograph on the cardboard and picked up the razor. My hands were clumsy; I had not done any drawing for a long time. It was a matter of finding the right grip, not too loose, not too tight. I pressed the razor against the cardboard and began making the stencil for the stamp.

It didn't take long to cut it out, but it was hard to predict how successful it would be. I placed the stencil on a blank sheet of paper and brushed ink over it. The result was satisfactory. Nehir had dried the plastic cover and the passport with an old electric fan that had stood unused in the living room since I had taken the apartment and which miraculously still worked. Zuhal's maimed photo lay on the table. I tore it into tiny pieces.

"Why did you have to do that?" Nehir rebuked me. "You could have kept it as a memento."

"I have another one," I said.

"Right," she said.

The next stage did not prove to be much of a challenge. I cut the young woman's photograph to size and glued it in place. She was younger than the date of birth printed in the passport made her, but it should not present her with a problem. Then I placed the stencil on top of the photograph and brushed it with ink. The ink was fresh, so it was a little darker than the original. The only other flaw I could spot with the naked eye was that the two parts of the stamp did not line up to the exact millimetre. But, as the saying goes, even the sultan's daughter has blemishes.

The final stage was the most dangerous. Reattaching the plastic cover to the page with an iron. Too much heat and the plastic would melt. I checked the iron several times with a moist finger and when it reached the temperature I believed was just right, I pressed it down on the cloth covering the passport.

The plastic was in place, glued to the page, securing the photograph of a new woman and with it, perhaps, her fate.

"I knew you were an artist!" Nehir exclaimed.

I took the passport and held it up against the light. The cover was in place, but the edges had acquired a yellow tint in sharp contrast with the rest of the clear plastic. I knew I had failed. It could survive only a superficial inspection; it would not stand much of a chance at closer scrutiny.

"My, gorgeous, gorgeous artist," Nehir said, and kissed me.

I wondered if I should give her my true opinion of the passport, but I knew I could not bear to disappoint her.

"Now. What was it you wanted to do to me?" she whispered seductively.

25

1 March, 1981, by the Black Sea

The group had set up camp in two shepherds' huts on a mountain pasture after several days of trying without success to find the other guerrilla units in the area. Perhaps they had passed within a few kilometres of each other; they would never know. They had agreed to join forces in order to confront the enemy as one. But little was going according to plan.

It was safe to light a fire, at least; these were shepherd's huts after all. They had endured long cold days of rain, sleet and snow, and they had had to take chances in order to survive. Zuhal was worried about discipline. Kemal had taken two of the peasants to a nearby village to find food, leaving her in command. At the end of her first day in charge, she realized that she had tried to do everything exactly as he would have done. This was not necessarily a problem; it confirmed that she knew the routine and her comrades seemed happy that someone was keeping the camp organized. Apart from the three men from Ankara. They were determined to show her that she was an unworthy deputy for Kemal. They snorted and made pointed remarks about "women's work" when she ordered them to prepare meals. She handled the confrontation badly and became irritable, but the others supported her. Suddenly the group had split into two factions, something that had never happened with Kemal in command. She realized that she was close to losing control, but she did not know how to get out herself of the situation without losing face. To her surprise it was Lucky Luke who smoothed over the ruffled feathers. Suddenly he was in favour of gender equality and insisted that all tasks were on a par in a guerrilla camp. But though the confrontation had been resolved, Zuhal knew she could no longer trust the men from Ankara.

She went to lie down after completing her inspection and posting the sentries. The women were billeted in the smaller of the two huts. The two women, exhausted after a hard day's work, were already asleep. For all that her body was tired, Zuhal found it hard to get to sleep. She had slept badly since she came to the mountains and woke with a start several times during the night. She was still awake when the door to the cabin was opened and the light from a torch fell on her.

"Are you awake, comrade?" a voice whispered. She switched on her own torch. It was one of the sentries.

"What is it? What's happened?" she asked choked by fear and her growing sense of inadequacy.

In the light from the torch the man's face was an ashen-grey mask.

"I was about to wake up the next guard, and that's when I discovered that . . . they . . . the three . . . the three guys from Ankara . . . . they've gone," he stammered.

A sense of catastrophe, of things falling apart, kickstarted her brain.

"Wake everyone. Prepare to evacuate on my command and send Hamit to me."

She took her gun, woke the girls and explained what had happened. When she had finished Hamit entered, ready for action. Everyone had gathered outside. She felt just as confident and assured as she used to before a speech to the student union.

"Comrades. The worst that can happen to a guerrilla group has happened. Three of our own have deserted the camp. My first task is to find and punish the traitors. Yours is to stick together and keep calm. That's why the main group will retreat to the woods. We need a machine-gun position at the edge of the treeline. Hamit and I will start tracking the traitors immediately. You'll wait for Kemal and the others and for our return. If none of us have turned up by noon tomorrow, you're to leave your positions and retreat deeper into the woods. That's all. Good luck."

Hamit needed no instructions. He tracked on all fours like a hunting dog and soon discovered three sets of footprints. The thick blanket of snow on the ground was nature's helping hand in the winter darkness. The open terrain was surrounded by woods on three sides, and sloped down to a river that flowed towards the nearest villages. In the dark it was hard to make out the surroundings, but the footprints led clearly to the west, into the trees. It would seem that the deserters had kept to the fringes of the woods, like the crew of a ship afraid to lose sight of the coastline. Zuhal tried to imagine what the three of them had in mind. Had they been planning to desert for a long time, waiting for the right moment, one that had come about through Kemal's absence? Or had the recent confrontation made their mind up? What was their intention now, switching sides to join the enemy? This would be a severe blow to the group as they had managed so far to create the illusion that they were stronger and better organized than they actually were. Or was it for personal reasons, a desire to return home to something dear and much missed? It troubled her that she had already condemned them as traitors. But it was too late now. And regardless of their motives, she had to find them and make an example of them to show that it was unacceptable to risk the lives of comrades through irresponsible acts. The three men had not taken any weapons, just a little food and water, so she did not anticipate any resistance, but she grew more enraged with every second that passed. Every branch that swiped her face and every stumbling step in the dark woods brought her closer to a point where she was ready to kill in cold blood.

The woods were a hostile, oppressive place at night. The darkness was like a thick blanket, almost impenetrable. It was dangerously quiet, as though the trees were sleeping and would rouse themselves to snarl at intruders who disturbed them. The animals were sleeping, too; only the mournful howls of a lonely wolf in the distance cut through the silence. Zuhal was grateful that Hamit was with her; she knew that she would have given up and returned to the camp had it not been for him. The woods laid traps for them, raised invisible obstacles in their path. Zuhal stumbled and fell, again and again, on the slippery ground. After one particularly heavy fall she stayed down with her face in the mud. She decided to lie there and perhaps sleep for a while.

"Stand up, comrade. We still have a long way to go," Hamit said from above in a soft and paternal voice.

"Tell me. Do we have any chance at all of catching them?" she asked without lifting her head.

"We might be lucky, you said so yourself when we left the others. So, with a bit of good fortune, we might."

She climbed to her feet and Hamit supported her until she regained her rhythm. They were brothers in arms, she and Hamit. She trusted him. She wiped the mud off her face with her handkerchief and laughed.

"What are you laughing at, comrade?" Hamit frowned.

"And I'd just washed my hair!' she said, still laughing. "Alright. You're in charge. You decide whether we give up or go on."

There were still some hours to go until dawn. No light filtered through the canopy to leaven the darkness. Zuhal hurried on, sustained by her last reserves of willpower. Suddenly Hamit sunk to his knees, as if he were saying his morning prayers. He gestured for her to stop and leaned forwards with his eyes glued to the ground in front of him. Then he stood and told her to wait until he came back, before disappearing silently between the trees. Zuhal went to have a look at whatever it was that had appeared like an apparition before Hamit's eyes. The footprints of the three men, which had up till that point been clearly distinct, had converged in a chaotic dance. She soon realized why. One of the footprints no longer left a regular pattern and a trail across the ground was visible as if a lame foot were being dragged after the body. Zuhal sat down under a tree and closed her eyes. She only dozed lightly; she was restless and constantly vigilant. Yet she dreamed all the same. In her dream she was at home with her father. They were sitting on the balcony watching the stars. It was a silent dream and nothing else happened. She awoke when the air pressure around her shifted minutely and she sensed that her surroundings had changed. Hamit, supple and silent, a born predator, was standing over her.

"I was dreaming," she said.

"It must have been a short dream," he said, grudgingly sympathetic, as though he blamed her for falling asleep.

"They're just ahead of us," he continued. "Around five hundred metres. They're talking. Arguing possibly. One of them is lying down. He must be a heavy burden to carry. We need to hurry before they go their separate ways."

He led the way. Zuhal felt wide awake and strangely refreshed. Her hands gripped the gun tightly, she did not feel the cold so keenly, she was warm, alert and light-footed. It was as if she were still in a dream where actions had no consequences. She lost her sense of time and space, and Hamit was forced to repeat her name to get her attention. The noise alerted the men. She could see their silhouettes, but not their faces, and as she watched two of them turned to flee. Hamit ran in pursuit and left her to deal with the third man. He was sitting on the ground with his back against a tree. She bent down to study his face. Lucky Luke did not look happy. Pain was deeply marked on his face and there was more to it than physical suffering alone. Then they heard the first shot, the report echoing and ricocheting from tree to tree. Another shot followed.

"What was that?" Lucky Luke said, flinching. His eyes were fixed on her gun.

She did not reply. He looked as if he wanted to talk – about anything at all – as if it were his last wish.

"Please help me back to the camp," he said.

She wondered where he had been injured. She had not brought her rucksack. How would they dress his wound? Hamit returned with his gun slung over his shoulder and a freshly lit cigarette in his mouth.

"They disappeared," he said without waiting to be asked and passed the cigarette to Lucky Luke.

Hamit looked at her. She turned to the wounded man.

"What's your name – apart from Lucky Luke?" she asked.

"Barış. Now you know. You can't kill someone with that name, can you?"

Her heart froze; her finger on the trigger too. He was right. She could not.

"Come on, comrade." Hamit's voice was taut with impatience.

"Leave him alone. We're going now." She turned, satisfied with her decision. Every step would take her further away from a cold-blooded execution. Then she heard a third shot. She thought she screamed, but she could not hear her own voice. Her ears were still ringing. She turned, ran and fell into Hamit's arms; he pressed her head to his chest.

"Don't worry. I'll take the blame on Judgment Day," he said without a hint of irony in his voice.

For a while they walked in silence, each absorbed in their own thoughts. Hamit stopped to light a cigarette. She would not necessarily have refused it had he offered her one. But he did not. Not out of rudeness; in his world women could kill, but they did not smoke.

"Everyone's got a name. Just so you know," he said, and walked on.

Zuhal wanted to call out to him and explain. But it would probably just confirm what he was thinking. He was a simple man with simple solutions, which probably made him a better survivor than her.

The morning brought with it the first fine late winter day. A warm sun melted the thin wet snow and revealed the grass – not yet green, but burnished brown. Sunlight sparkled on a river swelled by the thaw and birds hovered over the surrounding marshland. This was the scene that met them when they emerged from the woods, once more in sight of the shepherds' huts. Zuhal scanned the landscape with her binoculars. She could see the machine-gun emplacement on the far side of the clearing, and behind it, Kemal in conversation with the others. The relief that came over her when she recognized Kemal's familiar figure – his long hair, flowing in the wind, and his patchy beard, a relic of a time long past – was short-lived. The cry of birds and the beating of countless wings drew her attention to the marshland, where, barely visible through the reeds, a hunched formation of soldiers marched. She pointed in their direction without taking the binoculars from her eyes. Hamit knelt and studied the same area through his gunsights. The soldiers disappeared from view, only to re-emerge a moment later from the thick scrub. She could not tell how many there were, but they clearly outnumbered the guerrillas.

"Take out the man in front," she ordered.

Hamit fired. The man buckled and collapsed. Mayhem followed on the marshland as the panic-stricken soldiers retreated into the ranks behind and flocks of birds took to the air. Zuhal caught sight of Kemal in her binoculars again. He had assessed the situation through his own binoculars and was busy issuing instructions to the machine-gun crew.

The bullets from the first salvo fell short, whipping up mud and water but injuring no-one. It was enough; the soldiers, who had reached dry land, threw themselves on the ground. Zuhal and Hamit skirted the edge of the woods at a run. The last few hundred metres between the two wooded areas was open terrain. They hurtled on without stopping, leaving behind the cover the few last trees provided. She knew that they had been spotted and that they would draw enemy fire, but so far it was only the wind that tore past her ears. The machine-gun was now firing continuously to provide them with cover. Her legs felt leaden in the muddy soil. She expected at any moment to be hit in the back by a bullet and flung forwards. Her vision began to blur and all she could hear was the sound of her own breathing. When she felt the last of her strength spent, she would throw herself forwards and cling to the earth.

"I knew you would make it," Kemal's voice said.

Everyone had crowded around her and Hamit. She struggled to gain control of her breathing and managed to focus her eyes. Kemal was busy organizing their withdrawal. He asked for two volunteers to man the machine-gun and cover the retreat.

"Me," Hamit said, stepping forward.

"And me," one of the girls said. "It would show a lack of respect to leave my uncle."

They smiled at each other. Zuhal had not known that they were uncle and niece; they had never given that impression. She took Hamit's hand and hugged him.

"Don't worry. We won't be far behind you. I promised my brother to take good care of her," he said.

The soldiers had reached the huts and taken up positions behind them. The guerrillas split up into smaller units and started retreating into the woods. In daylight, the woods offered sanctuary. Zuhal walked alongside Kemal, staring at him to draw a response.

"What is it?" Kemal asked.

"Hamit and his niece," she said.

"Don't worry. Once they're inside the woods, no-one will be able to hurt them."

She walked on, reassured by the still audible grind of the machine-gun. She knew that the soldiers would not dare to cross the open terrain under heavy fire. As she walked, a new sound reached her ears, different from the sharp sporadic cracks from the soldiers' rifles and the familiar bursts from the machine-gun. It sounded as though a huge engine was working hard to get going, but failing to increase the revs above idle. *Tocka-tocka-tocka-tocka*. Suddenly she realized it must be the rotor blades of a helicopter. She stopped to listen. The machine-gun kept on going as if it were in competition with the helicopter's blades. He had not abandoned his position. She knew he never would. She wanted to run back to bring him and his niece to safety in the woods. She was first aware of it as an angry hiss eating its way through the air, then as an explosion that sounded like nothing she had ever heard. The flames, which rose instantly, threw an artificial glare over the woods. An ominous silence descended upon the world.

26

5 March, 1981, Istanbul

"I'm sorry," the young woman said. "It's unforgivable, but I've forgotten your name. After everything you've done for me, I ought never to forget it."

I, too, had forgotten her name soon after Nehir's brief introduction and had referred to her as Deniz's girlfriend ever since.

"My name is Barış," I said curtly.

"A nice name. After all, peace is what we need most right now, don't you think?" she said.

I was already focusing my faltering attention on the newspaper I was holding, so she turned and sighed as if peace was a lover who had disappointed and betrayed her. I do not know why my parents had chosen this name for me, but I have always found it problematic to be called "peace" in a world that was the scene of so many crimes. It hinted at unfulfilled utopian dreams. This was why Zuhal had refused to use my name; we did not need peace, but a fervent will to fight. Our names have an eerie tendency to play tricks on us, as Zuhal's and mine had done. But Nehir suited her name. She was a river; calm, wild, shallow, deep, lovely and unpredictable.

Nehir immediately got the wrong end of the stick when I mentioned to her that I wanted to travel with the young woman. I was surprised by her reaction.

"You've finished with me and now you're going, is that it? You want to get out, you've wanted to get out for ages, haven't you?"

I do not know why she reacted like that. Perhaps she was scared that I would leave her. I explained patiently that I only wanted to accompany the young woman to safety because she was surely one of the loneliest people in the world right now. That was true, but it was not the whole truth. I could not tell Nehir that Deniz's girlfriend was setting out on her fateful journey with a dubious passport, leaving me with a moral obligation to escort her to safety even though I had no idea what I would do if anything went wrong. Like the sea after a storm, she settled down eventually and drowned me in a multitude of tiny kisses.

"You're my hero," she sighed.

Yes, a reluctant hero. And my sense of duty was pulled as taut and as tense as my nerves. I hoped it would not snap at the last minute.

I had to confide in someone, someone besides Nehir. The Professor was the only person I trusted implicitly. And she ought to know what I was doing, in case I did not come back. It turned out to be a wise move. The Professor had good advice for me. We should avoid the airports, where the security forces were on a state of high alert. Going by bus was the least risky way to leave the country, but we should avoid the Bulgarian border. Their government had a policy of oppression towards their Turkish minority and tended to question all Turks in detail. The Greeks on the other hand might turn a blind eye to refugees. Greece held another advantage; the Professor would give us the address of a good and trustworthy friend she knew through Yorgo. Vasili Andoniadis was himself an immigrant from Istanbul and owned a bookshop in Athens. She would write to him and inform him of our arrival. The decision had been made. I spent the next few days getting together money for the trip. I still had some of Soldier's cash, saved for emergencies, and the Professor and Nehir's family also made generous contributions. I bought the bus tickets, a return ticket in my case, and exchanged the rest of the money into U.S. dollars to be used for buying the airline ticket in Athens.

Nehir came with us to the bus terminal. We sat in a café – the same as when I said goodbye to Gülnur after Levo's death – drank tea and waited for the bus to be made ready for the journey. This time it was my turn to board the bus while someone waved me off outside. I called out that she did not have to wait. Nehir could not hear me, but she understood what I meant and gestured back that she would stay until the bus left. We could not take our eyes off each other. We were both sad, but she was on the edge of despair, though she tried and failed to hide it behind a brave smile. It was only then that I realized the full extent of her fear that this bus would take me away from her and never bring me back. I wanted to get off the bus, embrace her and stay with her, but the frayed, stretched ties of duty that bound me to the woman beside me held strong. Tears I could not suppress rolled down my cheeks. As we pulled out of the depot I caught a glimpse of Nehir running after us like a late passenger who had just missed her bus.

The driver told us to head for passport control and queue to have our passports stamped when we approached the border. My body was stiff after the trip. I felt nervous, but I tried my best to relax while we waited in the queue. My companion was standing in front of me. From time to time she would turn and give me a questioning look. Up to that point, deliberately or otherwise, I had curbed my brain from thinking about the consequences of being stopped. We should have agreed a story together. I cursed my stupidity, but it was too late to cry over spilt milk. I smiled to encourage her. Then it was her turn. My heart skipped a beat when she slipped her passport under the window. The moments that followed felt like an eternity. When her passport was finally returned to her and she turned and walked briskly back to the bus, which was waiting for us in the transit area, I was so relieved that I felt I could cope with anything.

"This photo doesn't look like you," the policeman behind the glass said.

"I'm sorry?" I said, wrongfooted by the unexpected confrontation.

"You don't have a moustache in the photo," he explained, showing signs of impatience.

"That's correct. I grew my moustache later," I said, furious at my slack attention to detail.

"I see," he said in a tone that hinted that he was far from convinced. "I notice you have travelled in and out of the country a lot."

"I live and I work in Germany," I said, more relaxed this time. It was part of my backstory, as we both had German visas – fakes obviously.

"Why have you decided to travel through Greece this time?"

"I didn't fancy going through Bulgaria, where those bastards force our brothers to change their names," I said.

He liked that. I could tell from his eager, affirmative nodding that the Greeks, who only a moment ago had been his worst enemy, were completely forgotten. Bulgaria had taken over that role.

I got my passport back, the policeman wished me a pleasant journey and I thanked him. I started to walk the few metres back to the bus. The young woman was standing by the door waving to me.

"Hey, you. Come back," the policeman called out. My heart stopped. Armed guards were patrolling the area. If I ran, I had no chance of reaching the Greek side. I slowly retraced my steps.

"You. Would you do me a favour?" he asked, not at all patronizing this time, but smiling, friendly. "Please would you buy me a carton of cigarettes from the duty-free shop? Oh hell. Where did I put my wallet?"

"Forget it, officer. Please accept it as a gift from me," I said. It was all too easy to become corrupt in my euphoria. I ran to the duty-free shop.

The Greek customs officers waved us on. Exhausted, I slept for the rest of the journey.

We took a cab from the bus terminal. Athens was a very different from Istanbul, but the dense traffic made me feel at home. Vasili Andoniadis welcomed us with open arms into his cool, subtly lit bookshop, where books lay scattered across shelves, tables and the floor. He was an old but sprightly man with thin, greying hair, a thick moustache and a round, jovial face.

"How good to have visitors from Istanbul," he kept saying in an accent that went back generations – almost a distinct Turkish dialect, though one on the verge of dying out

He ignored our protests and closed his shop early, leading us to his home a few blocks away. Auntie Maria, which she immediately told us to call her, was the very ideal of a mother, just like the ones we knew from our neighbourhood in Istanbul. Their hospitality was deeply moving, even more so when their son, Lefter – named after a famous Turkish football player of Greek origin – came home from his job as a social worker at an asylum reception centre just outside the city. We sat down to eat. The table was decorated with exquisite dishes, as though my own mother had been in the kitchen with Auntie Maria. While the Andoniadis family drank the rakı I had brought, we tasted their ouzo and agreed how slight the differences between us were. The meal lasted as long as the conversation, which to start with focused mostly on the old country and the changes Constantinople-Istanbul had undergone, in our distinct but similar eyes.

Eventually the conversation shifted to the military coup and our own situation. Lefter, a dark-haired thirty-year-old bachelor still living with his parents, had left Istanbul in 1960 when he was nine years old, and as a young man had experienced a darker side of his new country when he was imprisoned by the military junta. His internment had lasted four years until the collapse of the junta in 1974, and once released he had he left his job as a teacher to work at the newly established asylum reception centre for Turkish refugees. He advised us against applying to stay in Greece as the conditions at the asylum centre were – to put it mildly – unsuitable for a young woman; limited space, limited freedom, frustration, internal conflicts between rival left-wing radical factions and very little chance of being granted asylum. He suggested we try to send Deniz's girlfriend to Germany immediately, and thanks to his old cellmates, who were now working for the police and customs authorities, it was a matter he thought he could resolve.

"What about you?" he asked me. "Wouldn't this be a good opportunity to get away and wait until things change in Turkey?"

It was a tempting thought. I was unhappy in my home country, disillusioned, my hopes crushed. I had been planning my escape for a long time, with Zuhal, admittedly. Getting away and starting a new life in another country might save me from eventual despair. Nehir could follow me; we could be reunited in better place.

"No, thank you. Fortunately I still have something to return to," I said.

Throughout the evening Lefter sat by the telephone calling his friends. When he had finally arranged guaranteed safe departure from the airport, he booked a one-way ticket on the early flight the following day. I sat down to write a letter to my mother in Germany asking her to take good care of the woman who had handed her the letter, who would need kind people in her new and intimidating surroundings. That night I slept with a clear conscience on the mattress on the floor, a makeshift bed Auntie Maria had made up for me.

We rose early the next morning. After breakfast I said goodbye to the young woman I had not managed to get to know. Lefter drove her off to her new future.

Vasili insisted on coming with me to the border to make sure that I got through customs. Auntie Maria provided each of us with a packed lunch, wept maternal tears and threw water after us in the hope of a speedy reunion. Vasili entertained me with amusing stories from the booktrade. At the border he chatted to the customs officials, who greeted me kindly, called me neighbour and carried out their checks without difficult questions. Vasili and I embraced each other for a long time and promised to meet in Istanbul soon. Everything went without a hitch at the Turkish border where a female customs officer welcomed me. I read the book that Vasili had given me as a leaving present on my way to Istanbul and called Nehir the moment I arrived.

27

11 March, 1981,
by the Black Sea

When they heard on the radio that the first death sentences following the coup had been pronounced and that the executions would swiftly follow, they sat down to discuss what they should do. They had not yet recovered from the loss of Hamit and his niece. Kemal had not criticized her in public, but he had made it clear in a brief, private conzversation, showing no interest in her version of events, that she had displayed poor judgement when she had been in charge. It was not until then that she understood the gravity of the incident and realized that she was responsible for the deaths of three people. She was desperate to prove herself in battle again – showing courage and a willingness to sacrifice herself was the only way she could clear her conscience. With this in mind she had proposed an audacious attack on a military out-post, assigning herself an almost suicidal role.

As usual Kemal weighed up the plan objectively. They were down to ten men and could not expect reinforcements for the foreseeable future, having failed to make contact with the other units. An open attack on an enemy position garrisoned by at least twenty well-armed soldiers was neither strategically nor tactically viable. No-one else backed her and the idea was dismissed. She felt cheated and punished. This was unreasonable – even she could see how risky her plan was – but cold logic did not prevent her from feeling deeply hurt. She followed the rest of the discussion with diminishing attention and participation. Only when one of the peasants told them about a nearby N.A.T.O. base, a small communication centre where two Englishmen worked, did she intervene to say she was against hostage-taking. Yet again she found that her views were ignored. The target was tempting. From a military point of view it was manageable and it appealed politically both as a gesture against Western imperialism and as a strike against military rule. They decided to send three men to carry out the necessary reconnaissance work.

It felt as if she had lost control and was being carried along by an unpredictable current that she could not resist. Everything was happening so quickly, right before her eyes, without her having the chance to make a difference. She felt useless and she missed Istanbul. At the same time she was overcome by an unfamiliar and depressing anxiety, convinced that everything outside her control was doomed to end in disaster. She longed for the city even more. If she were to have a mental breakdown, it ought to happen in the city she knew inside out, where she could hide from prying eyes. She wept in her sleeping bag that night, for the first time in many months, partly because she felt sorry for herself, but mainly out of frustration. It helped a little, and in the morning things looked brighter.

The reconnaissance team reported a minimal level of security around the base, which was occupied by a night watchman and the two Englishmen. All three lived on the base, but the team did not know if they ever went into town. They decided to attack immediately.

They set out at sunset. It was almost spring, but the air was still cool. The refreshing evening breeze cheered her up and she experienced that pleasant feeling in the legs that comes from finding your rhythm on a long march. She was a part of the group once again and ready to accept their decisions regardless of her personal convictions.

Everything went well. Much better than she had anticipated. They met with no resistance, either on the road or in storming the base. The guard was an old man equipped with an obsolete pistol – the only weapon in the place. Despite their uniforms, the two Englishmen were not soldiers. From the first moment fear carved deep lines on their faces and there they remained. The old man's behaviour was the complete opposite: he was relaxed and chatty.

"You must be the famous anarchists, but I hardly think that you would kill an old man," he said.

"Don't you be so sure of that," one of the peasants snarled, irritated by his compatriot's good humour.

"Very well. I have nothing to fear but God," the man sighed.

Zuhal and some of the others chuckled at the unintended comedy of the situation.

"Listen, old man. We'll be taking you to some godforsaken place if you don't hold your tongue," Kemal intervened.

"I'll only slow you down, son. My legs are not what they used to be," he said, encouraged by the laughter around him. They taped up his mouth and tied him to a chair. They left behind a written statement demanding that the regime stay the executions and release all political prisoners.

The episode with the old man had generated much amusement. They retraced their steps with renewed vigour. Even Zuhal felt more positive. With a little luck and pressure from world opinion, they might be able to outmanoeuvre the junta. Kemal stopped the group when they reached the woods.

"Comrades. The enemy will search the forest. We have to climb up higher into the mountains," he said.

Zuhal quickly assessed the situation. Kemal was right about one thing. The woods would become more dangerous. But all vegetation thinned out and eventually disappeared the higher into the mountains they went. This would rob them of the protective shield of the trees, restricting their movements in daylight.

"I don't agree," she started, but Kemal interrupted her.

"I've made up my mind," he said, and turned to leave.

They climbed in silence. The woods had long since revealed their secrets and traps, but the arduous trek across bare rock in the dead of night was a new challenge for Zuhal. It helped to focus on finding somewhere to secure her footing. The physical effort enabled her to push her unease to the furthermost corners of her brain. When they finally made camp in and around a cave, she stayed as far as she could from Kemal and the two hostages. She did not want to see their faces, did not want to talk to them. She needed to avoid getting to know them, avoid feeling any sympathy and, above all, avoid witnessing their fear, for which she was partly responsible. Zuhal had asked Kemal to be excused from any dealings with them. She knew he had other plans, that he wanted to make use of her language skills, and it was a reasonable expectation in the circumstances. But she also knew that he would not order her to do something she did not want to. So he took on the job of interrogating, reassuring and comforting the two men himself, even though it sat ill with his role as a leader.

Zuhal began to realize with some curiosity and misgiving that words were not enough to calm human fears. Since she had taken up arms, she had continued to hope that this could be a more or less painless war. But deep down she had known from the beginning that this was naïve and had started to accept death as a natural consequence of her actions. She drew the line at inflicting unnecessary pain, both physical and mental, especially on innocent people. But the line was a fine one, and it was only a question of time before it would be crossed. This was why she had suggested that they release immediately any prisoners

319

they might take. She could live with killing soldiers and sending her men to their deaths, but not with tormenting innocent people.

All she wanted to do now was to fall asleep and forget her troubles.

28

13–14 March, 1981,
Istanbul and the Black Sea

It was black, pitch-black in front of my eyes, but not for the creatures who accompanied me. They seemed confident and knew their way around as though they were natives of the night. I was scared, but also curious. I did not dare to look into their eyes, which glowed like cats'. Their touch on my arms felt a little rubbery, but smooth and friendly. I do not know how long we walked for, but eventually we reached a clearing between the trees. And just at that very moment, as though by prior agreement, a vast saucer-shaped object appeared above my head. However, I cannot be entirely sure of its shape because all I could see was its heavy outline. My escorts tightened their grip on my arms as though to reassure me. I did not have time to get really frightened before a pale yellow beam of light fell on me. It suspended gravity and I floated in the air like in a dream to wherever fate had decreed that I should go . . .

I laughed. I had a fit of giggles and kept on laughing. There was something hysterical about it, I had not laughed that hard and for so long in ages. I had finished the translation of yet another U.F.O. story. It was incredible that I could get paid for translating such drivel when I could do it in my sleep. Nor did I bother with dictionaries or other aids. If I came across new, unfamiliar words, I would simply invent a suitable solution. On a good day I could translate at a speed that would put Mr Ford's assembly line to shame. Luckily I would not be doing this for the rest of my life. The Professor had promised me a temporary job as a translator at the foreign-news desk at a newspaper. I inserted a fresh sheet of paper into my typewriter. The next job was a ghost story.

I was halfway through it when there was a knock on the door. I was meeting Nehir later that afternoon to go to the cinema. It could only be the Professor. I stretched my arms, arched my stiff back and went to answer the door. I could not have been more surprised if one of the junta had been standing outside. It was Zuhal's father.

"Oh, General, sir. Come inside, please," I said.

"I apologize for disturbing you," he said as he passed me. "I called the Professor before coming. She assured me that you were at home."

I took his coat and hat and asked him to sit down. Slowly he sunk into a chair and sighed deeply as though the act had been a great effort, smoothed his hair and looked weary.

"Would you like a glass of tea?"

"If you've already made some. Otherwise please don't trouble yourself."

I smiled and gestured to my glass in the middle of the table. Cigarettes and tea were my faithful companions in my lonely occupation. I fetched the teapot and a clean glass from the kitchen and poured tea for us both. Quietly, in order to give him time to compose himself and his thoughts. He was a proud man who would not have knocked on anyone's door unless the matter was important. I was in no doubt that his visit was about Zuhal. I myself needed all the time I could get. His body language suggested that he would find it hard to express what was on his mind. I tried to control myself, to suppress the fear that threatened to paralyse me. Nevertheless I managed to sit down on my chair rather than slump into it, as he had. But I needed the artificial composure that only a cigarette could give me.

"Would you mind if I smoke?"

"No, no. Not at all. In fact, I think I'll have one myself."

I offered him a cigarette from my packet and lit it without my hand noticeably trembling.

We sat opposite each other, smoking in silence before he started talking.

"They came early this morning," he said. "A colonel and a major from the army. I feared the worst when I opened the door to them, like you probably did when you saw me. They assured me that she is still alive. Everything they told me was in confidence and has been withheld from the media."

He inhaled deeply and crushed the cigarette stub in the ashtray.

"Zuhal was involved in the kidnapping of two Englishmen from a N.A.T.O. base by the Black Sea."

He paused briefly to give me time to digest the news. It sounded like a cock-and-bull story. Zuhal, of all people, must know that a guerrilla movement stood little or no chance without popular support.

"I find that hard to believe," I said. "She rarely leaves the city. Besides, how can they be sure that it was her? This is pure speculation. I wonder if they're up to something."

"That was my initial reaction, too," he said dryly. "They brought with them a letter from a general, once my subordinate. I think I can trust him. In the letter it said that the guard on the base had identified Zuhal without any hesitation. Anyway, that was not the reason they had come. They were here to ask me to go to the area and negotiate with the kidnappers. If they release the hostages, my daughter and the others will be given free passage to any country which would be prepared to offer them asylum."

"You run the risk of being misunderstood," I said, choosing my words very carefully. "She might have an emotional reaction. She might regard it as a betrayal."

I did not wish to provoke his anger, but this was surely the last thing he wanted to hear. Then again, I still had no idea why he had come and what it was that he did want to hear.

"I'm aware of that," he said, not in anger, but with all the despondence of a helpless man. "I'm here to ask you to come with me. If she sees two men she is fond of together, she might change her mind."

Wrong, I thought. She will hate us both. She will hate us for the rest of her life. But I was not a father myself. A father with no hope might believe anything. Faced with this man I was in a situation not so very different from the time I was forced into the police minibus and invited to betray Zuhal. Clearly unthinkable, now as then. Not even so honourable an intention as saving her life could make me side with her enemy. So why had I not rejected this man instantly? Why did I wait, why did I meet his eyes, pretending I was considering his request? Because I saw this as my chance to finally cut my ties with Zuhal. I knew I could go there and expose myself to her uncompromising and merciless wrath. It would be enough for me to stand there with the uniformed representatives of her enemy for her love for me to turn to hatred. And when she had ripped me out of her heart and forgotten me, then, only then, could I be with Nehir without being haunted by a ghost from the past.

"When are we leaving?" I said.

"As soon as possible. Whenever you're ready," he said, visibly relieved.

I packed a small suitcase and went outside to telephone Nehir. I told her I had to go on a journey to meet Zuhal and why.

"Hush," she said. "Don't explain anything. You will know what your heart wants when you come back."

We drove in the General's car though gloomy weather, dark clouds and showers of rain. I rarely ventured outside the metropolis, so everything along the highway was a novelty. Each fleeting impression made me realize how little interest I had shown in the rest of my country. While Zuhal even as a student had torn herself away from her safe urban existence and explored other parts of Turkey, I had been content to stay within the city walls, seduced by its decadent history, beauty, grandeur and not least by its liberal mindset, which was like a refreshing breeze when compared to the depressing conservatism of the countryside. I had mocked and teased Zuhal, half in jest, half in earnest, about my plans for separating Istanbul from the rest of the country and forming a city-state after the revolution. Needless to say she found this absurd, always thinking in terms of people, not cities.

The sea was dark and rough with a heavy, aggressive swell. When I was growing up I always associated positive thoughts with it. It was there to give you inner peace. We would catch the boat to the islands on a summer's day, sit in a café and watch the sun go down, slowly at first, only to drop suddenly into the sea like a ripe orange. The Black Sea was not a gentle lover caressing the feet of her beloved; she was a brutal mistress, terrifying, and she would kill without hesitation. We lost sight of the sea every time the road cut inland, but it would always come into view once more, just as marvellous and dominating as before. From time to time the sky would clear and dark clouds raced down the mountainsides revealing a carpet of green, wet and luscious; I had never seen woods like these before.

In contrast to the sea, the woods were inviting: they softened the harsh expression of the waves, nature's point and counterpoint. People were secondary: they had made themselves as invisible as possible and lived at a respectful distance from each other. No roofs dominated the terrain – mankind had been wise enough to blend in with the landscape. It was never monotonous. I looked out across the terrain that

Zuhal had chosen as her last stronghold until the twilight erased the colours and blurred the contours.

We reached our destination, a small coastal town, just before midnight. The General's I.D. card worked wonders every time we had to stop at a roadblock. Officers and soldiers alike stood rigid to salute the retired General. The receptionist at the hotel did likewise, but he lacked the uniform and training of a soldier and made something of a spectacle of himself. At first I felt sorry for him: he was just another sad example of how the whole country had been turned into a garrison. But his pitiful state, his deference to authority, his awe towards a retired soldier, irritated me. I wanted to kick him in the backside when he turned to leave, one final salute later.

Perhaps it was anger that kept me awake once Zuhal's father had gone to bed. With every passing minute it seemed less and less acceptable that I had agreed to come here to ask her to surrender. How could she live with such a betrayal? Betrayal. It had characterized my life. And now I had no hesitation in betraying Zuhal in order to be rid of her. I thought about her, about the chance meeting that had brought us together. About the extraordinary circumstances that forced us to live each day like tightrope walkers treading a fine line between life and death. And when death was an acceptable consequence, feelings intensified. Fear and happiness, pessimism and enthusiasm blended into one another. It became easy to love and easy to hate. I had not managed to see that we did not owe each other anything, that I neither had to love nor betray her. I did not even know if it had meant anything more to her than just one night with a man. My last thought before I fell asleep was that I had to speak to Zuhal's father and persuade him to give up on our mission. I suspected that he might feel only relief at avoiding meeting his beloved daughter in these circumstances.

We were woken at sunset by an army captain. He was polite but distant. He regretted that he did not have any news for us. His orders were to inform us that communication problems had arisen between the headquarters in the town and the section leaders in the field. As a result no-one was sure what they should do with us. We were asked to remain where we were until more information arrived. The region in which the kidnapping had taken place had now been designated a restricted area. As soon as the situation changed, we would be escorted there. However, for the time being, all he knew was that Special Forces had retaken a village that the guerrilla group had recently used as its base, and a message had been sent expressing a wish to negotiate. He left us shortly afterwards. I sat back, sensing that much had been left unsaid and that there might be others besides myself who were having second thoughts.

29

15 March, 1981, by the Black Sea

Hers was the last guard shift before dawn. As she slept, she dreamt about her father. He was wearing his uniform and was having his photo taken in a studio. She was sitting on a stool instructing both the photographer and her father. It was comical and she laughed.

"You're laughing in your sleep," the guard who roused her whispered.

She took her rucksack and her gun and padded downhill, feeling a little irritable, towards the guard post furthest from the camp, from where she would have a good view across the approaching paths. It was still dark when she sat down on the damp earth. She sighed, longing for spring, summer, heat. Then it would be lovely to take the dawn shift, hearing the sounds of nature stirring. She raised her head to look at the stars, but the sky above her was dark and limitless. The dream about her father had reminded her of something he had said about her and Saturn. She retrieved the diary from her rucksack. It was difficult to write in the dark, but she tried her best to scribble down the few sentences churning around in her mind.

She was glad that she had had a heart-to-heart with Kemal yesterday. Even though the conversation had been just as emotional as she had feared, it had cleared the air between them.

Afterwards they had evaluated the situation together. Kemal was not scared to admit his mistakes. Seeking higher ground in the mountains had been the wrong decision. A reconnaissance aircraft had flown overhead several times during the day and they had good reason to believe that they had been discovered. For all this, Kemal did not fear an attack – the army would not carry out an armed raid as long as there was any risk of the hostages getting caught in the crossfire. When the two men they had sent out to check the terrain returned without having encountered enemy activity, they decided to seek shelter in the woods. Then one of the Englishmen had twisted his foot during the descent and they had to camp for a while, construct a makeshift stretcher and continue their journey early the following day.

They needed the dark hours before the grey light of dawn to cover the last stretch towards the woods. It was time to wake the others. She was about to sling her rucksack over her shoulder when she heard the sound, at first vague and distant, then louder and louder, the sinister sound of helicopter rotor blades. It was hovering somewhere before her in the darkness, suspended in the air like some enormous and disgusting insect. The machine flew without any lights, so she was unable to judge the distance. At that very moment an intense swathe of light lit up the sky. The strong searchlight blinded her, passed over her head and swept in a curve along the ground, as though a desperate lighting technician were searching the stage for the missing lead actor. She fired a salvo with her gun towards its source, the sound of the bullets drowned out by the noise of the rotor blades. The searchlight was now falling in a steady beam across the camp. She screamed when she saw the flash and heard the angry hiss. All she could do was watch the white smoke pour out from the tail of the rocket that was accelerating towards the camp. Flames lit up the mountainsides and the aftershock from the explosion shook the earth beneath her feet. She threw herself behind a rock when she heard the second hiss. The explosion sent a shower of soil and shards of rock raining down on her. She waited as the searchlight scanned the terrain one last time – the rotor blades spinning faster and faster – and the helicopter turned through its axis. The noise grew increasingly distant and everything went quiet.

She ran towards the flames. She had to get there as soon as possible and help the wounded. She would need to assist Tarık, a medical student and her friend from Istanbul, who was responsible for the group's health. He had drilled her and the others in basic first aid. In her head she quickly listed what kind of equipment they had in the camp. Bandages, analgesics, syringes, scissors, scalpel. In her rucksack she also carried bandages, analgesics and disinfectant. She had to stay calm, think methodically, be organized, make sure airways were clear, perform heart massage, stop the bleeding, treat burns. She had to stay calm, she had to breathe slowly.

She was met by thick smoke and the smell of burnt flesh. She fell to her knees and vomited. Once her convulsions ceased, she tied a handkerchief over her mouth and entered the camp, braving the thick, coarse smoke. Everything was quiet, apart from the low crackling of burning bushes and bodies. She recognized the two Englishmen from what was left of their uniforms. Piles of rubble, burnt clothes, severed limbs everywhere. No signs of life, no breathing, no cries of pain. She wandered up and down with only one thing on her mind. She searched the piles systematically looking for Kemal. Everyone was there, in bits and pieces, everyone's remains except for Kemal's. She did not dare hope, but he had to be there somewhere. He could not have been vaporized or blown into a million pieces. She had to find him. She climbed up higher, switched on her torch and checked behind every rock.

He was lying on his back at the foot of a slope, some ten to fifteen metres from the camp. He had no visible injuries – he must have been killed by the shockwave and the rocks he would have hit when the blast knocked him off his feet. She sat down next to him, held his hand, caressed his hair and beard and looked right into his eyes, wide open and baffled, focused on some distant sector of the sky.

"There. There's a light!" a voice called out.

Her survival instinct overcame her wish to meet her fate at her Kemal's side. She switched off her torch, kissed him on the forehead as a last goodbye and forced herself to her feet. The reports from several guns filled the air. She could see the flashes from the muzzles and the orange glow of tracer rounds and hear the bullets whipping past. She turned to the right, keeping her finger off the trigger. In order not to give away her location she had to resist the temptation to return fire. Searchlights tore up the terrain in frantic haste as though they had become self aware but were out of control. She did not panic, but ran at a steady pace to conserve her energy. The shooting started to die down. The darkness had become her ally.

Inside the woods she stopped to get her breath back; she did not have time to rest properly, she knew they would come after her. She was no longer running, but taking great strides with a sense of purpose. She was confident that she knew the woods better than her pursuers. A couple of hours after dawn she heard dogs barking in the distance. When the barking began to fade away, she knew they were on the wrong track. However, she took no chances and for a while she waded through a stream that reached up to her knees. At noon she sat down to eat some bread and drink from her water bottle. After that she allowed herself short breaks at regular intervals and walked like a machine with her brain ticking over and her attention focused on the terrain, the compass and any sounds that disturbed the silence.

At nightfall she reached the area where she had met Kemal when she had arrived in the mountains from Istanbul. At the outskirts of the woods she could see light coming from a house in the valley below

331

where she had met her comrades for the first time. She sat down by a tree to rest.

Her thoughts were clear. She would seek shelter with friends there and with their help she would return to the city. She would not find comfort in revenge, but nor would she forget. She wanted only one thing: to return home.

She got up, carefully gathered her hair in a tight ponytail, looked back at the woods one last time and started walking down towards the house in the valley.

Epilogue

March 2005

I sneaked out of bed, carefully so as not to wake her. She was lying on her stomach, hugging the pillow. She liked to sleep naked no matter what time of year it was, obviously proud of her delicate body – the years had been kind. I wish I could say the same for myself. The mirror had grown heartless recently, revealing a very ordinary, middle-aged man. And having decorated my upper lip for years, my thick, but far-too-grey moustache had gone. She had protested when I shaved it off.

"That's childish," she said. "Your age has never suited you better than it does now."

I did not know if she was telling the truth. Recently I had started suspecting her of saying things she herself would like to hear from others. If this was the case, her efforts were unnecessary. Everyone already adored her.

I shuddered inside my winter coat when the wind hit me in the deserted streets. The air was never purer in this city than early on a Saturday morning when there was little or no traffic on the roads. I breathed deeply and took the first step towards the car, towards polluting the environment. It was odd to think that pollution had been an unknown concept thirty years ago. But there had been other priorities in those days. When I turned the key in the ignition, I could not help smiling as I thought of Soldier. He had once said, perhaps in an attempt at self-aware irony, that anyone who got into a car and turned the key was a potential killer. I sat quietly and stared at the dials on the dashboard as though they had something to tell me. Then I remembered. When I had parked the car last night, I had left a C.D. in the stereo. I pressed the green button. The voice that came from the speakers was deliciously old-fashioned. The sound was authentic, transferred from a gramophone record without any technological wizardry. The voice belonged to a singer from the '60s. She was long dead and forgotten. Perhaps the song was too.

I pulled in to the empty car park and got out of my car. Shivering in the open, I turned up the collar of my coat. There were no car park attendants in sight. I took the book and the bouquet, closed the door and locked the car, hoping to find it intact when I returned.

No-one had done anything to mend the old iron gate. The two doors hung loosely from their hinges, like rusty scrap metal. This might be just as well because they guarded a world that was indifferent to earthly concerns. Hardly anyone ever came here. I walked along the overgrown path, surprised yet again how spring was marching in and how green it was here, like a forgotten forest.

I always experienced a sense of exhilaration before I reached the hilltop, just before I saw the granite memorial, carefully carved in her image. She was just as young, her hair gathered in a tight ponytail, as in the passport photo in my wallet. The last steps were always the most difficult – that was when I struggled to suppress my tears. Age makes you strangely sentimental.

"Hello. It's me," I said, placing the bouquet at her feet.

Zuhal very nearly escaped. She reached the house as the commando team that was billeted there was preparing to leave, having received the news of the guerrilla group's destruction. She had not tried to flee, but had opened fire instead. It had been a brief exchange. She was hit several times in the arms, legs and chest. The General gave her diary to me. He thought I was its rightful heir.

We took Zuhal's remains back to Istanbul and buried her on a hilltop with a view of the Old City. It was my idea to erect a sculpture of her, carved from granite.

Five years later I married Nehir. We waited until she had completed her studies at the Conservatory and until Deniz was released from prison. We needed time for the wounds to heal. Nehir lost her father shortly after the wedding and found it hard to recover from the loss of a man to whom she had been so devoted. In time she achieved considerable success as a songwriter and singer. The passion in our relationship lasted a long time and by the time it had fizzled out we had long since become inseparable. Fame did not go to her head; she remained down-to-earth, open, loyal and genuine. As a result I never felt that I lived in her shadow. Her career was incompatible with having children and as I had ambivalent feelings towards parenthood, I was content with having Nehir.

I never finished my studies and soon realized that my skills as a musician were limited, to say the least. Instead I became a journalist – an arts journalist – a job which the Professor guided me towards, perhaps deliberately, perhaps not. I review films, theatre productions and exhibitions for various newspapers and magazines. In a neutral fashion. Politically correct. But professional and factual.

Soldier was given a restaurant as a thank-you present from "the family". He decided to live a quieter life, and in time he became the respectable owner of a fashionable club in the city. Nehir lights up the place and sings there on special occasions, such as when Soldier, divorced from his first wife, had married Leyla.

As I had not heard from Semra after my last letter, I made no attempt to re-establish contact with her. Rumour has it that she settled down in England. I hope she found the happiness she deserves.

We lost the Professor two years ago. A huge gathering said a fond farewell with celebration, songs and poetry when she was carried to her final place of rest.

Soldier and I helped Deniz leave the country after his release. He went to Germany and now lives with his wife in the same town as my brother. My brother married a German girl, and they have three children. He and Deniz have become good friends.

I am lucky that my mother is still alive. After the death of the Professor, I call her "the last woman". She returned to her beloved Istanbul, and is here still, in her old, spartan flat, always reminding me where I belong.

I take out the diary the General gave to me. A diary that consists of only a few sentences. I open it. I have always wondered at the handwriting. It is not illegible, but the words rise and fall, they intertwine as if she wrote those few lines in darkness.

I have not managed to write a single word so far. What is the point? I cannot see the stars. And I am no Saturn. At this very moment neither the struggle nor my loved ones are in my thoughts. Only black sky, black sea. But I am happy.

IZZET CELASIN was born in 1958 in Istanbul. He went to Norway as a political refugee in 1988, having been imprisoned in Turkey for his left-wing activism after the 1980 military coup. He now works as an interpreter in Oslo. Remarkably he wrote his first novel, *Black Sky, Black Sea*, in Norwegian, his adopted language.

CHARLOTTE BARSLUND is the translator of the Inspector Sejer novels by Karin Fossum and *The Dinosaur Feather* by Sissel-Jo Gazan.